A Journey, a Reckoning, and a Miracle

First published by O Books, 2009
O Books is an imprint of John Hunt Publishing Ltd., The Bothy, Deershot Lodge, Park Lane, Ropley,
Hants, SO24 0BE, UK
office1@o-books.net
www.o-books.net

Distribution in:	
UK and Europe Orca Book Services orders@orcabookservices.co.uk Tel: 01202 665432 Fax: 01202 666219 Int. code (44)	South Africa Alternative Books altbook@peterhyde.co.za Tel: 021 555 4027 Fax: 021 447 1430
USA and Canada NBN custserv@nbnbooks.com Tel: 1 800 462 6420 Fax: 1 800 338 4550	Text copyright K. J. Fraser 2008 Design: Stuart Davies ISBN: 978 1 84694 206 8
Australia and New Zealand Brumby Books sales@brumbybooks.com.au Tel: 61 3 9761 5535 Fax: 61 3 9761 7095	All rights reserved. Except for brief quotations in critical articles or reviews, no part of this book may be reproduced in any manner without prior written permission from the publishers.
Far East (offices in Singapore, Thailand, Hong Kong, Taiwan) Pansing Distribution Pte Ltd kemal@pansing.com Tel: 65 6319 9939 Fax: 65 6462 5761	The rights of K. J. Fraser as author have been asserted in accordance with the Copyright, Designs and Patents Act 1988. A CIP catalogue record for this book is available from the British Library.

Printed by Digital Book Print

A Journey,
a Reckoning,
and a Miracle

K. J. Fraser

KJ Fraser

Namaste

BOOKS

Winchester, UK
Washington, USA

dedicated

to

the great powers of healing,

that are called by many names

with
deep gratitude to
my parents
Barbara and Stewart
and
my husband
Andy

and for inspiration from
Charles, Mark, and the two Franks

Red Lake• •Itaska
Black Hills• Winona
Pipestone
Laramie•
Littleton• Hannibal
Great Sand Dunes• Cahokia
Oklahoma City•
Dallas•
Crawford• •Waco
Killeen•
New Orleans

Mississippi River

North

Spring

Chapter 1

Enveloped by the utter darkness of a cave deep in the earth after his last match had burned out and the flashlight had died, George stood alone without an inkling of hope. His hands found his face and he squeezed and tugged as if to check whether he still existed. Collapsing, he cursed when he hit the rocky ground. He slumped over, clutched his body, and groaning, curled into a fetal position and whimpered prayers. All he could wish was that death would come soon.

An eternity passed, and then he felt vibrations through the earth. This might have cheered him but he knew somehow these weren't rescuers. Something terrifying was coming. Something even worse than the absolute darkness. He opened his eyes and saw figures, glowing with a reddish menacing aura, advancing. Horrified, George pushed himself to his knees, then stood with arms outstretched, vainly trying to ward off their approach. Some were missing legs, others arms. Many were without eyes, fingers or toes. Some crawled on stumps; a few were being pushed in wheelchairs. Some of those pushing were headless. Many were children, and they, too, were missing arms, legs, and heads. A few adults and older children held babies with limbs either gone or shredded. They cried, like babies everywhere, and some of those with heads shook them back and forth, looking for nipples which they never found, because the mothers' breasts were gone. The maimed got closer and closer. Detached body parts approached too, in slow motion, as George cowered. He screamed for help but no one responded.

George woke up, gasping for air, sweat pouring down his face. He sat upright in bed and clutched his pillow. The same damn nightmare he'd had for weeks now. Just as horrifying as the first time: He was always alone in utter darkness with the horrible wounded zombies coming to get him. It was such a relief to find himself in his own bedroom, his wife sleeping soundly beside him. Tonight a new moon shone in through the window, and as he'd done after each nightmare, he got up and looked out over the yard, to make sure the frightening figures weren't there. He felt a tremendous sense of relief to see nothing but the same trees, bushes, seasonal flowers, and a couple of goofy little yard gnomes that had been gifts from his daughters. No horrible wounded people anywhere. Thank goodness. Thank Jesus Christ in heaven. Thank the Son, the Father, and the Holy Ghost.

He wanted to wake his wife just to hear her tell him everything was okay, that he was fine, "Go back to sleep, dear." But he wouldn't. She needed her sleep. He would deal with this himself.

"Please Lord, deliver me," he prayed. At times like this he often wished for a drink. Maybe *un dos equis, una margarita*, or even one of those horrible sweet southern bourbons. Some moonshine or *pulque* would be fine. But there wasn't any alcohol in the house. And, after all, he'd been the most powerful man in the world for eight years. He should be able to deal with a stupid recurrent nightmare. But every single night; it was getting to be too much.

George scanned the room, looking for something to hold his attention. On the night table he saw a *Newsweek* with that fucker Osama's face on the front page and a *USA Today* with a story of the latest casualty figures from the Iraq War. They were both too light for what he needed. He kept looking until his gaze fell on the armoire, on top of which sat the Bible. Yes, that would do. And beside it, the Alcoholics Anonymous *Big Book*. That would work, too.

George went to the armoire. Picking up his Bible, he weighed it in his right hand, then he picked up the *Big Book*, left over from his AA days, in his left. He gripped each book tightly. He lifted them up. If nothing else, he could strengthen his biceps.

As he pumped the books up and down, he thought about taking one of the many pills in the bathroom cabinet. A doctor friend had gotten them for him. George was well connected; he would never have to rely on prescriptions from Walgreen's or Wal-Mart. Nor would he ever have to worry about leaving a telltale paper or electronic trail that might suggest that he was a wacko or weak. He couldn't help imagining what it would be like if he did have to depend on a regular pharmacy. He could see himself walking through the store's automatic doors, accompanied by a full Secret Service detail to protect him from all the disgruntled idiots out there in the world. Everywhere he went, it seemed, people gave him dirty looks. His wife said he imagined it. Easy for her to say; everyone loved her.

Right hand, Bible up. Left hand, *Big Book* down. Up and down, left and right. After about a half hour of lifting, George was able to go back to bed and snuggle next to his warm wife.

* * *

Earlier that evening, in New Orleans, several hundred miles away, an old woman sat on her back porch, looking west. The sun shone on her dark skin and eased the arthritic pain in her knees. Soon it would be night and time for another nightmare for that man. It was inevitable. What goes around comes around. If not in this lifetime, then the next. But might as well happen in this one. Abbie had put a frightening curse on that damn Dubya, and it wasn't going to end until there'd been a reckoning. Martin, her younger grandson, had died in Iraq, and his sister, Judith, had been horribly mutilated by a bomb in Baghdad. She was still alive, but in one of the back wards of the Veterans Administration Medical Center in Dallas. No arms. No legs. No sight. Horrible enough for a man, but for a woman, completely grotesque.

Abbie groaned thinking about her beloved granddaughter. The elderly lady was immensely proud of Judith's military service, but in some ways Abbie could only imagine men in battle, and men as wounded veterans. However, she also considered herself a feminist, and although she might be old, she was still very smart, a graduate of the University of Alabama, precinct member of the Democratic Party since 1975, captain since 1989, and she paid attention to all the news.

She'd gone with her whole family, including Judith, who had not yet joined the military, to see the movie *Fahrenheit 911* the first weekend it came out. The sight of the horribly wounded man who'd lost his limbs and appeared blinded was both its worst and its most compelling moment. And to think of her sweet, beautiful, talented granddaughter mutilated like that crushed Abbie's heart and enraged her soul. Although they probably never saw *Fahrenheit 911*, Abbie wanted the horrifying image of that living wounded man to be pressed upon the minds of Bush, Cheney, Rumsfield, Wolfowitz, Rice, Fieth and all the rest of those bastards so they would never forget what they had done. Abbie wished that every time they walked past TV sets, the images of wounded and dying people with their shrieks and moans would blast and haunt them for the rest of their goddamned days and nights.

During her last visit at the hospital, the doctors said that Judith could talk, as they'd heard her mumble words at night in her sleep, but she never spoke to anyone during her waking hours. Not even when her grandmother sang to her, or massaged her head and face, during the weekly visits she made to sit with her. But the doctors held out hope that Judith would communicate again.

As she sat on the porch, Abbie composed herself, turned her thoughts away from the evildoers, and focused them on healing prayers for Judith.

Judith's whole family went on rotations to visit their beloved. They kept trying to reach her, and summon back the little girl and vivacious woman she had been. Every week a cousin from Tyler would bring roses, always the most fragrant, sometimes dozens, sometimes only one. A niece who lived in Denton brought CDs to play for her aunt. She'd figured out that Judith liked Arrested Development, Lauren Hill, Sugar Hill Gang, Black-Eyed Peas, and somewhat inexplicably, Lyle Lovett, Robert Earle Keene, and the Dixie Chicks. As painful as it was to observe this, the niece noticed which music rocked by watching to see whether her aunt twitched her stumps (stop it), or almost imperceptibly bobbed her head (keep it going). Judith's remaining brother Ben, a lawyer who worked in the Dallas D.A.'s office, had initially been reluctant to visit. It was so painful to see her degraded. But with encouragement from the other family members he thought back to when they were kids and remembered how much she'd enjoyed it when he read to her. So he'd decided to bring books and read to her again. Ben had started with little kid books, and he found the ones with rhymes, especially Dr Seuss, made Judith bob her head. Later he read William Carlos Williams and Alice Walker. Sometimes he just read or sang the lyrics of songs from the CDs left behind by his niece. Often he was overcome with emotions and unable even to talk. He wished Judith still had at least one hand left, so he could hold it.

Occasionally Ben ran into their great aunt, who brought homemade pies. The elderly lady would share them with the staff and any other visitors who happened to be there. Then she'd enter the young woman's room and feed her a piece. There was no end to the variations of pies she made. It was the only time Ben allowed himself to eat dessert. He couldn't tell if his visits did anything for his sister, but sitting in her room with the beautiful fragrant roses and reading out loud, often after eating a piece of pie, did something good for him. Ben kept visiting Judith, at least a couple of times a week.

Then there was the mechanic, Joseph, a white guy with whom Judith had served in Iraq. The family was somewhat suspicious when he first showed. He was the kind of rough-looking redneck Texan of whom generations of African Americans had learned to be wary. And he did have a red neck, and grease-stained hands, although he always wore clean coveralls. He'd bring a well-worn Bible and read scripture to Judith.

The family knew they'd served together and had become friends in Iraq. They'd come from two small towns in Texas, one mostly brown, and the other mostly white. However, they had the same accent, and had both attended Baptist churches in their separate towns.

Joseph had told Judith's family that he used to fix the Humvees and Bradleys she'd drive, for that was her job over there. He put extra armor on the vehicles, but he'd been sick with a mysterious viral illness the day she'd been injured, and she'd taken out the last vehicle available. It was the one the guys called Handi, because it was kind of a handicapped Humvee. It had been disabled a few times but was patched back together so that it functioned, more or less. If he'd been at work and known that it was the last vehicle available, he would have done something to totally disable it. Then she wouldn't have gone on that patrol, and she'd still be the lovely woman he remembered dancing, singing, laughing and joking around.

Judith-before-the-accident had a wicked sense of humor and could do great imitations of anyone, including the president and some of the generals who'd come through to inspect the troops. He remembered how she'd laughed so hard when Al Franken performed on a USO tour. She did a great imitation of him. Even their lieutenant, a usually grim, serious man in his fifties, had cracked a huge grin seeing her mimicking Al. Joseph recalled their amazement when this lieutenant, still beaming, told them that in college he'd watched every *Saturday Night Live* episode, and had especially enjoyed the then young Al Franken's skits. Judith and some other female soldiers had found burkas and re-enacted Al's hilarious cheerleaders-in-burkas skit for the lieutenant. The rest of their tour, until Judith was injured, was a breeze for everyone under that lieutenant's command.

Joseph had often thought about how humor and laughter could change people. But that seemed like another lifetime, very ancient history. There was no humor in Judith's room. During one visit he found himself studying the book in his hands. No humor in the Bible either, for that matter. He vaguely wondered why. Why couldn't there be a religion in which people laughed a lot? Judith would have liked that idea. He wished he could talk with her about it. Instead he turned to the first letter of Corinthians 13:4 and read: "*Love is patient and kind; love is not jealous or boastful; it is not arrogant or rude. Love does not insist on its own way; it is not irritable or resentful; it does not rejoice at wrong, but rejoices in the right. Love bears all things, believes all things, hopes all things, endures all things."*

He paused then and wiped his eyes. Her head nodded, which he'd come to realize was her way of saying, "Go on, don't stop, read me some more." He kept reading; *"Love never ends; as for prophecies, they will pass away; as for tongues, they will cease; as for knowledge, it will pass away. For our knowledge is imperfect and our prophecy is imperfect; but when the perfect comes, the imperfect will pass away...Faith, hope, love abide, these three; but the greatest of these is love."*

Joseph inhaled the smell of the roses. The scent mingled with the odor of grease on his hands. Not a bad combination. Flowers and oil. Something ancient, something modern. Joseph loved machinery and he could fix anything. He was especially fond of his motorcycle, an old Harley that he'd rehabilitated. He looked out the window and saw it parked near some blooming red and pink azaleas. In Iraq he'd often told Judith how, when they got back, they'd go for long rides in the piney woods. He knew that would never happen now. She had no hands with which to hold on to his back.

Joseph rode his bike to the hospital just about every day after work. He'd salute the old guy who held guard at the entrance to the building. Wearing a battered jungle camouflage cap and vest, indicating his Vietnam vet status, the guard was not on the VA payroll and was probably a patient who lived in the domiciliary. But he took his position seriously and would examine every visitor, to make sure they passed muster. He'd salute everyone, and even the old ladies would salute him back. One day, Joseph had been told, the vet had actually tackled a young guy to the ground to keep him from going into the rehab building. The old man had gotten arrested for that, but later it was revealed that the visitor was high on meth or crack and could have wreaked havoc on the wards. The guard was soon released, no charges filed, and he went back to his post of guarding the entrance to the abode of seriously and permanently injured veterans. Joseph enjoyed giving him the crispest salutes, out of ultimate respect for the older man.

Now the mechanic looked back at his friend in the bed. Except for where her eyes used to be, Judith's face was still beautiful. A headshot of her wearing sunglasses could still easily come from a fashion magazine. Judith had had the longest eyelashes of any woman Joseph had seen up close, and he missed her deep green eyes, a color he'd only seen once in a river in Tennessee. But now there was only puckered skin where her eyes had been, scrunched up scars. Joseph took one of the roses, a light purple one he knew was named Angel Face, inhaled it, and then held it up to Judith's nose. She was breathing, but he desperately wanted her to inhale deeply, so all those molecules of rose could penetrate her brain and wake her up. Damnit, he wanted his friend back.

She kept breathing, but there was no deep inhale or miraculous awakening.

He kept the rose in his hand as he returned to First Corinthians 15:51-54: *"Lo! I tell you a mystery. We shall not all sleep, but we shall all be changed, in a moment, in the twinkling of an eye, at the last trumpet. For the trumpet will sound, and the dead will be raised imperishable, and we shall be changed."*

Joseph shut the Bible, closed his eyes, and inhaled the essence of Angel Face.

"Son, I am glad you're here. Have a piece of this wonderful key lime pie I made this morning," said an elegantly dressed, white-haired lady as she entered the room. He smiled at her. Mabel had been the only one in Judith's family to accept him right off. And lucky for him, as she made the best pies in Texas.

"Sure, ma'am, I'd love a piece."

And they sat there, inhaling the scent of the roses, mingled with the tartness of the pie. As Joseph ate, the elderly lady took the last piece of pie and fed the filling, slowly, to her great niece. No crust, just the filling, as the nurses had told her a long time ago, nothing that needs chewing. They were on the east side of the hospital, and it was getting to be twilight with so many colors of green, and the tops of trees outside shimmering in the western light. Judith didn't move, except for breathing and swallowing. The rough-looking mechanic, holding the Bible, and the old black lady, holding the empty pie pan, sat quietly, looking at Judith and the swaying trees in the light outside her window.

* * *

George walked near his property line carrying his clippers. The Blackwater security guys had told him he needed to stay at least two hundred feet away from the perimeter, because otherwise sensors would set off alarms and a whole chain of reactions would occur, including many of his one hundred and three Secret Service agents yelling "Down, Tumbler" and jumping all over him to keep him from being shot by the offending intruder.

Despite these worrisome security measures, George loved his ranch of more than a thousand green acres with beautiful trees, streams, and a trout-filled pond. The wildflowers in the spring were the best that Texas had to offer, meaning the most beautiful in the whole wide world. He always invited his most honored guests in early April to show off the bluebonnets. He persuaded them to pose in the flowers, crouched down like little children. Some of them didn't get it, and indeed the bluebonnets didn't look like much up close. It was the big picture of those sweet indigo flowers that brought amazement and awe to most people. Pooty Poo, for example, had loved them. It hadn't just been looking into the Russian's eyes that had enabled George to see the other man's soul. But the ones who weren't astonished never got invited back. This had caused a few problems while in office. Dick had told him several times, "You've got to get over this bluebonnet thing." Then he'd said something about bluebonnets not being a "roarch shat" or "raw shock" (whatever that was) test for good people with good hearts. Oh well, Dick didn't appreciate the small treasures of nature. Yeah, he liked big mountains, manly fly-fishing, shooting small birds and other creatures, but not flowers. Well, damnit, this Texan liked his bluebonnets, and he wouldn't take the entire range of Rockies in exchange for his blue Texan flowers.

"Dang, another cholla," he muttered. He hated those damn cactuses from New Mexico, a few that had somehow, unbelievably, found their way to his ranch. The cholla reminded him of another New Mexican nuisance, a man whose meddlesome interfering a few years back with the North Koreans had made him, the president, look like an idiot. Even when George's advisors had told him that the New Mexican Governor's intervention had saved the world from a possible nuclear attack, George felt peeved that someone else had gotten credit for this achievement.

His advisors had tried to mollify him, suggesting that it was just luck that Bill Richardson had met the North Koreans while smoking cigars after UN dinners and had connected with them on some deep genuine basis. But George found out later that Bill had access to super secret historical reports written between 1960 and 2000 by a mysterious Boisho Erskine Shushmanov. The B.E.S. papers analyzed fundamental aspects of North Korean society and included intriguing details about the key players. Bill had evidently absorbed this information and used it in his dealings with the North Koreans. Although George had access to these reports, he hadn't read them. Since leaving office it had dawned on George that it was reading and thinking, just as much as luck, that had enabled Bill to accomplish his miracle.

But George preferred to think about his own successes, when the whole world looked at him in awe. Successes that didn't need books or much thought to comprehend. Like when he stood at Ground Zero, smoke still in the air, and gave his speech with the whole world admiring him and looking on with sympathy. Or after he'd landed on the USS Abraham Lincoln and celebrated in front of the big sign reading "Mission Accomplished." Or right after Kerry had conceded in November 2004 and George gave his victory speech, boasting about the capital he would spend and publicly thanking his "Architect." Yes, those were fine moments, and thinking about them gave him the strength to begin whacking at the cholla.

Unfortunately, the cholla, with its devious vicious thorns, stabbed George's hands and arms, causing him to drop the clippers. When he bent over to pick them up, he got another big piece of cholla in his scalp. He howled in frustration, and still struggling, he managed with some difficulty to rip the cholla pieces out of his hands and arms. But he couldn't get the piece out of his head without a mirror or some help. As he stalked back to the house he swore, "Damn New Mexican chollas."

While George was wrestling the cholla, Laura was reading a book to a group of visiting school children, all of whom had been vetted by the Secret Service. She had picked one of her favorites by Tomie dePaola, about the Comanche legend of the bluebonnets. Like George, she also loved the streams of pretty blue flowers in the Texas springtime, and every April she would invite over small groups of students to whom she would read. She had already explained that the Comanche Indians first occupied Texas, and of course when the settlers came in, there was tremendous fighting and fear between the two groups. But before the white man came to Texas, the Comanches lived pretty much like any other Indians. They hunted, gathered, made clothes, constructed dwellings, raised their families, honored their dead, and practiced their religion. They were just people trying to live the best they could, like everyone else.

In the story, the southwest was plagued with a horrible drought. And as anyone who's ever lived through a drought knows, the lack of rain eventually becomes unbearable and the focus for the whole community. Many prayers were sent up, but there was still no rain. Everything was drying up, water holes were cracking apart, and animals were becoming scarce.

One little girl in the drought-afflicted region had lost all her family to disease or old age and had only a small doll made by her mother when she was a baby. This doll was the last connection the girl had with her family. But when the elders said a great sacrifice would have to be made, she knew right away that her beloved doll had to be cast into the fire that night. Saying prayers to her ancestors and for future generations, she threw her doll into the flames, and while watching it burn, she fell asleep.

The next morning the rains had started, and according to the legend, the land was lush with grass and the lovely blue of the first bluebonnets. But the little girl and her doll were nowhere to be found. Eventually the people realized that the girl had sacrificed not only her most beloved possession but also herself for them and for the earth's transformation.

Laura finished reading the story and looked over the children's sweet upturned faces. "Children, when you think about everything you have, would you be able to give up your most precious possession? What you loved the most, to have the possibility of rain, or something else necessary for everyone to survive?" Laura didn't say anything about sacrificing themselves. Maybe in church she would have brought up Jesus, but this group might have a few non-Christians. She knew there were some in Texas.

Laura gazed around. The kids looked a bit worried, not really wanting to give up anything. Laura smiled at them sympathetically. "It *would* be hard to give up your favorite doll or action figure and just for the *possibility* of re-...er rain." Laura blanched. She had almost said "redemption."

She was so worried about her husband. She knew he was suffering from the difficulties with the Iraq War and she knew the country was also suffering. Maybe fifty years from now there would be democracy in the Middle East and George would be redeemed, but it wasn't looking good for happening in their lifetime. She really didn't want them to spend their retirement suffering and experiencing a feeling of horrible failure.

Laura gestured for the children to go play in the spacious backyard. As she watched them, she thought about sacrifice. She wondered if there was any sort of sacrifice she could make to help her husband and the country. What was her dearest belonging? Besides their daughters, who of course weren't really possessions, their most precious belonging was their ranch, their home, especially in the spring with all the bluebonnets. Yes, she had wanted to move to Dallas, but the ranch had been their home for years, and she knew how much her husband loved it.

In truth, Laura wasn't sure she could give up the ranch and all these beautiful flowers if that sacrifice was required of them. It was so peaceful after all the difficult years. It was the loveliest place she'd ever lived. People who'd never been to the Lone Star State couldn't really appreciate how beautiful the Texas countryside could be, especially in springtime. The wildflowers made up for the oppressive heat and the often unbearable sun of the rest of the year. The bluebonnets especially. Yes, they had a home in Dallas, but all rich Texans had their ranch for retreats. No, she wouldn't want to give this place up. Besides, what good would that do? It wouldn't bring back all those soldiers who had died or mend the wounds or minds of those who were injured. It wouldn't bring down the national debt.

She had been reading the papers and it really bothered her that people blamed her husband for the quagmire in the Middle East and the economic downturn from the enormous national debt due to the war and everything else. Laura recalled her mother-in-law's comment right before the Iraq War started in March 2003. The older woman had cautioned against examining the costs too carefully: "Why should we hear about body bags and deaths? Why should I waste my beautiful mind on something like that?" Her intention was to shield *her* husband, George Herbert Walker Bush, from what she considered to be *his* unnecessary suffering, but her remark had seriously offended those who *were* thinking about this obvious outcome of the war to other people. Maybe Laura and her mother-in-law should have talked with their husbands about the costs of war. Maybe talking could have prevented suffering. Maybe not. Now they had to deal with reality, and just like the little Comanche girl had done, there might have to be a major sacrifice to make things right.

Laura pursed her lips at the bluebonnet book. She hadn't realized this story would set off this train of thought. She placed the book on a table and picked up another. Oh, dear. She sighed. Something about sheep and goats. And that reminded her of that terrible day, September 11 2001, for the country and for her husband. He'd been reading a book to some school children about a pet goat when an aide interrupted him to tell him about the first plane hitting the World Trade Towers. The cameras were rolling, and later the whole world would see his confused reaction. That moment had been so unfair to him, Laura thought, and of course, no one knew at the time that this was anything more than a terrible accident.

She flicked the offensive book off the table, flipped through the rest of the stack, and soon found a suitable story about George Washington written by her friend, Lynn. Maybe two hundred years in the future someone would write a heroic book about her husband, and another First Lady would read it to twenty-third-century children. Laura called the children back in to read to them this story which would make the kids think of all the "good" Georges, including her own dear husband. Books were so powerful. They could have such an influence on young minds. Even old minds, she thought in passing.

Chapter 2

Lucy knew she was going to have to leave her home. As an only child, her parents loved her well enough, and she loved them, but things had happened during her senior year in high school. Her home was Killeen, Texas, the nearest town to Fort Hood, the major military base in the state. Lucy's family lived in one of a group of nondescript apartments with a concrete courtyard less than a block from the main drag with its McDonalds, liquor stores, Wal-Mart, pawnshops, and honky-tonks.

Many high school kids in Killeen looked up to the soldiers just as high school kids in college towns often admired college kids. And this was especially true for some high school girls, although not Lucy. The soldiers frightened her.

She was glad she was slim with long mousy brown hair, unlike most other teenage girls who had big hair, tight jeans and clingy low-cut camisoles, curvy creatures who attracted lots of attention. Even if they had dressed in rough feed sacks and hadn't washed their hair in a week, these teens who appeared to be in their twenties would attract young military men. Lucy would occasionally run into a few of them at the public library, where they went after school before their parents finished work. They would talk a bit about novels they'd read and movies they'd seen as they applied makeup, something Lucy was not allowed to wear. But increasingly there was some Larry, Tony, Donny, Frankie, or Sammy they had to go meet. Lucy was left behind with all the library books. But at least she had books, though the library books were quite different from the ones she had at home.

At home she had the Bible, several versions of it, and the whole *Left Behind* series (the adult and the kid versions), the bestselling books by LeHaye and Jenkins which fictionalized the tribulations and Rapture of the Bible's Revelations. Lucy's parents were completely absorbed in the coming Rapture. As her mom had told her, and as she'd heard many times in church, suddenly, with those others saved by Jesus, Lucy would be taken up into heaven. All the sinners would be left behind (hence the name of the series) to face the tribulations and the hell that would unfold on earth. There would be a few more chances for those left behind to repent and get raptured themselves, but the first group sent to heaven would remain the really special one. Lucy wanted to be in that group.

Lucy was sure she'd be chosen along with her mother and father. Many times her parents talked about how none of Lucy's classmates would be raptured, as they hadn't been saved. Lucy knew that some of these girls from school did things — maybe had sex with their Larrys, Tonys, and Donnys — but not all. And even some of those "sluts," as her father called them, helped out with the poor, attended their own churches, and believed in Jesus Christ.

Her parents had said that everyone in their church would be raptured together, but Lucy had begun to wonder. She knew that it was wrong to doubt, but she'd seen a few of the church parents slapping their kids around, and huge red-faced Deacon Pinkins was to be avoided at all costs. He acted perverted with girls her age, and once he'd even tried to fondle her in the church kitchen, though she hadn't dared to tell anyone about this as she thought it must somehow be her fault. She didn't think her parents would believe her, as they really respected that man. She thought about telling her friend Darrell, but he admired the deacon too and he wouldn't have believed her either. Sometimes Lucy found it hard to believe it herself and wondered if she'd just imagined what had happened. But she knew the deacon had pressed up against her, hard against her back, as she washed dishes. Lucy often thanked Jesus that approaching voices had scared him off. She felt sick every time she thought about him and made sure she was never alone at church because she feared he might corner her again. She really didn't want to be raptured with Deacon Pinkins.

Lucy had never had a bad experience like this in the town library. Her favorite place to sit, where she could see the librarian, Mrs Ethel

Weiskopf, and the librarian could see her, was at the end of a long row of stacked books in a huge rose-covered armchair under a poster of a famous Steinberg *New Yorker* cover "View from 9th Avenue."

When Lucy paused from reading, she'd often slide forward so that she could turn and look at the drawing. The bottom half of the poster was devoted to a couple of city blocks bounded in the middle by the Hudson River, and the top half showed a view looking west across America with a scattering of states and cities mentioned in a narrow strip: Texas, Los Angeles, Utah, Las Vegas, Nebraska, Chicago, and Kansas. This was topped by the Pacific Ocean, and finally China, Japan and Russia were shown as little blips on the horizon underneath the huge letters *The NEW YORKER*.

The poster had been hung by Mrs Weiskopf, who had grown up in a tenement in lower Manhattan and ended up in Texas with her military husband, who was now deceased. She had told Lucy that east and west coast people sometimes referred to the middle of the United States as "Flyover Country." Mrs Weiskopf had said that the description was dismissive and implied that nothing of interest could happen in that space save for the few places named on the poster, and even those names were only penciled in as random after-thoughts, maybe places the artist had visited as a child. Although a librarian, Mrs Weiskopf had a wild anti-authoritarian streak, and right above the word "Texas" she had written in "Killeen" in pen. Others had also written in names of towns that were significant to them. Making sure no one was watching, Lucy had once written her own name in small letters right above Killeen, Texas, and then imagining Mrs Weiskopf as a seventeen-year-old right before she married her soldier and moved west to become a librarian, Lucy had written "Ethel" above a little figure on 9th Avenue.

Lucy read all sorts of books in the rose-covered armchair under-neath the poster, including all the books available on Jesus, even those written by self-proclaimed non-believers. It was hard for Lucy to read what they wrote, as much of it was quite different from the teachings at church and in the Bible and the *Left Behind* series. But as she was so curious to learn everything she could about Jesus, she read them anyway. She became especially intrigued with the story of Jesus' travel in the wilderness and his missing years, including when he was seventeen, her age. Did he really travel about the Mediterranean, to Egypt or France, as some authors wrote? If Jesus had traveled, maybe there was something holy about journeying.

Lucy's disgust at Deacon Pinkins' actions, the influence of the odd map of the United States, and thoughts about Jesus' missing years were factors that contributed to her plan to leave home. But there was something else guiding her thoughts. Lucy's mother had often recounted the miracle of how she, while pregnant with Lucy, had escaped death in the 1991 Luby's Restaurant shooting in Killeen. Hardly anyone except the relatives of the victims and the survivors themselves remembered this shooting, but to Lucy this was a huge event in her family's history. Lucy's mother had been saved by Jesus, while others had died in terror during a crazed man's rampage at the restaurant. Then when Lucy was nine years old, the 9/ll disaster occurred, and when people in her church had talked about this national tragedy as the beginning of the tribulations predicted by Revelations, Lucy began to suspect that there was a connection between her mother's (and hence her own) escape from death at Luby's and the events predicted in the Bible.

At age twelve when she began going to the library after school, Lucy went straight for more information on the Luby's Restaurant shooting and 9/11. She was shocked to learn that there had been many more random mass killings in other public settings in America. They had actually started before Lucy was born, with the 1966 Texas tower shooting in Austin, but it seemed mass killings had intensified after her birth. Men and male teens had gone mad with killing all over the country: Waco, Oklahoma City, Columbine, Red Lake, the Amish school in Pennsylvania, Virginia Tech and countless other shootings of innocent, randomly chosen people. She'd also read about Hurricane Katrina in 2005, which the books described as caused by natural disaster and human ineptitude, although her father had said

New Orleans, a city of filthy homosexuals, was destroyed by an act of God. In the 9/11 books she read that the events of that day were inflicted on America by foreign terrorists. But if a hurricane could be brought on by people's sins, it seemed likely that 9/11 could have something to do with sin as well. Lucy was mystified by all of it.

During her senior year, it occurred to her that she should make a pilgrimage to these places to pray for the dead. This plan came through prayer, not as a sudden vision like lightening, but over several months, like gentle waves gradually shaping a beach. As she couldn't go everywhere, she decided to focus on some of the places where Americans had killed other Americans since her birth. Lucy would pray for the souls of those who had died and the miracle of those who had survived. Accompanied by her mother, she'd often gone to the former Luby's Restaurant, where her own family's miracle had unfolded. It was now a Chinese buffet, but she could still imagine it as a homey cafeteria. Being there was as spiritually rewarding as sitting in church. Lucy thought that by going to other places of violence, she'd find that same source of spiritual renewal. And she'd get away from horrible Deacon Pinkins. And see a bit of America, like Jesus had seen his world.

Lucy decided to call her journey the "Flyover Pilgrimage," based in part on what the librarian had told her about the Steinberg poster and in part on a dream she had shortly after she'd first begun to envision her pilgrimage. She dreamed about an angel flying, in a clockwise fashion, over the central part of the country, marking doors in Killeen and other towns, including those written on the Steinberg poster. Lucy knew the Old Testament story about Moses and the Hebrews, and how the angel of death had spared them and killed the Egyptians. She didn't want anyone to be killed, but her dream was clear. When the Apocalypse arrived, only people in the Flyover would be saved, just as the Hebrews had been saved. And her journey had to be clockwise too. She didn't understand why, but she knew that this was the correct route. She'd go to Waco first, then Oklahoma City, then Columbine in Littleton, Colorado, and then across to Red Lake, Minnesota. Then, perhaps, she'd go east from there, to the Amish school and Virginia Tech. And then she'd travel southwest back to her home in Texas.

Sitting under the poster one afternoon Lucy considered the logistics of leaving Killeen. She had a little money saved from her McDonald's job and babysitting, and she had found some camping stuff in the garage. She had been planning to go on church missionary work with one of two groups over the summer. She was supposed to decide and leave the next week. Her parents were away caring for elderly relatives and would still be away when she left. She hated to deceive them. That was wrong, but the pilgrimage message from her prayers was insistent, and after the dream of the angel Lucy knew her plan was directly from God. Her parents would eventually understand. She would tell each missionary group that she was going with the other and tell her parents she'd go with a third group. In a way that was true, although it was a group of one. She would send her parents postcards once in a while and they wouldn't worry because they'd believe she was with other Christians. And if the Rapture happened while she was gone, that would be fine, because they would all be reunited in heaven, no matter where she was in America. She didn't have to be in Killeen to be raptured. She sincerely hoped Deacon Pinkins would be left behind. Surely Jesus would know what he'd done and not allow him into heaven. She felt a little lonely thinking about her Flyover Pilgrimage, but she knew God would accompany her, and even though there would be difficulties, everything would basically be okay.

The only person Lucy had told about her dream was her friend Darrell. They had been waiting for Lucy's parents to pick her up after Bible study (Darrell had his own motorcycle but Lucy hadn't been given permission by her parents to ride it), and Lucy had described her dream to Darrell in a way that didn't reveal her plans for a pilgrimage. He had responded enthusiastically, especially when she mentioned that many doors in Colorado Springs were marked by the angel. He adored Colorado Springs' Focus on the Family Church, and feeling that it was the most blessed place in the country, he planned to join a youth ministry there later that year. Like Lucy, he was gradu-ating early, and apart from some work in a family business, he was taking time off before the next stage of his life.

Darrell had stood up and preached, "Just like Revelations said, the tribulations will come to us, but those who love Jesus will be saved." Lucy enjoyed watching him. He was almost six feet tall and broad-shouldered but lean and he wore a short-sleeved white button down shirt, tucked into khaki slacks. He had crew-cut cropped hair and he gestured with his large hands as he spoke. His morning glory-blue eyes blazed brightly whenever he said Jesus' name.

After he finished with an "Amen," Lucy considered whether to tell Darrell that she planned to travel to all those places the angel had marked. But she didn't think he'd approve of a single young woman going off on such a journey. She wasn't sure about that herself, but the message from her prayers and the dream was clear and she felt sure God would protect her.

Just then Lucy's parents had pulled up in their battered truck covered with old "Lubya Dubya" and "Viva Bush" bumper stickers. They, along with the other adults in the church, had voted for George W Bush twice and still prayed for him, now in his post-presidency. If anyone asked Lucy and Darrell, they would have said they planned to register and also vote Republican. The two young people concluded their conversation about her dream, and as she climbed into her parents' truck, Lucy said goodbye to Darrell and left him behind.

* * *

"Dad, wanna watch this old movie with us?"

Two pretty women in their late twenties sprawled on the leather couches in the spacious comfortable family room. A 60 x 90 inch ultrasupraplasma TV screen dominated the room with sensu-sound built into the walls and some of the furniture. This entertainment center was the latest in electronic wizardry and made the watchers feel they were actually just a few feet from the performers. When the viewers watched football, baseball, or basketball (or even golf or tennis), they had that giddy sense that they were part of the action. For some things, like the Super Bowl beer commercials, the feeling was kind of gross though, so there was a feature on the remote to turn the sensation part off, and just watch, if they cared to, the stupid advertisements.

"Yeah, Dad, come and watch this movie. I remember the first time I saw it I was babysitting for the Florida cousins. They'd gone to bed, and none of the help were around. I was thirteen. I popped it in and scared the living shit outta myself." The sisters grinned, laughed, and threw a few pillows at each other.

"Young ladies, stop throwing those pillows. If you hit my TV screen, I'm going to kill you. Cut it out. NOW!!" George cried.

"OKAY, Dad."

They looked at each other.

"NOT!!"

And they threw a bunch of pillows at their dad.

After he threw the pillows back at them, he asked his daughters what they planned to watch.

"Dad, it's a really good movie from the 1960s, *Night of the Living Dead*. Have you heard of it?" His curly-haired daughter handed him the cover box.

George shuddered in horror. Not only had he already seen the movie, but he may have been in it. He'd been drunk so many times in college and had so many misadventures, that it stood to reason that this could have been one of them. And now through the mists of time he didn't know if it had really happened or had just been a horrible nightmare. In his memory he'd been driving north of Pittsburgh, visiting some buddies, and they'd driven onto the movie set the night they were calling for extras. They were intoxicated and being in a movie seemed like a cool idea. They were told (or so his memory suggested) to put on rags, roll around in the dirt, and act like they were zombies, people brought back from the dead. It had been fun for a while, but soon the adrenaline had worn off and he'd reached that post-drunk stage. The set manager had growled at him when he'd asked if there was anything else to drink. Hung over, dirty, and freezing cold in the rainy night, he felt immensely relieved when they were dismissed the next morning and George fled with his friends back east to Yale. Months later he went to see the movie but it made him feel so sick, he'd had to leave the theater. He'd suppressed the experience, if indeed it really happened, with more alcohol, time, and the rest of his life. Playing a zombie, or even suspecting he might have played one, felt like death. It was the closest he'd ever come to the end of life, as a young man. If he'd thought seriously about it, which he didn't, perhaps he'd have concluded that it had been this experience that bolstered his intention to avoid service in Vietnam at all costs. George didn't want to die.

Not wanting to die is not an original thought, but it is one of the most profound. And sometimes it is so intense and occurs with such frequency that a person will do whatever it takes to prevent death, no matter what that entails.

Recalling the horrible zombie memory and looking at the DVD box cover reminded George of the nightmares he'd been recently suffering. The thought of watching the *Night of the Living Dead* with the overwhelming sight, sound, and sensation of ultrasupraplasma sensu-sound made him feel ill and light-headed.

"Dad, are you okay?" one daughter anxiously asked while trying to lead him to the couch.

"No, I'm fine," he said, resisting her. "I think I'll pass on this one."

He pulled himself together and smiled wanly. George was glad his girls had never played zombies. At least he hoped they hadn't.

"Okay, Dad, but you're going to miss a scream." The women settled onto the couch and started pushing buttons on the remote, giggling as the sensu-sound kicked in.

George staggered down the long corridor to his bedroom. It was difficult to walk as his usual confidence was greatly diminished by the overpowering presence of zombies, past and present. His daughters had put up old movie posters on the walls. Thankfully there was no *Night of the Living Dead* poster, but just as he was thinking that, he came face to face with Jack Nicholson in *The Shining*. George almost threw up, right then and there, but he managed to make it to the bathroom, just in time.

"Jesus fucking Christ."

He wiped the vomit from his mouth and looked at himself in the mirror. Utterly exhausted, he appeared like one of those zombies in the movie, or even in those horrible nightmares he suffered. He knew it was going to be an extra tough night. Maybe he should take those pills the psycho-nut quack had given him. He looked at the bottles trying to figure out which one would help him most. In the end he decided on some kind of natural herbal pill thing which his wife had found. He always trusted her; this stuff would probably work real good, he thought as he swallowed a couple of green pills.

* * *

> *Amazing Grace, how sweet the sound,*
> *that saved a wretch like me,*
> *I once was lost, but now I'm found,*
> *was blind but now I see.*

The two little girls finished the song for their auntie. Their mother stood behind them and looked at her cousin with a grave but gentle expression. They had been as close as sisters, and her daughters had called Judith Auntie soon after they'd started talking. The girls' notes hung in the air and seemed to envelope the woman on the bed. The stumps of her limbs calmed. They had visited so often they were no longer disturbed by the changes in their auntie, who in some ways reminded them of a beloved, battered dolly.

The air conditioning had broken, but this was an old hospital building and it still had windows that opened. It was humid and warm, but not unbearably so, especially at dusk on the east side of the building. Fireflies flitted around the trees and bushes outside. The little girls went to the window and one of them pulled up the screen. They had not turned on the lights and some of the fireflies got in, delighting the girls.

"Mommy, look, the fireflies have come to say hello to us." They gathered a few in their hands, watching them blink on and off. "Too bad Auntie can't see them."

"That's right, girls. Your Auntie used to love fireflies." As she said this, she wondered if her cousin could still love fireflies, whose blinking lights she'd never see again. Judith would have memories, of course, but would she want to be reminded of something she'd never behold again?

Their mother felt very sad and could see her daughters' spirits sagging. Being a mom and needing to put out a positive spin to outweigh reality, she said to the girls, "Well, let's tell your Aunt Judy a story about the fireflies, so she can see them in her mind again."

And the three sat on her bed making up a story. The little girls stroked their aunt's hair, and their mom contributed ideas when the little girls faltered. It was a wonderful story that included a princess and a daring rescue, although it was the princess rescuing a man rather than the other way around. The fireflies featured in every angle and became the little helper heroines illuminating the passage to freedom. Just as one of the girls was dramatically announcing "the end" of the story, the other noticed some June bugs who'd come through the window.

"Mommy, look, June bugs!"

"June bugs? This is April. I've never seen June bugs in April. Come to think of it, I don't know that I've seen fireflies in April either. Another sign of global warming? We'll have to start calling them April bugs."

The little girls played with the bugs on their hands and arms and giggled as they crawled over their skin. "Oh, Mommy, Auntie loved

June bugs. April bugs. Such cute tickly little things. Can we put some on her?"

Their mom didn't know what to think. Putting June bugs on a woman with only stumps for limbs, who didn't speak and couldn't see...? But her girls looked so enthusiastic, and she recalled enjoying the feeling of June bugs crawling on her skin when she'd been a kid.

"Well, let's ask her," she said as she quietly closed the door, making sure none of the hospital personnel were coming towards the room.

"Can we put the June bugs on you, Auntie?" the little girls asked. They looked at her face, and then grinned hugely at each other.

"Mommy, she smiled," they both said simultaneously.

"Are you sure?" their mom responded. She knew that Judith hadn't smiled since right before the IED had exploded underneath the Hummer. Joseph had been told by the other soldiers that she'd just finished telling a joke when the bomb went off. And no one had seen her smile since.

"Oh yes!" The girls both nodded, their eyes shining.

She gave them the classic skeptical mom look. She studied Judith's face, which had the same expressionless look it'd had for months. But when her girls nodded back at her with their most earnest, shocked-that-you-would-doubt-us look, she said, "Okay, let's roll."

Crap, the mom thought, Why do I keep saying that? This situation was the complete opposite of the one from which that now famous statement had come.

But maybe it wasn't. The girls put the June bugs on their aunt's upper chest and shoulders and they crawled around tentatively at first, but then picked up some momentum.

"Mommy, they're moving like fireflies," the younger girl said.

The mom didn't see it at first, but then she did, and she recalled a firefly experience she'd had as a kid in Tennessee, where the fireflies seemed to be dancing. She didn't know that June bugs could dance too. How strange and beautiful.

"Auntie's smiling again."

Their mom's mouth dropped open. It was true. "Hallelujah, praise Christ in heaven, she is smiling."

The June bugs crawled slowly on Judith's skin and the fireflies twinkled on and off, just as the stars did outside. While the little girls started singing a song about their aunt, their mother sat back in her chair in wonder at the healing power of June bugs and her sweet little girls — and Judith continued to smile as the bugs crawled over her skin and back over the skinny arms of the giggling children. And pretty soon their mom was giggling, and the whole room was filled to bursting with giggles, including, finally, sounds of mirth from Judith.

Chapter 3

Lucy put her Bible in her backpack. It had been wrapped in special Oaxacan cloth given to her by her beautiful friend Maria, who, a little older than Lucy, worked as a nursing assistant in the nearby VA hospital. Maria's folks had crossed the Rio Grande to get to *los Estados Unidos*, and the story went that she had been carried over on her dad's back. Her parents were still illegal, but Maria was able to get through school and had since gone to work as a nursing assistant to help her family. She was the only person in whom Lucy had confided about her journey. Maria had lit candles and offered prayers for her friend's safety. She didn't quite understand why Lucy felt compelled to go, but many of her own relatives made pilgrimages in Mexico, and the journey to *él Norte* was kind of a pilgrimage. The beautiful cloth that Maria offered Lucy for the trip had come from Maria's relatives in Oaxaca. She hoped it would protect Lucy and her Bible.

Other items that went into the small backpack: a radio, a couple of T-shirts, a pair of jeans, some underwear, toiletries, and another gift from Maria, a small plastic figure of Mary with baby Jesus at her feet.

At the last moment Lucy threw in a ballet skirt of indigo blue sprinkled with twinkling stars. Her mom hadn't let her take dance lessons in recent years, but Lucy had kept the skirt as a memory of something she'd done in the past, the only time when she felt as beautiful as Maria.

Lucy wrote out a note for her parents to find when they returned. She looked around her room once more, fixing in her memory the familiar items of childhood and her teenage years. She hoped everything would still look the same when she came home in a few months – if it was a few months. Lucy wasn't sure how long her journey would take. She put on her faded Cowboys cap, stuffed her jacket at the top of the backpack, and closed her door quietly.

The family's big yellow lab was stretched out in front of the door that led from the kitchen to the driveway. The old girl thumped her tail, lifted her head, and stretched, but didn't move away from the door. "*Rosa, despierta te, mi perra favorita,*" said Lucy, bending to pat her good dog one last time. The dog, which had belonged to Maria's family up until it was discovered that her brother was allergic, only responded to properly pronounced Spanish. As a result, Lucy had gotten pretty good at rolling her rrrr's. Even her parents, who couldn't speak any Spanish, had learned to roll their rrrr's by saying "RRRRRRosa."

The dog reluctantly got up, stretched, and then sat patiently while Lucy fondled her soft ears. That was when the tears started to fall. This was going to be tougher than she'd thought. Lucy wished she could take Rosa, but the dog was old and wouldn't move further than the backyard. She'd made arrangements with the neighbor to care for her pet until her parents returned. Rosa would be okay. "*Adiós, amiga, Rosa amiga de mi corazón.*"

Lucy placed the note for her parents on the counter and then closed the door behind her and stepped into the soft Texas darkness. It was about four in the morning, and even though they lived near the main drag, it was pretty quiet. Lucy wasn't looking for rides. She planned to walk the whole way. She stepped away from the apartment without looking back and turned north on Old FM 440, walking out of the life she knew and into another.

* * *

While Lucy walked out of Killeen, a few miles away, George tossed restlessly in his sleep, if the state he was in could even be called sleep. He was back in the cave and the armless, legless, eyeless, moaning, groaning bodies were lurching towards him. Some clutched the injured arms of others, and more than one carried a hand or foot they had lost, extending them like offerings. Many of them were wrapped in barely recognizable tattered and bloody American flags. George's dreams appeared in black and white, but he could tell that the blackness was blood.

The zombies came towards him, advancing in a semicircle. The fact that the creatures weren't coming up behind him offered him a glimmer of hope. But they were getting closer, and hope faded entirely when he saw with horror that a woman with her lower abdomen cut open was holding out a dead baby. The baby was only partially developed, but it was trailing a bloody limb, missing a foot, and the mom was having a hard time walking because she didn't have any feet.

"Oh, Christ, please, Lord, save me." George dropped to the ground. He stretched one hand out in front of him and cupped the other over his eyes.

"It's pretty awful, isn't it?" The deep quiet voice came out of the background, somewhere beyond the zombies. The voice rose over the moanings and groanings, and George felt as much as heard it. It was more than just the vibration of the voice that he felt, though; some unspeakable sensation that he couldn't even identify accompanied it, causing him to shudder. It seemed worse than the zombies themselves. He definitely didn't want to be touched by this creature he couldn't even see.

"*Es muy feo, sí?* Very ugly, right?" Again the power behind this force was more intense than anything he'd ever felt before. He knew this was something completely different, exponentially (he knew that word!) more powerful than all the American military might combined. More almighty than anything he'd experienced as the most powerful president of the most powerful nation that the world had ever seen.

"Are you...God?" There was silence.

"I thought you'd spoken with me before." The force let out an awesome sigh. Lightning flashed and the sky turned greenish black as the two figures, George and the other, were enveloped by a cool moist wind.

All the zombies had disappeared.

George looked up, then back down quickly, eyes shifting right and left, wishing he had one of those little speakerphone earplug thingies that connected him with other men.

"No, we don't have any of those here. You're on your own."

George lifted his head slightly and glimpsed flowers, surprisingly, near two bare beautiful healthy feet. Behind them he could see a small brook. And then he saw robes, some kind of cloth he'd never before seen, something that almost seemed alive. His eyes traveled up the living fabric which glowed with health. He then saw God's hands. Big, strong hands, nails square, and a little dirty like his wife's fingers when she'd been in the garden. Hands that could do anything. Then looking further up he saw long strong arms, draped in more of the shimmery cloth. He gasped as his eyes traveled further up. Breasts? Wait, this was God. God doesn't have breasts. George felt a stab of anger and almost snorted indignantly.

More lightning; a whirlwind of greenish black air twirled around his body. The indignant thought vanished instantly. He groaned and looked down again.

"Go ahead. Look at my face."

George whimpered. But finally he looked up and beheld the most wonderful face he'd seen in years, ever since he'd fallen in love with his wife. A face that could make all suffering worthwhile and endurable. A face that would look different to everyone who looked upon it, but with an inherent fundamental connection to the universe. Not a young face either, but mature and grave. Her hair was amazing, like a living organism from another universe with a rainbow of colors — yes, he was seeing colors now! — which rippled like river whitewater. Her eyes, though, were almost impossible to look at. They were like glowing green jewels, but molten, alive at the moment before hardening. George averted his eyes again. He almost wished for the return of the zombies.

"Are you really God?" he mumbled, trembling.

She almost smiled. "Well, many people would call me Mother Nature but some call me God."

He was amazed, and a little frightened. George had pondered God often, and this strange figure, a woman, wasn't at all whom he

31

thought he'd prayed to.

"You are really in a mess now, aren't you?" Waves of power rolled out of her body. The flowers at her feet seemed to turn their little heads sympathetically, expectantly, towards him.

He whimpered.

She observed him with just a glimmering of sympathy. "You know who the zombies are, brother, right?"

He shook his head.

"They aren't zombies at all. Perhaps they're just a projection from your own mind. You know, like projective tests. Rorschach tests."

He looked puzzled. He didn't know what she was talking about.

"Remember, you called them 'roach shat' or 'raw schock' tests when you and Dick debated about the significance of the bluebonnets. Tests some psychologists would have loved to give to you."

He was still puzzled.

"Never mind. We don't have a lot of time."

More thunder, lightening, and a cool, moist wind.

"No, they aren't zombies or projections. They're the souls of all the people who've died in the war you started. The unnecessary war."

He furrowed his brows, confused.

"The Iraq War? The war you started in March of 2003?"

Now he looked peeved.

She continued: "They've come to see you because you aren't paying attention to them. They are attached to you, as you are to them, because you caused their deaths."

George studied her, almost defiantly. "They died in the cause of freedom, democracy, making the world a better place, and ridding the world of tyrants." He stood up and started to do the swagger-from-the-helicopter walk that he'd perfected, a holdover from his cheerleader days at Yale. "It's too bad about those civilians..." (He couldn't bring himself to say mothers and children) "...but our soldiers volunteered. Lots of them volunteered after 9/11. We needed to fight the terrorists before they got to our own shores again. And Saddam had weapons of mass destruction that he was going to use—"

Mother Nature gave George such a withering look that he backed down. He knew there weren't any weapons of mass destruction. And he knew Iraq had no connection with Osama, that bastard, who still hadn't been found. But George would continue to tell anyone that the invasion of Iraq had been the correct strategy to fight terrorism. He started to make this point, but got another very dark look from the woman. A few snakes hissed and slithered towards him from the flowers at her feet.

"You know, you don't think very deeply about the consequences of your actions. Although I guess most people don't. However, I have a deeper vision." She flipped her amazing hair over her shimmering robe. The flowers stood up higher and preened a bit. She looked down at them and they pretended not to notice her.

"Look, brother, you're a Born Again Christian, and you have sinned against a lot of people. It's pretty simple. You now have to acknowledge your sins, ask for forgiveness from those you've hurt, and atone. Only then will the nightmares leave you and the souls rest in peace. It's not brain surgery or quantum physics, although they are connected."

George still appeared puzzled and somewhat defiant.

"Hmmm. This is going to be tougher than I thought. Think about it. Pray. Take some walks out in nature. Go to church. Talk with your wife. Watch for other women who will help you. Women have always helped you, George. God will help you too. And you can think of me in whatever form helps you. You aren't really a nature lover, are you?" And before his eyes she transformed into an Old Testament prophet with long white hair, tattered robes, a staff and a stone tablet on which the Ten Commandments were inscribed.

"Is this more like it?" she, in the form of a he, thundered. And with more lightning and a sudden, torrential rain, he/she vanished.

George realized right away that he was completely soaked, but it took him a few minutes to understand that he was standing outside on his own lawn, surrounded by familiar terrain. The dawn light was just peeking over the horizon and he could make out his daughters' funny little lawn gnomes. The scent of his wife's roses filled the soft air.

More time passed as he absorbed the vision of his blessed backyard. Surprisingly, he felt better than he had in months. The content of the dream was already slipping away, but its essence, like a seed, had taken hold deep within. Suddenly he found himself remembering a Saudi crown prince whose hand he had held in this very spot. Unconsciously he shook his left hand. Then he walked back to the house, stopping to urinate on some ugly bush he wanted to get rid of. George was just a man, after all.

* * *

Ben felt so angry he thought he'd better walk around outside the hospital a few times before he went in to see his sister. This crappy, shitty world sucked. He loosened his tie as he stalked around the building. Shortly after his sister had been wounded, one of his friends from college had given him a book on Buddhism. He'd tried to read it but it was way too sissified and passive. He'd thrown it away. The only thing that he agreed with was that the world was full of suffering. Damn sure it is.

He thought of the stupid criminals he prosecuted in his Dallas office. Such dumb shits, most of them, especially the ones who thought they could get away with their crimes. He wanted to smash their ugly faces. But the white collar criminals were even worse. One of them had actually gone to own his alma mater, Dartmouth. That guy had been an asshole in college, and he'd become an even greater asshole after going to Harvard Business School. He'd stolen more money from his corporate job than all the common criminals Ben had prosecuted together. But Mr MBA got caught and now was in the Dallas jail just like all the drug dealers and other scum. Ben would have liked to whip that guy's ass. But this was one of the reasons he'd gone to law school. A teacher in high school had really impressed on Ben the concept of the rule of law and how societies could be run so much better with rules thought out ahead of time rather than reactive retaliatory violence. He also recognized his own volcanic nature and he didn't want to end up like some of those assholes he prosecuted. Ben took karate classes to contain these urges.

He did a few katas on the grass with some lethal kicks aimed at some imaginary Iraqis. He would never know the people who'd put the bomb together that had exploded under his sister's Hummer. If he knew them, he didn't think he'd be able to use his legal expertise or his karate. He'd start by ripping their eyeballs out, and then he'd take a two-by-four and smash their limbs until they were nothing more than stumps like his sister's. Then he'd leave them there to die. Suffer, raghead shits. He did a few more kicks and soon felt calmer, at least under control enough to enter the hospital. After he'd finished he bowed to a straggly little bush near a dumpster. The principle of recognizing the opponent before and after a fight was well ingrained. That bush, to Ben, represented the Iraqis, the good and the bad.

Before Ben entered the hospital he also bowed to a couple of beautiful willows. One represented his sister and the other the spirit of their little brother who'd died in Iraq. Marty was in peace. Their sister, though, was still alive to suffer. But also to be loved. Ben could go see Judith now.

A few minutes later he walked into her room. Oh shit, he thought, that redneck mechanic Joseph was there. The other man had his back to the door, so Ben could see that the white man really *did* have a red neck, the red contrasting with the white of his skin just above the blue line of his shirt. Joseph was reading from the Bible, Psalms 103: 15-18: "*As for woman, her days are like grass; she flourishes like a flower of the field; for the wind passes over it, and it is gone, and its place knows, if no more. But the steadfast love of the Lord is from everlasting to everlasting upon those who fear her, and her righteousness to her children's children, to those who keep her covenant and remember to do her commandments.*"

"It's man, his, and he. You can't change the Bible like that," said Ben, and he gave the white guy a withering look, his hands on his hips.

Joseph turned and smiled at Ben. "I thought Judith would like it. She always talked about how much she loved being a Christian but the religion and the Bible were way too male. She wanted to change all the male words to female. That would begin to balance out two thousand years of male domination. I didn't really understand why it was such a big deal to her, but that's what Judith wanted."

Joseph gestured to the empty chair next to him. "Want to sit down?"

Ben glared at the other man. "No, I really want to spend some time with my sister alone. You don't belong here. Get out."

Joseph looked sad, but he didn't look cowed. "You know, your sister would have been the first to tell you to stand down, man."

"You fucking shit."

All the karate and laws were forgotten as Ben lunged for Joseph and pushed his chair over. Joseph grabbed Ben and fell over on top of the lawyer. They wrestled on the floor, kicking over a lamp and night-stand. A vase full of flowers crashed to the floor. The close quarters favored Joseph, who had been a wrestler in college, and now that it was happening, he seemed to relish the fight.

A nurse came running in. "What are you doing, you idiots?" The men got in a few more punches and then stopped, looking up at her from the floor. Both men registered that she was pretty attractive, taller than most women with long legs and Asian features, her long dark hair pulled back in a ponytail.

"STOP THAT and GET UP," she ordered, glaring. "Now, don't do this again. Look at your sister, your friend. She's crying." The nurse, Amy, frowned at them. Men, what idiots, she thought, always fighting, fighting even in a hospital. Both men got up, warily glanced at each other and approached the bed. Judith was, in fact, crying, tears streaming down her face.

All the animosity drained from the men's faces.

"But she's never done that before. At least not here," Joseph said with amazement. Ben put his hand to Judith's face, then bent over and put his cheek to hers, whispering something. When he pulled away, his tears were mingled with hers.

Joseph picked up the lamp and nightstand and set the Bible down. Then he gathered up the flowers and broken pieces of the vase. He filled a plastic cup with water and placed the flowers on her nightstand. He really wanted to stay, but he'd been there for a couple of hours, and it was Ben's turn to be with Judith. Joseph retrieved his Cowboys cap and said, "See you, man." Ben glared at him. Joseph turned to Judith and gently whispered, "Bye, Judith, I'll be back tomorrow." Then he and the nurse left the room.

Ben sat for a long time, looking at his sister, his face softening. He put his hand up to her cheek and felt her tears. At some point he picked up the Bible. *"O give thanks to the..."* He paused. *"...Lady, call on her name, make known her deeds among the peoples! Sing to her, sing praises to her, tell of all her wonderful works! Glory in her holy name; let the hearts of those who seek the Lady rejoice."*

Judith looked so calm and peaceful now. Ben could see a little smile on her face. Glory, glory, hallelujah, he thought to himself. Weird, he hadn't thought of that phrase in a long time. Maybe something their grandmother used to say. Ben hadn't seen that old lady in a while as she lived in New Orleans, but he was thinking, maybe he needed to go visit her. He thought on this for a while, then he kissed his sister and placed the Bible by the flowers next to Judith's bed.

Chapter 4

Lucy got a couple of miles out of town before the sun was up. She trudged along the road, and the few cars that went by didn't bother her. At one point she came over a hill and had to stop. The fields of bluebonnets stunned her. They looked like her idea of heaven.

She realized she hadn't seen such an abundance of bluebonnets in a very long while. Killeen had a few small patches, but the town was mostly concrete and asphalt. Some of her favorite childhood memories were trips to view the bluebonnets. The field trips had stopped by middle school and her parents hadn't taken her in years. Lucy wasn't allowed to date and she didn't drive. Family excursions to the countryside seemed to stop after her parents became interested in the Rapture. Looking at the beauty of the scene Lucy recalled the words of her preacher, which now puzzled her. He often quoted Anne Coulter: "God said, 'Earth is yours. Take it. Rape it. It's yours.'" This had frightened Lucy, as it seemed like such a strange and scary statement from a woman. The preacher disliked flowers and wouldn't allow them in church. She wondered what Anne and the preacher would think of this field of bluebonnets. She shivered to think of the bluebonnets being raped.

Lucy had never traveled outside of Texas and she didn't realize some people from other places planned vacations in early April to see the bluebonnets. She just knew they were a welcome relief to the Killeen concrete and asphalt, rolling streams of blue interspersed with green. Suddenly tired, Lucy took off her backpack, pushed it over a wire fence and then climbed over herself, glad the fence wasn't made out of barbwire. She aimed for a huge oak. When she got there, she saw a few old condoms on the side of the tree away from the road. She knew what they were because she had learned about them in health class in school, although the ones displayed in class were new while these were obviously used. Maybe one of those girls from school had been here with Larry or Tony or one of the others. She shoved the condoms away with her shoe, picked a bluebonnet and sat with her back against the tree. The closer she examined the delicate flower, the more ordinary it looked. She wondered how something so plain could look so astounding when joined together with others strewn through grass along rolling hills. This image of fields of bluebonnets tumbled in her mind as she fell asleep.

* * *

"Well, whatta we got here, Cal?"

Before she opened her eyes, Lucy felt the metal boot tip jabbing her bottom. Two big guys loomed over her. She couldn't see their faces as the sun was behind them, but she saw flabby lower bellies, dirty jeans, and scuffed cowboy boots. They smelled of sweat, beer, cigarette smoke, and something else that Lucy couldn't identify. She tried to get up, but they pushed her back down.

"We're gonna have us some fun, now, Bobby, aren't we?" Cal leered at his friend. Each man must have weighed at least 250 pounds, and Lucy was barely 110. She knew she didn't have a chance to get away. She clung to the wilted bluebonnet she'd picked a few hours before. The preacher had often said that unmarried girls had to be virgins to get into heaven, and it didn't matter if they'd been raped by a boyfriend or molested by a pervert. Lucy was horribly frightened by these guys, but her first thoughts were that now she'd never be raptured, and she'd never see her parents again. Her next feeling was pure terror as she wondered if these men would kill her. And where, she wondered, was God?

Cal put his hand up her shirt and grabbed at Lucy with his pudgy sweating hands. He howled, "This is gonna be great!!" Lucy screamed and the other man clamped his hand over her mouth. They dragged her a few feet away from the trunk of the tree.

Two other men on motorcycles were traveling down the same road Cal and Bobby had been on. Alan and David were good friends from college, now married lawyers in their fifties, both fathers of teenage girls, and both enduring midlife crises. Alan had suggested that David come down from Chicago and they ride motorcycles together through the hill country. In April it wouldn't be too hot and the fields of bluebonnets were otherworldly. David hadn't ridden a motorcycle in twenty-five years and didn't really like Texas, but he needed a break from his life and had taken Alan up on the offer.

The friends had been going along just fine until David ran over some cactus pieces on the road and his front tire started to go flat. They cruised to a stop near a pickup truck parked by a field of bluebonnets. "Fucking cactuses. I knew I shouldn't have come to Texas."

"Hey, it's part of the adventure, dude. Shut up, and let's fix it."

Just after dumping out the tool kit, the men heard Cal's chilling howl, and a shrieking young female squeal. Being the fathers of girls, they knew exactly what was going on: their worst nightmare on the other side of the fence. Leaping over it, tools in hands, they ran towards the tree as fast as they could.

They got there in time to see Bobby holding the girl down and Cal approaching with his pants down to his knees, his penis erect and bobbing. David hit the half nude man in the back with a wrench, and Alan tackled the other. Although smaller than the thugs, the lawyers were fit, had weapons, weren't drunk and were enraged. David got in another solid whack to Cal's arm as he vainly tried to pull up his pants with one hand and ward off the wrench with the other. Bobby was a tougher opponent for Alan and he got in a punch to Alan's gut, which brought the lawyer to his knees. But when Bobby charged like a bull to mow him over, Alan quickly rolled away and Bobby hit the tree instead, knocking himself out. Breathing heavily, Alan helped David subdue the other man. Then they pulled the pants off the assailants, and using a knife they'd found in Cal's pocket, the lawyers cut the pants into strips and used the strips and the men's belts to tie up the thugs.

Then they turned to the girl. She was lying on the ground, frozen like a baby rabbit, her shirt still pushed up around her armpits. When she didn't move, David gently pulled her shirt down and said, "Are you okay? We won't hurt you. Those guys aren't going to hurt you, either."

Dazed, Lucy sat up and burst into tears. The lawyers helped her to stand, and Alan picked up her backpack and walked with her to the road. David stayed behind and looked over at the tied-up men. He couldn't believe how good he felt to have whipped their asses. He had never done anything like this before. Viciously he kicked the bastards. That was for all the rapists who'd ever lived and gotten away with their crimes. How could anyone want to rape someone else? He'd never understood that. An ugly, sickening thing to do to another human being. David kicked each of the men once more and thought about crushing their heads in with the metal tools after smashing their genitals.

But he saw Lucy walking through the bluebonnets towards the road, and he thought of his wife and daughters back in Chicago. He knew he could spend the rest of his life in prison if he did any more violence to these assholes. That would be a real midlife crisis. David backed away from the rapists but stared at them for some minutes before he walked back to the road.

"Hey, dude, come on," Alan called. "Help me fix the tire before those guys can get untied. This is Lucy, here, and I had her take this knife and destroy their tires, so if they do get up before the cops get here, they won't be able to go anywhere. My cell doesn't work out here, so we're going to have to ride towards Waco to get reception. Pretty lonely spot. Probably won't get any rides, especially without any pants." They all started laughing, nervously at first, but then hysterically.

When the laughter died down, Lucy announced that she was glad they were going to Waco as that was where she was headed too. She'd gotten her sense of assurance back surprisingly quickly. Both men wondered about that, but neither felt it was his place to question her. They fixed the tire and finished repacking the tools and mounted the bikes, David with Lucy and Alan with her backpack.

A few hours later, they were finishing off some incredibly high calorie comfort food in an International House of Pancakes (IHOP) in the middle of Waco. They'd been to the police and were later informed that the creeps had been picked up. The lawyers looked anxiously at the young woman. "Are you sure you're going to be okay?" David asked.

Lucy pushed her plate aside and took out her Bible, which she unwrapped from Maria's Oaxacan cloth. After opening the book, she began reading from Ezekiel 34:25-26: *"I will make with them a covenant of peace and banish wild beasts from the land, so that they may dwell securely in the wilderness and sleep in the woods. And I will make them and the places round about my hill a blessing; and I will send down the showers in their season; they shall be the showers of blessing.*

"Thank you, you are my blessings." Lucy rewrapped the Bible and returned it to her backpack. They all stood up and she gave both the lawyers hugs. Then she walked out into the afternoon sun towards a nearby motel, where she'd promised she'd stay that night.

"Wow." The two men looked at each other. "Very intense girl. Weird trip she's on. Glad we were there to help her. Best damn legal team in the world." They laughed. It was the best work they'd ever done. David said, "Let's take the long road back to Austin tomorrow, see more bluebonnets, but then I need to get home to my wife. I'm going to surprise her and take her out to this place we used to visit in northern Michigan."

"Yeah, me too."

"What, with my wife?"

"No, asshole, with *my* wife," Alan said. "But for us it's down to Cabo, where we went before having the girls. There's some stuff we have to work on." He paused and looked at his old friend. "Cool, man. Texas motorcycle pilgrim bluebonnet therapy. Who would have thought?" And they laughed and laughed, until the waitress came over and asked if everything was okay. Yes, indeed it was.

* * *

The police officers had just put the handcuffed men into the squad car when another young man came over the hill on a motorcycle. Darrell stopped and pulled over. He watched the squad car make a U-turn and head down the road towards Waco. Noticing the two prisoners in the back seat, he tipped his cap to the officers as the car went by. He was puzzled as to what had occurred and now was really worried about Lucy. Where was she? Could something have happened to her here?

Darrell had been following Lucy since she'd left Killeen. He had gone to her home that morning and had been surprised when no one answered the door. Looking through the window in the kitchen door he'd seen the note on the counter. It was close enough that he was actually able to read it. When he read that Lucy had left with a church group, he was initially puzzled. He knew that Lucy hadn't gone with either of the church groups because he'd helped them pack the chartered buses. All at once, he realized that she must have gone on the pilgrimage envisioned from her dream. He was shocked knowing that she'd be heading to Waco and then Columbine. Darrell wasn't due in Colorado Springs for a few weeks, and his own parents were away on a mission. He decided to follow Lucy and persuade her to return to Texas with him. He knew that Lucy felt her dream was a dream from God. But the real America was dangerous. He had to find her. He'd gotten some things together and sped out of town. He'd hoped to catch up with her before she got to Waco. Now he hoped he wasn't too late.

Darrell frowned and walked over to where the police car had been parked. He saw a large tree, and after crossing the fence, strode towards it. Pacing around the tree, he noticed a small cross earring and picked it up. It was Lucy's. He felt very worried. What had happened to her? He hoped those prisoners hadn't done anything to her. He got down on his knees and prayed that she was safe. Rape: the word came into his mind. No, they couldn't have raped her. Not that. Not Lucy. He didn't want to think about that possibility. It would be too terrible for her, for him, and for her parents. He didn't think she could get raptured if she'd been raped. Unmarried women needed to be virgins.

Darrell felt disgusted at himself. He wished he'd prevented Lucy from going on this journey in the first place, even though it seemed inspired by God. While he thought it best that all women stay home, marry and have children, he knew that sometimes righteous people went on pilgrimages. Darrell prayed again that she hadn't been raped. He wanted a virgin for a wife, and her parents would be devastated if their daughter was hurt. Darrell worried that maybe they'd blame him for not telling them about her dream.

Why hadn't he contacted them? He knew the answer. He wanted to be alone with Lucy. He figured he'd catch up with her, and having saved her, she'd fall in love with him. She seemed to like him, but they'd never been truly alone together. This trip was the big opportunity. Maybe that's why this had happened. He'd selfishly wanted her alone, and now maybe she'd been hurt.

He held Lucy's little cross tightly between the palms of his hands and thought about Jesus, and how he died for everyone's sins. "Lord in heaven, Jesus on the cross, hear me, please hear me. Please forgive me for being selfish, and please help me find Lucy and find her safe." When he finished his prayer, he returned to his motorcycle and drove as fast as he could towards Waco. He figured if she'd been hurt she would have been taken to an emergency room.

He found a hospital easily and some time later left the building feeling both relieved and discouraged. Lucy had not been there as a patient, nor at any of the other hospitals the clerk had checked, so surely she was okay, he imagined. He'd like to find her to make sure, but he felt his prayers had been partially answered. Lucy was likely still a virgin. God had been looking out for her and for him. Darrell could still marry Lucy if he could find her. The YWCA, of course, was the place for decent girls to stay. Darrell would return to the hospital to ask where the Ys were in Waco.

It had been hours since he'd last eaten, and he was suddenly tremendously hungry. Darrell looked up and saw a billboard ad for an IHOP just a few blocks away. The youth church group ate at the Killeen's IHOP after Sunday school. Darrell *loved* IHOP food. He knew that Lucy liked IHOP, too. Maybe she'd be in there. He could borrow a phone book there just as well as at the hospital. He got on his bike and rode down the expressway, salivating when he saw the familiar orange sign.

Darrell parked his motorcycle next to a couple of Harleys. As he admired the bikes, the owners approached. The two middle-aged men were laughing, and as they got closer, Darrell observed that one was wearing a gold chain necklace with the Star of David. Jewish. Two Jews on motorcycles in Waco, Texas at the IHOP. You didn't see that every day. He wished he wasn't so hungry. They looked friendly, and he knew the preacher had said that 144,000 Jews needed to convert to Christianity for the Revelations prophecy to be fulfilled. The conversions were supposed to happen after the first Rapture, but there was no harm in getting started. There were different estimates as to how many Jews had been converted already, but surely lots more were needed. Darrell had hardly met any Jews, so he hadn't really had the opportunity to evangelize. And now it was here. Convert Jews to Jesus or eat? Find Lucy or eat?

Darrell was ravenous with hunger and really wanted to find Lucy too. He reluctantly watched the men get on their motorcycles and peel out of the lot. He hoped maybe there would be other Jews on this journey whom he could convert. Besides finding Lucy, that would definitely justify the trip for him. He'd get Lucy to fall in love with him. His prayers were working. Thank the Lord, God in Heaven. And thank sweet Jesus Christ. He kissed Lucy's earring and put it back in his pocket. All he needed was a double stack of pancakes with syrup and bacon. Then he'd go find Lucy. And then he'd find more Jews.

* * *

George had just finished another Republican fundraising speech.

Now, as he sat in his Denver hotel penthouse suite, he watched himself on CNN. Not a bad speech, he thought, and another $200,000 for less than twenty minutes work. However, it was getting tougher to put a positive spin on Iraq. He saw the CNN ticker tape of the official American death toll since March of 2003. "Four thousand, seven hundred and eighty-four dead, 31,631 wounded, 16,286 wounded seriously." Those numbers were always followed with the statement, "There are no accurate figures for Iraqi dead and wounded." As he continued to watch the CNN story, he became infuriated all over again when he saw those damned Code Pink ladies drop a huge pink slip over one of the convention center balconies with the words, *Apologize, George.*

"Feminist bitches," George swore as he removed his grandfather's treasured cuff links. He'd ended his speech and was just turning from the podium when Code Pink dropped their enormous sign. The Secret Service had rushed him off so quickly that he'd missed seeing these words live on the huge pink slip, but he'd heard the applause diminish and some laughter emerge. He felt absolutely livid that CNN showed the sign on national TV. Apologize? What in the heck did he have to apologize for? Code Pink and Mother Nature had a lot of nerve. George pulled his shirt over his head, and when he tossed it on the floor, he knocked his cuff links off the nightstand. He bent over to pick them up, and straightening, hit his head on a sharp corner.

"Goddamn it!" He rubbed his head and thought about a recent medical report he'd come across from the Surgeon General. It included an article from *The New England Journal of Medicine* that summarized not only the CNN figures from the last six years but also all the estimated suicides, domestic violence incidents, homicides, and other convictions for rape, assault, and robbery by Iraq and Afghanistan veterans. It also stated that without the advances of modern medical care, at least 15,000 of the wounded would have died of their injuries, which would have made deaths from the war closer to 20,000. The report confirmed that the VA system was vastly under-funded and described episodes of violence as a result of veterans not being able to get appointments or help for their problems. It also mentioned that these figures didn't include the National Guard troops, so all the statistics could be doubled. Damn statistics, George thought, and damn *The New England Journal*, likely full of Democrats who'd tried to discredit the war effort from the beginning, like that other inflammatory medical journal, *The Lancet*.

He hated thinking about these numbers, just like he hated thinking about the draft that would probably be instituted soon and would be blamed on him. Soldiers had retired from the military and volunteers had dwindled as the Iraq War dragged on. The new draft would include men and women. Women had performed so well in Iraq and Afghanistan and there was no way a draft could be instituted without them. Everyone capable was needed in the fight against terror. George was glad that his daughters had passed the age of twenty-six and couldn't be drafted. It would have been horrible to have one of his beloved girls killed or wounded. He rubbed his sore head and decided to think of something enjoyable.

George really liked speaking with high school audiences about patriotism, service to country, and sacrifice. He'd even used his wife's bluebonnet sacrifice story a few times. It went over really well in Texas, which boasted the greatest numbers of volunteers for the military. He felt immensely proud of *that* statistic. The only problem with those school talks was that they let those damn liberals set up tables. Unlike when he was president, at the last few schools at which he'd spoken, he'd been forced to see and hear the ACLU and Amnesty International. Free speech was great but he didn't want to hear it, especially irritating liberal ideas such as young people serving the country by being teachers, doctors, nurses, musicians, parents, librarians, ministers, writers or almost anything else besides being soldiers. Liberals advocated a draft for service, with military service only being one option. And to avoid the pending draft, many young adults were not only going to Canada, but also to Mexico where many had relatives. George still couldn't believe the big neighbors to the north and south had refused to participate in the

Iraq War, and now they were taking in cowardly Americans.

He turned off the TV right before they showed Obama talking about yet another plan to save the economy. George grudgingly admired the new president but absolutely hated watching anything to do with the failures of the economy. A never-ending catastrophic nightmare, even worse than all those zombies.

His head still hurt and he couldn't get these depressing thoughts out of his mind. He was going to have to take a pill for pain and another for sleep. George walked into the bathroom and regarded the array of medicines on the counter. He wished his wife was there to advise him. Opening a couple of different bottles and pouring a few pills from each into his hand, he tossed them down with water.

Hours later George suffered a horrific nightmare. The zombies were really howling, their blood spurting bright red, and there were more terribly injured children and babies than there had been the last time. And now he could smell vomit, feces, burned flesh, and rotting corpse smells. He'd never smelled these things in real life, so he didn't know why he could in his dream. But he could, and it was more terrifying than anything he'd experienced. George tried to run, but he was frozen.

Mother Nature appeared abruptly in the midst of the zombies, who didn't disappear but calmed down when they saw her. "Yes, and you're stuck there, until you atone, George."

He trembled and shifted his eyes.

"It takes you a long time to learn and change, doesn't it? Well, you aren't that different than most people." She looked seriously at him. "But you've had a religious conversion before, and it's possible for you to have another. I'm TRYING to help you." Her eyes glowed and a few lighting bolts flashed and thunder boomed.

"What can I do?" he asked peevishly. "I can't start any other wars. I don't have power over the military anymore." He sighed. He really missed that power. He recalled again, briefly, the tremendous feeling of landing on the Abraham Lincoln off Virginia, signaling, just a few months after it started, that the war was basically over and won. He loved being a pilot again, and landing on a ship was a huge rush, something he'd never done while in the Texas Guard. It was also fun being naughty, as he'd performed this stunt against the advice of Laura and the Secret Service.

Zap. Pow. ZZZZZST. "Ouch, that hurts!" Lightning singed his hair, and once again he was completely drenched. As he shivered he noticed some gross moldy stuff growing around his bare feet.

"OKAY, George, let's start with the wounded, a very good place to start. Look around you."

George averted his eyes. He wished this was just a movie and they were all actors. Until he'd met wounded soldiers in the hospital, he'd never been around sick or injured people. He truly admired the soldiers for their courage, although he didn't really understand the mental cases with PPD or PPWEE or whatever it was. If only they became Born Again Christians like him, they would get over whatever problems they claimed to have.

Suddenly George found himself flat on his back, completely naked, in that grim, horrible place where he'd first encountered the zombies. He couldn't see out of one eye, and when he put his hand up to investigate, all he felt was bloody mush. He screamed and tried to get up but half his foot was gone. Shivering, sobbing, and screaming in incredible pain, he was completely without hope.

"And this is just the beginning," Mother Nature said walking slowly around him. "Imagine being nineteen years old and like this for the rest of your life. Sure, if you're found in time, the doctors will stitch you up, keep your infections at bay, and get you to rehab where they'll do what they can. But you'll still have only one eye, one hand and one foot, and, believe me, you'll have PTSD. Post... Traumatic... Stress... Disorder. Very high incidence in injured soldiers. Almost anyone can get PTSD when traumatized enough." She paused to let that thought sink in. "And you'd be one of the lucky ones."

George wailed.

She recalled many young men and women who had endured even more before they were found...or died. She had been there with every one of them and remembered everything. She had comforted those she could, and helped many die quickly when she knew help would not arrive in time. Finally she threw George a towel and let him get up.

He whimpered. The pain seemed to recede a bit, and he could see outlines of his hand and foot returning. "What can I do? I'm not a doctor or nurse or minister. I can't take them bike riding because they don't have arms and legs and are blind. I guess I could donate money to some veterans' causes." He paused and thought. Hmmm, and that would get tax relief too.

George was instantly flattened back on the ground, howling again, this time with no eyes, no hands, no feet and in even more excruciating pain. Mother Nature let him stay there a long, long time, watching him suffer as so many others had. Finally she stopped the pain, as she wanted him to pay attention. No towel this time, though.

"You know, we could debate the need for taxes, to protect the weak, educate the young, preserve the environment, etcetera, etcetera. Lowering taxes isn't to give the wealthy more jewelry, another Lear jet, luxury vacations to Antarctica, 10,000 square-foot additions to their 8,000 square-foot homes, or expeditions to Mount Everest. People, especially people like you, should be proud to pay their taxes, to help the disadvantaged." She glared at him. Why didn't he get it?

George, whose body had been restored again, looked at her with a slight glimmer of understanding. He'd found another towel on the cave floor, an old dingy grey thing, and wrapped it around his waist. "Why, you sound a bit like my wife, when we started dating." They had met in high school, but hadn't dated much until years later. He seemed too wild for her, and after she'd accidentally killed a pedestrian while driving, she'd had enough of her own sorrow to deal with. Laura had gone into the world of books and become a librarian. When he called her up to date again, they were in their mid-twenties. It took several calls before she would go out with him, but he convinced her that he had changed. He'd told her he wanted to run for office, maybe governor some day. She thought about all the libraries and schools he could support, and that she would be able to help people with their daily problems, which she often overheard as she checked books in and out. Many patrons had found her to be a sympathetic person, possibly because of her own trauma, and many of the problems they talked about could be solved by good government, which meant taxes. He hadn't thought about this in years, but Laura had favored taxes.

"Yes, George, you've got a very good wife, and no doubt she's going to help you with your problems."

He nodded.

"Apologies. Let me say it again: APOLOGIES. The Code Pink ladies are right. Very powerful stuff. You've apologized before, to Laura at least, and you can do it again. Although this time it will be on a scale that you'll find hard to imagine, and in public." Mother Nature took off the backpack she was wearing today and pulled out a book. "Look what I have here. You know this book really well." She handed him a well-worn copy of the *Big Book,* the book used by alcoholics everywhere trying to achieve sobriety.

"Why, it's my book! How did you get this?"

"It's hard to explain, but when someone needs something, the right book appears. Books change lives, brother. You know that from reading the Bible."

She looked at him, waiting. He *was* still handsome, especially when pondering thoughtfully. She knew he and his wife were *very* satisfied with each other, and that this relationship was fundamental to his recovery, and that of the nation. She thought of the reverse of the oft-used phrase "for the want of a nail, the kingdom was lost." For the presence of a good marriage, the world was saved. She wasn't sure what had been going on with their marriage during the Iraq War planning. Maybe his wife was distracted with raising their daughters, who were her priority. And George wasn't supposed to have become the president. If he'd remained the Governor of Texas, the Iraq War never would have happened. Eyes glowing, she flipped her robes and there were more flashes of lightening and thunder accordingly. The five Supreme Court justices who'd sided with the Republican lawyers and decided the fate of so many people would also suffer. They were all religious people, so they'd have their own reckonings.

Mother Nature calmed down and turned back to George. "Turn to page 76 of the *Big Book*, and please read me the third paragraph, starting with the words '*Faith without works is dead*.'"

George found it: "*Faith without works is dead. Let's look at Steps Eight and Nine. We have a list of all persons we have harmed and to whom we are willing to make amends. We made it when we took inventory. We subjected ourselves to a drastic self-appraisal. Now we go out to our fellows and repair the damage done in the past.*" He stopped reading but repeated those last words: "*Now we go out to our fellows and repair the damage done in the past.*"

"There you go. It's all there, George." And with that she vanished.

* * *

Ben slouched against the wall outside Judith's room, his eyes closed. He'd had a long day and some tears rolled down his cheeks. He was waiting while Judith finished up with some kind of new age organic enzyme treatment. Sounded kooky but if it worked, so be it. He slid to the floor.

"Hey, man." It was Joseph. He had a huge bouquet of roses in one hand and a book of hymns in the other. He squatted next to Ben and pulled a clean faded purple bandana out of his shirt pocket and offered it to the other man. Ben looked at the cloth for a while, but then he took it. "Thanks."

A half hour later Amy came out of Judith's room and, smiling at Ben, indicated that the men could go in. Entering, they found Judith lying on her bed, covered in white sheets and dressed in a soft blue-green gown. Ben gave her a kiss. Joseph would have kissed her too (as he had many times), however he refrained due to Ben's presence. He placed the flowers in the new vase he'd brought, setting it close so that Judith could smell their wonderful scent. He sat down in one of two adjacent chairs, the one further away from Judith.

"Let's see. What do you think she'd like to hear?"

Joseph flipped through the hymnal. *"For the Beauty of the Earth? Morning Has Broken?"*

"Good songs but not quite right." Ben took the hymnal from Joseph and turned the pages. "This one. This is our grandma's favorite hymn and I know Judith loved it." He moved his chair over to sit by Joseph and they began to sing:

> *Wake, now, my senses and hear the earth call;*
> *feel the deep power of being in all*
> *keep, with the web of creation your vow,*
> *giving receiving as love shows us how.*

Ben and Joseph sang the next verse and then a remarkable thing happened. Judith opened her mouth and began to sing too. Her voice was scratchy and slow, but she was singing:

> *Wake now, compassion, give heed to the cry,*
> *voices of suffering fill the wide sky;*
> *Take as your neighbor both stranger and friend,*
> *praying and striving their hardship to end.*

Ben and Joseph were almost too astonished to continue but they sang the next verse with Judith and finished the hymn together:

> *Wake, now, my vision of ministry clear;*
> *brighten my pathway with radiance here;*
> *Mingle my calling with all who will share;*
> *work toward a planet transformed by our care.*

Ben was the first to break the silence. "Judith, you sang!" he cried softly. "You sang. You sang." He couldn't say anything else.

"Hey, Ben. 'Wake now." Judith's voice was still croaky. "Joseph. 'Wake now."

Joseph moved his face close to hers. They could feel each other's breath. Judith mumbled something which he couldn't understand. Months later she would tell him that her awakening by their voices singing the ancient Irish melody was accompanied by a dreamy vision of soft green spring leaves fluttering and filtering sunlight as she floated beneath in a comfortable hammock. She wouldn't remember what she said, just the feeling of aliveness and returning to voices she loved, singing a hymn she'd known forever.

Chapter 5

Lucy awoke refreshed from her night's sleep. She'd dreamt of bluebonnets, lawyers, and motorcycles. Alan and David had been raptured with her from a field of bluebonnets, riding their motorcycles up a rainbow road, spiraling up into heaven. God was a little surprised to see folks arrive by motorcycle, however he welcomed them all through the pearly gates. Lucy had noticed the Star of David necklace one lawyer wore and recalled that they'd sent back their plates upon which was unordered bacon. She realized that the men must be Jewish. She wondered if she'd missed her opportunity to try to convert the two men. She must have been truly overwhelmed by her ordeal. She knew that 144,000 Jews were needed to be baptized into the Christian faith for the prophecy to be fulfilled. In spite of this disappointment, Lucy figured her dream meant these nice Jewish lawyers might convert in the future. They certainly had done God's work in her rescue.

Lucy was still thinking about converting Jews as she walked out of Waco towards the site of the former Branch Davidian compound. About an hour after she left the motel, she reached the fenced-off site. Lucy looked out over acres and acres of bluebonnets, then brought her gaze to rest on the simple plaque beside the road. Nearby were a couple of nuns, two conservatively dressed young blonde men carrying Bibles, and some sad looking older men and women. All were facing west towards the site of the tragedy.

The plaque offered the barest details: four Alcohol Tobacco and Firearms agents and eighty-two Davidians, including twenty-seven children, had died, most of them in a fire on April 19 1999. Lucy recalled other information from the internet at the Killeen Library. There were conflicting arguments as to who was responsible for the tragedy. Many believed that the leader, David Koresh, and some of his followers had set the fire as federal agents raided the building in a vain attempt to rescue the children. They believed that David was an insane sociopath who had amassed an arsenal of weapons. Others felt that the government had unnecessarily interfered in David's personal affairs and in his religion. They blamed the federal agents for the deaths of everyone in the fire. Lucy couldn't figure it out from reading the endless internet accounts. All she could conclude was that guns didn't belong in churches.

Lucy wondered whether the tragedy could have been prevented and how far back one would have to go. David had been born to a fourteen-year-old unmarried mother and raised by his grandparents. Dyslexic and teased by classmates, he dropped out of high school and at age twenty he got a fifteen-year-old girl pregnant. He wanted to marry her but his church refused permission. Quoting scripture, he'd argued with the elders, but to no avail. David was kicked out of church and twelve years later he connected with the Branch Davidians, and eventually took it over. Lucy wondered if things would have turned out differently if the church had allowed him to marry the mother of his first child. He was trying to create a different story than that of his own mother. Or, what if he'd renounced guns and violence after he became the church leader? The Branch Davidians could have become a peaceful retreat, known only to locals and pilgrims.

It could have been like St Alcuin Community Church, another church Lucy had read about in the library. Founded in Dallas about the same time that David was reforming the Branch Davidians, St Alcuin was organized by a Father Albert Achilles Taliaferro. In mysterious synchronicity, Father Taliaferro had died the same year David Koresch died, but in contrast to David's legacy of bitterness, the former Episcopalian minister left a lasting legacy of peace and good deeds still rippling across the country years later.

Lucy imagined how horrible it would be to die in a fire. She wondered what the Davidians had thought when they realized they would be devoured by the flames. Maybe they believed they'd be raptured into heaven, as David had promised them. It would have been merciful if they had believed this. She knew that some of the victims, mostly children, had been shot before the fire reached them, their bodies fused by flames with the larger bodies of adults. Maybe those parents had whispered to their little ones, "Close your eyes, my dear, and I'll see you in heaven," before they pulled the triggers. But this wasn't how the Rapture was supposed to happen. Everything Lucy had been taught at church and read in the *Left Behind* series indicated that the Rapture would happen in an instant and would not be due to gunshots or immolation. All children under twelve would disappear as would any others whose lives had been exemplary and who accepted Jesus.

As Lucy looked over the now peaceful fields, she knelt and then cried. Even if they hadn't been raptured, the children were surely in heaven, along with whoever had tried to protect them. She sincerely doubted, though, that David was with Jesus, and whoever it was who'd set the fire was also likely in hell, continuing to burn. Lucy took off her backpack, pulled out her Bible and read Psalm 102 out loud. Maybe one of the Branch Davidians had said this prayer before dying:

> *Hear my prayer, O Lord; let my cry come to thee!*
> *Do not hide thy face from me*
> *In the day of my distress!*
> *They will perish, but thou dost endure;*
> *They will all wear out like a garment*
> *Thou changes them like raiment, and they pass away;*
> *But thou art the same, and thy years have no end.*

The nuns approached Lucy and knelt beside her. They took out their Bibles and read other verses. The women were kneeling on the very spot where a Gulf War veteran, Timothy McVeigh, had stood some months after the Waco disaster. Waco had apparently been a tipping point in his mentally and emotionally dysfunctional life. He had brooded about the cause of the Davidians' deaths and apparently believed that if the government hadn't intervened, these people would have lived. Their deaths enraged Timothy. However, his was an inner hidden rage and he was a very controlled person who knew how to plan. And that's what he did; using a massive ammonia fertilizer bomb, he acted out his fury exactly one year after the Waco disaster in Oklahoma City at the Murrah Federal Building.

Lucy knew about Timothy, and as she looked around at the nuns and the others, she wondered what would have happened if someone had become aware of his grief as he stood at the Waco site that day. Perhaps he could have explained that he didn't know anyone personally, but that the Davidian deaths had affected him as if all his own relatives had been brutally murdered. Then the two mourners might have gone to a nearby Shoney's Big Boy and talked over a meal of hamburgers, fries and pecan pie. Maybe something in their conversation would have helped Timothy think differently about his grief, and maybe he could have found some other way to deal with it. Maybe he could have written a book, or welded sculptures of all the people who had died there. Or joined a seminary and become an evangelical preacher. Or done something else creative and non-violent to channel his grief and anger, instead of planning and carrying out one of the worst American terrorist attacks of the twentieth century.

Lucy and the nuns finished their prayers and got to their feet and hugged one another. The ladies offered Lucy a ride to Oklahoma City, where they lived. After the motorcycle-riding lawyers had helped her, Lucy had decided that she would accept rides when they were offered. She wouldn't be able to walk the entire distance. The nuns had a very old Pontiac, which they said ran on prayers. They offered some before they turned on the engine. The prayers must have worked, as the car started and Lucy fell asleep in the back seat and didn't wake up until they stopped outside the convent.

* * *

"Honey, look at our garden. Something terrible's happened." George frowned. All the flowers seemed to be dying, and all at the same time. Flowers do die back, but the couple had arranged to have successive waves of blooms, so the garden would never appear completely dead. Now all the flowers were wilted, and some of the trees and bushes were dead. The only thing that looked healthy was the damn bush he peed on every night. George wondered if he was going to have to go around peeing on all the other plants to get them to grow again.

Laura regarded the garden. "You're right. How sad. I guess we better call for help from the Lady Bird Johnson Wildflower Center. They know everything there is about flowers. I'll go call them right now." She walked back toward the house.

"Honey, can you also ask them if they know how to get rid of that bush I hate and some of those chollas over there?"

Laura nodded her head. It hadn't rained since February and George was getting worried. It was shaping up to be the hottest spring on record; would probably even beat 2006, which had been pretty awful even for Texas. He remembered reading some reports on climate change during the last year of his presidency and wondered how global warming might affect his retirement in Texas. He still didn't think that human activity was to blame. Mother Nature was going to do whatever she was going to do. And what can you do about the weather?

The serenity prayer came to mind. Change what you can, accept what you can't and have the wisdom to know the difference. Well, that would come in useful if the Lady Bird folks were without any ideas.

Acceptance of a dead garden would be tough, however. George clenched his hands and strutted angrily across the lawn. Why couldn't everything just stay the same? Why couldn't he just get to enjoy his retirement like any other American? Why did things that he'd worked so hard on have to die? He went over to the shed and picked up his chainsaw, an act which always made him feel better. I'll go out and cut down something, he thought. His mind flashed to the west coast forests where, in his opinion, there were far too many trees. George wished he could be magically transported to the California redwoods. Although it had probably never been done with a handheld chainsaw, it would feel really great to cut down a huge Sequoia. George started to feel better. He strutted over to that bush he hated and pulled the cord to start the engine.

A few minutes later, Laura heard his screams and ran outside. She found him lying on the ground, howling, the chainsaw still running, dangerously close to his leg. She pulled it away and turned it off. "Honey, what happened? Oh no, you're bleeding," she cried as she noticed blood spurting from his shoe.

"OWWW. I tried to cut that bush, and that damn chainsaw just jumped out of my hands and landed on my fucking foot. OWWWW!"

Laura helped George remove his shoe. She used the dishtowel in her hands to bind the wound. Then she ran back into the house and called for the Secret Service, who quickly arrived. One agent called for a helicopter as the other held the towel on George's foot. Minutes later, as he was lifted into the helicopter, George noted that the pilot, who was wearing shorts, had a prosthesis on his left leg. Probably a war vet, he thought. In spite of his own pain, George wondered why the heck they had to send him a disabled pilot.

The pilot noticed him staring. "Oh, don't worry, sir, I am triple A certified, highest rating a helicopter pilot can have, and under the Americans with Disabilities Law, God bless it, they've fitted helicopters for guys like me, so we can have jobs. Listen, sir, let's go, otherwise you're going to need one of these bad boys for yourself." George, who was feeling faint, suddenly vomited. As one agent strapped him in, another grabbed an oily rag from the floor and wiped the vomit from his face and chest. The helicopter rose from the ground. They'd be in Fort Hood in just minutes, the pilot promised.

But the agent's cell phone rang and he frowned as he heard the news that some sort of radiation leak had just occurred at the hospital there and all emergencies were being diverted to Waco, which had the closest civilian hospitals. He informed George.

"Wherever you want," he cried. "Just get me some help. The pain is killing me."

They soon arrived in the Waco Hospital parking lot and the agents hustled the president into the emergency room waiting area. George looked up from the stretcher. The waiting room and hallways were packed with patients and their families.

"What are all these people doing here?" It was more crowded than a typical Republican fundraiser. But unlike the folks at one of those festive gatherings, these people looked poor, tired, worried and ill. There was a long line to check insurance or lack of it, and other long lines for nurse triage and seeing a doctor.

"Make way, make way, we've got a president here." The crowd of people opened up for the stretcher and George looked at their faces as he passed through. They were all ages, male and female, Anglos, Hispanics, African Americans, and Asians. He hadn't been in a non-military hospital for years. George had no idea how crowded public emergency rooms were and felt immensely relieved that as a VIP he was moved to the front of the line into a private room. George felt fairly certain that he would live. A nurse took his blood pressure, pulse, and temperature, and checked his oxygen level with a small clip on his finger. Then she said, "Here. Blow into this." She put a small whistle-looking thing up to his lips.

"What is that?" George growled suspiciously.

"It's to check if there's any alcohol on board. Routine screening, sir. We get so many intoxicated patients that we like to know up front in case someone goes into withdrawal, and then we can make a referral to substance treatment when they're ready to leave. It's a mandate from the new Texas Driving While Intoxicated law that Mothers Against Drunk Driving got passed. It's really put a dent in DWI deaths and injuries."

"No, I won't have that silly test. Get that out of my face." George tried to bat the breathalyzer away.

"Well, sir, I can't make you take the test, but I'll have to fill out a form confirming that you refused, and right now our computer is on the blink, so you'll have to wait longer. Our administrators have told us that the breathalyzer has to be done, or refusal paperwork completed, before we can administer care, unless of course the person is dying." The nurse beamed at George. "The nurses insisted on that exception. Listen, sir, you think about it. I've got to go take a break. All the doctors are dealing with multiple motor vehicle accident victims, much more seriously injured than you." The nurse didn't say it, but once under the control of medical personnel, at least in this hospital, there were no VIPs, just human beings, and they were triaged and treated in order of medical severity. He wasn't bleeding and his vital signs were stable. "When I come back, you tell me what you want to do." The nurse flipped her cornrow braids, covered with colored beads, and started walking towards the door.

"Hey, you can't leave me alone. Are you going to take a smoke break? Come back," George yelled angrily.

The nurse turned around, hands on her hips. "No, sir, no one smokes here. We are a one hundred percent smoke-free hospital. But it is time for my break and I'm going to our hol-ka room."

"Your what? Polka room?" What kind of hospital was this? George was really wishing he'd gone to Fort Hood.

The nurse said over her shoulder, "H-O-L-K-A." She didn't have time to explain to this man, who would need a lot of explaining. He didn't know how lucky he was. Another nurse would have sewn his ass to the gurney the minute his attitude became apparent. Sighing as she reached the hol-ka, she slipped off her shoes and placed them in a rack under a small sign which read: *Hol-ka: a room for rejuvenation. Idea came from a dream in Dorothy Bryant's classic tale,* The Kin of Ata Are Waiting For You. *You are welcome. There is a place for you in our hol-ka.*

The nurse stooped down, crawled down a carpeted passageway and entered the hol-ka, a sort of meditation, yoga, relaxation room with ethereal soft music and padded floors without any furniture. She could sit quietly, do a few yoga or tai chi positions, rest on her back with her feet up the wall, or simply lie on the floor in "shivasina," a state of relaxation. Like most people, she only needed to be in there for five or ten minutes, and she would come out refreshed, ready to tackle new problems with calmness and clarity. Hol-ka use had replaced smoke or coffee breaks for medical staff, and had helped hospital staff manage otherwise impossible levels of stress.

The nurse, feeling so much better, emerged from the hol-ka and returned to help the unruly patient. George sensed her calmness, and when asked again, he cooperated with the breathalyzer test, which showed 0.00, as he knew it would. He hadn't drunk any alcohol in years. A doctor in blood-spattered scrubs appeared and in no time George's wound was irrigated and stitched up. After antibiotic and tetanus shots, he was given a couple of Percosets and soon felt much better. George thanked the nurse.

"No worries, sir. If you like, check out the hol-ka before you leave. Most people really like it."

No thanks, he thought. Sounded way too weird.

"Namaste, sir. *Adiós*," said the nurse, bowing slightly and folding her hands at her heart as if praying. She left the room as a Secret Service agent entered.

No mass day? This was a really weird hospital, he thought. What did that mean? It sounded like Spanglish, but why would she say that, and why bow? George asked the agent, "What did she mean, 'no mass day'?"

The Secret Service agent happened to have done yoga for years to help him deal with the tension of the job and prevent recurrence of back pain. He was the right person to ask. "'Namaste,' sir, means 'I salute the divinity in both of us,' and '*Adiós*,' of course means, 'go with God.'"

George looked surprised. Namaste was a really nice thing for her to say. He'd never been namasted before and he'd forgotten that "*adiós*" meant "go with God." He felt a lot better and he didn't think it was just the Percosets. He was soon buckled up in the helicopter and flying into the sky.

"Namaste. *Adiós*." As he closed his eyes and slumped back in his seat, George whispered those words. "The divinity within both of us. Go with God...."

* * *

Miguel worked with Joseph. Also a veteran of the Iraq War, he had lost both feet to an IED. In the garage they worked as a team with Joseph doing repairs which needed a standing mechanic, and Miguel, lying on his back on a trolley, fixing stuff underneath the cars. He got so good at scooting around the garage that he'd leave his prostheses in his locker. Miguel's arms were massively strong and he'd learned to walk on his hands in the rehabilitation hospital with the help of a very creative physical therapist, who'd once been a circus acrobat. Miguel enjoyed having people look at him with amazement instead of pity.

Miguel could also play the guitar really well. It was a miracle to him that he hadn't lost his hands in Iraq. He could even remember that this was his first thought, right after the explosion. "*No mi manos, Diós*, not my hands, *por favor*," he'd screamed. His mates in the Humvee had looked at him in horror, as blood gushed from his legs, his feet obliterated. But Miguel was yelling with joy that his hands were still there. He had recovered relatively quickly once back in Texas and had become an even better guitarist than he'd been before the accident, as he couldn't easily do other activities. He played all kinds of music, but he particularly liked playing in his family's mariachi band.

They played in weddings, *quinceañeros* parties, graduation ceremonies, and at restaurants. Miguel's favorite experiences were when they serenaded young women in the middle of the night. He'd last done this a few months ago, at the request of a cousin, Javier, who was completely besotted over a girl, Carmelita. They'd gotten to her home after midnight and quieted the dogs, who knew the cousin. Miguel sat in a chair and started playing *Cielito Lindo* while the others stood under Carmelita's window and sang. Seconds later the young woman flung open the window and pulled her robe around herself, but not before the young men saw her alluring figure visible through her nightgown. Javier sang with ardor, and Miguel remembered feeling awed at the power of love, which brought out a voice he'd never heard coming from his cousin.

At work in the garage, Miguel had been talking with Joseph about doing a mariachi serenade for Judith at the hospital. Joseph had confided how much he loved Judith and had told his friend that her wakening at the singing of the hymn had turned out to be only a temporary return to complete consciousness. She hadn't communicated since, although she appeared aware of visitors and smiled in the presence of those who loved her, as might a nine-month-old baby. Miguel was convinced that a mariachi serenade would be just the thing to wake her up for good. Joseph wasn't too sure about this, thinking it would rouse the whole hospital, and bring that crazy guard running to tackle the band.

"No, *hombre*, chill. It'll be great. No woman can resist mariachi music when played for her, just for her. *Es mágica, amigo.* She'll wake up and she'll love you so much."

Joseph was mostly of Scottish ancestry and he'd considered getting a bagpiper for Judith. But bagpipes weren't the music of love. Rather, their doleful haunting sounds honored sorrow and made people think about eternity. Bagpipes were profoundly emotional, hair-raising and very effective at funerals and other serious ceremonies. But this obviously wasn't what was needed for Judith. Maybe Miguel was right, but Joseph wasn't sure that Judith even liked Mexican music. It was one thing, amazingly, that they had never talked about. What if she hated it and woke up angry?

"*No te preocupes, chavo.* No worries, guy. Mariachi music, she'll love it. Think about it, *hombre*." Miguel, acting like a playful puppy, pretended to bite his friend's ankle, and then wheeled himself under the suburban Humvee they were working on. They didn't really enjoy working on these Humvees. The huge vehicles reminded the men of the war, and it seemed stupid to have Humvees in suburban

America — although, ironically, they'd gotten their jobs partly because they knew how to work on these lumbering vehicles from their time in Iraq, even though the Humvees in America were like Rolls Royces compared with the utilitarian vehicles used in the war. But even more than the vehicles, what really steamed Miguel and Joseph were the Hummer owners.

Sometimes it was an extremely well dressed, serious man, always fit, with a Blue Tooth hooked to his ear, and a very curt manner with service people. But more often it would be the wife who returned for the tuned-up Humvee. Almost always extremely attractive, she'd be wearing a tight-fitting short skirt, high heels showing off sleek legs and sculpted calves, big Texas hair, movie star sunglasses, a little bit too much make up for daytime, and tits like jet engines. Nevertheless, the woman's smoldering sensuality was usually tempered by a scornful smile and disdain for the world in general and service people in particular. Be that as it may, Miguel was often still on the roller when the woman showed up, and he had a great view up the long legs and short skirts. This, he didn't complain about.

It almost seemed as if these women wanted to be seen by him. One time he was pretty sure the woman he found himself beneath had no panties on, and he glimpsed her bush. Miguel was so shocked he pushed the roller back under another car and ran into the wall on the other side, hurting his head. Joseph, meanwhile, was trying to avoid looking at the woman's cleavage, which was tough as she kept arching her back. After she left, both men looked at each other and laughed. They both had boners.

"We are fucking pathetic, bro."

"It's evolutionary biology, *hombre*. Can't change millions of years of what brings on hard-ons. That's why Hummers sell. Sex and power."

It had happened often enough now that the men were able to anticipate their reactions and mostly prevent them. It made them look forward to the more sensible cars, driven by more normal men and women most probably wearing underwear. Sex was good, but not in a garage, not in a Hummer, but at home, in a soft, comfortable bed with a loving partner who had been turned on by another human being, not a Hummer. It might have been different for other vets, but for Joseph and Miguel, they wanted no more association of war with sex.

Sometimes though, these Hummer owners were decently dressed parents with the cutest kids, sitting solemnly in the back, dwarfed by the huge leather seats. The little girls almost always wore pink, and had rosy backpacks with fuzzy white rabbits attached, while the boys wore Thomas the Tank Engine outfits and carried Barney backpacks. Joseph and Miguel had talked about these families too and concluded that maybe they loved their kids so much — and feared the world so intensely — that they had come to feel that anything less than a Hummer would fail to protect them. Still, with gas prices soaring and all the scornful looks people gave them, these gas guzzling vehicles didn't seem worth the $55,000 price tag. Besides, Al-Queda didn't seem likely to attack north Texas, and even if they did, these vehicles would quickly run out of gas. They'd seen several Hummers with fake bumper stickers, "GRDY PG," plastered on by environmentalists or outraged motorists, perhaps when the Hummers were parked in two spaces where parking was hard to find. The mechanics predicted that soon these monsters would disappear like the dinosaurs. Hummers were odd last gasps of the reign of oil addiction, Joseph thought as he looked over at his motorcycle, which got eighty miles per gallon.

At the end of a day of dealing with Hummer owners, Joseph relented and agreed to listen to Miguel's mariachi music. He didn't really like mariachi music himself, but he couldn't squash Miguel's enthusiasm for a musical miracle for Judith and that of his musician *compadres*, who insisted on the awesome power of a moonlight mariachi serenade. All they needed was a full moon and Joseph's agreement. But he couldn't decide right then. After Joseph left the disappointed musicians, Miguel said, "I just hope he doesn't choose bagpipes for Judith. That would kill her." And they spent the rest of the evening deriding Anglos for their love of sad, serious music.

Chapter 6

After thanking the nuns for the ride, Lucy found her way to the site of the former Murrah Federal Building in downtown Oklahoma City. It was now a memorial with a grassy lawn, shady trees, and a glistening reflecting pool. One hundred sixty-one chairs, some occupied by teddy bears and draped with flowers, represented the people who had died that day in April of 1994 when a massive fertilizer bomb exploded. The bomb destroyed the front part of the building, decimating the people inside. The worst part had been that the building contained a day care center, and at nine in the morning, the center was filled with the employees' young children, including babies.

Many children were killed right away, but some were horribly burned and lingered in agony for days before dying. The image that remained in people's minds was of one particular burned baby, carried from the smoldering ruins by a burly firefighter covered in soot, the baby still alive. No one could think of these babies without feeling horror, and seeing a child's name on one of the chairs, Lucy began to weep. The man who built and detonated the bomb had said he didn't know there was a daycare in the building. She wasn't sure if he'd added that he wouldn't have set the bomb there if he'd known, but surely he would have found another place to direct his rage. And inevitably there would have been a group of elementary students on a field trip or some other innocent people who would have died because of his beliefs.

Lucy knew that Timothy McVey had been executed in prison after a long trial. She had a hard time praying for his soul but she had been taught in church that all sinners had the chance for redemption, if they accepted Jesus Christ into their lives, and if they truly atoned. She didn't think Timothy had come to Christ in prison before he died, but maybe if he'd been kept alive, he would have. And she wondered if maybe people would have learned something from him that might have helped to prevent other deaths someday somewhere else. Lucy had heard that such lessons had been learned from two other American terrorists, Eric Rudolph, the Olympic Park bomber, and Ted Kaczynski, the Unabomber, who were both imprisoned for life for the crimes they had committed. Lucy wondered if revenge and perceived justice were worth more than the kind of knowledge that has the power to prevent future tragedies while at the same time providing a means of redemption for the sinners.

Lucy walked slowly through the rows of chairs and prayed for each individual. Noticing the items left in memory of the dead, she tried to absorb something of each person. The chairs held bouquets of roses, marigolds, heather, gerberas, carnations, sunflowers, blue flax, and daisies. One child's chair held dandelions, perhaps for a kid who had liked to blow the delicate white fluff into the breeze. Lucy closed her eyes and imagined angelic children playing with dandelions.

When she finished her prayers and looked back towards the open grassy area, she saw a strange sight. A group of people was doing some kind of strange flowing exercises. She went closer and noticed the peaceful expression on their faces. A man beckoned her, and Lucy shyly joined them. With her ballet background she was able to follow the movements, and after some time she got the hang of it. She followed along at the end when they bowed to each other, saying, "Namaste." She didn't know what that meant, but she had the same feeling as when she prayed with her family in church.

* * *

By the time George returned home from the hospital it was 110 degrees. Something about coming of age in west Texas had made him just love heat. The hotter, the better. Maybe it was part of why the news of global warming didn't really bother him. George loved going for a fast walk or bike ride on his property with heat shimmering off the roads and trails, although with his injured foot he was going to have to disappoint the few Secret Service men and women who seemed to enjoy hot exercise as much as he did. Some of them had served in Iraq and Afghanistan and would always say, "The heat in Texas ain't nuthin' like that over there in the Middle East." George still longed to go there himself in the middle of summer to see if they were exaggerating. But this was not possible, as there were plenty of people over there who hated him, and those folks bore grudges for hundreds of years.

That night George tried some of the tea his wife had made for the Chinese who'd visited a few years back. He felt better as he remembered the success of that meeting. Even *The New York Times* and that Seymour guy at *The New Yorker* had been impressed with him. The Chinese leaders had arrived in a very controlled, angry mood with demands regarding Taiwan. But Laura had served the Chinese leaders her special new tea, and they had visibly relaxed. And, as much as she and George hated people smoking, they had even let the Chinese smoke indoors to help decrease tensions. That and Laura's special tea had created an atmosphere that enabled them all to talk reasonably. Then George took them on a bike ride around his ranch. They had all ridden bikes as young men in China but hadn't used them for years. Once they got accustomed to the American mountain bikes, they threw their arms in the air and gleefully shouted "Hands off" in English followed by a torrent of cheerful exclamations in Chinese. The accompanying American negotiators, whose hands had remained firmly on their bars, noted these details and later agreed that the afternoon had been a peaceful tipping point in the relationship between China and the US. As unbelievable as it seemed when later discussed by diplomats and historians, special tea served by a kind woman, relaxation of the smoking rules and a fun bike ride were the pivotal points that eased these world leaders away from the brink of disaster for billions of other people. Yes, he thought, it was too bad everything else hadn't been so easy. He snorted at the thought of his dad inviting Saddam to Kennebunkport or him inviting Ahmadinejad to Crawford.

There were no zombies that night. Instead, Mother Nature appeared with a woman who looked like George's wife did in her twenties when they'd started dating. George immediately liked her, although Mother Nature remained intimidating. "I've brought someone to talk with you, brother. She's a librarian."

They were in the ranch library, which, sarcastic internet jokes aside, had a great deal more than two books. It contained all the classics and books recommended by the *National Review*, though the truth was that George hadn't read many of them.

Mother Nature continued: "You know, librarians and others have been thinking about books that they wish you had read in high school or college or afterwards. Perhaps you'd have done things differently if you'd read some of the world's great literature and thought about other people's ideas. Once you became president, you still could have taken time to read some of these books, but reading just doesn't seem to be one of your passions."

"I do like to read," George insisted. "Let's see, I read Camus' *The Stranger*. That was strange, heh, heh, but I did read it. And I read a great book about Abraham Lincoln around the same time. And Cormac McCarthy's *The Road*. Oprah sent Laura a copy and she gave it to me." He didn't want to admit that he'd only read part of that book. It reminded him too much of the *Night of the Living Dead*.

Mother Nature interrupted. "I'm glad you like to read. And now that you've finished being president, you'll have more time. My friend the librarian wants to recommend some books which will help you with your nightmares. And they'll help you to decide what to do with the rest of your life."

If this monster bitch would just leave me alone, George thought, that would help me. I know what I'm going to do with the rest of my life, thank you. He planned to encourage people to have healthy habits, like exercising, not drinking, and not smoking. He'd enjoy reading books on exercise and health. He'd be better than Bill at shaping up the country with his *own* healthy habits campaign.

"Okay, what sort of books are you recommending?" George

studied the librarian. She wore a dress which had multiple copies of a strange woman's face with one dark eyebrow depicted on the material. The librarian wore sturdy sandals, and she must have just stepped out of the garden, or she'd been painting outside, because he could see smudges of dirt and paint on her hands. She was holding a piece of paper and gazing intently at him, as if she'd waited a long time to talk with him, and now the time had finally come.

Mother Nature stood back. She really wasn't a book person herself, although she wouldn't admit this to George (or the librarian). The librarian was exactly the right person to talk with him about books. The little flowers at Mother Nature's feet looked up expectantly at the other woman, whose face was glowing like a huge sunflower.

"I'll hear you out," said George. Librarians were so much better than zombies or Mother Nature.

George wanted to listen, but there was this association in his mind that was so painful, he had to force himself to pay attention. His first memories of reading were of struggling with his mother over this task. She had tried to get him to read more, and if his little sister hadn't died of leukemia, just at a crucial time, George might have developed a love of books and reading. But his sister had died, and as many families did in those days, they had buried their grief. George's overwhelmed mother had given up trying to help him to learn to love books. However, George had married a librarian. His wife had filled this void. Over the years she had encouraged reading, and he did read more. But George had missed out on so many books which could have expanded his mind and imagination, books which could have made all the difference in the world for him — and as the future unfolded, for everyone else on earth.

The librarian put on her glasses and unfolded the piece of paper. "These are all good books, and many of them you probably have right here. The others you can order off the internet, or get from the library." A small paperback appeared in her hands. "First, I suggest *All Quiet on the Western Front* by Erich Maria Remarque. A book about

World War I, it's written from the perspective of a German infantry man and is probably one of the best books ever about the reality of war."

George had heard of this one, but hadn't read it. Mother Nature hadn't read the book either but she didn't have to, because, like Death, she'd been there, as she had for every war.

"Every man, because it usually is a man, should read this book before he starts a war. This is the book you should have read at least ten times before deciding to go to war in Iraq," she said.

George smirked and folded his arms over his chest. He really didn't want to be reminded of Iraq by Mother Nature. He still felt he'd made the right decision to order the military into Baghdad, or Babylon, as he preferred to think of that biblical land.

Mother Nature was starting to feel irritated. The flowers at her feet put their leaves over their petal faces. "All life is born to die, brother. I know that better than anyone. But I hate wasted lives. People killed in an unnecessary war is a horrible waste. If I ruled the world…," and she smiled, because in a way she did, although she couldn't control these crazy humans half the time, "…when leaders decided to go to war, I would send *them*, not their armies. So with the Iraq War, you could have picked, let's say, three of your top advisors. Perhaps Dick, Donald, and Condi? And Saddam could have picked his three top aides, probably his two sons and the red-haired commander who's still on the loose. Then you two and your entourages go fight it out. No holds barred. Kind of like that *Fight Club* movie with sexy Brad Pitt and even sexier Edward Norton. Sizzling!" Mother Nature wolf whistled. She liked that movie a lot, as it confirmed her views of humanity. Also, she thought George might have seen that film.

George was in pretty good physical shape but he hadn't been in a physical fight in years. He found it impossible to envision Condi scuffling with Uday, but he actually liked the thought of himself wrestling Saddam Hussein. A high noon gunfight might be even better, but he'd have to practice shooting first. Suddenly he shook his head. What was he thinking? That was a ridiculous idea: instead of a war to have some sort of all-star wrestling match between two leaders and their chief advisors?

Mother Nature and George, both with their hands on their hips, stared defiantly at each other.

The librarian quietly said, "Sir, please just read *All Quiet on the Western Front*. Think about the soldiers in that book. Imagine what they would have wanted. Imagine what their families would have wanted. Imagine what the families of those who died would have wanted. Imagine what the wounded would have wanted. Imagine yourself in their shoes."

George had a sudden image of boots, all the boots of the dead soldiers from the Iraq War. Imagining, he shuddered.

"Next, *Slaughterhouse-Five* by Kurt Vonnegut." It mysteriously appeared in her hand. "Now this is really a good book. One of the classics of the twentieth century." The librarian looked over her glasses at George. "Vonnegut's book takes place in World War II and it's about the fire bombing of Dresden which happened in February 1945. The city was filled with civilians and the war wounded. The British bombed Dresden and the firestorm that erupted killed half a million people. It's probably the worst single massacre in history. Kurt Vonnegut was a young American soldier who'd been captured by the Germans and could have died in the firestorm, but he lived, as he'd been ordered into a fireproof slaughterhouse. As a POW, the Germans forced him and others to bury the bodies which had been burned and dismembered by the fire. Kurt was never the same again. He started writing after he returned from the war, slowly putting into words what he'd seen and experienced, finally pouring the whole thing into the novel. His main character, Billy Pilgrim, had PTSD. Post Traumatic Stress Disorder. Probably Kurt Vonnegut had PTSD too. How could he not? How could anyone not after such an experience?"

The librarian and Mother Nature regarded George. Could he imagine being a young Kurt Vonnegut, a young soldier, a prisoner, forced to look at, dig up, and re-bury the corpses of burned-up, mutilated old men, women, children, and babies? And do this day after day after day?

George had only been a three-year-old in 1945. If his family had been living in Dresden then, he and his mother might have been among the thousands who died in that burning inferno. Or if they had lived, they might have had PTSD for the rest of their lives.

The librarian continued. "Imagining yourself as someone else. That's what great literature does. It puts you into the lives of the characters, makes you feel what it would have been like to be them, and then changes you forever."

The librarian and Mother Nature exchanged glances and wondered. Did George have this sort of imagination? Had it been squeezed out of him? If it had, could imagination be revived this late in life? Even if he read these books, would the stories affect him as they had so many millions of other readers?

George continued to feel perturbed. PTSD. What did those letters mean? Yeah, he knew it meant Post Traumatic Stress Disorder. But what did it *really* mean? Why couldn't soldiers just pull it together? Why did they have to be so emotional?

Mother Nature honed in on his thoughts. "PTSD is part of your nature, brother. Something traumatic happens to someone. People react differently, but almost everyone can be traumatized badly enough to get PTSD, with the right combination of factors. If you had been a solider in Vietnam, shot down and captured like, say, John McCain, what do you think you'd be like today?"

George appeared puzzled and uncomfortable. He just didn't imagine things like that. It was a waste of time. It was not worth thinking about something unless it was actually happening. "I like John McCain. Good man." George thought to himself, John *was* the better man, which was why the Architect had to slime him in the 2000 campaign. Otherwise, John might have become president and....

Mother Nature looked at him with some respect. "You do have an imagination."

"Everyone has an imagination," said the librarian. She gave

George the Vonnegut book. "Just try to imagine yourself as Billy Pilgrim."

George took *Slaughterhouse-Five* reluctantly. It was a slim book, however, and he figured it wouldn't take too long to read.

The librarian went on. "Something else interesting about this book. The events happened in 1945, but the book didn't come out until 1969 during the Vietnam War. It was actually banned in a few states. People thought it was unpatriotic. Even though Kurt was just telling the truth."

Hearing this, George wanted to fling the book out of his fingers, but it seemed stuck to his skin.

Another volume appeared in the librarian's hands. *"War is a Force That Gives Us Meaning* by former war correspondent Chris Hedges. A non-fiction, it's a bit heavier, but Chris has written something I think you'll appreciate." She pondered on how it was that this book described the powerful psychological attraction war holds for people, even many of those who are anti-war peace activists. Reading the book the first time, the librarian had felt her own adrenaline rising, and even though she loved children, gardens, and books, she began to have wild thoughts of ordering safari clothes, buying a camera, abandoning her life as she knew it, and flying off to a war zone to cover the story. That fantasy was completely insane, but such thoughts were exactly what Chris described in his book. People are attracted to the insanity of war, even when they know better. Even when they are librarians who know that wars are very bad for libraries, which are often burned or ransacked. Although, ironically, she thought, wars provided the material for many of the books in libraries.

George took the book. "I like the title: *War is a Force That Gives Us Meaning.*" He was The War President, after all.

Mother Nature and the librarian glanced at each other with raised eyebrows. George didn't get it that this was a passionately anti-war book, the title ironic.

Mother Nature said, "You people can't help it. Aggression,

offensive or defensive, is part of who you are. You wouldn't be here today if it wasn't for your aggressive instincts. The War President, indeed," she mumbled, turning to the librarian.

George relaxed a bit. Maybe this female did understand him. He liked being known as The War President. "Yes, The War on Terror. The War in Afghanistan. The War for Iraq Operation Freedom. The War against Iran. The War against China. The War against...."

"Whoa, cowboy. The war against China? When did that start?" Mother Nature tried to keep up, but a war against China was news to her.

"It's only a cold war, so far. Just like Ronald Reagan had the USSR, the Evil Empire. And the next great war will be against China."

Before 9/ll some of his advisors had told George that China was a potential threat and a novel he'd read had predicted a Chinese invasion. "Heh, heh, didn't you read Eric Harry's great novel, *Invasion*?"

The librarian and Mother Nature looked at each other. Neither had heard of that one.

"Sure, great stuff. He writes kind of like Michael Creighton. *Invasion* is in the future." George used his fingers as quotation marks. "Heh, heh, Eric Harry has China invading the US from the Gulf of Mexico. It's kind of like imaging the Civil War being re-fought in our time, but now between the Americans and the Chinese, on American soil."

"Oh Lord." Mother Nature sighed. It was bad enough to want to have wars "over there." She didn't really think George wanted a war on American soil, but she couldn't put anything past him. He really did seem to want to be remembered as The War President, although he'd never fought as a soldier in a war.

"Okay, before anyone starts a war with China, or recommends it..." (she knew that former presidents had the ear of the current president and other influential people) "...please read this anti-war book, and the others, and think about them. Remarque is long dead and unfortunately Vonnegut died recently, but you could invite Chris

Hedges to Crawford. Invite him to a place at your table."

George looked abashed. That was an absurd suggestion.

The librarian said, "Let's move on. *The Invisible Man* by Ralph Ellison."

"Wait, I thought we were doing anti-war books," said Mother Nature with surprise.

"*The Invisible Man* is one of the best books ever written. It describes how people get erased, even as they continue to live. This story makes you think about the worth of every single human being. Wars erase individuals. The daily grind of life can erase individuals. However, paying attention, giving erased people a chance to speak, can bring them back to life."

"How could reading a book about an invisible man bring anyone back to life?" This book was probably as weird as Camus' *The Stranger*. George looked genuinely puzzled. He sincerely wished he could bring all the war dead back to life and heal all the wounded. But he wasn't a doctor. He wasn't a minister. He wasn't a miracle worker.

Mother Nature was all three, and more. "*You* need to think about all those people, individually, whose lives *you* affected by *your* decision to go to war, and then, for the ones who are living, *you* need to go talk with them."

George contemplated her with dismay. "That's not possible."

"What? Thinking about them? Or going to talk with them? Sure, you could do either. You can do both. You have all the time in the world now. What else are you going to do?" Mother Nature examined him with curiosity.

The last couple of years in office, George had really anticipated his post-presidency time, when he wouldn't have to work anymore. Although he loved the power and respect he'd received as president, he hadn't cared for the actual work. It had been easy initially, but after things went sour with Iraq, and his polling numbers plummeted, he'd had to work hard at things that were quite difficult. The last year in office he'd been counting down the days, looking forward to January

20 2009 and the rest of his life: bike riding, working on his library, writing a memoir, fundraising for Republicans, spending time with his daughters and wife, fishing with his father and friends and maybe even trying some standup comedy with Steve Bridges. That really was fun at the White House Correspondents dinner in 2006. Sunny as ever, he had repressed the second half of the show when he'd been skewered by Steve Colbert and Helen Thomas. Thinking back over the last few months, however, he hadn't anticipated zombie nightmares and having to deal with Mother Nature.

She read his mind and shook her head. "I'm thinking about you meeting individual soldiers, the wounded, and the families of the dead – including the anti-war families. Not at some big, staged meetings, but one-on-one. Going to their homes, or hospitals. Or invite them to Crawford. Have a post-presidency ministry, if you will. God will help you, if you decide to do that. And if you really want to do comedy, you could audition for the *Colbert Report*."

George felt insulted. "That's utterly ridiculous." He hated Colbert and that humiliating video with Helen Thomas asking questions about the Iraq War. The memory of the second half of the correspondents' dinner flooded his mind now, and he felt as though he might explode with anger.

Mother Nature persisted. "What's ridiculous? That God would help you? That they'd let you on the *Colbert Report*? I don't think so. She or he, however you envision the Almighty, will certainly help you. And I bet Colbert would have you on, as long as you make people laugh." Mother Nature smiled and the flowers looked up at him. "A *Colbert Report* appearance would really be good publicity for helping wounded veterans and the families of the dead."

George folded his arms across his chest and fumed.

"Just read Ralph Ellison's book, sir," said the librarian, and after handing it to him another appeared. "*The Veiled Kingdom* by Carmen bin Ladin."

"Bin Ladin? I don't want to read any crap by a bin Ladin," George replied. This woman was outrageous.

The librarian looked over her glasses. "Carmen made the mistake of marrying one of Osama's brothers and can't help what her last name is, or was, as she eventually changed it, but that's the name on the book. She has a lot of observations to make on Osama bin Ladin's early life, and how perverted a society, in this case, Saudi society, becomes when the contributions of women are crushed."

"I've promoted lots of women!" George had raised his voice. "I love women. My wife, my daughters. Karen. Condi." George actually thought that the veiling of women and excluding them from public life was stupid and creepy. However, those Saudis had power and oil and you had to deal with them. But a book by a bin Ladin? It really, truly bothered him that Osama hadn't been caught yet, and he didn't want to be reminded.

Yet when the librarian held it out, *The Veiled Kingdom* flew into his hands. George held the books uncomfortably as another volume appeared.

"*The Fifth Sacred Thing* by Starhawk."

Mother Nature looked respectfully at the other woman. She loved this book. *The Fifth Sacred Thing* was a truly inspired work, far ahead of its time. It was shelved under women's fiction in the library, which was too bad, as few men might venture into that section. *The Fifth Sacred Thing* belonged with books about Mahatma Gandhi, Martin Luther King, Nelson Mandela and Wangari Maathai.

"Non-violent resistance to injustice and war. One of the hardest tasks in the world. People with passionate goals but they don't resort to violence to achieve them, even though they have every reason in the world to become violent. *The Fifth Sacred Thing* is a futurist book set in California in this century when the oil runs out. America fractures in two. Ultimately the survivors prevail through peace and non-violent resistance. They invite the enemy to the table."

George appeared befuddled, then angry. "How could you invite someone like Osama or Saddham to the table? That would have been like inviting Hitler or Stalin to dinner." George equated the first two with the latter and identified himself with Abraham Lincoln and

Winston Churchill.

Mother Nature looked at him incredulously. "I knew Abraham Lincoln and Winston Churchill, and you, sir, are neither."

George stared at her, his lips trembling.

Mother Nature glared back. "Sometimes you do have to fight. I'll grant you that," she snapped. "Sometimes, but not always. And books like this push your imagination to try harder and think of alternatives. I don't think Osama would have wanted to sit down at the table, if he'd been offered a place, but the invitation could have been extended."

"And we'd seat him in between us, wouldn't we?" The librarian smiled. She really would enjoy seeing Osama, squirming between herself and Mother Nature. He would just have to get used to sitting and talking with women in a civilized manner. The librarian gave Starhawk's book to George.

"The table? What are you talking about? And why would I want to sit down with Osama, of all people?" He didn't want to sit down with Mother Nature either. The librarian might be okay, as long as his wife was there to make conversation.

"Sure, Laura can be there too. Your daughters. Anyone you want." Mother Nature really didn't want Cheney, Rove or Rumsfeld there, but in the spirit of *The Fifth Sacred Thing*, even they could have a place at the table, as long as they listened at least half the time to the others.

The stack of books was getting higher, and harder to hold. People can only absorb so much. It would not be good to overload this man. The librarian looked at her list. So many good books to choose from. Which ones could have the biggest impact? Ahh, she thought as she noted one title. "*The Grinch Who Stole Christmas* by Dr Seuss. Seuss' real name was Theodore Geisel. One of Dartmouth College's most famous and influential graduates. Seuss was his mother's last name, before her marriage to Mr Geisel."

"Hmm, didn't know that, but, heh, heh, I like that book. I read it every Christmas to my daughters when they were young," George said enthusiastically.

The women regarded him with bewildered expressions. Did he really not get it, that *he* was considered by many to be the Grinch? That many parents who voted against him in 2000 and 2004 had read the book to their children those following Christmases, substituting George's name for that of the Grinch? The librarian thought this was one of the most psychologically astute books ever written. No matter how big, bad and powerful someone is, he or she can never entirely take away everything from the little guys. They still have their love for one another and their own creativity, singing, in the case of the Whos. And in loving one another and creating, the people also have the awesome ability to change the big, bad, and powerful. To be sure, this didn't always work, but it worked sometimes, and it was good to remember this idea when absolutely everything else is taken away.

The librarian looked at George, the Grinch to so many people. She really wanted to sit down at the table with him, and have him "carve the roast beast," *after* he'd had a change of heart through the awesome power of forgiveness, love and creativity. She didn't know if other people would feel the same. But that's what was so powerful about this story. The Grinch, horrible as he was, could change and be welcomed. His heart could grow. It could happen with George, too. Anything was possible. She firmly believed that. The librarian read from her list. "*The Quiet American* by Graham Greene and *The Ugly American* by William J. Lederer and Eugene Burdick."

"Ugly, quiet Americans? They sound extremely unpatriotic. I won't read those books."

The librarian glared at him, and Mother Nature thundered and threw a few lightning bolts around.

"Okay, okay, I'll force myself."

Still miffed, as those were really good books, the librarian went back to her list. "*1984* and *Animal Farm* by George Orwell," she said.

"Hey, I think I read those in high school." Or at least the Cliff Notes, he thought to himself.

"Better read them again, carefully, brother. This time the originals, please," said Mother Nature.

The librarian continued reading: "*The Swallows of Kabul* by Yasmina Khadra, aka Mohammed Moulessehoul."

"A book by Mohammed? I didn't know he wrote books, like Jesus did."

The librarian felt sad. Jesus did not write the Bible, just as Mohammed did not write the Koran. Perhaps they should have written their own books, but that wasn't how people did things back then. She wondered if people these days wouldn't be so mixed up about religion if these great prophets had written their own books.

"No, he didn't write this book. *The Swallows of Kabul* is a tragic book about a travesty of nature." She gave George the book.

"*The Kin of Ata are Waiting for You* by Dorothy Bryant." The librarian held up another book. Mother Nature smiled. This librarian was good.

George hadn't heard of *The Kin of Ata*, but then, most people hadn't.

Mother Nature stepped forward to describe it. "It's about a man who does a nightmarish thing and ends up on an island where the society is based on dreams. It takes a while, but he finally learns to dream, heals himself in the process and adds his creativity to the community." Mother Nature closed her eyes, breathed deeply and whispered, "Dreams are incredibly powerful."

The librarian nodded. "Think about what's happening now."

George looked surprised. "Now?"

"Sure, this is a dream, sir."

"It is?" This was the realest dream he'd ever had. At least this dream wasn't like those horrible zombie nightmares. He took the book from the woman.

"Also, you're going to have to stop reading Tom Clancy and Clive Cussler. Fun as they are, they, and others like them, promote war. You can keep reading Ken Follett, though, if you need a break. His stuff really moves along, but he also shows the folly of war," said the librarian.

And Mother Nature added, "Michael Creighton's early books are okay, but that book he wrote, poo-pooing global warming, infuriated me. Although, I am a great fan of the First Amendment. But you need to realize that book is complete fiction and utter contrarian nonsense."

George liked that book and began to argue but the librarian interrupted.

"Oh, of course, how could we forget?" She put her hands to her forehead. "All the world's great religious texts."

Mother Nature reached into her backpack and pulled out twelve volumes of different sizes. "There are more, but these are pretty representative, all translated into English with good appendices, so you can think of a topic, like forgiveness, for example, look it up and find out what each religion has to say about it. All religions have something to say about just about everything that's important. And you have your own Bible." She respectfully gave him the stack of religious books, and the librarian put the list inside the cover of the top book.

"Now, we know you like to read in the bathroom. Please don't do this with these sacred books. Wash your hands before you pick them up. Treat them with all the reverence that you treat the Bible and the American flag. And don't, I say DON'T, flush any of them down the toilet."

George looked hurt. "I would never do that. That would really screw up the plumbing." He had never understood those reports of the Koran being flushed down the toilet at Guantánamo. If someone did that, he or she was a complete idiot.

Strong as George was, he was having a hard time holding the stack of books. "I don't think I can read all this stuff," he said, wincing. "Could I listen to some of them on audiotape?"

Mother Nature and the librarian exchanged a look. Mother Nature shrugged and the librarian replied, "Sir, you need to pay attention to what you're reading and sometimes when people listen to tapes, they're double or even triple tasking. However, I guess it's okay if you're driving somewhere, like that boring stretch between Crawford and Dallas."

George looked relieved.

Mother Nature added, "It would really be better to get a good Mexican hammock and set it up under a tree by the pool with a pitcher of lemonade. No interruptions. Focus on the task at hand. Good reading, brother. *Nos vemos. Adiós.*" And they vanished.

* * *

Since singing the hymn, Judith had continued to smile and open her mouth as if to speak, especially when fragrant flowers were placed near her nose or when sung to or touched. But she never said anything else. Joseph felt she was on the verge of awakening and his desire for her grew and grew.

It was this desire that finally convinced him to accept Miguel's mariachi serenade for Judith. Traditionally the midnight singing was for girls who'd turned fifteen, but Miguel informed Joseph that with the changing times, mariachi serenades had gained in popularity for women of all ages. It could be an amazingly successful strategy for romance, although often the neighbors were less enamored, especially if there were several suitors and multitudes of mariachis. The cops would be called, but they usually delayed their arrival so the mariachis could skedaddle. The police just couldn't arrest people for showing their *amour con música*. Besides, some of the officers had arranged for serenades for their own sweethearts.

One Saturday night Miguel's mariachi group traveled to the VA hospital. There were four violinists, one *vihuela* and *guitarro* player each, two trumpeters, a folk harpist, and two singers. Miguel held his *vihuela* as tenderly as one might hold a baby. It was just past midnight when they arrived. The mariachis clearly weren't supposed to be on the grounds, but once they explained their mission, the crazy unpaid guard escorted them to Judith's side of the building. They parked their van so they'd have a quick getaway. They knew the night staff was settling in, not expecting anything out of the ordinary and hoping the patients were sedated enough so they'd sleep through the shift.

Amy was the only RN on that night along with a couple of nurses' aides for a ward of forty multiple amputees, some of whom were blind like Judith. Others had serious head injuries and required total care. The nurses did their best and parents, siblings, spouses and church groups all contributed to helping the injured. But it was very hard. The amputees weren't going to grow back limbs, and those with serious brain damage couldn't be rehabilitated. And for some of the wounded, their families had given up. It was too demoralizing to see their loved ones permanently traumatized.

The staff used humor when they could. They couldn't work there without occasional laughter. Amy was repeating a joke Ben had told her to one of the nursing assistants as they went over some paperwork. "The pope, Bush, and a school age boy are in a private plane with one pilot flying in the sky. Suddenly there's a problem with the engine and the pilot says, as he grabs one of the three parachute packs available, 'We're going down. I'm outta here.' And he jumps out of the plane. Bush grabs a pack, and after putting it on, saying, 'I'm the leader of the free world,' he jumps out too. The pope and the little boy look at each other. The pope says, 'I am a very old man. You take the last pack, and I'll go down with the plane.' The little boy says, 'No, we can both be saved. There are two parachutes left. President Bush just jumped out with my backpack.'"

Amy and the nurses' aide giggled. It was a funny joke and perfectly illustrated the selfishness and stupidity of the former president. Amy figured maybe she'd tell it to Judith's grandmother if Ben hadn't told her already. The old lady could do with a good laugh. Amy knew she hated Bush too, as she held the man responsible for Judith's injuries and her brother's death.

All of a sudden the booming sound of mariachi music burst through the hallway to the nurses' station. The two women ran towards the sound of *El Rey* and found Judith wide awake and smiling. They looked outside the window where the mariachis stood in a semicircle. Traditionally, the serenaded girl or woman would come to the window, in a diaphanous nightgown. Joseph knew Judith couldn't do this, but he anxiously hoped she liked what she heard.

The nurses got busy. They knew exactly what this was for. Love. True Love. Sometimes even more effective than antibiotics for healing. They got Judith into her wheelchair and pushed it towards the window. The window was constructed in such a way that Judith's shoulders and head were visible to the men below. Joseph could see Judith smiling, and he thought she looked beautiful. Feeling elated, all his anxiety vanished. He began singing his solo.

The mariachis played and sang for a half hour. Joseph felt trans-formed and would have stood there all night, but the guard ran up and said with a hoarse whisper, "Security's on its way. Better scram, guys." The musicians gave one last blast with their instruments, and dragging Joseph with them, they ran off to the van.

As Joseph yelled out "*Adiós, mi amour,*" Judith opened her mouth and cried out to Amy, "Joseph, Joseph." She kept saying this as Amy and the aide settled her back into her bed. Joseph's voice and the mariachi music swirled through her mind and Judith had the most wonderful dreams that night, of dancing, swimming, and making love with him. She had her arms, her legs and her sight. It was as if they'd met before they joined the Army, before the Iraq War, when they would have had a chance at a very different life. Judith actually hadn't liked mariachi music before she heard it at her hospital window. But it had been a better choice than bagpipes. From then on mariachi music would remind her of Joseph's love.

Chapter 7

Leaving Oklahoma City, Lucy got a ride from a Cherokee family driving north. By late afternoon she had reached Wamego, Kansas, the home of the Wizard of Oz Museum. She'd seen a large billboard for this museum and thought she'd visit it before going on to Columbine. As a child, *The Wizard of Oz* had been her favorite movie, but after her family joined the new church, her parents had thrown away the DVD. Lucy hadn't thought about it in years, but when she saw the billboard, she knew she'd have to visit. Lucy had loved Dorothy, and her three loyal friends, the Tin Man, the Scarecrow, and the Cowardly Lion, and their adventuresome journey. As a child, the Wicked Witch and her evil monkeys had been the scariest characters she'd seen in the movies while Glenda the Good Witch embodied everything Lucy aspired to.

Lucy bought some food in a deli, and walking out of town, she found an abandoned barn. Exploring it, she found stairs and climbed to the second floor, where she could look out at the night sky. Lucy noticed a rope connected to a strong hook from the top of an open window. The rope easily looked long enough to stretch to the ground, and she thought about swinging out on it. But she was too scared. If it broke, she'd be injured without any help. She wished she had a friend traveling with her. Maria would have been a good traveling partner, but she didn't really understand Lucy's religious beliefs. Darrell would have understood her beliefs, but he wouldn't have wanted her to leave her parents. She wondered how things might have been different with either friend by her side. Later, before she went to sleep, Lucy whispered the Lord's Prayer and Psalm 23: *"The Lord is my shepherd; I shall not want...."*

Lucy, like most Americans, didn't know that prior to the Civil War, Kansas had been the site of ferocious fighting between abolitionists and slave owners. Perhaps there had been a particularly fierce battle on the site of this farm, for Lucy dreamed of soldiers, all of them weeping, sitting in a field of wildflowers. The ballet skirt she found herself wearing in the dream suddenly transformed into a gossamer gown as if she were a butterfly. Lucy reached out her hands towards the soldiers. One of the men crawled to her and clutched her skirt. She stroked his hair and he stopped weeping. The flowers began to grow and transform into women. Once they were fully realized, they all began to comfort the men, as Lucy had. The dream's last remnants had the flower-women humming a strange lyrical tune and the men helping one another to their feet.

In the morning, Lucy wondered why she'd dreamt of soldiers. Flowers she could understand, but she hadn't thought much about soldiers, except to be a little afraid of those in Killeen. She'd known a few kids from school who had enlisted. One had died in Iraq, but she didn't know him well. The dream left her with a good feeling, however. Perhaps something miraculous would happen during her time in Kansas. But the very thought of a miracle brought along its counterpart. She shivered and imagined the possibility of wicked witches and evil monkeys.

The other visitors at the museum were mostly families with children. The area where the kids could try on costumes and act out their favorite parts from the movie was extremely popular. A face painter sponged on green makeup for those who wanted to be the Wicked Witch of the West. Seeing several green-skinned cackling witches, Lucy felt uneasy. Halloween celebrations were forbidden by her church, and acting like witches was especially sacrilegious.

Lucy remembered dressing up as a witch once when she was little, when her Aunt Diana, a theater seamstress, had visited. She was en route from Atlanta to Los Angeles and had many costumes, which Lucy had enjoyed trying on. Lucy remembered how much fun she'd had.

Lucy laughed. How silly not to put on a costume. What harm could there be? She was going to do it, too. No one knew her here and, besides, she recalled Aunt Diana telling her that most witches were good women with deep knowledge of the forces of nature.

Sadly, the societies they lived in couldn't tolerate powerful, intelligent women, so they killed them. And as the movie had shown, not all witches were old and ugly. Glenda, the Good Witch of the North, reminded her of Aunt Diana. Lucy looked at the flowing pink dress hanging on the rack. She *was* going to try on the Glenda the Good Witch dress.

The costume assistant helped her slip the glittery pink dress over voluminous stiff petticoats and then placed a gold crown on her head and gave Lucy a magic wand. Looking at herself in the mirror, Lucy appeared transformed. She had become Glenda. Waving the wand, she playfully gave out wishes to several children who had gathered around to admire her. "And you'll get a cute kitten some day," she said to one young girl. "And you will definitely get your horse, even though you may be grown up before that happens," she said to a chubby, sad-looking girl, who smiled shyly back at Lucy. She felt the magical power of the wand and her words. Weirdly, it seemed as if she were in church again, although the preacher would have definitely disapproved.

After a while the kids left. Suddenly tired, Lucy wanted to sit down, but she'd have to take the gown off first. There was no sitting for Glenda while wearing that billowing dress. Lucy closed her eyes and wished she could disappear into a magical snow globe, as Glenda did in the movie. Lucy imagined floating to a beautiful green place on the other side of the snowstorm, removing her dress, soaking in a warm bath and then slipping into a deep forest-green dressing gown and relaxing with some warm tea in front of a fire. It was exhausting work granting wishes and righting the world's wrongs.

"Well, what have we here, my pretty? Eh, eh, eh."

Lucy started. Standing before her was the Wicked Witch of the West, green skin, hooked nose, evil laugh, and broomstick, which she brandished menacingly at Lucy.

Without hesitation, Lucy thrust her magic wand in the witch's face, and with Glenda's tinkily high laughter cried, "Hah-hah, hah-hah, hah! Be gone, you have no power here." She waved her wand aggressively towards the green woman.

The Wicked Witch cowered and said those classic lines that almost every kid in America knew by heart, "I'm melting, I'm melting. Who would have thought a pretty little girl like you could destroy my beautiful wickedness? Oh what a world, what a world." And the witch seemed to shrink and then mostly disappear into the floor.

Lucy looked at her wand with astonishment. Whoa! She was going to have to buy one of these for her journey. A real magic wand would come in handy.

"Lucy, help me up. Come on, give me a hand."

What? The Wicked Witch was smiling at her, and Lucy could see she was trying to get part way out of a hole in the floor. She looked at the witch more closely.

"Maria! What are you doing here?" Lucy helped pull her out and tried to give her a hug, although it was difficult because of her outfit. One could see why Glenda had to be so distant and disappear in a snow globe. The Wicked Witch's outfit, on the other hand, was made for traveling and hugging, at least when worn by someone like Maria.

"Lucy, I couldn't take Killeen after you left. My parents were driving me crazy. I wanted to go on an adventure like you, so I quit my job and I followed you, to where I thought you'd be going. When I heard about this place, I knew you'd come here. Remember all those Wizard of Oz games we played as kids? And here you are, and here I am." Maria took off her witch's hat and pulled her long hair down. She removed the green robe, revealing a purple leather jumpsuit.

Lucy shed the Glenda outfit and felt the transformation that brought her back to being a girl from Texas in a T-shirt and jeans. She still held the wand though. It was hard to put that down. She looked curiously at Maria's outfit.

"Oh, yeah, these," Maria said, gesturing to the leather. "Well, there have been a few other changes too, *amiga*. Let me introduce my friend, Charlie."

A woman stepped out from the shadows of the room. Lucy hadn't noticed her before. She was also incredibly attractive, although different from Maria. An Anglo with very fair skin, short hair spiked up with some type of gel, she looked kind of like a mountain lion. All in black, she wore a leather vest that showed her sculpted arms, and her legs were encased in skin-tight leggings plunging into combat boots. Charlie had a watchful look on her face.

Charlie said nothing but stuck out her hand, which Lucy shook. A surge of power went through the handshake, but Lucy stood her ground, and it was the other woman's turn to look a little surprised. This little girl had some power, too. Now she understood, a bit, why Maria had insisted on following this kid. Also she knew right away that there was no threat from Lucy. Charlie relaxed a bit.

Lucy regarded Maria curiously.

"Let me get this green stuff off," Maria said quickly. "I hope it comes off, otherwise, I'll have to take the costume with me and keep scaring the bejesus out of everyone we meet." Maria laughed; she spun around and grabbed a jar of cold cream from a shelf against the wall. Then she turned to the full-length mirror and started rubbing her face. Lucy and Charlie stood awkwardly and watched Maria transform herself back from the green-skinned witch. Lucy reluctantly replaced the magic wand in a box and glanced at the Glenda dress, not wanting to forget how she'd felt wearing it. A few minutes later Maria said, "Let's go into the tea room and I'll explain *todo, amiga.*"

The pink-themed tearoom was a little girl's fantasy parlor. Lucy, Maria, and Charlie ordered some Red Zinger and Maria began talking. "Charlie got out of the army a few months ago. They would have kept her, she won every award they had, but she flipped out, almost killed an officer, and ended up in the psych ward in the Fort Hood hospital. I was there as a nursing assistant, as you know, and I used to take her on escorted walks around the hospital grounds. I know we weren't supposed to, but we fell in love. I guess that's happened before with nurses and patients. I quit my job before we did anything about it and waited until Charlie got out of the hospital." She took Charlie's hand and said, "We're lovers, Lucy."

Lucy felt faint. "No, Maria, please don't be gay," she pleaded. Charlie was staring at Lucy defiantly but Lucy had her hand up to her face as if trying to shield herself from Maria's lover.

Her best friend a lesbian? No, no way. Lucy didn't know any homosexuals; the preacher and her parents said homosexuality was an abomination. But she loved Maria, and Lucy knew she was a good person. How could she be a lesbian? And so pretty, she could have any guy she wanted. But apparently she didn't want any guys.

The tea arrived and Maria kept talking. She explained that right after Charlie got out of the hospital Maria heard that Lucy had left town. She and Charlie didn't have anything better to do, and so they'd followed her. Charlie folded her arms across her chest and looked at Lucy sullenly. Maria touched Charlie's arm and, looking back at Lucy, she whispered, "True love." Lucy had never felt this herself, but she'd read about it and her parents had told her about their own love. And they had talked in church about falling in love with someone else who had been saved by Jesus.

The three women moved out to a porch and Lucy sat in a rocker while Maria and Charlie swayed on the porch swing. They were holding hands, and at some point in the conversation, Lucy had a glimpse of their souls, and her beliefs about gays and lesbians shifted a little bit, but enough. The couple saw it in Lucy's face the moment it happened. Maria smiled and Charlie relaxed a little more.

This had been exhausting. Change was hard work. Even the beginning of change was hard work. "Let's go find a place to stay. We have some bucks, and we'll spring for two rooms." Maria winked at Charlie. "We need our privacy." Lucy looked a little worried again, but then nodded. It was hard to be upset with True Love.

As they walked to the motel, Charlie pushed their motorcycle. She could have ridden it, but she liked to work her muscles. Lucy didn't know much about motorcycles, but she saw that it was a Harley, like the ones the lawyers had been riding. Charlie pushed it into a space near the motel. When they were told it would be a short wait until they could check in, they sat down on a bench outside the office.

As Lucy watched them, Maria leaned over and kissed Charlie. Lucy didn't realize that her eyes were filling up with tears until Charlie got up and stomped off.

Maria let her go. "Don't worry. You'll get used to it. It may seem strange, but this really is True Love. Just like *The Princess Bride*, but the lesbian version." Maria laughed.

Charlie turned her head at the sound of her laughter but kept walking.

"She's okay, now, just a little tense. The docs say she has PTSD, Post Traumatic Stress Disorder. She still takes meds, at least some of the time. Charlie just has to go a little crazy in the ERs and they'll give her whatever she wants. She's a hundred percent service connected." When Lucy looked puzzled Maria explained that meant she'd get all her medical care paid for.

Maria and Lucy watched Charlie, who really did look like a mountain lion. But she'd been fed and was being fed regularly. She wasn't dangerous, at least not to these two.

* * *

It was the hottest day of the year in central Texas. Electricity was failing. Elderly people were dying in Dallas and Fort Worth. George knew this from the news and he was glad his own parents were safe in cool green Maine. He still loved the heat and felt he could live without air conditioning. But he knew his wife and visitors needed cooling.

George was really upset with those landscapers, though. They hadn't been able to do anything with his trees and plants. Half of them were dead, and the rest looked pitiful. The water level in the lake had gone down and a lot of the fish were dead. It stank. He'd had water trucked in, but it was sucked up into the air as if by a giant vacuum cleaner.

One of those damn gardeners had the balls to mention global warming and tell George he should have signed the Kyoto Treaty. The fool tried to suggest he read Gore's *Planet in the Balance* or see that goddamn documentary *An Inconvenient Truth*. George cursed him off of his property and yelled at his supervisor, who listened but didn't take any action. Actually, he thought the whole crew must have been a bunch of environmental freaks. Global warming. What a load of crap. Michael Creighton had it right in his book debunking global warming.

George looked around. The only thing that seemed to be thriving was that damn shrub. His wounded foot throbbed as he glared at it. He'd been peeing on it every night, but it just seemed to get hardier. Maybe he'd burn it. Tonight, when it cooled down a few degrees, he'd get the hose out, soak the ground all around, then put some kerosene on it and get rid of it once and for all.

Meanwhile, he had been trying to read *All Quiet on the Western Front*. He'd forgotten that it was written by a WW I German veteran in 1928. George had never read any books by the enemy. He thought that his father might have read it. They'd had a few conversations about the first Iraq War, but mostly arguments about the second. George and his old man really didn't see eye to eye. At least his dad respected him now. George W had been a two-term president. Perhaps he would even get his likeness carved in stone like those at Mount Rushmore. Except George would be carved into Texan granite at Enchanted Rock, not far from Crawford. His dad hadn't even attempted such glory in Maine. Of course, those Down East Mainiacs would have lawyered his dad to death with all their regulations, restrictions, and covenants. Texans didn't have that many rules and George was pretty sure he could get around any damn Austin environmental lawyers.

He pictured his own face blasted right into the middle of Enchanted Rock. In the spring he'd be framed with bluebonnets and remembered forever. Like the Easter Island faces, people would look at him for the next thousand years. He smiled.

George had gotten to the part in the book where the gases in the dead bodies make noises. Yuck! It reminded him of the zombies from his dreams. He hadn't been bothered by them too much lately except when he had stopped reading for a couple of days. Then he'd had a humdinger of a nightmare. He realized he had to keep reading to keep them away.

Thinking about books reminded George of something irritating from earlier that day. He'd gone with his wife to the local library where she'd read a book about Cherokees and strawberries, the fruit of kindness and forgiveness, to a group of school children. George decided to check out some books. It wasn't too much of a hassle to get a card and find books he wanted, but then he noticed the librarian making a copy of the names of the books he was checking out. The librarian turned to a file cabinet and placed the list in a folder.

"What are you doing? It looks like you copied my books," George exclaimed. "Why did you do that and why are you locking it in that file cabinet?" George felt really paranoid. Where was his wife? He could hear her talking about strawberries.

"Sir, we do this with everyone." The librarian lowered his voice. "We even have a system to record fingerprints to prove, if necessary, that suspects really did check out specific books."

"But, but, but…that's not American!" George sputtered. Wasn't the right to privacy somewhere in the Constitution?

The portly, bearded librarian looked surprised. "But sir, this was a law you supported as part of the Patriot Act of 2001. Congress tried to repeal it in 2005, but you vetoed that effort. Don't you remember?" The librarian appeared concerned. This was the biggest issue that American librarians had ever dealt with apart from book banning. Most librarians hated the so-called Patriot Act and many defied it. This particular librarian thought it was reasonable, but should apply to everyone.

"I am not one of the bad guys!" George shouted. "Give me back that list. Here, take these stupid books, too." He threw them at the librarian.

A group of school kids waiting to check out books for summer reading regarded George, their eyes wide with surprise. They knew that books should be treated with respect, even if you didn't like what was in them.

The librarian also was shocked, then angry. What was wrong with this man?

By this time Laura had come over and bent to pick up the books. She put her hand on her husband's arm. "Honey, calm down, they're just books." She looked at them. "And real good books for your summer reading." She smiled at everyone. "Let's check them out under my card. I don't mind if anyone knows what I read."

Later that night reading the Remarque book, George realized that the grotesque passage about dead bloated bodies reminded him of war protest signs he'd seen outside the last talk he'd given. He'd been in Kansas where he thought there wouldn't be any protestors. But there were, and some had even lain down in the road, pretending to be dead. He did think briefly about the dead in Iraq then. Pretty unpleasant stuff. But he remembered that his mom had advised the nation on the eve of the war not to think about these sorts of things. Reading the Remarque book about the long dead was preferable to thinking about the recently dead.

Later yet George woke from a dreamless sleep and went out into the yard. He peed on the bush that he hated. Then he stared at it, thinking that maybe getting rid of it would somehow turn things around with his property.

A minute later he was sloshing kerosene on it, taking care not to get any on his hands. He found some buckets, filled them with water and placed them nearby just in case. Then he stood back and threw a lit match on the bush. It caught easily and within seconds was flaming. George felt immensely satisfied.

But then, in spite of the fact that there was no breeze, the fire flared towards him, and he had to back away. And worse, next an apparition appeared in the flames. George was used to strange beings in his dreams, but he was certain he was awake. He dropped to his knees. The roaring terror hovered over him and began to speak.

"You know who I am, right?

George quavered. "Yes, yes, you're G—" The entity roared up, and George fell back.

"Yes, I am who I am."

George thought he'd heard that before. He replied carefully, "And I am who I am." There was silence. Then George continued, speaking with more confidence. "If you are who you are, then you must be God, and that means I'm…I'm…like Moses." And George just knew what was going to happen next. "Are you going to give me some new Commandments?"

The fire roared up. "You don't need any new ones. Just obey the old ones. The rules of righteous conduct. What's the sixth, eighth, and tenth?"

George straightened. "I know them: Six: you shall not murder; Eight: you shall not steal; Ten: you shall not bear false witness against your neighbor and you shall not covet your neighbor's house, wife, slave, ox, or ass."

"Good. You know them but you haven't taken them to heart. Also they didn't have anything but olive oil back in those days, but now you can add fossil fuel oil to that list of things not to covet. Lies and murder, however, are pretty much the same now as then. Bush lies, people die."

"I never lied."

The fire roared up and singed George's hair and clothing. He fell to the ground.

The apparition laughed. "You did lie. Yes, you did lie. I'm not sure which lie was the worst, the one about Saddam being an imminent threat, the one about weapons of mass destruction, or the one about a possible nuclear threat. And then repeating these falsehoods so much that even when the media corrected itself, half the people still believed those lies. You used your power to convince people of things that were not true. And calling this war against terror a crusade! Were you completely insane?"

George looked shaken. He had really believed these threats, but that was because he had already decided to invade Iraq and deal with Saddam before reading reports that could have dissuaded him. Besides, in retrospect, some of these reports gave him bad intelligence. It wasn't his fault. And maybe Osama had been in Iraq, instead of hiding out in Pakistan or Afghanistan.

"Lies, lies, lies." The apparition flared up and towered over the man. "Many people would say it's too late for you. You've sinned worse than almost anyone living today. However, you still have time to conduct yourself righteously. Look at the *Big Book* and the AA rules about apologies and making amends for your mistakes where possible."

A few seconds of silence passed, and then the fire flared again. "And don't tell people I told you to go to war. That was Cheney. And he's not, I repeat, NOT God." The flame flared even higher, and with a tremendous roar, disappeared into the night.

George stared at the bush, which was still there, unsinged. If anything, it seemed more alive and vigorous than before the burning.

How could he apologize? He hadn't done that since he apologized to Laura years ago for his drinking. Apologies wouldn't bring back the lives that were lost, or the limbs and brains that had been destroyed.

George curled up on the ground and wept. He hadn't cried this hard in years. Eventually he felt drops on his face and he realized that it was raining. Raining. Thank God. He pulled himself to a kneeling position and folded his hands in prayer. "Oh, Lord, please help me. I truly have sinned. Please, please, please, help me." For a long time he remained kneeling, weeping and washed by the rain.

* * *

The nurses had put Judith back to bed, turned out the lights, and closed the door. Judith could feel the breeze from outside, and she could smell the roses that her cousin had left earlier. Tears ran down her face. Damn that Joseph! How could he leave her here like this? Her breasts and the curve of her hips were untouched by the explosion. She couldn't see them, but she could touch them with her arm stumps. But she couldn't reach between her legs, and that certainly wasn't anything she could ask the nurses to do. It hadn't really bothered her until recently. But now that damn Joseph and his stupid mariachi music had really aroused her. And there wasn't a damn thing she could do about it. At least not tonight. But she was going to have a talk with him and ask him for what she needed. "Joseph, Joseph," she whispered to herself.

Judith remembered the first day she'd met Joseph. They'd been thrown together in basic training because their names were close alphabetically. They had liked each other instantly, but it wasn't lust like she'd felt for her high school boyfriend. She and Joseph had the same sense of humor and they could laugh about almost anything. In Iraq, he helped relieve the tension of the patrols, and he'd laughed at all her comedic efforts. He'd even written a song for her to sing and a couple of routines for her to perform. She hummed a few verses of that song now and thought about their first kiss, in a dark garage. There had been other kisses, but they'd never consummated their love. Neither of them had wanted their first time to be in the back of a Bradley in Iraq, likely to be interrupted. Joseph wanted it to be in a quiet guest house in a city like New Orleans where an interracial couple would be welcomed. Fresh sheets. Flowers on the bed stand. Smell of coffee and beignets. Slowly removing each other's clothing. Clean clothing. No dust, no grease, no sounds of ordnance or warning sirens.

And now here she was, no arms below the elbows. One leg amputated above the knee, one below. Blind. Destroyed, but now filled with desire.

Eventually she stopped crying. She'd talk with a nurse about birth control. Maybe Amy would assist. She seemed to have something for her brother, and she wasn't the type to blab.

Judith opened her mouth to speak again. She wasn't sure she could say anything besides "Joseph." She tried.

"Help me," she whispered.

"Help me." It came out stronger the second time.

Judith smiled. She was pretty sure how it was going to end, and if he still liked her, continue. She fell asleep and dreamed of herself with arms and legs, making love with Joseph in that New Orleans hotel where true love was welcomed.

Chapter 8

Maria and Charlie bought a sidecar for Lucy the next day. They handed her a pink helmet and put her backpack in the rear storage container with their stuff. Charlie told her to stay away from a certain metal container and Lucy promised not to touch it. By the time they had taken care of all these details, it was late afternoon. They wanted to spend the night by water. They looked at the map and saw a lake not too far away. They checked their belongings one last time and then roared out of Wamego heading northwest towards Tuttle Creek Lake.

While they had been readying the Harley, eighteen men traveled across Kansas. Proceeding in all sorts of beat-up, dirty, noisy trucks, cars, motorcycles, and even an old Hummer, they were a grim group. Many had lost limbs. Others had facial deformities like the worst cases of adolescent acne. A couple were without genitalia, and some wore totally crazed expressions: An American Mad Max group.

But all were men with brains and hearts and feelings — albeit mostly feelings of sadness and anger. And they all shared a sense of purpose and were moving towards a common destiny. All Iraq War vets, mostly young men in their twenties, they had been terribly traumatized from the war.

These men had met in the PTSD ward in the Houston VA, where a young researcher had started a program for hardcore PTSD patients. The vets had been referred from all over the US for the researcher's project. The program teamed the veterans together in pairs, a mostly able-bodied one paired with one with missing limbs. Meds were prescribed but much of the treatment was a new type of cognitive behavior therapy. Vets were offered instruction in creative tasks, such as writing, acting, or painting (even if they had to hold the brushes in their mouths), and all participated in some form of physical rehabilitation that involved yoga or breathing and meditation techniques. The vets really liked their doctors, nurses and therapists and were finding moments of peace and meaning in their suffering. They were discovering hope again. But then, halfway through, they were told the program would be terminated. Something had happened in Washington and the money had run out. Money was needed for some new war or some boondoggle projects such as, one of the docs suggested, redecorating hospital adminis-tration offices. The newspapers had almost daily stories about the huge deficit from the Iraq War and the oil/energy and economic crises. There wasn't enough money for the mental health, physical rehab and job development programs necessary for the traumatized vets. The researcher and her assistants were laid off – but they would find jobs elsewhere. The vets had nowhere to go.

A few days before the end of the program the clinicians and patients had gathered for a prayer circle. One of the nurses, a former Iraq War medic, was Sioux. He'd performed a special prayer for the vets, reminding them of their duty to return to themselves, so that they could return to their families and their communities. The healthcare workers told them not to give up, to use what they'd learned to continue to recover. The vets listened but they seemed terribly demoralized, as if they had lost their spirit.

Later that night, one of them came up with a plan. Henry from Kansas had been a Boy Scout and then an Eagle Scout. After 9/11, he joined the military, as he loved everything American and wanted to fight for his country. Henry and his family and friends, like most people in Kansas, had voted for Bush in 2000 and 2004 and believed everything he said. Henry had even shaken Bush's hand at a rally during a home leave. What a high that had been. But all this meant he had further to fall when he did.

Henry's best friend in Iraq had been a guy called Surfer Dude, from California. Surfer Dude had saved Henry's life once in an ambush and they'd become good friends. Still, they argued constantly, with Surfer Dude insisting on showing him news articles about the lies contributing to the buildup of the war. Surfer Dude said that once he got out, he was going to learn everything he could about the peaceful resolution of problems. There were other ways to deal with terrorism. He wasn't anti-war and he heartily agreed that a military was needed, but, he argued, soldiers should never be misused.

A week before Surfer Dude was due to leave, a mortar hit the base and he was killed. Henry was devastated. He couldn't believe that his friend was dead and all his lofty plans were gone. And then when some idiot, one command level above him, demeaned his friend, saying, "That's what happens to peaceniks," Henry went berserk and beat the shit out of the officer. He was restrained before any permanent damage was done but he was discharged shortly thereafter.

When Henry returned to Kansas, he was congratulated for his service. His family and friends tried to get him to run for office and marry his hometown sweetheart. But he just couldn't do it. Everything felt completely false. Henry started reading books which had come out since 2003 and was appalled to realize that Surfer Dude had been right about the lies that started the war. His patriotism had been horribly misused. Henry wept constantly for his friend, and for the other dead and wounded. He tried to help a few homeless Iraq vets but they were mired in drinking and fighting. He started a few courses at the local community college but he couldn't concentrate on anything. His rage and despair grew and grew into a raging case of PTSD.

One of his teachers, someone Henry had confided in, had heard about the new treatment program for vets with PTSD and encouraged him to give it a try. Henry had made his way to the Houston VA and he'd experienced a glimmer of hope, until the program came to a grinding halt. Then all his rage returned. He thought about going to Crawford or Maryland and making Bush or Cheney pay for what they'd done, but in the end he realized he had "caught" some of his dead friend's peacefulness and he really didn't want to hurt anyone else. He reasoned that the noble thing to do was to kill himself. And he knew exactly where he would go to do it: the

Boy Scout camp where his path to the military had begun. In Henry's mind, his death in the camp would be a chilling message to those who encouraged boys to become soldiers.

The armless guy Henry had been teamed with in the hospital was Rusty, from Hawaii. Rusty had never made it home. He'd gone from Baghdad to Landstuhl to Walter Reed and then to Houston. His mother had come to visit him, but the rest of his family had one excuse after another. He'd been a high school football hero and a champion surfer, and they couldn't cope with the thought that their wonder boy now had no arms. Rusty desperately wished for the Hawaiian ocean. He wished they'd sent him home to Hawaii from Walter Reed, but the doctors had told him that the Houston program offered the best chance for long-term recovery.

Rusty had developed great intuition since his injury, something that happens when someone is reliant upon others for almost everything. "You're thinking about killing yourself, right?" Rusty asked one evening after it had been announced that the program would be terminated.

Henry seemed only slightly surprised. He was used to his friend's mind reading by now. All the vets had noticed it amongst the limbless.

"Yep, buddy. It's the end of the line for me." Henry looked at the floor. It was hard to admit this, especially to a guy without arms.

"Well, I want you to take me with you and do me, then yourself."

Henry's expression was suddenly grave. He started to speak but Rusty interrupted.

"No, before you say anything, just listen. I obviously can't kill myself, and I've tried everything they suggested to get better. If my family had accepted me back, I could have lived like this. Put me on a raft and tow me out to sea. Kind of like water skiing without arms. That would have been great, man. But they didn't. They won't. Take me with you, dude. Don't leave me here."

Henry regarded his buddy a long time then finally nodded.

Over the next few days and nights, in quiet conversations, many of the vets came to the same conclusion. Little by little the able-bodied agreed to help the limbless. Henry, who was used to organizing, told them he knew just the place for it to happen.

They surprised the staff with their sudden improvement in demeanor, which solved the problem of placement. The vets without obvious physical injures told the staff that they would take care of their limbless teammates. This was true but not in the way the staff imagined. Some of the guys had vehicles with enough room for those without wheels, and inside them, locked up securely, was an arsenal of weapons. For this group, the method of suicide was a no brainer.

A few days later, the vets were discharged. With the staff waving goodbye, the disabled men departed in their strange-looking convoy. The vets felt lighthearted. There were no more hospitals in their future.

* * *

George threw *The Fifth Sacred Thing* across the room. He had gotten to the place where the soldiers had ordered the families to go home or they would be killed. A young child came forward and said, "There is a place at our table for you." A soldier shot the child dead. Another child, trembling, came forward and also said, "There is a place at our table for you." He shot that child dead too. Yet another one came forward and started to say the same thing. The soldier, aghast, threw down his weapon and ran off screaming.

George wasn't going to finish this book. "Useless feminist bullshit!" The theme was completely ridiculous. As inane an idea as offering a place at the table to Saddam or Uday.

George went outside and began walking. About two-thirds of the landscaping was dead. The temperature was hitting 120 degrees. He wasn't wearing a hat and he hadn't brought any water along. He walked down the road away from the house. His foot was almost healed, and in spite of the heat, it felt good to be exercising. After a while, George felt his head burning and was about to turn back when he stumbled and fell. "Jesus Christ," he yelled, hoping he wouldn't screw up his knees.

George was still on the ground when he realized that suddenly it wasn't hot anymore. He felt comfortable, except for a slight headache and his thirst.

"Here's some water for you, son." A man with long hair and a long beard handed him a dipper. As he drank, he noted that the man was strangely dressed. Long, rough robes. Old, worn sandals. How did this guy get on the property?

George looked around for some familiar faces, but the man said gently, "There's no one else here but you and me. And you've asked me to come help you. So here I am."

"Jesus! It's really you. I'm sorry I took your name in vain."

The man in the rough robes threw back his head and laughed. "It's okay. I like being recalled in times of pain, if it helps. Usually it doesn't, though. They keep making the same mistakes." He pulled a book out of his backpack and gave it to George.

George, who wasn't about to refuse anything from Jesus, took it. He looked down and saw it was the Starhawk book. He groaned.

Jesus looked at him. "You've got to keep on reading *The Fifth Sacred Thing*. You've reached the most crucial part in the whole book. I like this book a lot. It reminds me of Mary, my wife."

George squinted at Jesus. "Little kids getting shot? Offering a place at the table to soldiers who've just killed your relatives? I don't want to be blasphemous, but I'm not going to read any of this bull crap." Even as George was speaking he was actually thinking, Did Jesus just say something about having a *wife*?

Jesus unfocused his eyes for a moment to better observe George's soul. He didn't weep on this occasion, but he felt like it. Starhawk. Mahatma Gandhi. Nelson Mandela. Ang Sang Sui. Rigoberta Menchu. Wangari Maathai. Martin Luther King. Every one of them would have offered a place at the table to their enemy, if they had the chance. At some point people had to start talking and stop fighting. That's what Mary had said. Jesus didn't understand why people didn't get that. He didn't understand why they hadn't included the Gospel of Mary in the Bible. It was the most important gospel, in his opinion. The last two thousand years might have been quite different. But that was another cross to bear. Not this man's problem. Jesus sighed and a single tear rolled down his radiant cheek.

"Oh, Jesus, you're crying." George found a worn but clean bandana in his pocket and handed it to him.

Jesus spoke again. "Has all this recent reading combined with your dreams made you think of doing anything differently?"

George thought a bit and said, "Well, you know, reading all these war books has made me think more of our soldiers who died. Maybe I should start visiting more cemeteries on holidays."

Jesus gazed at him with compassion.

George knew he needed to do more, a lot more. "The wounded, all the wounded. I've got to go see them, right? Thank them for their service. I always went right before Christmas, your birthday, heh, heh, and I've visited the wounded other times, too. I could go more often. That would make them feel better, right?"

Jesus kept his gentle expression trained on the other man.

George recalled his dream of the night before. Apologies. Is that what he was going to have to do? To tell them that he had been wrong, that there had been no need for this war that had taken away their limbs? Was his pride worth more than their limbs? It was one thing to go into a room with all the presidential aura and spend a few minutes thanking a soldier for his or her service, trying not to look at the space in the bed where a leg or arm should have been…but to apologize?

Jesus continued to contemplate George.

As George looked back at him, he felt the other man's radiance and compassion, and a sense of grace swept through him. "Okay, I'll do it. I'll see more wounded vets in the hospitals or at their homes. I'll thank them and I'll, I'll…." He stopped talking. It was really hard to think about apologizing, and he knew he would need to sit there for a very long time with their families. And they might want to show him the place where they no longer had a foot or an arm. They might want him to touch them. That was what Jesus was asking, and how could he refuse? But how could he do it? It was impossible. He looked at Jesus with a stricken face.

"A place at their table, son. You'll have a place at their table." Jesus put his hand out to George's brow and wiped it gently with the bandana. George closed his eyes, and when he opened them, he found himself alone in the middle of the road. He could hear an engine getting closer, and he was just pushing himself up as his wife came over the hill on the ATV with the "Boycott France" stickers on the back.

"Honey, what happened?" Laura cried.

"I'm okay. My prayers were answered. Jesus. My wife. Thank the Lord." George climbed onto the ATV and slumped in the seat, but he felt good. As soon as he recovered he was going to start calling around and figure out how to visit the veterans and the families of the dead soldiers. He knew it had to be done quietly and with dignity. Jesus. Jesus Christ! Jesus actually came and talked with him. Jesus! That was amazing. He'd have to tell Laura and his preacher. He wasn't sure about telling them, however, that Jesus had been married to Mary. That would be just too unbelievable.

* * *

Judith regained her voice rapidly and amongst the conversations she had, she had talked frankly with Amy, who understood entirely. While others might have been disturbed by the idea of the disabled having sex, Amy had been a nurse long enough and a sexually active woman even longer. She made sure that Judith had a massage and arranged for a hairdresser. They found a beautiful new gown for Judith to wear. Amy brushed and flossed Judith's teeth and put on some light makeup that enhanced her lovely face. And later that afternoon Amy inserted a diaphragm. It was going to take a week for the birth control pills to work, and Judith didn't want to wait any longer. Sex would be complicated enough without getting pregnant. Amy would put up the "do not disturb" sign, and a tough ex-Army female nurse would help maintain the perimeter. She had done this for other wounded vets; this wouldn't be the first couple to make love in a hospital.

When Joseph showed up, he was a little surprised at the quietness in the hall. The lights had been dimmed. There were more flowers at the nurses' station than usual, and the large gruff nurse had set up a desk between the station and Judith's room, as if she was guarding that area. Joseph was pleased when she gave him a smile, and he saw that she must have been quite pretty when younger and weighing two hundred pounds less.

Joseph opened Judith's door and was stunned to see her sitting up in bed, in a beautiful purple gown, her hair up around her face with flowers to one side and a teasing smile on her lips. Under soft, low lighting, he could see the outline of her breasts and he felt a good sensation in his groin. As he closed the door, he noticed the "do not disturb" sign. He placed his flowers in a waiting vase and popped the CD that was sitting out into the player: Sade. Beautiful, sexy music poured into the room.

After placing a chair firmly against the door, Joseph walked over to the bed and kissed Judith. Instead of backing away afterwards, he was drawn, as if into a whirlpool. He settled in closer. A real kiss. A kiss like the last one they'd had in Iraq.

Judith touched Joseph with the stubs of her arms. He kept kissing her as he unbuttoned his shirt. They'd never been skin to skin before. After he removed his shirt, he slowly untied her gown. All the while they continued to kiss. She was wearing a bra that released from the front, and he soon unhooked it and her beautiful breasts swung free.

Slowly Joseph ended the kiss. He took her face in his hands and whispered, "Is this what you want?" It sure was what he wanted. A room in a hospital wasn't a New Orleans Bed and Breakfast, but it was better than the backseat of a Bradley in Baghdad.

Judith smiled. "Of course, Joseph, of course."

He settled in with another kiss and gently began pushing her gown apart until he could see her whole torso. She was gorgeous. He kissed her nipples and she moaned. "Touch my belly." He started to touch her belly, rubbing in slow clockwise circles. She definitely liked that, and he started making bigger circles.

Joseph pulled away to remove the rest of his clothes. It felt great to be naked in her room. He hoped he wouldn't act like a teenager, but he was too much in love to worry about that, and he knew Judith would give him a second or third chance if it was all over too quickly the first time.

Joseph eased himself beside Judith. The sensation of her arm stumps touching his shoulders and chest was strange, but not horrible. Different, but not repelling. A variation on finding a tattoo or a scar on a new lover. The thought drifted away and Joseph returned to focus on the sensations. He pulled her gown down so it was like a pool of water around her waist. He fondled and kissed her breasts, which were about the most perfect and beautiful breasts he'd ever seen. His hands went towards her legs. If he'd looked at her, he would have seen a look of ecstasy on her face.

Judith had not been loved like this in a very long time. Another man had loved her, but he'd been killed by a drunk driver a few years before she joined the Army. It had shocked her so much she'd never let herself fall for anyone until Joseph. Judith couldn't believe how good this felt. She regretted that she had barely any limbs to touch him, but she soon forgot her missing body parts. She had all she needed.

By this time, his fingers were inside her, and he'd moved back to kissing her on the mouth. Joseph asked her permission one more time, and Judith nodded. He pushed the buttons to lower the bed and lifted his body over hers. She was ready for him, and a few minutes later they experienced the miracle they'd both been waiting for.

Chapter 9

Lucy, Maria and Charlie had run out of gas. It was getting dark and they were on a dirt road, somewhere near the river, which they could hear through the forest.

"Well, looks like we'll need to camp here tonight. We have enough water and food," Charlie said. They'd pushed the motorcycle towards a clearing under some trees. They had one tent, which Maria and Charlie would use while Lucy slept under the stars. Maria got a small fire going and began to warm up some beans in a pan. They were just about to eat when they heard the sound of a truck approaching. Immediately alert, Charlie ran to the motorcycle and returned with a service revolver.

"Are you crazy?" Maria shouted. "We're not in Iraq, it isn't the enemy coming down the road." She ran over and pulled on Charlie's vest to get her attention. Lucy got to her feet and ran towards the couple.

Charlie ignored them both. Meanwhile, the lights of a truck loomed closer. The driver must have seen the three women. The truck slowed and the engine stalled. The driver tried to restart the ignition but he did it too hastily and the truck just sat there.

The truck's occupants had been trying to find the state park that night. Jesus, a hefty Mexican American middle-aged grandfather, and his friend, Kenzo, an African Filipino, were carrying a load of paper products from Los Angeles to Kansas City and wanted to rest in a park. They peered through the window trying to figure out the three women: a tall tough-looking well-built short-haired woman, holding a very big gun, a Mexican with beautiful black hair, and a slightly-built girl with mousey brown hair.

Jesus sighed. He expected this sort of trouble in LA, but not in Kansas. He yelled out the open window, "We're okay." And looking at Maria, he added, *"Buenas noches, señoritas. No hay problemas. Somos buena gente."* Jesus was sweating now. "Please put down the gun."

"That's right, Charlie. Put down that stupid gun." Maria was practically jumping up and down with anger.

Charlie lowered the weapon. "Okay. You can get out of the truck slowly, and close the doors and put your hands up. And stay right beside your vehicle." She could still remember the words in Arabic, but she didn't need another language now. Jesus and Kenzo got out and did what she said. They stood there with their hands up looking warily at the women.

"*Buenas noches, señores.* I'm Maria, and this is Charlie and Lucy," Maria said. She gave Charlie a stern glance and strode forward to shake the hand of the driver.

"*Con much gusto, señorita.*" Jesus bowed slightly as he took her hand. Maria immediately liked him. She turned to Kenzo and they shook hands. Charlie, who had put her weapon down, nodded at the men but didn't approach. Lucy stepped forward and shook their hands.

There was a little small talk, but Charlie was still suspicious and insisted on knowing what they had in the truck. This was just the same size truck that would be used in Iraq to hide the enemy. "You have to show me. Open up the back."

Jesus looked at her. "It's nothing dangerous, *señorita*. I can assure you. Paper products."

Charlie raised her weapon and pointed it. "Open the truck."

"Oh, Charlie, don't be crazy," Maria began, but when she saw the gun swing in her direction, she stopped talking abruptly. Where was the caring lover now? Charlie hadn't told her everything about Iraq. She was certain of that now.

Jesus observed them calmly. "Sure, *señorita*. I open the truck for you. You see, *no problemas*."

Charlie indicated that Jesus and Kenzo should walk in front of her to the back of the truck. She was more concerned about Kenzo, as he moved like a martial artist. She stood a few feet away from him with the weapon trained on his back while he and Jesus opened up the double doors. A few moments later, Maria and Lucy heard laughter coming from the rear of the vehicle. They hurried over and saw Charlie on her knees, her gun in the dirt, laughing hysterically. She pointed into the truck, and then the other two women started snickering. Jesus started laughing, too. Kenzo's eyes had crinkled up and he smiled.

It took Charlie a while to stop laughing. "Well, girls, we are definitely in luck with these guys. Where were you when we needed you in Iraq?"

The truck was filled almost completely with cartons of light, medium, and heavy tampon boxes. Kenzo had opened one of the cartons so that Charlie could see that the contents matched the description printed on the outside. Charlie glanced down at her weapon and then considered the men. She could have shot them dead over a truck filled with tampons. She put the safety catch on her gun and got up and walked a short distance away. She wondered if she was going to be this screwed up all her life.

A little while later the group sat with a meal of refried beans laid out before them. Lucy said she'd like to offer a prayer. Jesus took off his Angels cap and he and Kenzo looked on respectfully. "Thank you, Lord, for this food and company before us. Thank you too for a truck load of tampons." Lucy couldn't help but smile. "We are blessed with your presence, especially Kenzo and Jesus, and in this nourishment. All are welcome. Amen."

Charlie recalled her family's usual speedy prayer before meals when she was young, "GodisgoodGodisgreatthankyouforthisfood -Amen." She hadn't thought about her family in a long time. They hated the fact that she was lesbian. Thinking about them made her sad and mad all over again. She grabbed a few tortillas and strode off into the darkness, saying she was going for a walk.

"She'll be okay," Maria said, watching her go.

"*Ojalá*," said Jesus and crossed himself.

Over the next hour or so, Maria and Lucy described their friendship and recent reunion. Lucy talked about her pilgrimage and her plan to go next to Columbine High School. Jesus talked about his family. He had children spanning thirty years, some grandchildren and some foster children. Kenzo just listened. He was the first to hear Charlie coming back as she moved quietly through the woods.

"Soldiers, we have a situation, about a ten-minute walk from here." Charlie had assumed a military bearing. She'd gone towards the river, she explained, and at some point crossed a dirt road with a sign that said "Boy Scout Camp Windego." Hearing sounds from the camp, she'd followed the road cautiously and soon saw a strange sight.

"I saw a bunch of vehicles. Real beaters. Some Bradleys and Hummers. Some bikes," she said, thumbing towards her own motorcycle. "And there were all these soldiers, well, ex-soldiers. Vets sitting around a huge campfire." Even if they hadn't been in uniform, or parts of uniforms, she would have been able to tell them a mile away. "And the weapons they have. Oh man, they have everything." She proceeded to list what she'd seen, an arsenal of weapons of the types they'd used in Iraq.

Lucy looked very worried. She wondered if the vets were going to attack someone. She knew there had been episodes of violence by vets in the past. Or maybe they were planning something worse, like Timothy McVey. Then suddenly she began to wonder if she had been sent there by the Lord to prevent an attack. That would fit with the dreams she'd had about her pilgrimage. But what could she do? She didn't know anything about weapons.

"Oh, yeah, a lot of those guys are crips. Missing legs or arms. Only some would be able to shoot."

While the others were puzzling over all this, Charlie and Kenzo suddenly became very alert. Charlie was about to run for her gun again when a young man stumbled out of the woods. Dark curly hair, dark eyes, average height, dressed in faded Desert Storm gear and old beat-up boots, he looked desperate. "You have to help me," he cried. "They're all going to kill themselves. We have to stop them." He looked at Charlie and saluted. "Bill Stein, third lieutenant honorably discharged due to medical reasons. Those crazy fuckers want to kill themselves and we've got to stop them."

"They aren't going to attack anyone?" Lucy asked hopefully. He was handsome, but looked exhausted and on the verge of collapse.

Bill regarded Lucy for a moment. "No, they're just going to attack themselves." He took a step forward and quickly explained about the abrupt closure of the VA researcher's PTSD program, the demoralization that had followed, the vets' decision to kill themselves at the old scout camp, and how he had decided to follow them and try to stop the mass suicide. "I was there myself at the VA, and I've been following them, trying to figure out how to keep them from killing themselves. But I can't stop them on my own. Then I saw you guys and thought you might help...."

Bill had never been this tired, even in Iraq. When a tear escaped, he angrily wiped it away. Maria approached him and put her arm around his shoulders. The image of Mary and Jesus came to Lucy's mind. A young-man-Jesus, not yet famous, who was just trying to do some good, and Maria, the comforting woman bolstering his fading courage.

While Lucy watched the scene unfold before her like a Bible story, Charlie, Kenzo and Jesus looked at one another. Then they made a little circle and began to whisper. A few minutes later, Charlie approached the others. "Okay, listen up. We have a plan."

Charlie took command. She described what she had in her small arsenal on the motorbike and what Jesus and Kenzo could contribute. Bill spoke up, saying that, as a friend of a former medic, he had some supplies of meds, including Ryphenol, known as the date rape drug.

"Oh, what were you going to do with those, Billy boy?" Charlie said sarcastically. Lucy drew away from Bill, recalling the men in Texas who had almost raped her.

"I would *never* rape anyone," Bill said furiously, drawing himself up. "I figured these guys, some of them, at least, would start drinking and maybe I could put the roofies in their drinks. They'd pass out and I could get their weapons away from them."

Charlie studied him intently and finally nodded. "Okay, that's actually a good idea. Let's roll, guys." The plan was that Jesus would drive the truck as close as possible. One of those new hybrids, it had a quiet engine, along with good gas mileage. They hoped the noise the soldiers were making in the camp would mask their approach. Bill and Charlie had noted some bleachers on one side of the clearing where the vets were gathered. There they could take cover. Bill planned to go back into the camp and do what he could to put the sedatives in their drinks. This would disable some of the guys, but as the first to drink began to pass out, the others would become suspicious. That was where Charlie's knowledge and equipment would be used. Lucy, Maria, and Jesus would be with the truck and they would come in last.

Bill wasn't too sure about the plan; he knew these guys and he knew how serious they were, and also what type of weapons they had, but Charlie's eyes were sparkling. She *knew* this was going to work. She *loved* this type of stuff. Heck, if the military didn't have so much bullshit, she wouldn't have left. As she got ready for whatever was going to happen, she realized she hadn't felt so alive since being in Iraq. She looked at Maria and softened a bit. Yes, she felt alive with her. But that was a totally different way of feeling alive. Charlie needed aggression and competition. She saw a spark in Maria's eyes. They grinned at each other. Maria knew this was going to work, too.

* * *

From a monitor backstage, George surveyed the crowd at the Albuquerque Marriott. This was going to be a lot harder than he thought. He really wanted to say something about his recent revelations, but he just couldn't do it before these people. How would all these wealthy, cheering Republicans respond if he explained that he'd been wrong and wanted to apologize to everybody he'd hurt? That he wanted to spend the rest of his life atoning and that this would be the last Republican fundraising speech he ever did? He had countless speaking engagements scheduled and there didn't seem to be much time to go see wounded veterans. Besides, his closest advisors wanted George to minimize the visits to the wounded. Even his former advisor, the Architect, who George still spoke with occasionally, complained that it called attention to the continuing chaos in Iraq. The Architect advised George to keep visiting military bases with their young healthy attractive cheering soldiers. Or go to high schools to keep up recruitment. It was okay to quietly visit a wounded veteran or speak with a family of a deceased serviceman at church, but it was not okay to put too much time into it. Perhaps once a month.

George was still needed to fundraise for the party, to keep on message that Iraq was part of the bigger war against terror. And that's what George spoke about in Albuquerque. Between their cheers and the presence of his backstage advisors, George managed to stick with his speech and earned over a million dollars for the party that afternoon. After the orgy of handshaking, George went for a bike ride along the Rio Grande River. The lovely cottonwoods and murmur of the river uplifted him and returned him to thoughts of his recent revelations. As they pedaled along, George told the Secret Service agents that he wanted to go to the VA hospital and pay an impromptu visit to a wounded Iraq vet. The agents heartily approved, as they had friends who had been killed and wounded in Iraq. The soldiers and their families who had been visited *by a president* would talk about the experience the rest of their lives. It would help them get through all the painful rehab, the difficulty with prosthetic limbs, the sadness at not being able to play basketball or run marathons, and for some, the agonizing rejection by family, friends or lovers who no longer wanted to be close to this man or woman missing one or more limbs.

With one call to the VA, the request for a visit without fanfare was quickly arranged. The chief of the hospital told George they had a young man who had lost both legs and part of one arm. He was pretty depressed and they thought that the former president could really cheer him up. President Bush could come over right after regular visiting hours and have as much time and privacy as he wanted with

Harry.

On the ward a nurse walked into Harry's room and told him and his visiting family that a special visitor wanted to talk with him. The young man groaned. He didn't want any older vets or candy ladies or well-meaning teenagers coming by. The shrink was okay, but he didn't want her to meet his family. They were so opinionated about Iraq and he knew her empathy would bring this out. He couldn't deal with all the drama or "affect," as the psychiatrist called it.

Harry's father, a Vietnam vet, hadn't actively encouraged his son to enlist, but after 9/11 the young man had signed up with the Marines and his dad had given his approval. Harry's mother, on the other hand, was a social worker, and had tried to dissuade her son from enlisting. There were many ways to serve one's country, she'd told him, and what was needed after 9/11 was intelligence, diplomacy, detective work, and creative thinking. But she couldn't keep him from becoming a soldier.

Defending the homeland was so fundamental, backed up by millions of years of evolution. And when the Iraq War began, she had believed President Bush, and along with her husband and seventy percent of Americans, had supported the war.

His older sister was an anti-war, anti-globalization activist. Jez had been protesting for as long as Harry could remember and had opposed the Iraq invasion from the first whispers of war. Harry knew she was just as idealistic as he was, but her idealism was in the opposite direction. She had tried to argue him out of joining the military and told him improbable but true stories: the Texan town where Comanches and settlers traded without any violence, the 1914 Christmas Eve truce where the young Germans and English soldiers sang *Stile Nacht, Silent Night,* near the trenches, and the Israeli daycare in a pre-1948 Palestinian home which cared for children of all religions and nationalities. Jez could go on forever with such stories, the voices of hope. But for Harry they didn't outweigh all the epics, libraries of books, films of war, and violent video games that glorified battle. He'd joined up, and now he was a depressed disabled veteran.

Harry's mom had changed her mind about the war with the Abu Ghraib prison news and his dad had changed his mind when he first saw his son missing half his body. They didn't talk much with Harry about this, as he still felt the mission was just, and he was thinking about his buddies back in Iraq.

Today was his twenty-third birthday. With the help of the staff they had snuck the family dog into the hospital. The grinning black labrador lay on the hospital bed in the place where Harry's legs would have been if he'd still had them. The dog was all they could easily talk about, and as they told funny dog stories, Harry pulled softly at her ears with his remaining hand.

The nurse who had knocked on the door had been told that the former president only wanted to visit a veteran, not meet the family. She opened her mouth to say, "The rest of you need to leave now," but then she changed her mind. She wondered what it would be like to sit down and talk with a president, even a former president. Well, here was an opportunity for this American family to do just that. Now that he wasn't "the decider" anymore, maybe he could be "the listener" and "the learner." And maybe he could help bring this young soldier out of his depression.

The nurse smiled and said, "You have a very special visitor. I think you will all want to talk with him." She closed the door, walked down the hall, and announced to President Bush and his two agents that the young man was ready.

George told the agents to wait outside the room. There was no threat from a disabled vet laid up in a hospital bed. George wanted to see the welcome surprise on the young man's face, which would surely be altered if he were to enter the room after a couple Secret Service agents.

When George walked into the room and saw the young man's family and dog (who growled at him), he almost walked out. But he pulled himself together and presenting himself with dignity, walked forward to introduce himself, as if they didn't know who he was. First he greeted Harry, who extended his hand and did his best to straighten up, then the father, who also held his hand out. The mother was hesitant, but then she shook George's hand, too, though with a grave expression on her face. The sister folded her hands over her chest and scowled at George. He faltered; he hadn't seen such up-close disdain from anyone in years.

"My name is Jezebel," the sister said aggressively. She couldn't stand this man. Jezebel took off her vest to make sure that George saw her T-shirt with a map of the United States and the words: "Weapons of Mass Destruction: We Found Them!"

"Jezebel, right," George said, then he turned to the young man.

There weren't enough seats. Harry's father, a retired doctor, gave up his so the former president could sit. Harry's dad knew it was always important to sit down, especially in a hospital, if you had something serious to communicate. Standing implied that you had other places to be, and the person being addressed was not really that significant. The dog had stopped growling but still looked ready to leap off the bed and bite George at the slightest provocation.

"Harry, thank you, son, for your service. I appreciate it and your country appreciates it. I'm sorry you were wounded. We'll try and do everything we can to help you." George said these words with heartfelt sincerity. "Would you like to tell me anything? I'm here to listen. Take as much time as you need." He relaxed a bit, realizing this was really true. He wasn't going to leave until Harry and his family asked him to. George was going to make *their* time more important than *his*. He hadn't experienced this sense of humility in years. Since his youth, George's time had *always* been more important than anyone else's.

The dog thumped his tail and grinned. Harry patted the lab's head and started to speak. "Sir, I joined the Marines after 9/11 like a lot of my friends did. We wanted to defend our country. I especially wanted to go to Afghanistan to get Osama. I was there for a year, and was damn happy to get the Taliban, those fuckers. Oh, sorry, sir, didn't mean to swear."

George chuckled. "Don't worry, I've said the same thing about those fuckers myself."

Everyone in the room nodded, even Jezebel.

"We almost had him, sir, in Tora Bora, but then this weird sand snow storm came in. We couldn't see anything, all our weapons and radios were jammed up, and we had to retreat. We never got that close again, and a few months later I got sent to Iraq. I kept hoping they'd get me back to Afghanistan, but it never happened." All at once Harry smiled. "You know, it was the last time I got to ride a horse, when I was over there. It was like being back in the 1800s, sir."

The family looked at one another with some hope. This was more than Harry had said in months. The president was helping just by sitting and listening.

"So, Iraq. Well, I got sent there with a few of my buddies. We figured you knew what you were doing. Weapons of mass destruction, nuclear attack, imminent threat. Sounded pretty bad. Maybe we'd find Osama in Iraq. Bad guys stick together, right?" Harry spoke sincerely.

George averted his eyes. The dog frowned at him.

After long seconds of silence the former president lifted his gaze and pondered the young soldier. Was this how he was going to start telling the truth? Well, he had to begin somewhere. "Well, Harry, I have to say, no. No, there was nothing to link Saddam and Osama. No more than there was to link Rumsfield and Saddam."

Harry's family looked stunned. Even Jezebel lost her sarcastic expression. Harry registered that this was an incredible revelation. The dog whimpered. George continued. "Yes, I can see you look surprised. Although I did admit this in a press conference a few years after the war began."

Jezebel, who had already regained her attitude, said scornfully, "Just once."

George glanced at the young woman. She was about the same age as his daughters. But she was so different. "Yeah, Jez, you're right. It was just once. And once wasn't enough to counteract the thousands of times people had heard otherwise on FOX."

George looked embarrassed. Jezebel wished she had her cell phone recorder on. Harry's parents were speechless. Harry perceived the awkwardness of the moment.

"Well, I'm glad we got Saddam, sir, and those bastards, Uday and Qusay," Harry continued, "although I'm sorry we killed the grandson. But I guess with the pre-emptive attack philosophy, maybe it was right to kill him, too." Harry said this to the former president with a questioning look.

Jezebel and her mother were both thinking that so many other people, including children, had been killed in prior efforts to get Saddam and his sons. Jezebel started to say something, but her mother stopped her. "Wait," she mouthed to her daughter.

Jezebel slouched back in her chair.

"Well, I've got to say, son, that the pre-emptive military strategy, on this scale, was… It was…." Boy, this is hard, George thought. "It was wrong, also." And he bowed his head.

There was a collective gasp. Even the dog raised his eyebrows.

And so it went. Although George continued to defend his belief that democracy could replace dictatorship, he admitted that the war in Iraq would never have happened if not for the Iraqi oil resources and the desire to gain strategic military control of the area and to make a good profit. As a former oil man, George told them, he really couldn't see the American economy running on anything else besides oil, and he knew that control of the energy supply was essential to keeping the US powerful.

At this point Jezebel leapt in and told him she had plenty of information about conservation, alternative and renewable fuels, a national campaign to get people to change their ways, and all kinds of incentives for research. "Like a Manhattan project to completely overhaul the energy policy of the United States. People would really get behind it, because it truly would be a plan for their future and their children's futures. This could be one of the great things you could do as an ex-president," she said enthusiastically. She hesitated.

Then she added, leaning forward in her chair, "Please."

This was the first time Jez had said that word in years. It was quite incredible for her parents to hear her politely ask for something from "The Antichrist," as she had referred to him most of the time.

Harry's mother noticed her son's energy fading and knew it was time to bring this historic meeting to a close. The nurse at the door had been listening for some time and she also realized that Harry was getting exhausted. She'd seen healing before, but not quite like this. She poked her head into the room and said, "Harry, I think it's time for you to rest." Harry's mother nodded.

"Could I say a prayer for you before I leave? For all of us?" George asked. Everyone, including Jez, nodded back. The former president got down on his knees and began to pray.

* * *

Love, in all its forms, had awakened Judith, but she still struggled. It was tremendously difficult to recover from loss of a limb, much less all four, and adapt simultaneously to sudden blindness. People born without limbs, or who lose their sight at an early age, have years to learn how to cope. Their growing brains are astonishingly flexible and responsive to the interplay between their bodies and their environments. She had her moments of despair, mostly when she was alone, but Judith was determined to succeed nonetheless.

For inspiration, one of the physical therapists read Judith the story of a young man born without arms and legs but with an incredible strength of will. In high school he played football and was really good at tackling opponents. And his personality was such that he had many friends and he took a beautiful girl to the senior prom. Judith wondered if he lost his virginity with her. It was hard not to think about sex with all the lovemaking with Joseph. While a couple of prudes disapproved, most of the nursing staff was very supportive of Judith and Joseph's conjugal visits. Some of them were a bit jealous, admitting to each other that Judith "got more" than they did at home.

But they didn't begrudge her time with Joseph. And they did what they could to protect their privacy.

Ben did surprise them once. In spite of the hymn singing, Ben remained aloof from Joseph. His rage and anger at those who had hurt Judith somehow got channeled towards Joseph. Ben did knock, but he didn't wait for an answer, and when he saw Joseph's clothes strewn across the floor, and the couple cuddling underneath the bedcovers, he went berserk. Screaming, swearing, and kicking furniture, Ben would have attacked Joseph, who'd gotten out of bed, holding a pillow over his nakedness, if Amy hadn't entered the room.

"Walk with me," she said quickly, and she grabbed Ben's arm. He calmed down enough to accompany her. She motioned to the other nurse that she was taking him outside. On the east side of the hospital, away from the setting sun and under the trees, it was cooler. Amy led Ben over to a bench and they sat down. "What's wrong with you? Your sister is happy. She's getting better. She and Joseph are in love. What's wrong with that?"

He put his head in his hands and rocked backwards and forwards on the bench. "Oh, shit, I don't know. You're right. I'm an idiot. I just hate what's happened to her." He removed his hands from his head looked down at them. "At least if she still had hands, I think I could stand it." Amy placed her fingers on the inside of his forearm and moved them slowly towards his hand. He gasped. He'd never felt anything simultaneously so erotic and so kind. She smiled and he saw a little gap between her front teeth that he'd never been close enough to notice. He wondered how long her hair was, as it was pulled into some kind of elaborate arrangement on her head.

"It goes down to my waist."

Ben looked surprised.

"I know what men think when they look at my hair. I'm a nurse, and I'm also a beautiful, confident woman." She smiled again.

Ben wanted to touch her head and take down her hair. He couldn't remember if it was the Thai or the Vietnamese who didn't want their heads touched. He lifted his hands, but then dropped them to his thighs. "You've gotta understand that my sister was the most beautiful, talented, smartest girl and woman I'd ever known. And so kind. She helped everyone feel better, be better, do better. I looked up to her so much, and so did our brother." Ben put his head in his hands again and suddenly he began to sob. "I miss Martin so much too. He was so much like her. But at least he's dead. He's not suffering anymore."

Amy stood with her hands on her hips. "That's what you think? That it's better to be dead than wounded? Better dead than missing something?" Incredulously, she regarded him.

Ben looked up at her. "Sure. I mean who'd want to live without arms and legs, and no sight?"

They glared at each other for a few moments and then Amy sat beside him again. "You're wrong, guy," she said more gently. "I'll tell you a story from my parents. They came from Vietnam, they escaped on a boat in 1979 after all their brothers and sisters had died from torture, disease, or broken hearts. My parents fell in love in a refugee camp, and they found the strength to leave. They suffered a lot. They finally got to the states, and a church helped them. They suffered more; all bad thoughts still there in their dreams. But they got better. Not whole, but better. They had me and my sister. Every day they pray to our ancestors and our relatives who no longer live. They know they'll be reincarnated someday, whole and happy. It's inevitable. Life goes on."

Ben still felt sad but he was no longer sobbing.

Amy placed her fingers lightly back on his inner forearm. "Your sister, she wants to live. She is living. All of us lose something as we get older. Some lose more than others, but always there is hope. Where there's life, there's hope, and it comes in all forms. Even hope for you, guy." She smiled.

Ben stared at her beautifully manicured nails moving up and down his arm, the tips of her fingers sending warm sensations through his body. He relaxed a bit. Maybe something in his life was going to get better. Maybe she was right. He took her hand and slowly moved it to his cheek, where she wiped away his remaining tears.

Chapter 10

Contrary to what Bill had told Lucy and the others, the soldiers did not intend to drink. Henry had told his mates that their suicides couldn't deteriorate into a drunken mess. Drunks with guns could result in injuries instead of deaths, and this last mission was supposed to be about the end of their suffering. Besides, there had to be order, similar to Boy Scout and military rituals. Seated around the campfire, Henry had the veterans check their weapons. Then he asked the ones who had all their limbs to make sure the others were comfortable.

He looked around the group. Besides his buddy from Hawaii, there was Walt from New Hampshire, who was missing his right leg and left arm; he'd been hit in Falluja. Luis from Florida had only one eye and was missing his right hand, the bones were still in the soil somewhere near the Syrian border. Skipio from Minnesota was missing all his limbs, the victim of a massive bomb in Baghdad that had killed everyone else in the Bradley. Jimmy from Kentucky was taking care of Skipio. He didn't look wounded, but he had horrible scars on his abdomen and groin and had no genitalia, except what the reconstructive surgeons had given him for urination. He'd also been injured in Baghdad, with a different bomb. And so it went, with each one of the soldiers missing something physically and mentally and their hearts broken.

"OKAY, are you ready, men?" Henry regarded each one in turn. He wanted to see the answer to his question in their eyes. They all nodded. They each planned to say something, like they'd done in group therapy at the VA: something about why they were there and why they didn't want to live any longer.

Henry began. "I loved my country so much. Everything about America made me so damn proud." He went on to talk about his childhood, and what it had been like to become an Eagle Scout, and how that had led to military service. "I miss myself — that young guy who thought we were the greatest in the world. I miss Surfer Dude. He was right. The war was wrong. We were misused by guys who had never gone to war themselves." Henry sighed. "I'm ready to die."

He turned to Barry, who was from Pittsburgh. Barry had no legs, but incredibly strong arms. "I miss running, man. I used to love running." He had run cross-country in high school and in college before he dropped out to join the military after 9/11. He still dreamed about running, but the race always ended in a fiery crash, the same explosion that took his legs. Barry tried wheelchair basketball and skiing for the disabled, but it wasn't the same.

Barry gestured to John, a Mormon from Utah whose face was mangled from a previous suicide attempt. He told the group that he was thinking about his family and everyone in his church. His parents built him a small house behind their own and people kept bringing him meals and offering him jobs. But they didn't want to hear about his painful experiences in Iraq. They didn't want to hear about the checkpoint he'd been manning when the car came towards them and the driver didn't seem to understand the order to stop. He and the other guard had fired, and when the car wrecked, they ran toward it yelling in Arabic, "Stop. Get out of the car." They'd been shocked when a little girl, covered in blood, staggered out and fell at their feet. Beyond her they could see other small kids, all bloodied, one still alive, screaming. And worse had been the sounds of the parents in the front seat, mortally injured, whimpering for their kids, unable to comfort them in their last moments.

John had barely made it back to the base before he flipped out. He tried to kill himself that night, but he'd been saved by medics and sent off to Germany. No matter what medications the doctors gave him, every night he re-lived the death of the family.

John was definitely ready to die. He knew he wouldn't get to heaven but he hoped the Iraqi family was reunited there — even though as a Mormon he wasn't supposed to believe that Muslims or other non-Mormons could go to heaven. This was yet another thing his family didn't understand.

John looked miserably at his hands. He tipped his head to the next guy in the circle.

Jimmy from Kentucky said, "Ya'll know how much I used to love ridin' horses." He was small enough that he'd even jockeyed some, but he mostly loved riding on trails through fields around his small town. He could have ridden without a leg or an arm, but the injuries to his abdomen where his legs joined his body had left him in incredible pain, and there was no way he could even sit on a horse. He'd tried with an incredibly gentle Tennessee walker, but he couldn't make it around the paddock without screaming with pain. He'd fallen into the arms of his parents and high school sweetheart, and he recalled all of them sobbing while the puzzled horse nuzzled him, trying to get him to get up and try again. Remembering this, Jimmy choked up and motioned to the next man to speak.

Propped next to Jimmy, Skipio from Minnesota still had a sense of humor. He called himself "the Monty Python knight" from the famous scene where the knight who had his legs and arms cut off screams at his opponent, "I'll still fight you. I'm not dead yet." He was part Chippewa, and before joining the Marines, he'd canoed all over Minnesota and parts of Canada. He still dreamed of canoeing and wished to hell that the explosion had left him with at least one arm. He had envisioned using a kayak paddle in a specially built canoe, but he just couldn't figure out how to do it without limbs. "This knight is ready to die, guys." He pictured the Monty Python knight finally falling over, going still and silent. Skipio was satisfied to know that Jimmy would put a bullet right through his eye, killing him instantly before he shot himself.

Mario, from Guatemala, hadn't said much because his English wasn't too good. He'd come to the United States on foot, via Mexico. He'd worked in a chicken factory in Iowa before he volunteered in 2006. He'd heard that volunteers could become US citizens, and that's what he desired more than anything in the whole world. Mario had lost a foot in Iraq.

Mario wasn't sure that he belonged here with these suicidal vets. He was here for Skipio, who knew some Spanish and had become his first real American friend in Germany, where they met in the hospital. They had been reunited in the PTSD program, and Skipio had inspired Mario to keep trying, to get over the lingering pain from his amputation, his doubts about being able to work again and worrying that he'd lost his opportunity for citizenship.

Mario had also been friendly with Bill, who he didn't see right now. He knew Bill had his doubts about this group suicide plan. Mario wished the hospital program had continued. Some of the staff spoke Spanish and he had even started to think that maybe he could go to nursing school on his veterans' benefits. But when the hospital program ended, and Skipio lost hope, Mario lost hope also. When his friend said he wanted to suicide with these guys, Mario decided that he couldn't desert him. Some of Mario's Mayan ancestors had come to him in his dreams, and he knew they would welcome him in the afterlife. Mario said, "I miss jungle where I from. Iraq no jungle, just hot and sand. Jungle lots of water. Waterfalls. Swimming. Pretty flowers. Pretty girls, too."

He smiled and some of the other guys did too, thinking of girls and water and fun. "And *loros*, parrots," Mario added. "*Adiós, loros, chicas, flores, agua.*" Mario bowed his head.

The rest of the guys told their stories, each of them taking as long as they needed. The fire was dying down by the time the last one finished speaking. They looked at one another and those who could stand stood up and saluted. In their eyes was the same look that they'd had when they'd been inducted into the services. Someone observing them would have seen beyond the wounds and losses a very distinguished group of men. And they were. All true Americans.

Lucky for them, there *was* someone looking at them. Charlie, Kenzo and Bill waited in the shadows behind the bleachers. Charlie held contraptions that looked like TV remote control channel changers. She was aiming and punching buttons furiously in the direction of all the soldiers.

Kenzo had to stifle a laugh. "What are you doing?" he whispered. "Trying to change the channel from 'Real Men Kill Themselves' to 'Lesbian Eye for Suicidal Soldiers'?" Kenzo reached for one of the channel changers. "Let a man do this job; remotes are for men, not women."

"Shut up," Charlie hissed. "You wouldn't know how to operate these even after a million years of instruction." She concentrated on the weapon furthest away. Lying next to Henry, it was the group's most lethal weapon. She figured he'd be first and last. First to kill the armless Hawaiian, and last to die himself, after he'd checked each guy to make sure he was truly dead.

The veterans were starting to pick up their weapons.

It was time. Bill pulled out his harmonica and began playing taps. The soldiers froze at the sound. Only one continued to go for his weapon. But Charlie quickly punched a few more buttons on the remote, now aimed at his weapon, and then she smiled, satisfied.

"You've forgotten something, men." Kenzo emerged from behind the bleachers and boomed in a large voice. He'd done some radio theater and often spoken in the church where he'd gone with his family when they'd still been alive. It all came back right then. "You have forgotten the other part of the therapy." Not only had he studied psychology, but he'd also done some therapy himself, which had helped *him* not kill himself. "The other part of the therapy is to say why *not* to kill yourselves, what you have to live for, and what you *can* do with the rest of your lives." Kenzo thought back to what Bill had told him about the men. Bill hadn't shown himself yet to the group, but he was still playing the harmonica, now something hauntingly reminiscent of Bruce Springsteen.

"You, Mr Hawaii, you want to go in the ocean. Get Mr Kansas there to take you. He needs to broaden his horizons." He'd been told by Bill that the vet from Kansas had never swum in the ocean, even though he was an excellent swimmer. In one of the hospital therapy sessions he'd admitted a fear of the ocean, perhaps the only fear he had. "Yeah, you, Mr Kansas, the final badge, the last medal, the one that's really worth earning. Take your friend to Hawaii, and get some flippers for yourself and a comfortable raft for your friend. Paddle out to sea. That's what he wants, and that's what you need."

Mario was looking happier. He didn't get all the words but he grasped what the new man was saying. *Esperanza.* Hope. Mario reached down to his weapon and pushed the safety.

"*Y, tu,* Luis de Florida. *Hay mujer que te quiere. Esta en tu casa. T'espera.*" Kenzo was fluent in Spanish from his years in LA. "Yes, there's a woman in your home. She's waiting for you. She loves you." He paused. "She loves you so much, and I see five kids in your future." Kenzo had no idea where this thought came from, but there it was.

Luis looked at him with wonder. He had always wanted a lot of kids, the prospect of which was the one thing that could stop him from killing himself. He had no idea how this man knew there was a woman in his home. He had told her that when he got back from Iraq, he'd make love to her every day and they'd make lots of babies. Luis had been so ashamed of his injuries, however, he'd never gone home, even though she'd written hundreds of emails, pleading with him. Kenzo spoke again. "*Hijos, hijas, amigo, les piensa, por favor.* Sons, daughters, friend, think of them." Luis put the safety on his weapon.

"Who's going to take me canoeing?" Skipio asked. "They'd have to carry me, all the gear, and the boat. I'm a son of bitch to take care of."

Mario wanted to volunteer to help his friend, but he'd never been in a canoe and didn't know how to swim. Kenzo looked at Skipo intently. He'd grown up in New York City, but he'd gone to camp in upstate New York and spent many blissful hours in the water in canoes and kayaks. He hadn't done it in years, but all of a sudden he had the most intense desire to go canoeing. "I'll take you, dude."

Skipio looked surprised.

"I've always wanted to see Minnesota." Kenzo had a ton of money from the settlement after the fire that had killed his family, and he hadn't touched any of it. He knew his wife would want it spent this way.

Two of the men had been getting more and more agitated as they listened to Kenzo's solutions. Bert from Idaho and Paul from Georgia had become lovers in Iraq and were wounded from "friendly fire" – a "fragging for fagging." The "don't ask, don't tell" policy had been quietly dropped because there weren't enough soldiers to do the jobs, but there were still people in the military who hated gays, and Burt and Paul were the victims of that hatred. Like the others, Burt and Paul had served with distinction, but the fag-hating officer above them had done everything he could to deny their bravery. Luckily, most of the men in their platoon knew their value and valor, and they leapt up the chain of command to help Bert and Paul get their medals. It was a homophobic soldier in another platoon who took advantage of fierce fighting in Kirkuk one day and threw a grenade at the two as they walked forward into what they didn't recognize as a trap. It was deemed an accident by investigators, but Paul and Bert knew it was no accident. Their injuries weren't bad enough to require discharge, and they would have stayed in the military, but they knew that homophobia would kill them sooner than the Iraqis. So they'd asked for a discharge. They had wanted to live.

When they got back to the states, unfortunately, they'd encountered clergy and hospital administrators from the "great purge" at the Air Force Academy who also hated gays and did their level best to convert them to Christianity and heterosexuality. When Bert and Paul rebuffed these efforts, the Air Force administrators of the purge had attempted to undermine their rehabilitation. The two men found out about the Houston PTSD program on their own, and a sympathetic clerk had processed the paperwork for admission. They had been very hopeful about starting their lives over again, and when the program abruptly ended, they felt too demoralized to continue with life. Between their physical pain and general hopelessness, they really didn't see any other way out.

Paul and Bert picked up their weapons, although they didn't release the safety catches.

Charlie grabbed a couple of remotes and violently pushed the buttons. She frowned and tossed the remotes to the ground. "Plan B, guys," she ordered Jesus, Maria and Lucy, who waited next to a catapult launcher. Jesus was going to have to find another gift for his grandson.

"Fire on, soldiers."

Lucy hit a button and all at once four hundred tampons went flying through the air towards Bert and Paul. They and all the others hit the dirt. She hit the button again and more tampons flew through the air. Maria, Charlie and Lucy began to throw the rest of their stockpile by hand. Bill, Kenzo and Jesus looked a little uncomfortable, but the soldiers on the ground appeared terrified. They had never been so close to so many tampons in their lives. Most men were more afraid of tampons than anything else a woman could throw at them, and these soldiers were no different.

Finally some of the men on the ground, including Burt and Paul, sat up and started throwing the tampons back at their assailants, who by now had revealed themselves. They could see Bill, whom they all knew, and Rusty from Hawaii suddenly yelled, "Charlie, Charlie, is that you?"

Charlie looked at him. A broad smile crossed her face. "Yeah, it's me." She ran towards him to give him a hug. She had been the one to save his life, but they'd lost touch after he was evacuated from Iraq. He was the only man she'd ever made love with, as an experiment to see what heterosexual sex was like. He'd never made love to a lesbian, and he would have done it again, but she advised him to stick with straight women in the future; he would just get aggravated trying to compete with other women for a dyke's love. He'd laughed and told her he'd accept her advice. But there hadn't been other opportunities for sex in Iraq, and once he'd lost both his arms, he doubted there would be any action in the future. That was another reason for wanting to die.

"Okay, everyone, I think this operation is coming to an end." Charlie looked over the group. Kenzo, Bill, and Jesus had collected the weapons and were removing the ammunition. No sense in taking any chances. Some of the soldiers were still throwing the tampons around. "Okay, cut it out guys. Everyone able-bodied needs to pick up all these tampons and put them back in the boxes over there." Charlie laughed. "Aren't you glad we didn't throw used tampons at you?" The men looked grossed out all over again. Jesus had to smile. So did Kenzo. This woman was something else.

After they had cleaned everything up, Lucy and Jesus got out all the food supplies he and Kenzo had in the truck and cooked up a meal. They had just enough food for the group.

Lucy wanted to say a prayer. She looked through her Bible and found what she was looking for: "Psalms 100 (1-5): *Make a joyful noise to the Lord, all the lands! Serve the Lord with gladness! Come into his presence singing! Know that the Lord is God! It is he that made us, and we are his; we are his people, and the sheep of his pasture. Enter his gates with thanksgiving, and his courts with praise! Give thanks to him, bless his name! For the Lord is good; his steadfast love endures forever, and his faithfulness to all generations.*"

There were a few minutes of silence, everyone listening to the cicadas and sounds of the river. The wounded soldiers still looked sad and demoralized. None of them wanted to die anymore, but they weren't sure what they were going to do next. Jesus and Kenzo looked at each other. "*Get Up Stand Up,*" they both said simultaneously and then they started to sing the words of the old Bob Marley song, substituting the word "sit" for "stand."

Jesus took Maria by the hand and they began to dance. Warily, Kenzo approached Charlie, and she took his hand, too. Lucy had only danced in her ballet class and in a few small performances with other dancers, but she approached Henry and reached out her hand. Kenzo and Jesus kept singing as they danced. Bill picked up the tune on his harmonica. The vets who could stand did, and swaying, they tapped their feet. The remaining vets bobbed their heads. The music was hypnotic.

Mario and the other men with legs were dancing by the time the song finished while those who had hands clapped. Lucy asked, "Who wrote that song? That's beautiful. Seems like I should have heard it in church, but I never did."

"Bob Marley, one of the greatest songwriters of the twentieth century. From Jamaica but people all over the world love Marley's music," Kenzo answered. "This song could have been an anthem. Or a hymn." He paused and then said, "He was right about looking for your life on earth, not in heaven."

Kenzo smiled. He was just remembering another box he had in the truck. He retrieved it and opened it up in front of the vets. It was full of T-shirts. There were a few like Jezebel's T-shirt: "Weapons of Mass Destruction: We Found Them" with a map of the United States and all its deadly weapons. Others had the face of President Bush with a dark mustache and words: "Got Oil?" or that of Saddham Hussein captioned with "Weapon of Mass Distraction." Another depicted a map of Iraq: "What's Our Oil Doing Under Their Sand?" And yet another, showing fierce-looking Native Americans, said: "Homeland Security: Fighting Terrorism since 1492." Others from the box read "Peace is Patriotic" with a peace sign on the American flag, and a stern Uncle Sam saying "You Can't Be All You Can Be If You're Dead." The last T-shirt thrown out read "Honor Vets, Wage Peace."

The vets with arms put on the shirts and helped the others. They talked amongst themselves as they dressed but then fell silent. They had been prepared to die, and now that they had decided to live, there were practical matters to consider. Some had closed bank accounts and mailed checks to loved ones. Others had sent notes that their loved ones would receive in a day or two. Some notes had included instructions for favorite possessions to be given to various friends. And if the Federal government assumed they were dead, it might take years to straighten it all out. They wondered if there was a VA hospital nearby. If they all showed up in the ER and described what they'd almost done, they'd likely all be admitted. The mental health staff would straighten everything out.

But Jesus had a different idea. They could use cell phones to contact their loved ones and they could call the closest VA facility. "I want to suggest a pilgrimage," he said. "That's what we do in Mexico and what people everywhere have done for centuries."

"And I know just where you guys could go: the Great Sand Dunes National Park in Colorado," offered Kenzo. "One of my friends who came back from Iraq went there and told me that it helped him a lot. It's a healing place."

The Great Sand Dunes was a magnificent natural playground between two rugged mountain ranges, the San Juans to the west, and the Sangre de Christos to the east, with a beautiful strange river emerging from the mountains at the base of the sand dunes. "My friend told me, you cross the river, and you go from America back into the desert, as if you were crossing back into Iraq."

"Fuck Iraq," said Rusty.

Kenzo held up his hand. "But it's not Iraq. It's America. Even though you're slogging up the dunes, falling back, feeling hot sand under cool, and then cool sand again, there's no IEDs, or booby traps. And you won't need weapons or armor, just water bottles, hats, and socks with sandals. You can see forever in all directions. And for those who can't walk, the National Park Service, in their great wisdom, provides free wheelchairs with buggy-type wheels. Sierra Hotel, guys, just like you."

The vets smiled. Sierra Hotel was slang for "hot stuff." The Iraq War vets knew that the Vietnam veterans had their motorcycle trips to the Black Hills and their deeply moving memorial in Washington DC. Maybe the Great Sand Dunes could serve as a natural place of healing for the Iraq War vets. It would be up to them, of course, to create their own future unique memorials. This was just an idea. None of these vets had been to the Great Sand Dunes. None of them had even heard about it. But it wasn't very far away and it sounded better than a hospital.

Jesus wanted to follow them. But he knew he had to deal with his employer about the missing tampons. The truth might work if the boss knew the items were used to save veterans' lives. Kenzo convinced Jesus to call his boss, who was a veteran, and just tell him what happened. Jesus was an exemplary employee; he'd never been late with a delivery and never lost a load. Perhaps his boss would have mercy.

The vets used cell phones to contact their loved ones that night and early the next morning, and then they pulled out of the scout camp and headed west with the sun just rising behind them. It was the perfect temperature with a slight cool breeze at their backs. The soldiers rode in their beat-up vehicles, but they looked almost festive; they'd found some old flags in a cabin which depicted bears, bobcats, mountain lions, elk and moose. They'd attached these to the antennas and luggage racks.

Charlie and Maria looked stunning on their motorcycle. Charlie was wearing a T-shirt that said "Well-behaved women rarely make history," and Maria was wearing one of the "Weapons of Mass Distraction" T-shirts. As they drove, with Maria holding on tightly from behind, Charlie called something back to her about her two "weapons of mass distraction." In their sidecar rode Skipio, who wanted to feel the sun on his face and torso and the wind in his hair.

Kenzo and Jesus settled into the truck with all the weapons safely locked inside. They were going to turn them in to the next police station they found. As they pulled out of the parking lot, they put on a Bob Marley CD and sang with him about love.

Lucy rode on a motorcycle behind Bill. Before this day, Lucy had only ever ridden behind the lawyer who'd saved her in Texas, and then she'd been in such shock she could barely remember that experience. She felt a little shy when Bill asked her to hold on tight to his waist, and she tried to keep her body a few inches away from Bill's back. But she found herself relaxing against him as they rode to Trinidad, Colorado.

They planned to go north to Littleton while the rest of the group continued west to Great Sand. In the past, Bill had made decisions with caution, but he'd been unhinged by Iraq, and now that he'd accomplished his suicide prevention mission, he didn't feel he needed to continue with the others. While they were packing up that morning, Lucy had explained her pilgrimage and her beliefs. Bill wasn't sure about her trip, but he was intrigued with her. He'd never talked with a Born Again Christian girl or anyone on a pilgrimage. And she was cute, he thought, with her freckles and her soft straight hair, parted in the middle.

Bill said he'd take her to Littleton. That worked out well, because earlier in the morning Maria and Charlie had confessed they wanted to accompany the vets to Great Sand Dunes. Charlie wanted to talk more with Rusty and realized she'd been missing the company of soldiers.

Bill didn't understand Lucy's Rapture beliefs, but he'd heard that some fundamentalist Christians had to convert a certain number of Jews for the Revelations prophecy to come true. Maybe Lucy would try to convert him. After what he'd endured in Iraq and dealing with the suicidal vets, her efforts would be amusing, but it wasn't going to happen. He hadn't been to temple in years, but he'd always be a Jew. However, he wanted to protect Lucy after she told him about the bad guys and her rescue by the lawyers near Waco. As Bill drove the motorcycle, he was feeling really good about being alive with this woman at his back. Once he felt her small breasts press against his back, although she quickly pulled away.

Perhaps Bill and Lucy were too conscious of the proximity of their bodies to notice much more about their surroundings than that they were beautiful. If they'd been more observant, they might have seen the glint of binoculars from behind some shrubbery as they moved away from the camp. One set was held by Darrell, who had been hiding close to the vets. He had been heading to Columbine to search for Lucy, but he'd pulled off the road the night before to rest and couldn't believe it when he woke in the morning and heard her voice through the tangle of trees that separated them. He was furious when he saw Lucy ride off on the motorcycle with another young man. The Lord was truly testing him. He was still fuming as he started his bike, but he had to keep control so he wouldn't wreck. He was focusing so hard he missed seeing other men, also with binoculars, hiding in bushes on the other side of the road.

These four men, faces fixed in grim masks and bulging muscles under camouflage clothing, appeared frighteningly powerful. Somewhat puzzled and angry, they silently watched the first group leave and noted the solitary rider who followed. They had thought the vets would kill themselves, which would have solved their problem, and after collecting huge bonuses, they would have gone on to the next job. They were contractors who had met at Abu Ghraib in Iraq — two during the torture of a prisoner, the others in an interrogation. When Abu Ghraib became public, they were sent to another prison that the press knew nothing about. They'd had even more fun there, but eventually they had returned to the United States where they still worked for the same shadowy corporation. Their current assignment was to do whatever was necessary—including murder—to keep veterans from telling the truth about what they'd experienced in Iraq and Afghanistan. All of these vets had stories to tell, but as long as they were labeled "crazy" no one would believe their stories. And if they killed themselves or died in accidents, then no one would ever hear their stories.

The contractors' bosses really wanted some of these vets to die and they would be very unhappy when they heard that the mass suicide had not occurred. The contractors were particularly pissed off that Bill was still alive. He'd been one of the whistle blowers who had exposed their Abu Ghraib activities.

One of the men spoke into his tiny microphone. "Sir, they are all alive, heading west, with five individuals who interfered with their suicide pact. Another unknown is following them. They appear to be heading to Colorado." He listened and then spoke to the others. "Our orders are to terminate them, but to make the deaths look like accidents. These individuals are a national security risk." He had said this seriously, but then added, with a sneer, "We can do whatever we want with Bill, just so long as he ends up dead."

The four men gathered up their weapons and communications gear and trotted to their motorcycles, hidden a short distance away. They would have preferred a Hummer, but that would have been too obvious. They looked plenty intimidating no matter what they rode. They pulled out on the highway, one by one, and headed west.

Summer

Chapter 11

The former secretary of state frowned at her reflection in the mirror. To any observer, Condi appeared stunning, but she sometimes couldn't see it herself. This was going to be her first date in many years and she really wanted to look good. She liked this man whom she'd met at a recent Beethoven concert at the Kennedy Center.

That evening brought bittersweet memories, however, as there had been a reference to Beethoven's *Eroica* which many in the audience didn't understand, but Condi certainly did. In 1804, while Lewis and Clark explored North America, Napoleon was the darling of the French Revolution. Beethoven was as thrilled as anyone else in Europe who loved freedom, and he had composed a symphony to be called *Bonaparte*. But then Napoleon crowned himself emperor. Beethoven was intensely disappointed that a potentially heroic leader, possibly another George Washington, had succumbed to power and become even worse than the overthrown French royalty. He hastily changed the name of his symphony to *Eroica*.

The symphony director had just lost his son to suicide following his battle with severe PTSD from the Iraq War. Many of the orchestra members had watched this young man grow up, knew him well and also felt incredible grief at his death. When the director learned that some former Bush administration officials would be in attendance that night, he asked the orchestra to play *Eroica*. With a hasty rehearsal they rose to the challenge, and when the conductor introduced the symphony, he looked directly at the former secretary of state, the former minister of defense, and the former CIA director. They all heard the name Napoleon Bonaparte but they knew he was really talking about their former boss, who had put himself above the law and acted as though he was emperor. The orchestra played *Eroica* with all the fury that Beethoven must have felt, two hundred years before, when he realized he'd almost been duped into glorifying a dictator.

Condi had been so unnerved by this musical protest that she excused herself, and soon found herself pacing in the lobby. An elegantly dressed dark-skinned man with the physique of an athlete approached her and asked if she'd like to join him for a drink. His accent gave him away as Nigerian. Taking in his handsome face and gentle demeanor, she accepted his offer. As the sounds of *Eroica* filtered into the lobby, Condi and the man talked. She gave him her email address before they parted company, and she felt strangely strengthened when she returned to the hall, head held high.

Condi had a wonderful evening with Faruq Bashir, a widower with grown up children and grandchildren scattered between the United States, Great Britain and Nigeria. In his capacity as an investment banker, he shuttled between these and other locations. At the end of the evening, he took her hand and kissed it outside her front door. She wanted to invite him in, but the Secret Service were watching, and this was their first date. Condi smiled, said goodnight, and went inside humming *Ode to Joy*.

Like many other very busy people, she didn't often remember her dreams, but that night she had a very vivid one. At the piano, she was playing Beethoven's piano sonata in E, opus 109, when she heard a voice saying, "More subtly, more of a murmur."

Condi looked around, and there was Beethoven, nodding his head, his hands behind his back. She lifted her hands, but he gestured to her to keep playing, and she did, finishing the piece. It was the best she had ever played, and when she turned around to seek his approval, he was frowning.

"Yes, you played that beautifully, and remarkably, for me, I can hear again. My music really is awesome. But what does it mean? What is the significance of this music? What's the point of it all?"

It was unnerving enough to be talking with Beethoven, but he seemed angry at her. Well, other people had been mad at her, Condi considered, and she had handled them quite diplomatically.

"Your last music was subtle and serene, no longer heroic and overwhelming," she told him. She felt pleased to be able to discuss the nuances of his music with the great composer.

"Yes, exactly!" Beethoven thundered.

The former secretary of state blanched. Why was he so angry? She loved his music and could play it more beautifully than many professional pianists.

"I know a lot about you," he said. "I've followed you since childhood. I follow everyone who is attracted to my music, especially my piano music, as this was *my* instrument. I know about the little girls in Birmingham, and that one who was your friend. She would have been a great musician. She would have composed songs that would have rivaled mine." He looked very sad. "And the young man who killed himself recently, he also would have composed great music."

She looked surprised. What young man? A suicide? She never read those pages of the newspaper and couldn't think of anyone she knew who had killed himself recently.

"The son of the director at the Kennedy Center. His son was an Iraq War veteran. Before he entered the military they told him he could play music. Of course, they put him in the Army and made him learn how to kill people, which he did a lot, as a sharp shooter. He ended up killing a whole school bus load of kids when he shot at a suicide bomber standing nearby. The soldier completely lost it, his music vanished, and months after his return, he killed himself. His father found him; he'd hanged himself in their garage." Beethoven looked at Condi with scorn.

This was a terrible tragedy, but what did it have to do with her? These volunteers knew what they were getting into. Yes, things had not gone well over there, but like her husband...no, her boss (she shook her head in irritation at herself; she was still making this mistake in her mind) had told her, "Democracy is messy, it takes a long time."

Recovery from slavery had taken more than one hundred fifty years. Condi hoped it would take less time to recover from Iraq, but in the meantime she wasn't responsible for a soldier's suicide. "I'm sorry about that young man, but he was a volunteer."

Beethoven thundered the famous beginning of his 5th symphony, "Duh, duh, duh, daaaaaa!"

Condi cringed over her elegant Chickering piano.

"He didn't volunteer to die for a Napoleon wannabe." He paused to look around at her elegant home. "You seem to be enjoying your life, going to concerts and dating, as well as playing the piano. All the things that that young man, and many others, won't ever do again. Unfortunately I can't compose a symphony to these dead soldiers but I can keep coming here to tell you about the suffering of Iraq War vets and their loved ones. And I will never stop, Duh, duh, duh, daaaaaa, until you apologize and make amends for your role in this devastating unnecessary war."

Condi was stricken. She held up her beautifully manicured hands as if to quiet him. She was appalled to see blood dripping from her fingers.

Beethoven laughed. "That's going to keep happening whenever you try to play the piano, until you've acknowledged what you did. Talk to your 'husband'— your old boss. Find out what he's been going through, and what he's considering." Beethoven started to fade. "I'll be listening. I can hear everything now. And while you're at it, check out Steve Earle's song, *Condi, Condi*." He sang a couple of lines and Condi blushed. She'd heard this sexy song. It embarrassed her immensely.

"Before I go, some Bob Marley." And he sang of love for even the most hopeless sinner. As Beethoven disappeared, she heard him say, "I like Bob and Steve."

* * *

Judith's family threw her a Juneteenth celebration. Everyone was there: the cousin from Tyler, her aunt and little cousins, her lawyer brother from Dallas, Joseph, and even her grandmother from New Orleans. They brought a huge feast: fried chicken, okra, mashed potatoes with lots of butter, biscuits, coleslaw, lemonade, and pecan pie. Because the family had invited all the hospital staff as well, they had to have the party in the day room.

Many of the staff were descendents of slaves and had celebrated Juneteenth Day every year of their lives. Most white people, however, didn't celebrate the holiday or even know much about its history. President Lincoln signed the Emancipation Proclamation freeing the slaves September 22 1862, and the law went into effect January 1 1863. The news went to large cities first and filtered quickly to nearby plantations and farms to slaves eager for freedom. But in the days before technology, news traveled slowly to more remote regions. At that time Texas was at the end of the United States. The slave owners had conspired amongst themselves to maintain a wall of silence so that their slaves would remain slaves as long as possible.

It wasn't until June 19 1865, two and a half years later, that General Gordon Granger rode into Galveston with his soldiers and publicly proclaimed Emancipation as law. There was so much joy and celebration, most of the now former slaves didn't even notice the sneering looks of their former masters. And it wasn't until some days later that they realized that they had been forced to remain enslaved much longer than slaves elsewhere.

Some wanted to lynch their former masters. Some wanted to poison their livestock and rape their women. But cooler minds prevailed, and with the creativity and dignity that had enabled their ancestors to survive years of slavery, the former slaves decided to create an annual celebration. Juneteenth Day, as it came to be called, spread throughout Texas and was eventually taken up by other African American communities in solidarity with their Texas brethren. It still amazed blacks that some whites viewed this holiday as an example of the ignorance of the slaves, when in reality it showed the vileness of their former masters. The holiday was celebrated with strength, joy, and inclusion. Nicknamed the "Better Late Than Never" day, this holiday could include everyone.

Ben was still a little wary of Joseph, but the joy flowing from

Judith pretty much outweighed any weirdness from her brother. Also, Amy, wearing her sexiest, tightest nurse's uniform, chatted with Ben and flattered him. She'd discovered a long time ago how susceptible most men were to flattery, especially when it was genuine. She had learned that Ben was a merciful prosecutor, that he tried to find out the truth, sometimes to the detriment of his prosecution. Amy liked that.

Judith was telling "you might be a lawyer if you..." jokes. "You might be a lawyer if the shortest sentence you ever wrote was eighty words long." Everyone in the room laughed and Ben grinned. That was funny and true. Judith had regained her sense of humor, but she wasn't quite ready to joke about Iraq yet.

While her family was laughing and eating, then singing and praying, other families were visiting their loved ones on other floors of the hospital. These other floors were not for rehabilitation, just for compassionate nursing care of soldiers with irreversible brain damage from injuries in Iraq or from their serious suicide attempts. All the patients on these floors were DNR: Do Not Resuscitate. Most of the families asked for this, but for those who didn't, the doctors, nurses, and clerics spent a long time talking with them, mentioning the Terry Schaivo case from 2005. Hardly anyone wanted a state legislature or Congress deciding end-of-life decisions for their loved ones. Families who did want resuscitative efforts were very rare, and those patients were put on other floors. In this hospital, so far, none had survived resuscitation, but the full effort was made when that was what the family wanted.

* * *

Condi sat on the back porch with George and Laura. They had invited her for a weekend visit and the three were sitting outside, in the dark, talking. It was Juneteenth Day, a day of awakening to the truth, a "Better Late Than Never day," the newspaper quipped. George hadn't understood the real significance of this holiday until now. He wanted to talk with Condi about his thoughts but wasn't sure how to begin. She seemed tense. He thought a little piano music might relax her. "Would you like to play some songs for us, Condi?"

She looked down at her hands and frowned. Ever since the Beethoven dream, each time she tried to play the piano, blood oozed out of her fingers. When she placed her feet on the pedals, blood oozed from between her toes. It didn't hurt physically, but it was appalling nonetheless. The blood stopped when she lifted her hands and feet away from the piano.

Condi really missed playing music. It had been her way of keeping her sanity during the previous eight years, especially as the war worsened. She had tried wearing surgical gloves and slippers, but the blood spurted out even faster. It splashed onto her white carpet, and as she couldn't explain the blood stains to her house-keeper, she had painstakingly attempted to clean up the mess herself. However, the ugliness had begun to encircle the piano in an ever-widening pattern and she no longer allowed anyone into her music room.

Condi had seen a few doctors, but there were no pianos in doctors' offices and most didn't believe her frankly unbelievable story. One had the gall to offer her antipsychotic medication, which she refused. Another suggested the possibility of a stigmata, like that of Christ. That comment had left her speechless. Condi did have religious beliefs but she'd never felt she was like Christ.

She had to respond to George's request. "My arthritis is acting up a bit. Sorry. I'll have to pass tonight."

The three old friends lapsed into reminiscing about porches. George and his wife recalled porches in west Texas where they'd watched glorious sunsets in their youth. Laura mentioned a porch off the apartment where she'd lived while working as a librarian, back when she and George had courted. Condi described her parents' and grandparents' porches in Alabama. There had been songs, lemonade and happiness until the bombings had started, and everyone had had to move inside. It had become too dangerous to sit quietly with one's family on a porch. Condi remembered the suffocating heat of southern homes without air conditioning. This memory made her think about how she couldn't now sit outside on someone's porch, unless she happened to be in a secure location like this, as there were many many people who detested her. She wasn't hated as much as Bush and Cheney, but like others who'd championed the Iraq War, she knew she would have to live with the public's revulsion for the rest of her life.

Condi felt incredibly safe at the Crawford ranch. She loved this couple. Laura had forgiven Condi's gaffe during her introduction as the new secretary of state in 2005 when she uttered the first syllable of "husband" instead of "boss" or "president." Laura knew that the other woman's outstanding intellect and loyalty had been absolutely essential to George's success in office.

Laura was intrigued when Condi began talking about the Nigerian man she'd met at the concert. George listened with amusement and some relief. He really liked Condi and was happy to see her relax and enjoy life as he had. Early in their relationship he had kidded her about men, and tried a few times to set her up with guys he thought she would like. But she was *very, very* serious about her work, and soon he stopped trying. So the Nigerian suitor was good news.

Surrounded by darkness, Condi finally told her friends about the strange dream she'd had the first night she dated Farouq. She described it with sadness, as Beethoven was one of her musical heroes. She concluded by confessing that the great composer had told her that she had to apologize to the wounded veterans and the families of the dead. She didn't explain about the blood; she was afraid George and Laura, like that one doctor, would mention the stigmata of Jesus.

George looked at her in amazement. "But I've been having the same kind of dreams."

Laura turned to him in astonishment. He hadn't told her anything about this. She started to feel miffed that he was mentioning this for the first time to the other woman. But then she quickly realized that this was similar to other privileged information that George and Condi had shared.

"It was so real and so wonderful to see him," Condi lamented, "but he didn't want to talk about music, just the Iraq War and all the wounded soldiers." Her voice cracked and she started to sob.

This shocked Laura and George. They had never seen her cry. They didn't know it was possible. They both moved closer and put their arms around her shoulders. Then George said, "A horribly scary woman appears in my dreams. She's told me the same thing." He shuddered, and looked at his wife with some embarrassment. "I've been having these nightmares for months."

"Oh, honey, you should have told me. No wonder you've been so distressed."

He hadn't told anyone about the visit to the Albuquerque VA either. He'd made the Secret Service agents swear to secrecy. But he figured this was the time and these were the people to tell. It was always easier to talk with women. Gosh, Dick would be pissed. And the Architect, he didn't even want to think about him and what he would say. Well, those guys probably never had any dreams of zombies and or a horrible Mother Nature. Besides George was sick of having them tell him what to do all the time.

"I did go visit a vet in Albuquerque," George said. "A young man who'd been badly injured in Iraq and was very depressed. His family was there."

George had thought a lot about this visit. It was a spiritual experience, as awesome as when he had accepted Jesus Christ into his heart and renounced alcohol. There had been nothing else as powerful, not even anything that had happened during his presidency. And when he compared the time with the wounded veteran and his family to the Top-Gun-Mission-Accomplished flight, George felt completely sickened. That had been a pitiful pathetic stunt that reminded him now of being drunk. How could he have confused the power of the two experiences? Okay, deep breath, and move forward, he told himself.

"I talked with them for a few hours." He paused. "And I apologized for everything connected with the war. I told them that we knew Saddam was not really a threat, but we just wanted to get him for revenge, for the oil, and to grab power in the Middle East."

Condi looked at George in astonishment. She could understand some kind of general apology, and she assumed that's what Beethoven had been talking about, but to apologize for the specifics, oh no. That was really a bad move and, if recorded.... She swore silently and reverted to her serious, *very, very* serious former secretary of state demeanor. "Sir, uh, sir, were you recorded?" She hoped to God not. Everyone in the Bush administration had shuddered when Felt stepped forward, revealing that he was Deep Throat, the man who had deep-sixed Nixon back in 1974. They all hoped that various conversations of the previous years had not been secretly taped.

Suddenly, blood began to gush from Condi's fingertips and she could feel it oozing, sticky, in her shoes. Oh, Jesus, no, she thought. Luckily for her, it was dark. She wiped her bloody fingers on her dark skirt. Did Beethoven mean for her to apologize as George had, directly, to terribly injured veterans and their families? This would be impossible.

George sensed her discomfort, although he didn't know about the blood. "No, no, nothing was recorded. Just the family and their dog were present. Heh, heh." He grinned, thinking about the dog. Then he frowned, remembering the veteran's sister. Hmm, maybe she did have a tape recorder. Well, shit, if she did. But it had felt so good to confess, and that's what he needed to tell Condi. He'd almost forgotten about Laura. He took his wife's hand in the dark and squeezed it.

"Condi, you didn't know me back when I quit drinking and accepted Jesus into my heart. Besides meeting my wife, marrying her and having our daughters, it was the most profound experience in my life. Even more profound than becoming the president."

George had been thinking that if he was going to start being honest, he was going to have to acknowledge all the chicanery that had gotten him into office the first time, and contributed to his victory in 2004 as well. But that was for another conversation. The issue with the veterans and the Iraq War was clearly the most important moral mission of the rest of his life. "You know, my nightmares forced me to think about the wounded, but when I finally said something directly to these people I'd hurt, I had this awesome feeling of power, real power, and compassion."

What he said next would seem grandiose, but George let it come out anyway. "I felt like Jesus must have felt when he healed the sick and did his other miracles. It was incredible."

Condi just couldn't wrap her head around this new information. She realized that her mouth had fallen open and she was emitting short exhalations of disbelief. If she'd ever had a religious experience like he'd described, it was as a child, but those memories were buried deep within her soul after the Birmingham bombing killed her friend. It was hard to believe there was a God when something like that happened. However, she knew that George was genuine about his faith, unlike some of the other sanctimonious jerks she'd had to put up with in office.

Laura smiled with relief and love. None of what he'd revealed surprised her. It just confirmed what she'd decided many years ago. He could change when the stakes were high enough. She smiled at Condi too, and settled in to listen to the conversation that she knew was going to alter everything, for the good of these two people and the country. Thank you, Lord, she silently prayed with a gaze up to the stars. She had her own views, but she'd decided a long time ago that her main role in life was to support the man she'd married.

Chapter 12

After the first day on the motorcycle, Lucy felt physically exhausted but emotionally alive. She'd enjoyed holding on to Bill's waist. Taking the back roads, they'd sailed through beautiful fields of wheat. Sitting at a picnic table at a rest stop, Lucy was looking at Bill but thinking about Rayford Steele. He was not a church friend or some guy from her high school but one of the heroes in *The Rising*, the first book in the *Countdown to the Rapture* series written by Tim LeHaye and Jerry B. Jenkins. She'd read all the *Left Behind* books and she was in love with Rayford, who had become a pilot over the course of the series. *The Rising* traced his development from childhood to young adulthood, and she thought of him as the kind of man she'd like to marry. Bill seemed like Rayford, and as she'd ridden the motorcycle with him, she imagined them being raptured to heaven together.

However, she knew that Bill was Jewish. That was a problem. Lucy had never tried to convert anyone, but this young man had wanted to save those other men from killing themselves. That was the kind of heroics that Rayford would engage in. Could Bill be her soul mate? Maybe meeting him was another reason for her pilgrimage. Again she thought about how wonderful it had felt to hold on to Bill's back. Almost too wonderful. She knew her parents definitely wouldn't approve of this aspect of her journey. But if she converted Bill to Christ, her parents would surely be pleased.

While she mused about Bill and Rayford, Maria and Charlie negotiated accommodations for the group. It wasn't too hard to accomplish. Two beautiful women on a Harley pull into Small Town USA and ride slowly down the main drag looking for a modest motel with a vacancy sign. They park in front of the office where they see an attendant glance up and do a double-take as they remove their helmets. Maria shakes out her long black hair. Slowly the women remove their leather chaps and reveal beautiful long legs ending at a very short skirt, in Maria's case, and a very short pair of cutoffs for

Charlie. Then, looking at the clerk, Maria smiles. Not much later, they have rooms at a discount for the whole party. *No problemas.*

Later that night, Bill and Lucy sat with their backs to the motel and faced an empty pasture with millions of stars overhead and stared into the dying fire. The others had sensed the developing romance and drifted off. Lucy turned her gaze from the fire. "Bill, I don't know what your favorite books are, but besides the Bible, mine are the *Left Behind* series. I especially like *The Rising*. Have you read it?"

Bill turned to her with surprise. Not only had he heard of them, but he couldn't stand those books. He'd actually been fooled into purchasing one at an airport bookstore because on the shelf it looked like a cool thriller. At the time he'd never heard of LeHaye or Jenkins or the Rapture, but as he read the book on the airplane he realized it was a Born-Again-Christians-are-the-only-people-who-will-be-saved book. He was shocked to learn later that the books in the series were on the bestseller lists. Maybe the authors were buying up their own inventory to make it look like they had a lot more readers and believers than they really did. Maybe not. Maybe there really were millions of people out there who believed in the Rapture and sincerely thought that everyone else would burn in the hell that earth would become. Utter rubbish, he'd thought when he threw the book, half read, in the nearest trashcan upon disembarking.

Now Bill looked at Lucy's eager face. He liked her, so he said, "Yes, I have heard about these books. I read one of them. I think it was *The Rising*."

Lucy gushed. "Oh, I love that book. It's got such a great story and deals so well with the theme of good versus evil." She knew from her AP English class that this was one of the main themes of great literature. Her teacher, who also attended her church, had really liked an essay Lucy had written comparing *The Rising* with *Paradise Lost*, which they'd read in annotated form.

Bill went on. "Yeah, *The Rising*. Well, Lucy, you know, I like Bruce Springsteen's CD *The Rising* better. I don't know why they were called the same name, except they came out after the September 11th tragedy. Maybe LeHaye and Jenkins copied Bruce."

Lucy didn't know anything about Bruce Springsteen. "Is he Christian, Bill, like Mr LeHaye and Mr Jenkins?" Lucy didn't wait for an answer. "Maybe Bruce read the series and created his rising music in response. Accepting Christ into their hearts and souls helped people recover from 9/11. Maybe it would help you too."

Bill laughed. "I don't think Bruce thinks the same way as Tim and Jerry. And I'm afraid I don't either. I don't have anything against anyone's religion, but when they say that everyone else will burn in hell if they don't accept Christ in exactly the way they do, there's something wrong. Jesus, if he was here, would agree with me, I think." Bill searched Lucy's face to see if she understood.

"No, that's not true. Jesus is for everyone, if they just accept him into their hearts," she said, her voice rising.

"Sure, Jesus was a good guy," Bill agreed, thinking of a line in a John Prine song, *Jesus, The Missing Years.*

"A good guy?" Lucy sputtered. "A good guy? He was the greatest person who ever lived. The son of God. The Messiah. The Alpha. The Omega." And to think that Bill had seemed so like Rayford.

Bill observed her with resignation. "I think Jesus was a man, although a very good man. It sounds like he did a lot of good and obviously inspired his followers who inspired billions over the last two thousand years. But what about Buddha, Mohammed, or Confucius? And a bunch of others that we never heard about because no one wrote about them?" Bill surprised himself. He'd never articulated such thoughts. But in fact he had taken a religious studies class in college that helped him understand the Bible from a non-believer historical perspective. "And, Lucy, it was just *people* who wrote the Bible. Educated and inspired people, but still just *people.* Both the Old and the New Testaments. And those writers edited out stories they didn't want. The Gnostics, for example. Ever heard about them? The Gospel of Mary? Ever heard of that?"

But Lucy wasn't listening. She had this sinking feeling that she'd allowed herself to be tempted by the forces of Lucifer, by riding the motorcycle with Bill, and then starting to imagine him as Rayford. Sure, Bill had helped save all those vets and had offered to protect her on her pilgrimage. But not to believe in Jesus and just call him "a very good man…." That was too much. This is what the *Left Behind* books had said would happen. Lucifer can appear very attractive. Lucy stood up, hands on her hips, and said, "I am going to pray for your soul. Good night." And she stalked off to her room.

"Thanks, Lucy, that'll be fine. Happy to have someone pray for me," Bill whispered as he watched her walk away. He pulled out his harmonica and started singing and playing John Prine's song, *Jesus The Missing Years*, which told the story of a teenage Jesus bumming around the Mediterranean until he was beguiled in Rome by a sweet Irish girl.

After a few minutes Bill stopped playing and wondered if Lucy was Irish. He thought of a young Jesus meeting someone like Lucy in ancient Rome. He pulled his sleeping bag over his body and made a pillow of his jacket and soon fell asleep looking at the stars. Bill dreamed of dancing with Lucy in a small meadow surrounded by grass and trees on a hill overlooking Rome.

Feelings of attraction stayed with him after he woke the next morning. He went to greet Lucy when she emerged from her room, but she wouldn't look at him. Later on he wasn't too surprised when she got in a truck with a couple of the vets.

Charlie looked at Bill as the truck drove off. They were waiting for Maria. "What did you say to piss her off, guy?"

Bill smiled wryly. "We had a difference of opinion about Jesus."

"Dang that Jesus. He was such a good guy, but so many people have argued over him, and even killed each other over him. Fucking ridiculous." Charlie kicked her boot on the ground and wished she still smoked so she could pull out a cigarette now.

"Yep," said Bill. What else could he say? Maria emerged, looking stunning as usual. She got on the back of Charlie's motorcycle and they pulled out, following the others.

* * *

The nurses were worried. Everything had gone to hell since the Juneteenth party. In spite of all their good care, Judith had developed bedsores, one in her lower sacral area, and the other where her right buttock met the top of her leg. The nurses constantly turned her and her dressings were changed frequently, but the infection persisted. Eventually a culture came back as the dreaded MRSA.

MRSA stood for Methicillin Resistant Staphylococcus Aureus infection. It was something hospitals feared, because it was a bacterial infection that didn't respond to methicillin, one of the best antibiotics ever produced, and it destroyed flesh. Sadly, MRSA had been conceived in hospitals. Bacteria are living organisms, and like all other life forms, they must change when faced with challenges, or they die. Over many years' use of penicillins to treat deadly infections, staph aureus, a common harmless skin bacteria, had transformed into the monstrous MRSA.

As if it was not enough to endure blindness and the loss of four limbs, poor Judith now had this flesh-eating bacteria to contend with. She suffered episodes of delirium, although she usually recognized everyone who came to visit.

Joseph was frightened at the thought of losing Judith, after she'd come this far. He found himself getting really angry, emotions he hadn't felt since Judith was first injured. At work he yelled at some Hummer owners, a couple who complained that his repairs had worsened their gas mileage. He told them to go take a "flying fuck" if they didn't like what he'd done. While Joseph's curse left the wife speechless, her massive husband, standing outside the vehicle, growled and raised his clenched fists. Luckily for Joseph, Miguel, holding some heavy tools, wheeled up out of nowhere. The Hummer driver and his wife jumped into the vehicle and screeched out of the parking lot.

That evening after a badly needed gym workout, Joseph and Miguel, wearing his prostheses, went to their favorite bar. They had a few beers while they watched the Rangers get whooped by the Angels. Miguel was wearing some emblem from his Iraq days, and another man, wearing the same insignia, approached their table. He was holding an O'Douls in his hands. Same bottle he'd been holding for the past hour, only about a quarter of it sipped.

"Sure, go ahead, take a seat," said Miguel. They introduced themselves and the new man, Roberto, said he'd also been in Iraq. They traded a few stories, and the conversation came around to Judith. Joseph described her war wounds, and the dreaded MRSA.

Roberto looked at them intently. He hadn't known why he'd come to this bar this night, as he really wasn't supposed to be there. He was on probation from a Driving While Intoxicated (DWI). But something had made him come in, and something had made him sit down with these two guys. "Listen, I don't know if I can offer this, but I'd like to anyway. Maybe Judith could do with a healing ceremony." Roberto's mother was Navaho Arapaho, and his father a Sioux Scot. He'd mostly resolved his own issues with the Iraq War with some healing ceremonies that his relatives and friends had done for him. He'd had severe PTSD, which had made him start drinking. But he'd basically quit after the ceremonies. The DWI was so stupid. He hadn't been drinking anything at all for eight months. Then at his brother's birthday party he'd had a few too many, and he'd gotten stopped on the way home. He'd blown a 0.09 on the breathalyzer, with 0.08 being the legal limit. But at least the PTSD hadn't come back. The ceremonies worked, and he hadn't gotten discouraged with the DWI.

"Let me ask my brother. I think we could do a ceremony for your Judith."

"But we're not Indian, er, Native American," Joseph said, apologetically.

"It's okay. Some of the ceremonies are just for Natives, but others can be for anyone who needs them. And I think your Judith needs one. She was a soldier who was defending our country. We have a ceremony for all who love our country, no matter their ancestry."

Roberto had long resolved the differences in his own background.

His Sioux and Arapaho ancestors had been on this continent for over ten thousand years. They'd probably contributed to the extinction of the mammoths, but they'd had to eat. His Navaho ancestors had arrived just before the Spanish. They had fought with the Pueblo tribes who called them the "head bashers." And his Scottish ancestors? Well, they were the most difficult to fit in. He'd read about them, and learned that they'd been fighting the English for more than a thousand years, way longer than the Indians had fought the Europeans. And some of the Scottish were descended from Normans from France, who'd been fighting the English for centuries. Before that they battled the Vikings and the Romans. And someone else before that. Maybe all this fighting — futile fighting, it turned out — made the Scots quick to anger. He'd read that they had the highest blood pressure rates in the whole world. A lot of them drank too much. Some of them were even wilder than most of his Indian ancestors. But many of them had the gift of sight and healing. He'd finally resolved that they all belonged, at least within his own soul and body.

"Yeah, let me talk with my brother, and you guys talk to the nurses at the hospital. Figure out who Judith would want to be there. We need everyone who really loves her to help her recover."

"Thank you." Joseph looked down and started to sob. He hadn't done this in a long time, but he needed to now. Miguel put his arm around Joseph's shoulder and paid the tab. Then the three men walked out into the dark soft night.

* * *

Condi just couldn't see flicking over the house of cards that had been so carefully constructed over the last decade. She didn't mind visiting a few vets, preferably those with lower limb injuries. It would be hard to face the ones who had lost their hands or had facial deformities. It was too horrible to imagine losing her own hands or her looks. And she just couldn't admit that she'd been wrong, any more than she could imagine spending the rest of her life apologizing. She liked jetting around the world in Armani suits, pursuing diplomacy, a serious, intelligent woman whom governments world wide respected. She liked respect even better than piano playing.

A few days after her visit with George and Laura, Condi reluctantly called the former vice president and the Architect. She really didn't like Dick or Karl, and neither liked her, as they all envied the others' relationships with the former president. However, they could work together when they had a common goal on a major issue. Condi described the urgency of the situation, although she did not mention her own dreams. She simply told them that George was planning to publicly apologize for everything connected with the Iraq War.

Dick and Karl were livid, as she knew they would be. They found it hard to believe what Condi was telling them. "Jesus, I hope he wasn't taped. I can't believe he apologized to a vet," Dick sputtered. In his view there wasn't anything to apologize for. Denial, obfuscation, distraction, fear, and more denial had gotten them this far, and nothing had gone wrong for them.

They were in the process of writing the history of the last several years so they could be sure future generations were accurately informed. Dick's wife, Lynn, with her extensive contacts in the educational publishing world, was particularly involved in this effort. Karl was wondering why George had decided to deviate from their carefully constructed master plan. It had to be that damn religious thing. It had almost screwed things up before, several times. Actually, if Dick hadn't found some Bible passages to show George that the end justifies the means, they might not have been in the White House at all. And the Bible had come in very handy to justify many of his own actions. What in the heck was happening down there in Crawford? Karl was going to have to visit George and convince him to behave. Dick would accompany him. The big guns would be needed together this time. Dick and Karl hadn't seen each other since January, but it appeared to be a necessary rendezvous. At the end of June, Texas would be at its sunniest and hottest. Hotter than Hades. Both men hated the thought of visiting Crawford at this time of year. But they had to talk to George, and they had no doubt about the outcome of their planned intervention.

* * *

Darrell figured it was time to make his move. He knew that Lucy was headed for Columbine in Littleton, and he was sure that when he found her alone, he could persuade her back to his side. This pilgrimage had seemed odd from the beginning and he hoped she'd had enough now. He certainly had.

Darrell had a couple of his favorite *Left Behind* books in his satchel. He thought of himself as the hero pilot, Rayford. He wanted to be in the first Rapture group but he figured, like Rayford, he *might* be one of the ones left behind to help save people for the next Rapture. Since he also wanted to convert Jews to Christianity, he was pleased to note that Bill looked Jewish and that maybe there'd be an opportunity. He wondered if Lucy had been trying to convert him. Still, Darrell felt jealous thinking of her talking to him and riding behind him on the motorcycle.

That night the group reached Trinidad, Colorado. They would have preferred quiet but all the accommodations in Trinidad were close enough to highways to hear the hum. Now that Charlie and Maria knew that Lucy no longer wanted to travel with Bill, they wanted to take her to Columbine and then catch up with the vets after that, but Lucy refused their offer. She explained that helping to save the veterans had fitted in with her pilgrimage, but the attraction to Bill, an agent of Lucifer, had almost derailed her from her purpose. She needed to travel by herself now.

This time of year, Lucy would have long hours of daylight to walk north the two hundred miles between Trinidad and Littleton. At a nearby table in the motel restaurant, Bill listened to their conversation. Lucy hadn't spoken with him since the night of the argument.

Charlie and Maria knew that Bill would trail Lucy once she set off for Columbine. They wouldn't have agreed to leave her otherwise. But they didn't know how he'd follow her. It would be kind of obvious: a motorcycle traveling at two miles per hour about twenty feet behind a young woman walking? Oh, well, true love would find a way. Charlie and Maria wished they could see it all unfold, but they'd be with the vets at the Sand Dunes.

Jesus had finally reached his dispatcher, who told him that the boss had had an emergency and that he had been called in as deputy to take care of the boss's responsibilities. Jesus was good friends with the dispatcher, and when he told him how the tampons had been destroyed serving a higher purpose, saving lives, the dispatcher had laughed. The paper products were insured, and while some women in Kansas City were going to be out of luck this month, they would get another driver and truck sent out the next day. Jesus requested a two-week emergency leave, which was granted as he hadn't taken a vacation in ages. Kenzo and Jesus found a nearby Costco and an Army Navy surplus store, and using the veterans' discount cards and their own credit cards (this would be their charitable donation for the year), they filled the empty truck with supplies they would need for the veterans.

The next morning Lucy said goodbye to the vets, shook hands with Jesus and Kenzo and hugged Charlie and Maria. She ignored Bill, who was tinkering with his motorcycle. A few minutes after her departure, Bill told the group that something was wrong with his bike. He'd have to fix it and catch up with the others later. Maria gave him an ironic look but felt relieved knowing that he'd be right behind Lucy.

None of them noticed a young man across the street who was also tinkering with *his* motorcycle. And no one noticed four men watching all of them from a window table inside a nearby deli. The leader, Luke, ordered the other three to follow the vets. Luke would take care of Bill himself.

Luke swallowed the last of his coffee. He observed Bill following the young woman and then saw the other young motorcyclist following Bill. He didn't know who this woman and the other man were, but he'd take care of all of them, if necessary. Luke felt supremely confident. It would give him great satisfaction to destroy the man who'd ruined their fun at Abu Ghraib.

* * *

Lucy was so busy singing hymns as she walked that she didn't notice the clouds forming behind her, and later in the day, as she was trudging north along the highway, she was surprised when the sun suddenly disappeared and the first hard raindrops hit her. She ran towards an old barn she saw in the distance. Soaked, she squeezed through the heavy doors. Then she stood still until her eyes adjusted. The barn was empty of life but the hay stacked high against the back wall made the place smell sweet. Lucy settled herself in an empty stall to wait out the rainstorm. The rain hitting the tin roof was incredibly noisy, but the stall was dry and comforting.

Bill had seen Lucy running for the barn and decided it was as good a place as any to try to make peace with her. A pilgrimage would help his PTSD, he'd reasoned. Maybe that would convince her. He wanted to protect her. Plus he really liked her, in spite of her kooky Rapture beliefs.

Darrell, seeing Lucy run for the barn and Lucifer follow, aimed his bike towards them. He figured this was his opportunity to stop the evil one, collect Lucy and head for home. He hid his bike on the side of an outbuilding not far from the road and then ran off toward the barn. It was raining so hard that Bill didn't hear anyone running after him.

Luke, hiding behind a large roadside billboard, observed all three individuals go into the barn. He cricked his neck right and left and then spoke into his cell. "The girl has gone into a barn and the subject and another man are following. Subject doesn't seem to know he's being followed by this other man. The girl doesn't know they're following her." He listened, nodded, then clicked the cell phone off and put it in a pocket of his jacket. This was going to be interesting. He cracked his knuckles. He'd take care of Bill first, because that was his mission, and then he'd amuse himself with the other man and the girl. The possibilities reminded him of Abu Ghraib. That place had given him a lot of great memories for masturbation. He hadn't had a chance to try any of these out on Americans, but it looked like that opportunity was arising, just like his penis. Ignoring the rain, he grinned, and walked slowly toward the barn. After being in Iraq, he didn't mind getting wet; the wetter, the better.

* * *

The three men sat on the same back porch where George had relaxed with Condi and Laura a few nights before. They had been very close in the previous ten years, but hadn't been together since leaving Washington.

The Architect was enjoying a cigar. The other two didn't smoke, and they made sure to sit upwind of Karl. He dipped his cigar at Dick and indicated that he should speak first. "George, we need to talk. We've heard that you've been doing some new thinking." What an understatement, Dick thought. He plowed on. "We've all come a long way and don't want to change horses in mid-stream. Can't have you doing a Colin on us."

George winced and recalled his first secretary of state's repudiation of his administration just before the last election. He started to say something positive about Colin, but Dick interrupted. "We heard about your little speech in Albuquerque. The one at the VA." The former vice president and the Architect stared at George and waited.

"Oh, that one." George appeared a bit chagrined. He knew they wouldn't like that. "Well, I've been thinking and praying." Thinking of prayer increased his confidence. "It was God's will for me to start telling the truth. I—"

"The truth?" Karl interrupted. "What are you talking about?

You've been telling the truth all along. It's always been God's will." Karl turned away. He hated talking about God. Even he knew he sounded insincere.

Dick, looking at the two men, was thinking, thank God George didn't know about the anthrax experiment. He put on his wise older brother look. "You have to think of your legacy now. We accomplished everything we could have dreamed of in the eight years we had, and now all we have to do is make sure that history properly records our accomplishments." And allows me to keep all my wealth, Dick thought to himself. He wasn't going to let his place in history or his lifestyle be destroyed by George *or* God. "Now we have to stay the course and make sure the history of this time is written correctly. There's nothing to apologize for." Dick pursed his lips and patted the other man's arm in a brotherly gesture.

The Architect closed in. "Remember Machiavelli? One of the greatest men to ever live." His book, *The Prince*, was Karl's favorite. He had read it dozens of times. It was the one book that struck his heart as true. He had been the person to introduce it to George, and they had read passages together, interspersed with Bible verses. Karl had been able to find a surprising amount in the Bible that supported Machiavelli and vice versa. Thank God that fifteenth-century Italian prince had the sense to write his observations down and publishers had continued to keep it in print for the past five hundred and fifty years.

George replied, "But I've been hearing from God. I have to start apologizing. I've done some thinking and I've realized that the Iraq War was wrong. We never should have gone in there. It's hard for me to say it, but we should have just stayed in Afghanistan and gotten Osama and the rest of Al-Queda. Everyone would have loved me as much as they did right after 9/11. And we could have dealt with the terrorists with much less loss of life and limb."

George thought ruefully of all those negative articles written about him in *The New York Times*, *The New Yorker* and *The Nation*, to name just a few. Someone had given him statistics on articles written after 9/11 with columns labeled "positive" and "negative," complete with a graph. The "positives" had gone way up, but then come down like one of those waves in the famous Japanese wood prints, and kept going down from 2003 onward until his approval rating had slipped to twenty-four percent by the end of his presidency, the lowest ever of any president recorded.

Karl and Dick frowned at each other, and then at their former boss. They would have to try another tactic, the one they'd used a few other times when logic and Machiavelli hadn't worked. Karl said, "We've also heard from God. He's been very clear. Nothing is to change on what we've said the past few years. We've prayed hard. God has been completely consistent and on message."

George wavered. "But, but, God told me…." He drifted off and tried to remember exactly what it was that God had told him. Except for the burning bush, it wasn't really God, it was Mother Nature and Jesus who had done the talking. Now that he thought about it in the company of these two powerful men, Mother Nature clearly was not God, even though she thought she was. And Jesus was Jesus, the son of God. Maybe Karl and Dick had been visited by the real God, the one in the burning bush. George had always believed these men, who had been essential to his successes. George really wanted to ask what God had looked like to them, but that would be embarrassing.

The men kept talking and praying into the evening. Karl and Dick eventually convinced George, as they had many times before, that they were right. In some ways they were more powerful than God.

George hoped that the family at the Albuquerque VA hadn't talked with anyone else, and that Jezebel hadn't taped anything. He didn't recall any cell phones.

The three men gave the secret handshake. It was a variation on the one George had learned at Yale, but it had been modified for his inner core advisors. However, they had no idea that their modification would have had Lucifer laughing, because they had turned an ancient Christian form of greeting into a secret sign of evil.

Chapter 13

Loved ones and staff gathered in Judith's room. It was crowded and hot, but the group was quiet, waiting for the medicine man and woman to begin. Judith, no longer conscious, lay still on her bed, covered by a hospital sheet and a light, thoroughly-washed homemade quilt. With fevers spiking every day, she hovered between life and death. The doctors had considered moving her to the main hospital's intensive care unit, but she had requested Do Not Resuscitate (DNR) status when she'd been conscious, and they would honor her wish. In retrospect, some of the staff thought she'd been delirious when she made this decision. They'd thought about getting a psychiatrist to talk with her, but the rehabilitation hospital was trying to save money, and mental health services were limited. One cynical doctor, who should have retired a long time ago, thought that it was better that these severely wounded vets die. He felt they were just a burden to themselves, their families, and society, and they had nothing to contribute. He had happily signed Judith's DNR order.

Amy had made sure this doctor would not be around during the ceremony. Only the nurses who liked this patient were present that evening. Everyone there needed to be on Judith's side for this sacred ceremony to be effective.

The medicine woman, an attractive mature woman with grey streaked hair, a loose turquoise colored dress and necklace made of stones and feathers, asked for the holy spirit to enter the room. She turned to the east, asking for the power of new beginnings, then to the south, asking for forgiveness, then to the west for strength, and finally to the north for wisdom. The people in the room turned with her. The medicine man, meanwhile, held lit sage from sacred Changing Woman Mountain in New Mexico and pushed the smoke in the four directions. Smudging their faces and hands with the smoke, the medicine people invited the spirits of healing, saying, "All the doors are open; we welcome you here."

Summoning memories of ceremonies he had performed, mostly in the deserts of Arizona and New Mexico, at night under the illumination of the moon, billions of stars, and huge bonfires with the magical smell of *piñon*, the medicine man spoke: "This woman is a soldier who went far from her land, our land, to serve and protect those she loved, and those she didn't even know. She has given her limbs and sight for the rest of us. She doesn't need to give her life now, Lord." He used the language of her religion, knowing that to the Great Spirit it didn't really matter what words were used. But for the ill one, it was important to use language that spoke to that person's heart. "We need her here on earth, Lord. She has more work to do. We need her songs, her stories, her laughter. Hear our prayers, Lord, and make her well again." He didn't use the name of the super-bug as that would only empower the evil force infecting Judith. The word sounded evil to him, as the words "plague" and "smallpox" had sounded to previous generations.

Ben leaned over Judith's shoulder and stroked her hair. Tears rolled down his face. "I got you a special wheelchair," he whispered. "One that can move almost as well as you did when you danced. Get well, sister, so we can try it out." He sobbed and turned away. His grandmother, Abbie, hugged him.

Joseph came forward with freesias, delicate white, purple and yellow flowers with a mysterious, cleansing scent. He brushed the freesias over her body, and their scent filled the air. "Judith, we all love you, and I want you back. We are going to get married when you recover, and we're going to dance at our wedding." The family looked at him in surprise. They didn't know this was coming, but Abbie grinned. Ben looked at Joseph with some surprise too, but also with respect.

Abbie approached the bed and sang a sweet hug-a-bug song handed down from her family and one she'd sung to her granddaughter when she was a little girl.

Judith's nieces and their mother came forward with a library book on the lessons of flowers: *Take a Deep Breath: little lessons from flowers for a happier world.* Inviting Judith to sense flowers from memory, they took turns in reading the phrases:

"*Sunflowers taught me...to be proud of what makes you unique.*"

"*Dandelions taught me...to appreciate life, no matter where it takes you.*"

They pretended to blow at white puffy dandelions and imagined the delicate seeds floating over their auntie.

Each person in the room offered their hearts and souls to Judith. The medicine man and woman chanted in their own languages and smudged more sage and flowers over her body. As they finished by thanking the spirits, everyone in the room felt the connection with everyone else. Some actually saw a web of light arcing from one head to another in a great circle of life. They poured their life force into the wounded woman, and then one by one they left until only Ben and Amy remained.

They sat quietly feeling the ebbing currents of the healing ceremony. Amy noticed how sad Ben looked. She walked behind him where he sat and touched the back of his shirt, first somewhat tentatively, then with more conviction. Her capable fingers found sore spots of tension, and she kneaded them up and down, left and right, doing a four-directions healing massage. Amy could feel Ben's muscles loosening.

Since she had closed her eyes to better feel what she was doing, she didn't see his hands until he reached back and grasped her wrists, gently. He stroked them. She stopped massaging and let him caress her hands. Then Ben pulled her around in front of him and folded his arms around her waist, his head fitting just under her breasts, his cheek feeling her breath move in and out of her body. At first he held her as a drowning man might hold a life preserver, but then his hands slipped lower over her slick, tight nurse's uniform. She breathed in sharply but didn't move away. He pulled her down to sit on his lap, moving himself to accommodate her height. He looked into her eyes, really looked, and he was encouraged to see that they were smiling back at him. Ben leaned forward, touched her lips lightly, and then kissed her. Amy kissed him back.

"Oh, Jesus, this is disgusting." A short, chubby nurse had opened the door. She held her hands on the space where her hips would have been if she'd had a waist. Her words didn't fit the grin on her face though, as she liked both these people. "Hey cut it out, someone's coming. Some kind of special inspection." She jerked her thumb indicating the direction of the intruder.

Ben squeezed Amy's hand. She murmured her phone number, which he memorized as he left the room. Amy looked in the mirror to straighten up, then smiled at Judith. Before she left the room, Amy made an ancient sign of healing, something she recalled from childhood and her Vietnamese ancestors' worship, a sign which summoned all of Judith's and her own spirit-world relatives to enter this room to heal this woman.

* * *

The night after Karl and Dick's visit, George tossed and turned, and when he entered the dream world, he found himself on a strange dusty plain without trees beneath a dark red sky. He saw what looked like old Roman ruins off in the distance. A man in robes approached him. Was this Jesus again? No, it didn't seem to be. Except for his robes, which made him look like someone from about five hundred years ago, this man looked more like the many CEOs he'd met over the years. He was tall and thin, with a long nose and short dark hair; there was an impish look about him. George instantly thought of Daniel Day-Lewis in the terrifying movie, *There Will Be Blood.* He shuddered.

The robed man regarded him sternly. "You have to stop listening to those guys. They're wrong." George thought back to what the Architect and former vice president had told him the previous evening. The robed man continued to speak. "It's my fault, really. I'm responsible for a lot of bad things. It's amazing what the power of one book can do, for good or for evil. Unfortunately, I wrote an evil book, although I didn't intend evil." The man looked regretful.

Who was this man? What was he talking about? George groaned. It was probably another book he should have read in high school or college.

"That's right. You didn't read my book then. But Karl and Dick read it, and they took it to heart. And the ideas in it made them and you very successful, as it did many others." He removed a slim volume from his pocket: *The Prince* by Machiavelli.

"Sure, I've heard of this book. Machiavelli? You wrote it?" He looked at him in admiration.

"Don't look at me like that," the robed man thundered, and George fell back. Red dust flew up in a whirlwind. When the storm settled down, the former president was on his knees covered in grime. The other man looked exactly the same as he had before, his clothing was spotless.

"Yes, and call me Nic, by the way. I wrote these words after I was exiled from my home. They threw me out of Florence, and I wrote this book to try to get back in. It didn't work, however. They never let me return. It's quite ironic to me that tens of thousands of men have found this book helpful. Not for going home, but for gaining power. It wasn't until after I'd died and saw what happened because of my book that I learned of the evil I had spawned. And do you know who taught me? No, not Jesus or God or Mary. It was St Francis and St Therese of Lisieux."

Nic sat on a bench that appeared out of nowhere and cradled his hands between his knees as he gazed at the filthy man on the ground. "Sit." George got up off his knees and sat on the bench, but not too close.

"Almost everyone knows St Francis but not many know St Therese. Many non-Catholics don't know about her, but she's as beloved amongst Catholics as Mary, mother of Jesus."

George shrugged. He didn't know who she was.

"She lived at the end of the nineteenth century. She's the patron saint of France."

George groaned. He really hated France.

All at once another dust storm descended, this time with horrible chiggers that bit him all over, even into his orifices. Nic considered George with disdain. "What's wrong with you? We're talking about one of the most beautiful souls who ever walked the earth. You really don't get it, do you? Nationalities, cultures, borders, and ancestries have nothing to do with the soul. And just as everyone's soul is equal in heaven, they can be equal on earth as well."

George was itching all over, and the more he scratched, the worse he felt.

Nic regarded him with irritation. He took something out of a pouch and threw it at George. George stopped itching, but he was still covered in dirt and looked more bedraggled than ever. Nic resumed speaking: "St Therese of Lisieux wrote a book, *The Little Way: Story of a Soul.* Much better than mine. She had what she called a strategy. Her strategy was the complete opposite of mine. Hers was: surrender to gratitude, the art of becoming smaller and smaller, so that God would accept full responsibility for everything. I had to spend years thinking about this, but her philosophy finally got through to me."

George didn't like the sound of this. He liked being big and powerful, and he missed that aspect of his life before he became "the former...."

Nic kept talking. "You can learn this on earth. It's a lot easier to learn here than in heaven — if that's where you end up." Heaven actually wasn't the easy place it was made out to be. People who reached it were sometimes forced to go through more difficulty than they'd ever encountered on earth, or would endure in hell, if they chose to go there. Nic didn't envy the former president. George was going to have a tougher time than most in heaven. This man was responsible for far more suffering than he was — and that was saying a lot. "You still have a chance. A warning to you: those other two guys, your so-called friends, are going to spend an eternity learning from me and others we have in mind. That is, of course, if they choose to go to heaven."

George didn't understand at all. "What do you mean, choosing to go to heaven?"

"Sure, they can choose, but everyone's heaven is different. For many, heaven is hell, because it *is* other people, those they have to learn from. Sartre was right with *No Exit*, but only for some people." Nic gazed at George. He probably could learn a lot on earth, but Karl and Dick were going to suffer as much as all those unjustifiably detained had suffered in Abu Ghraib and Guantánamo. Missteps, indeed, Nic snorted.

"Here." Nic tossed *The Prince* to George. "You can have my personally signed copy, with annotations on what I would change, if I could write it again now. And here's St Therese's *Little Way*." He handed it carefully to George.

"Anyone can write a book about the way the world is, but it takes an angel from God to write a book about the way the world could be. If you like, you could even discuss these ideas with Karl and Dick. It's possible for anyone to change, although I think it's unlikely for those two. Just concentrate on St Therese, and my re-writes, the way I am now. We are WAY more powerful than the Architect or the quail-hunter."

Nic started to walk away, then he turned back. "By the way, *you* aren't *anything* like Winston Churchill. I *know* Winston Churchill. And the Iraq War is not World War II, my friend. I'd like to say more on this, however, our time is coming to a close. I will repeat what others have recently advised you. The only way you have of redeeming yourself, at this point, is to apologize for the mistakes made in your administration and make amends. Otherwise you go down in history like Hitler, Stalin, Pol Pot, or even your nemesis, Osama."

Nic faded out, and the former president woke up, lying facedown in his backyard. Covered in red dirt, the chigger itching had returned with a vengeance. George, who was wearing only a pair of boxer shorts, picked himself up, ran over to the pool and jumped in. The chlorine stung, but when he emerged, he felt like he'd been baptized again. Nic and St Therese would help him. George found a towel on one of the lawn chairs and wrapped it around his waist; then he sat down in the same chair and picked up the books. The moon was full, and although there were still hours to go before daylight, he was able to see well enough to read. The books seemed illuminated from within. Perhaps, he thought, it was their heavenly origin.

George read a few pages and then he stopped, struck with a memory. It was August 10 2006 in Wisconsin when he announced that the British had uncovered an "Islamic fascist terrorist plot" which could have killed thousands of Americans. If it had occurred, he, George, would have been seen as a complete utter failure. This was his first inkling of understanding that the war in Iraq had created even more Islamic fascists and made it *more* likely to have more 9/11s. Why hadn't he listened to his earthly father? Had God really told him to go to war? Or was it Dick?

Hubris. He was pretty sure it was the correct word. Magically, a dictionary appeared in his hands. He flipped the pages to the H and read out loud. "Hubris: insolence or wanton violence stemming from excessive pride."

"Wasteful."

George turned around. "Aw, shit."

It was her: Mother Nature. She smiled. She didn't mind being called another name for compost. She continued: "Wanton. Greedy. Fascist."

"I'm not a fascist," George said.

"Yes, you are. 'Fascist: a person who believes in a strong central government permitting no opposition or criticism, emphasizing aggressive nationalism.' But the word 'fascist' is associated with the Nazis, so we can just go back to 'wasteful.' Most people can under-stand that. Wasting the resources of your country. People. Money. Time. Good will. Honor. Legacy."

George felt a chill.

"Yes, you are going down not only as your country's worst

president, but also the man responsible for the decline of the United States of America, as in 'decline and fall of the American empire.' You've bankrupted your country, George. Huge tax cuts for the wealthy. A horrible, wasteful, unnecessary war that had nothing to do with 9/11, and has increased the likelihood of more terrorism. Massive debt to China. China!" Mother Nature smiled. "I like China. They've been around a long time. They also have very long memories. They know how to wait. They've got you by the balls, George."

Under his damp boxers he felt his testicles shrivel.

"Hubris is a great word. I'm sorry you didn't learn it in college or later. There is a reason for a liberal arts education. Anyway, I'm not that forgiving, but I am full of regeneration. Life always returns. Even possibly for you and for your country. And I've already told you, there's a way out of this mess: by helping those you have hurt. Maybe your change of heart will inspire others who are ultimately going to have to clean up your mess."

George whimpered. "What about Karl, Dick...?"

Mother Nature smiled. "Don't worry about them. Karma, George. That's real, too." She paused and then added, "By the way, they were lying to you when they said they'd talked to God." And she vanished.

* * *

Lucy heard someone enter the barn, and thinking it must be the owner, she froze.

"Lucy? It's me, Bill. Where are you?"

Lucy made herself smaller. She wasn't afraid of Bill; she just didn't want him there. Why had he followed her? She would demand that he leave. She sighed deeply. "Here I am," she said, but she didn't get up. He saw her and crouched down a respectable distance away.

"Why did you follow me? I don't want you here. Go back with the other vets. You belong with them, not me."

Bill didn't really know what to say. He couldn't believe what she believed, but he had an incredibly strong feeling for her, and he wanted to make sure she was safe and help her finish her pilgrimage. Even though her reasons didn't make sense to him, he agreed with the idea of honoring the dead and liked the thought of a spiritual journey. He might have chosen another route, perhaps north through the Sierras, then south through the Rockies, but this was her trip and he'd follow her.

Bill wasn't paying attention to her words. He really wanted to kiss her. Bill was looking at Lucy as a wolf looks at its mate, when he saw her eyes widen at something behind him. He glanced over his shoulder and was shocked to see another person in the barn, someone who had gotten close without a sound. A tall well-built young man wearing a cowboy shirt glared at him. Bill jumped to his feet and quickly moved to protect Lucy.

"No, Bill, I know him. He's fine." She gestured for Bill to back away as Darrell approached. "Hi, Darrell, what are you doing here?" Lucy had felt neutral towards him back at home, but now she felt some relief. Thank you, God, she said in a silent prayer. Darrell would help convince Bill to leave. Then she'd have to figure out how to get Darrell to go back to Texas.

"You know this guy?" Bill asked, confused.

"Darrell is from home. We go to the same church." Lucy smiled at Darrell. It *was* good to see him. "Thank the Lord that you're here, Darrell. I was just asking Bill to leave."

Darrell squatted beside Lucy inside the stall. Then he raised his hand towards Bill and made the sign of the cross. "Get out, thee, Lucifer. You are not wanted here. We are the people of the Lord, and you are not one of the saved."

Bill agreed he wasn't one of the saved, but he didn't like the possessiveness he saw in Darrell's eyes. It was obvious to him that this dude was just hoping to get into Lucy's pants. "Lucifer? Yeah, right. Listen, *Darrell*, my name is Bill. B-i-l-l. I'm not anymore Lucifer than you are, and I think you have something else on your mind." Bill leaned against the side of the stall, placing his hand on the post there, when all of a sudden he shrieked. Lucy and Darrell were horrified to see that another man had come from behind Bill and was now looming over the three of them. Broad-shouldered with a small head and short arms, rotten teeth, and dressed completely in black, the new man was utterly terrifying. He held a knife in one hand and grinned at a second knife, still quivering and pinning Bill's hand to the post.

Bill recognized him right away, that bastard Luke he'd gotten arrested for crimes at Abu Ghraib. One of the real sickos. But what was he doing here? As soon as Bill thought the question, he knew the answer. Luke was here to kill him.

Luke waved his knife menacingly towards Darrell and Lucy, who seemed frozen to the spot. Lucy was crying. Then he turned toward Bill and slapped his pinioned arm. Bill screamed and then retched. Luke grinned. "You thought you could escape us, Bill Stein," he sneered.

"You know him?" Lucy asked in a small voice. She hadn't felt such fear since she was almost raped.

Bill glanced at her. In spite of his pain, he wanted to protect her. He even wanted to protect Darrell. Luke was pure evil. "His name is Luke. Met him in Iraq."

Luke nodded, then hitched his belt up and rubbed his crotch. Darrell and Lucy noticed the bulge there. Bill hadn't taken his eyes off Luke's face.

How in the hell had they let the bastard out of prison? Bill was against the death penalty, but if anyone deserved execution, it was Luke.

Indicating Darrell and Lucy, Luke demanded, "You two take off your clothes. Now."

He shoved Bill's arm again, and Bill moaned in pain. Terrified, Darrell removed his shirt, and Lucy turned away to remove hers.

Luke shook his head. "No way. You turn around so I can see you. So everyone can see you." Lucy and Darrell were both crying by now. They began reciting Psalm 24:3: *"Yea, through I walk through the valley of death, I fear no evil...."*

Luke laughed. "Jesus freaks, huh? Where's your Jesus now?" He slapped his thighs. "You keep praying just as long as you keep taking your clothes off." He hadn't felt this good since Abu Ghraib.

Bill, meanwhile, was remembering all the rage that he'd felt in Iraq at the Americans who had abused prisoners. The travesties at Abu Ghraib and Guantánamo had been such perversions of patriotism that it had made him physically ill. But there had been a doctor and a chaplain who had helped him, and he'd learned to meditate, which came in handy now as he sought to ignore the ferocious pain in his hand and concentrate on what he had to do next.

Luke was mesmerized watching the young crying, praying couple take off their clothes, and Bill knew this was his best chance. He pivoted his body around, and employing a shoulder height karate kick, slammed Luke in his head. Luke screamed as he fell over. Bill was screaming too, in agony, as the knife in his hand torqued, but he fought on, kicking Luke in the groin and then stomping on his knee, which cracked and snapped under Bill's heavy boot.

Lucy, down to her underpants, sprang forward and grabbed the knife Luke had dropped. Bill held the squirming Luke under his foot, but he was beginning to tremble, his concentration wavering, and Luke would soon get away. In a flash, enraged with memories of Deacon Pinkins and under the oak with Cal and Bobby, Lucy plunged the knife into Luke's shoulder. Blood spurted out onto his shirt and into the air.

Bill stared at Lucy with amazement. Her chest was spattered with Luke's blood. Darrell appeared dumbfounded. She ignored their looks and pulled the other knife out of Bill's hand. He sank to the floor, grimacing and grunting. It was only after she'd bound his wound up with her bra that she remembered her nakedness and covered herself with her hands as she bent to retrieve her shirt. Once Lucy had found her pants and put them on, she checked Bill, who was now quiet, but breathing heavily in pain. By this time Darrell was dressed, too. The three stared at each other and at the moaning man on the floor. He was clutching the knife in his shoulder but didn't seem able to pull it out. Blood was seeping across the stall.

Darrell stepped forward to put his arm around Lucy. She shrugged him off. "What do we do with this guy now?"

"We can't just let him die," Darrell responded. Lucy nodded. She couldn't believe that she'd thrust a knife into another person with her own hands. But she was certain that he would have killed all three of them, after brutally degrading and torturing them. Bill needed medical attention, and the fact that he was wounded would provide evidence that they had been attacked. Darrell took out his cell phone and dialed 911. Then they sat and waited for the police and paramedics.

Chapter 14

Judith began to recover the next day. Her temperature came down until it was back to normal, and her skin sores started healing up. Her consciousness returned, and pretty soon so did her sense of humor. Almost two weeks had disappeared from her life. She was glad to be back.

Her first joke was kind of juvenile but it got a big laugh every time. She loved trying it on new doctors and other healthcare professionals. They were so serious, and it was good to get them to laugh.

She'd indicate the white napkin tucked in her hospital gown as she ate her breakfast, and say, "What color is this?"

"White."

"What color is this?"

"White," the doctor or nurse would repeat with a bit of irritation.

"What color is this?" Judith would ask with a grin.

"WHITE!"

"What do cows drink?"

"MILK."

Silence.

Then laughter all around. Cows drink water, of course, but responding repetitively to each question with "white, white, white" made almost anyone answer the last question with "milk," even those who'd heard the joke before.

Judith was trying to come up with some analogy to the lead up to the war with Iraq. It didn't hum along like the "white" joke, but there was still something there. Weapons of mass destruction. Imminent threat. Osama bin Ladin. All connected to Iraq and Iran.

"What do we most fear?"

"Another 9/11."

"*What* do we most fear?"

"Another 9/11."

"*What* do we most fear?"

"Nineelevenweaponsofmassdestructionimminentthreatosam-abinladiniraqirannineeleven."

"What do cows drink?"

"Milk."

"Auuwwwghh!!!"

Judith had told some jokes to the new psychiatrist they'd sent in to talk with her. Some emergency funding had come through, and they'd hired a part-time psychiatrist to help the vets. This one seemed super serious, like she really needed some joking around, especially if Judith was going to put up with her questions. Questions like whether she was suicidal. She wondered how the psychiatrist thought she might kill herself without any arms or legs.

Judith still had nightmares, and she startled easily at loud, unexpected noises. She hoped this new doctor could help her, and when the doctor answered "milk" and then burst into laughter, Judith thought she might enjoy seeing her again.

While the doctor was still laughing, Ben walked in with some flowers. He nodded to the doctor, kissed Judith and put the flowers in the vase. Judith started to smile. "Doc, meet Ben. He's a lawyer. Don't hold that against him, he doesn't do medical malpractice."

Ben and the doctor shook hands and murmured hellos. Then Judith cried, "How about some light bulb jokes, folks?" Without waiting for an answer, she asked, "How many lawyers does it take to change a light bulb?"

Ben knew all the lawyer light bulb jokes. "How many can you afford, sister?"

The psychiatrist laughed.

Judith spoke to her: "Dr Stern, how many psychiatrists does it take to change a light bulb?"

The psychiatrist, who couldn't remember jokes, said, "I don't know. How many, Judith?"

Judith turned toward Ben.

Ben said, "I just know lawyer light bulb jokes. I don't know much about psychiatrists. How many psychiatrists does it take to change a light bulb?"

Judith beamed. "Just one. However, it's expensive, takes a long time, and, most importantly, the light bulb has to want to change!"

They all laughed.

"This is great," Judith said. "I'm not going to have any problems if I can get you two to laugh."

"What are you talking about?" Ben asked.

Judith focused straight on Ben, as if she could see him clearly. "I want to be a comedian. Not a standup comedian, of course. A sit-down comedian. What do you think?"

Ben threw his hands up in the air. That was the most insane idea he'd heard yet. He glared at the psychiatrist. "You didn't put her up to this, did you?"

Dr Stern was horrified. "No, of course not. This is the first I've heard about it." Then she smiled. "But I like it. Her jokes are funny. I really liked the 'white' joke."

Ben studied the white psychiatrist. Had Judith been making racist jokes? That was okay to do with other people of color but not with whites. Maybe Judith didn't realize the psychiatrist *was* white. Ben mumbled, "The white joke?"

The psychiatrist started laughing and Judith joined her. Finally Ben cracked a smile, and pretty soon they were all laughing so hard they had tears rolling down their faces.

Dr Stern finally said, "Let's do the white joke on your brother, Judith." And she picked up a napkin from the food tray and put it under Judith's chin.

Judith grinned. "Ben, what color is this?"

* * *

Charlie and Maria escorted the vets to the Great Sand Dunes National Park. They'd stay in a campground close to the park where the Sangre de Christos Mountains swept east and the spacious San Luis Valley spread west towards the San Juan Mountains. The veterans had a hard time taking in the enormous beauty of the place. They could easily imagine mammoths — sabertooth tigers and other giants — roaming this valley thousands of years before. Now the only mammoths were huge RVs. Jesus and Kenzo had left the supplies with the vets and gone in to nearby Alamosa to get some work done on their truck. They'd called to say they'd have to spend the night there as the truck couldn't be fixed until the next day.

After setting up camp, the vets weren't sure what would happen next, but they all seemed to sense that something was about to transpire. They were lingering around the campfire when Charlie noticed a child approaching. "Look," she said quietly, and the others stopped talking and watched the boy come nearer. When he reached them, he said, "Hello. My grandfathers would like you to come join them at the amphitheater."

Driving in they'd noticed the amphitheater to the north of the campground. It was set into the mountainside with a small fire pit in the center between the speaking area against the cliffs, several backless benches to the west, and a sweat lodge erected nearby.

Maria and Charlie nodded at the boy and gestured to the men to follow. They walked, or were pushed, towards the amphitheater, and soon found two elders tending the fire. The old men looked at the group. Still wearing their "Funny Times" T-shirts, and missing arms, legs, eyes, parts of their faces, and in some cases, their minds, they might have seemed like a bunch of misfits. But the older men knew these younger men were warriors whose inner spirit still burned.

The older men were brown-skinned and had wrinkled faces and beautiful grey hair, plaited in a fat braid on one man, and in two skinny braids on the other. The man with the fat braid winked at Maria. She smiled her gorgeous smile and winked back. Charlie sighed and rolled her eyes. Then fat braid spoke: "We are Korean War vets, and we assume that you are Iraq War vets. We have been called here to help you. And you seem to have been called here for help." They studied the individual faces in the group, and most of the men, even those who seemingly had lost their minds, nodded.

"Let's invite the spirits in. Those who can, please rise."

Those who could stand, stood up and helped turn the others to face south. The older men invited the spirits in from the other directions, turning west, then north, then east. "You may sit now." Fat braid looked at Maria and Charlie. "You've helped bring these men this far, and you will be blessed for your help."

Maria, who understood that men and women needed to be separate for some ceremonies, said, "You want us to leave, right? It's a man-woman thing?"

Charlie interrupted: "No, it's a vet, non-vet thing. This group just happens to have all men, but if there were female vets, besides me, you'd have a grandmother warrior here, right?" she asked, looking at the man with skinny braids. The man nodded.

Maria regarded Charlie with surprise. Charlie hadn't appeared even the least bit angry, cynical, sarcastic, bitter, irritable, or sad. Charlie smiled back at her gently and said, "And I could stay, but, Maria, you couldn't. This is just for warriors, wounded warriors."

Both older men nodded. As she gazed at them, Charlie's eyes began to water. Damn it, she hadn't cried since she was twelve. She smiled at the men, straightened up, and gave the most sincere salute she'd ever given to anyone. The older men saluted back and Charlie took Maria's hand. "I don't need to stay. Our friends are in good hands." The two women strode off.

Some distance away from their camp, Charlie and Maria noticed another group, this one made up of mostly women and a couple of men who looked like pirates, all illuminated by their campfire. One of the men played a beautiful guitar with a strange haunting tune. A couple of the women, their bodies swaying, softly clapped. The others stood around with drinks and cigarettes. They were all attractive, striking rather than beautiful, many with long hair, big earrings, tight shirts, long dresses, and bare feet. Maria briefly wondered if they were some strange religious sect, but she'd never heard of a religion in which people drank and smoked and looked so sensuous. She noticed the logo on their van: "*Brujas Buenas*." "Hmm," she murmured, "Good witches."

"Oh, Jesus. They're smoking," Charlie said. Charlie hated cigarettes. She was a former smoker but had quit in basic training. All the soldiers were encouraged to quit — a reversal of hundreds of years of military practice when, as a rationed addiction, tobacco had been used to control and motivate soldiers. But the late twentieth-century military had realized the staggering health costs associated with tobacco use and imposed a "sticks and carrots" approach to get soldiers to quit. Of course, some soldiers relapsed when they went to war, but not Charlie. She conducted a personal crusade to ban smokers from within a fifty-foot perimeter of her. "No smoking" was the first thing she learned to say in Arabic.

Charlie was prepared to stride over and demand that the gypsies put out their cigarettes, or at least smoke them elsewhere, but Maria put her hand on her arm and shook her head. "Listen to the music, Charlie. I hate smoking, too, but right now, there's something more important. If you had asthma, I'd agree with you. Look, they're putting them out now anyway." Maria chuckled. "Good Witches, Charlie. Take it easy. They're bewitching me. *Vámanos, amiga.* Let's join them."

Charlie followed Maria doubtfully. As they approached, the man's music quickened. The women were clapping faster, swaying their hips, and tapping their feet on the earth below. One beckoned to Maria and Charlie, and the guitar player gestured at the bench next to him. They sat and waited to see what would unfold.

Suddenly, there was an unearthly howl from the man without the guitar. "Aaaaaiiiiiiiii. Aaaaaaiiiiiiiii. Aaaaaiiiiiiii!" he screamed.

Charlie jumped, all senses alert. The hair on Maria's neck stood on end, but she realized it wasn't a threat, just a howl from deep in the earth, a howl of respect for life, and an invitation to the spirits to inspire the musicians and dancers' *duendes* or souls. A couple of women clapped a strange rhythm intertwined with foot tapping and the others began to dance around the fire. Arms lifted, fingers curled in beautiful patterns that reminded Maria of huge flowers —

hibiscus, roses of Sharon, or poinsettias. Hips moved further left and right than Maria thought hips could go.

The women's bodies worked with the music. Flamenco was almost the opposite of classical music, and the voluptuous bodies of the flamencas contrasted with the lean almost anorexic bodies favored in ballet. These were *women*. Even the most gay man would have been entranced as they danced around the campfire. The women were like the earth, the music like the rain, and the two merging together created beautiful images of corn, beans, sunflowers, and hollyhocks. Though the women were focused inward, completely involved in their dancing, one invited Maria to enter the circle by curling her fingers towards her body.

The emotions inspired by the music, the singing, and the women dancing around the fire overcame Charlie. Something melted in her heart. Flamenco dancing was incredibly sensual and sexy but remarkably respectful and empowering, too. It was exactly the opposite of the strip shows Charlie had seen, and she'd seen a lot of them. She was stabbed by a thought: if all the strippers worldwide suddenly transformed into flamenco dancers, the whole dynamic between women and their watchers would shift like some kind of evolutionary wormhole. She had completely forgotten about their cigarette smoking.

Charlie watched Maria dance. The dancing revealed something that Charlie had only sensed in her lover in private. Flamenco was not a first date kind of experience, especially outdoor fire-inspired flamenco under a brilliant western star-lit theater. Charlie knew she was never going to enter a strip joint again.

Maria soon left the dancers and walked off with her lover. They had set up their camp at a distance, which was unfortunate for the flamencos. *Las Brujas Buenas* could have done with help from Charlie, but she was otherwise engaged when it all went down.

* * *

George woke up with a headache. His wife was away and there was no one else in the house as it was Sunday. He felt stuck between the proverbial rock and a hard place. On the one hand, there were all the dreadful nightmares pressuring him to change. On the other, his closest advisors were demanding that he stay the course. George loved the title "Freedom President" and still believed he would enter the history books of Afghanistan and Iraq some day as one of the founding fathers of their newly formed democracies. He hoped it would happen in his lifetime, so he could walk the streets with adoring crowds throwing him flowers and candy, instead of shoes.

"Ah, hell," he said to himself. Even he knew this was an unlikely fantasy. The Taliban had taken control of large areas of Afghanistan, and much of the rest of the country was wracked with violence. In most places girls couldn't go to school anymore, and they still hadn't found that asshole, Osama. Iraq was an utter hell hole of civil war, and the Shias had just instituted Sharia, a harsh form of Islamic justice that condoned cutting off of hands for thievery, stoning for adultery, and crucifixion for homosexual behavior. At least Saddam was gone. That was a personal achievement. But Osama was still at large. George imagined dragging Osama to justice in the dirt as the American Indian cowboy had done to the evil Saudi in *Hidalgo*. Heck, he'd pull that sucker all the way to Guantánamo. Or maybe to the World Court at the Hague. "Heh, heh," he chuckled, there wouldn't be much left of someone pulled in the dirt that far. George frowned. He couldn't go to the Hague. Some lawyers wanted to indict him for war crimes and he'd been warned by Condi never to travel to Europe. He doubted anyone could actually arrest a former president of the United States, but he knew what had happened to Pinochet and Kissinger. He didn't like Europe anyway. Except for splendid visits with Queen Lizzy and that last chat with Sark, Europe was just a bunch of old crap, nothing like Texas.

George noticed his Bible and his mood brightened. Religion had helped him before and surely God would help him again. He knelt and faced the bed, and glancing at the photos of his wife and daughters on the bureau, he prayed. "Oh, Lord, I don't know what to do. Please help me." He waited a long time with his head bowed but the only sound he heard was the hum of the air conditioner. Then he began to wonder if perhaps he'd find God at church, maybe one he'd never been to before. He reached for the phone book on the nightstand.

Although he'd been to just about every church in a twenty-mile radius, he hadn't gone to any Catholic churches, as he'd been irritated that the previous pope had actively preached against the Iraq War. The current pope was a decent guy, like his Russian friend, Vlad, and maybe George would find out something about this St Therese of Lisieux. As George got dressed he marveled that Nic's friend, St Francis, who'd been born almost one thousand years ago, was still remembered and loved by people today. Machiavelli was born about five hundred years ago and lots of powerful people still admired him, too. George hoped people would remember him in a thousand years. But would they recall him as St Francis or Machiavelli? He shuddered to think he could be remembered, as Machiavelli had suggested, as another Hitler or Stalin.

The closest Catholic church was St Eugene Church, just down the road in McGregor. The blurb in the Yellow Pages hadn't said anything about St Therese but did mention Our Lady of San Juan and St Philip. George didn't understand Catholics with all their saints but those two sounded nice and perhaps he'd ask the priest about St Therese.

George was a bit surprised when he arrived to find himself at the Spanish-speaking service. But he knew some Spanish and everyone looked friendly — though they didn't seem to recognize him. The priest had winked at George when he came through the door but otherwise gave no indication that he knew him either. George thought this was wonderful, to be in a church without everyone fawning all over him. "Thank you, Lord, I think you've answered my prayers this morning," he muttered.

He sat in a pew towards the back, again, an experience he hadn't had in a long time, as he was always pushed to the front of every church he entered. The Secret Service agents sat discreetly near the aisle, and a young mother in her Sunday best sat on the other side of him. She was accompanied by two young girls dressed in pretty frocks, their long black hair neatly tucked under flowered hair bands. The girls had three paper fans between them, and one of them offered the extra fan to George, which he graciously accepted as there was no air conditioning.

Opening up the fan, he saw a watercolor of a gentle-looking Mexican man, identified as San Juan de Lagos de Jalisco. This didn't seem like the same church but maybe they'd gotten these fans from a sister church. George had difficulty deciphering the Spanish but it seemed to say that Juan was the saint most venerated in Jalisco, and that a similar saint was sanctified and brought to the lower Rio Grande valley in Texas for the Mexicans who lived there. Expecting more about saints, he flipped over the fan — and almost dropped it, shocked at the drawing depicted. It was a picture of a church with a plane crashed through the roof. George looked anxiously at the ceiling.

As the service started, he read the miraculous true story, written in English, of the plane crash. Close to eight hundred people, many of them children, were sitting in the Hidalgo county church on Sunday October 23 1970, when a small plane inexplicably crashed through the roof. Small churches are built as economically as possible, and with the poverty of the lower Rio Grande Valley, their church had been built with great frugality. But it must have been built with great love and faith, because the plane hit the one rock-solid steel beam in the roof, and no one was killed or even hurt. Even the statue of la Virgin de San Juan was unscathed. It didn't recount what happened to the pilot.

George thought back to September 11 2001, when those other planes had crashed into the buildings and the earth. He wished there'd been a steel beam of love and faith strong enough to prevent all those deaths. Sweating and trembling, he began to weep. He had truly mourned all those 9/11 deaths, but there hadn't been time to really feel their loss, and now he was struck with the enormity of it.

He recalled all those photos in *The New York Times*, and the short bios that Laura had diligently read, even though neither of them usually looked at that newspaper. She'd said that it was a gesture of respect to read about these people, just as *The Times* had shown its respect by writing about them.

The priest droned on in Spanish and George looked around for something to distract himself. Along with saints there were huge photos of young men and women in uniforms on the walls. He was glad to see their photos, but then he noticed they were rimmed in black and each had dates underneath. Dates starting with 1983 and 1979 and even 1991, and ending with 2004, 2007, and 2009. Two thousand nine. This very year someone's son had died in the service. Sweat rolled down George's neck and his shirt stuck to his back. He looked at his hands, which had signed the death warrants for all these young people. His nose dripped. It seemed that he'd never felt so hot. Perhaps it had been an enormous mistake to attend this church. He wanted to flee.

The young mother next to George passed him a lace-edged hanky and one of the little girls gave him a piece of candy. He accepted both, cleared his throat, whispered "*Gracias*," and mopped his face. The priest had been talking in Spanish, but now he switched to English. Was it because he'd seen George's distress, or was this a part of the service? Either way, George would remember his words for the rest of his life.

"Luke 15:11-32." The priest paused and looked over the audience. In fact, he knew who George was. He had voted for him, the first time. But not the second time. He had agreed with the Vatican, that the Iraq War was deeply immoral. Earlier this week he'd been inspired to choose this famous passage from Luke. Now he knew why.

"You all remember the story of the Prodigal Son. The extravagant son. Remember 'prodigal' means extravagant, although we think the word means 'lost.' We have talked about this man many times before. The son who was given everything, but left home and squandered his fortune. He became a swineherd, the lowest of the low at that time, as pork was not eaten by Jews. Meanwhile, an elder son had stayed home to care for his father, and had used his inheritance wisely. Many years later, the younger son realized his mistakes, and decided to return home and ask for forgiveness. Without any hesitation the father gave his forgiveness and killed a fatted calf in honor of the youngest son. The elder son complained bitterly that he should have been given this great honor. He had stayed and done everything the father asked. But the father told him, 'Your brother was dead, and is alive again. He was lost and is now found.'"

The priest paused and remembered where he'd truly understood this story: in a halfway house where he'd ministered and seen true healing between people who'd been bitterly estranged for years.

"And just as the father forgave his son, so Jesus forgives those who make mistakes. Forgives the extravagant. Forgives the wasteful. Forgives the squanderers. Forgives and invites the prodigals to his table. Everyone is welcome at Jesus' table. Let us pray."

Everyone moved to their knees and bowed their heads.

As the priest said the Lord's Prayer, George, now on his knees, thought about the Prodigal Son. Wasteful. Extravagant. Squanderer. He'd accepted Jesus into his heart years ago, but he wondered now if Jesus had accepted him. Seeing himself as the Prodigal Son, he began to pray for forgiveness.

It was probably only minutes, but it seemed like hours had passed before George sat back in his seat and heard the next words of the priest. "Let us remember the dear soul of St Therese of Lisieux, the Little Flower. Her motto was, 'Love is repaid by love alone.' She told us that it doesn't matter what position a person has in this life, it's the place you've been given by God. Everyone can find his or her place. It's never too late. Let us pray."

George had stopped crying. Time seemed suspended. He felt the awesome and gentle power of Jesus and St Therese. Humility washed over him, as it had years ago when he'd quit drinking. He felt the same sense of grace. Yes. Amazing grace. "Thank you, Lord. Thank you, St Therese." He had found God through the Yellow Pages.

Chapter 15

The hospital staff had decided to do something different this year to celebrate Independence Day. At twilight all the patients who could be moved were brought outside where they heard and sang patriotic songs like *America, America the Beautiful, The Star Spangled Banner, The Battle Hymn of the Republic,* and even *Onward Christian Soldiers* (with the word "Righteous" substituted for "Christian" so no one was offended).

There also were songs of peace: *Where Have All the Flowers Gone? Christmas in the Trenches, Ode to Joy, Wake Now My Senses, For the Beauty of the Earth, In a Distance, This is My Song, Gonna Lay Down My Sword and Shield, Edelweiss,* and *Amazing Grace*.

Judith sang one of her favorite songs, *I've Got Peace like a River,* accompanied by her brother, aunt and nieces. The other patients and their families were stunned by the beauty and strength of her voice. The wounded felt like they belonged again; although they'd left their limbs, eyes, and in some cases, their minds, back in Iraq, they were still part of this nation, perhaps the best part.

As Joseph wheeled Judith back to her room, she continued to sing. She felt intoxicated by the experience of being with a group of people singing. She'd forgotten how inspiring that felt. It felt like a miracle.

During the celebration, Ben had seen Amy wearing not her nurse's uniform but a beautiful *ao dai,* the traditional costume of Vietnamese women. Although the graceful, sensual outfit almost completely covered her body, some skin showed at her midriff. Amy's long hair swayed free like a veil over her slim waist. Ben hadn't taken his eyes off her. As the crowd thinned, he approached, took her hand, and they walked to a bench away from the hospital lights. Fireflies circled around them and the scent of roses brushed the air like gentle waves.

"I want to sing you a song from my country," Amy said. "It's a song of independence also." She'd been inspired by the hymn *This is My Song* when she heard the line about the sky being blue in other countries just like it was here in America. She'd heard that hymn before and was so glad it had been included. She'd believed for a long time that just as one could love different people, one could love two or more countries, and even the whole planet at the same time. One could be proud of one's culture, but love a new culture, too. It didn't have to be either-or.

"Vietnam was independent for many centuries. Many Americans don't know that. We kicked out the Chinese. We kicked out the French. Then we kicked out the Americans. After the French and before the Americans we had twenty years when no one else was there, just us, like in our history for a long time before the Chinese. We have songs called *nhac tien chien,* songs to celebrate these times of freedom. One song I like from 1930s is *Giot Mua Thu* or *Autumn Rain Drops.* Written by Dan The Phong and Bui Cong Ky." She began softly, but her voice got stronger as she sang, first in Vietnamese then in English.

She continued, singing the whole song, and as she finished, it began to rain. Ben didn't have a jacket, otherwise he would have offered it to Amy. Her white *ao dai* started to get wet, and pretty soon it clung to her skin. It was dark but he could see her body clearly. His hands went towards the edge of her *ao dai.* Amy moved her arms to his shoulders. They were about to kiss when they heard the whistling of the crazy guy who patrolled the grounds. "I don't have to work tomorrow," Amy whispered, looking at Ben.

He replied, "I'm going to be real sick tomorrow." He smiled. He'd never called in sick.

The disturbed vet looked through the gentle rain and thought he was back in Vietnam again: a woman in an *ao dai* and a large African American man — lovers, like he'd once been. He felt frightened for them. A bomb had exploded when he'd been with his lover in Saigon, and it had killed her instantly. He had a flashback to the blood on her *ao dai.* Before that moment, he was normal, and after, he was not.

He almost screamed at the couple embracing on the bench, but all the years of being at the hospital stopped him. It was a healing place, and he had a holy patrol. He backed off and stood in the rain with one hand on his heart and whistled a tune from a John Prine love song, *You've Got Gold Inside of You.*

* * *

It was bad enough to be almost killed by that Abu Ghraib torturer who apparently would recover from the wound she'd inflicted, but now Lucy was stuck with Darrell and Bill — whose wound had been cleaned and re-bandaged. People who feel they are protected by God don't rattle easily, but such people often need solitude. Neither man seemed to get that Lucy wanted to be alone. She left them glaring at each other at the table in Shoney's Big Boy restaurant and went to the "cowgirls" restroom and sat on a toilet in the last stall. An ad on the door had phone numbers for Colorado Springs churches along with the message, "If you're pregnant and scared, call this number." There was also the usual graffiti: "Julie loves Benny." "Monica does it for free." She recalled writing on the Steinberg map in the Killeen Library. Maybe the girls who'd written here were trying to put themselves on their own maps.

She'd brought her backpack into the restroom as she needed to wash up and change. But now a plan was forming in her mind. She'd noticed a back exit door, and in spite of the sign that said an alarm would go off if the door was opened, it was already slightly ajar.

Lucy left the stall and regarded the young woman standing at the sinks in front of the wide mirror. She was a little taller than Lucy and about a hundred pounds overweight. Lucy looked away as the woman bent, the edge of her crack appearing on one end and her huge breasts almost popping out of her tube top on the other. Lucy blushed. Maybe this was Monica.

"Hi, hon, howahyuh?" she said as she straightened again.

Lucy smiled stiffly and started to wash her hands.

"There's no paper towels there, hon. Have some of these." She pulled up her tube top, grabbed a bunch of paper towels and shoved them at Lucy. "You from around here?" she asked as she began to apply mascara.

"No, I'm headed north, to, uh, Littleton, near Denver." Lucy dried her hands on the paper towels.

"You don't say? That's where I'm going, too. I'm going to see my mother. Been in Mexico for a long time and figured it was time to go home. My mom's not going to recognize me though." She grabbed the fat at her waist and started laughing. "All those *enchiladas y margaritas estan aquí*, all right here!" Mexican men didn't care how fat women were, just how often they were ready for love. Joy knew this little skinny girl would have a hard time south of the border.

God, thank you, Lucy said to herself. "Could you take me to Littleton?" she asked. "Uh, there's an ex-boyfriend out there, and I've got to get away from him." Lucy hated to lie, but she had to put her pilgrimage first.

"*Chica,* of course. I've had a few of those *pendejos* after me, too. My jeep's parked out back. I'll look to make sure the coast is clear." She opened the door and glanced down the hall. She gestured to Lucy, who followed after a quick look herself back to the dining room. Bill and Darrell seemed to be arguing. Whether about her or God, she didn't know.

"My name is Joy, and this is my Joymobile. Let's go do a Thelma and Louise." She grabbed Lucy's backpack and threw it into the rear of the jeep on top of a scuffed surfboard. Lucy told Joy her name and was still trying to buckle her safety belt when Joy roared out of the back alley and headed north for the freeway.

Pike's Peak loomed to the west. Until today the mountains had been obscured by clouds, otherwise Lucy would have seen it from Kansas. The base of the mountain was enormous and covered the entire sprawling west side of Colorado Springs. Now safely buckled in, Lucy craned her head around Joy to look. "Ohmygosh."

Joy grinned. "Yeah, it sure is beautiful. Colorado has the best mountains. And Pikes Peak *es mi favorita*. A little history for you, Lucy. Utes called it Tarakiev, Sun Mountain, first mountain of the front range to be hit by the rising sun. Very spiritual place for them. The Spanish called it *Almagre*, meaning red earth, my favorite name. And Zebulon Pike was an explorer." Joy swerved around a slow-moving semi and back into the right lane as another semi bore down on the Joymobile. Lucy gasped. "Sorry, Lucy. Ok, *basta historia, amiga.*"

No matter the mountain's name, Lucy felt awestruck. The peak was just like her dream of heaven. She relaxed. Pikes Peak — or Tarakiev or Almagre — was a good omen for the next part of her journey.

Joy had been listening to Mexican ranchería music before she'd stopped at the restaurant. Imagining what might have happened to Lucy, she'd thought about putting on Lucinda Williams' *Everything is Wrong*. But she looked at Lucy's face and decided to play *Ode to Joy*, her own special song. Back a million years ago, her father had told her that *Ode to Joy* had been written for her. But when she was sixteen, her drunk, recently-widowed mother informed her that she was really named after the yellow dishwashing soap.

Shortly after the cruel soap comment, Joy had left home and hadn't returned. Working in waitress jobs, she'd drifted east through the United States. Her only period of stability had been when she lived with a migrant Mexican family in Tennessee. She'd fallen in love with Jose, a decent guy who taught her Spanish. He lived with his parents and siblings, who were incredibly nice to her. Then one night, he didn't show up. He was extremely responsible, and when his worried family called Joy and she said he wasn't with her, everyone became concerned. They set out looking for him and converged on emergency vehicles, lights flashing, just as the paramedics were loading Jose's bloodied body into an ambulance. The family wanted to kill the drunk teenager, moaning in his wrecked car, but the cops held them back. They were later told that Jose was already dead.

Joy made it through the funeral and later gave almost all her belongings to his family. She only kept her secondhand jeep, some clothing, her keyboard, and Jose's surfboard. This was the only item he'd brought with him from Mexico, as a reminder of his Puerto Escondido home, not knowing that he'd end up in Tennessee where there was no surf. Her decision to bring the surfboard back to Mexico after his death was the beginning of her own odyssey.

"So hon, what's your *cuento, que es tu* story? You look like you're on *un journado* somewhere. Lucy.... That's a good name for someone on a journey, just like the original Lucy a million of years ago, out of Africa. Or Lucy from the Beatles' song. That's where those anthropologists got her name. *Lo sabes*?" Joy spoke very rapidly with accurately accented Spanish sprinkled in. She could speak Spanish and English correctly, but she enjoyed Spanglish, which she'd sometimes mix up with redneck southern or the equivalent from Mexico, *chuntaro*. Southern Spanglish, she called it. Kind of like *la música roja*, her own red music, a mixture of *ranchería*, classical, country and folk she'd started playing on piano. Joy had found pianos in some of the strangest places in little towns in Mexico and she'd made a living with her music. She'd also found *novios*, boyfriends. But when the attraction wore off or the man became possessive, Joy would leave and start all over again. During a period of self-imposed celibacy, she'd stayed long enough in the last *pueblo* to receive a letter from a friend in Colorado. The letter said that her mother had cancer and didn't have long to live. It was almost ten years since Joy left home, and they had not communicated at all during this time. Joy was surprised to learn from this friend that her mother had been sober all these years, and she'd stayed in the family house, hoping that Joy would write or return. "I've been on my own *journado*, Lucille. Will have to *informartele una vez*, tell you about it sometime. But, *primero*, first, *tu cuento*."

Lucy considered telling Joy about the violent incident in the barn, but she was still in shock about having knifed a man. Perhaps Joy would have asked her to get out of the jeep if she knew. Lucy replied, "Well, I'm from Killeen, Texas, near Fort Hood, not that far from Crawford." She looked at Joy. She wasn't sure how much she wanted to say about her pilgrimage.

"Yeah? What's in Littleton for you, *chiquita*?" Joy had a sudden thought. "You're not one of those religious nuts who've come to pray for us there?"

Lucy paled. "I'm not a nut. I'm on a pilgrimage for God."

Joy burst out laughing. She slapped her thigh and her tube top started to come down again. It was hard to pull it up while driving. "Anythang you say, *mi hija de Diós*." She patted Lucy's arm. "*Digame.* Tell me *de tu peregrinacion.* Mexicans like pilgrimages." Before Lucy could speak, Joy's thoughts flitted to Jose and his search for the perfect wave, which really, he'd told her, was a search for *Diós*, God. He'd left home as a teenager like Joy; however, he hadn't left in anger and he'd kept in touch with his family. After he'd earned enough money as a Spanish instructor to cute *gringas*, he'd helped his family move to *él Norte*. Jose's nickname for Joy, his beloved from Colorado, had been *Alegría Roja*, Red Joy.

Joy's eyes started to fill with tears. Her emotions shifted as rapidly as her speech. Fucking drunk drivers, *borrachos malcriados*, she hissed to herself. She pounded the wheel. And the kid had only gotten a couple of years probation. She'd never know how that murderer turned out. Had he become a poster child for Mothers Against Drunk Driving? Or was he now in prison after killing his third or fourth victim? One of life's little shitty mysteries. Joy breathed in and out. She knew, especially when driving, it was important not to give in to angry, sad memories.

Lucy looked frightened at the driver's sudden shift in mood. Joy reassured her. "*No te preocupes,* don't worry, *muchacha,* I'm okay. *Digame*, Lucy, your story." To herself she said, *Ayúdame*, help me forget my thoughts about Jose. Joy knew that all those meaningless affairs in Mexico had been an effort to find Jose again. But all she'd found was alcoholism, just like her mother. However, she'd had her last drink right before she read that letter, and she doubted she'd ever drink again. "It's okay, Lucy. I respect all religious beliefs. And I love God, too." She smiled.

Lucy responded, "Well, like I said, I grew up in Texas. I left home in April." She went on to tell Joy everything that had happened, including the incident in the barn where she'd stabbed the assailant. ("You go, girl," Joy said when she heard this.) It took almost the whole drive to Littleton for Lucy to tell her story. Joy was a really good listener, and Lucy felt relieved to recount everything, especially when Joy expressed her approval of Lucy's journey. Joy looked at Lucy with new respect, although she still thought the Rapture philosophy was the biggest bunch of *caca* she'd heard of since Scientology.

"Lucy, I got the pilgrimage part. I sort of did one myself in Mexico, but it wasn't like yours. Mine was all mixed up with *muchachos* and alcohol. And way too many *enchiladas*. But I don't understand this Rapture, uh…uh…philosophy."

Lucy's knowledge of the Rapture began with her parents, who grew up in families without any religion. They were still in high school when they fell in love and her mom got pregnant. Both their parents wanted Lucy's mother to get an abortion or give the baby up for adoption. This was 1991 and there were plenty of infertile women out there who wanted a white baby. Lucy's mom didn't make any decision; it was as if she were paralyzed, and her boyfriend, while loving, didn't know what to do either. "So my mom was pregnant with me," Lucy explained to Joy, "and walking down the street to have a meal at this Luby's in Killeen. And she was really tired from the pregnancy and her feet were swollen, and so she stopped about a half a block away at a bench to rest. She was about to get up, but an older woman sat down and started talking to her. She offered my mom an ice cold Orange Fanta. It became her favorite drink from then on. It's my favorite drink, too." Lucy paused. "Then the lady started talking about Jesus. And just a few minutes later, there was all this noise. They saw a truck crashing over the sidewalk into Luby's."

Lucy paused again to see if Joy was listening.

Joy nodded her head.

"My mom and the other lady sat there, stunned. Then the lady said she was a nurse, that maybe the driver had a seizure or heart attack, and she had to go see if she could help. She told my mom to stay on the bench, but my mom followed. The other lady moved faster though and got to the Luby's just as people were screaming and running away. My mom got knocked over out on the sidewalk." Lucy's voice quavered. "Getting knocked over saved her life. She had a hard time getting up because of being pregnant. She knew, by then, this wasn't a guy that had had a seizure. The driver had gotten out with guns. My mom heard the shots. She saw a policeman run in and chase the guy. My mom had gotten up by then and she saw all the people, screaming, moaning, covered in blood, lying on the floor." Lucy started crying. She hadn't talked about the event in a long time.

Joy knew what Lucy was going to say. She'd seen and heard enough suffering to know that Lucy's mother had found the nurse lady dead. Joy patted Lucy's arm and glanced at her little plastic *Virgin de Guadelupe*, who swung from the rearview mirror. Joy uttered a short Catholic prayer she'd learned from Jose for compassion for those who suffer. Pretty much everyone, she thought to herself.

"So my mom found the lady and she was dead. Lying on top of someone, who was injured but alive. You can imagine what happened to my mom. She hadn't been raised with any religion, but after this, she *had* to find out more about Jesus. She especially loved all those stories about his curing the sick and raising the dead. She and my dad visited all the churches in Killeen and they found this cute Baptist church where they got married right before I was born. The preacher there was an old man who was happy to marry them. He didn't care if my mom was pregnant." Lucy smiled.

"Was that where you learned about the Rapture?" Joy asked.

"No, that was later. Right before I started junior high. My mom and I had read a couple of *Left Behind* books by Mr LeHaye and Mr Jenkins, so we knew about the Rapture. But after 9/11, my parents figured that everything in Revelations was coming true and they knew we needed to get right with Jesus so we'd make it into heaven. We stopped going to that Baptist church." Lucy had a memory of the kind black preacher in their home, praying with her parents while she lay down on the floor outside the living room and listened. He was trying to convince them of something, but they didn't seem to be listening. Lucy fell asleep, and by the time she woke up, he was gone. She never saw him again.

"We joined a church where everyone was Born Again and would be raptured when the time came. We read all the rest of the books by Mr LeHaye and Mr Jenkins, and we read the Bible too, mostly from Revelations." Lucy felt herself going into a little trance. She closed her eyes and whispered, "Revelations 17:5-6: *And on her forehead was written a name of mystery: Babylon the great, mother of harlots, and of earth's abominations. And I saw the woman, drunk with the blood of the saints and the blood of the martyrs of Jesus."*

Joy snapped her fingers in Lucy's face. Lucy startled and opened her eyes. "It's okay, hon, you just had little spell there." Joy decided she'd heard enough about the Rapture. She needed to get Lucy to talk about something different. They were close to Littleton.

"Lucy, I'm older than you, but while you were reading about the Rapture, I was reading JK Rowlings' *Harry Potter* books and—"

"*Harry Potter*! Those books are evil. The preacher warned us about *Harry Potter* and JK Rowling."

"*Tranquille, amiga.* I listened to you. Please listen to me. Hermoine is one of Harry's best friends and a hero in her own right. When I read the books, I imaged myself as Hermoine, really smart and having lots of adventures. She helped me escape the weirdness of my home. Plus the books were so fun. Did they mention the Quiddish games in those sermons? Maybe not, as that's a reminder of witches on broomsticks."

Lucy looked askance. Joy continued, "Even Laura Bush likes *Harry Potter*. Bet you didn't know that, did you? You did read something else besides the *Left Behind* books, right?" Joy glanced at Lucy.

Lucy nodded. "Yeah, I wasn't really supposed to, but I went to the library in Killeen and read just about everything they had. Everything except the *Harry Potter* books. I felt kind of bad reading stuff I knew my parents disapproved of, but I just couldn't stop. I prayed on it, but that didn't work." Lucy looked sad.

"Oh, hon, don't you worry, *no te preocupes*, the truth is out there in a lot of forms. Maybe the Rapture is one form." (Not, Joy thought to herself.) "There's a lot out there, and one way to experience it is to read it. The other way is to live it. And if you survive that, well, maybe write about it." The thought occurred to Joy that this was what she needed to do next with her life. She began to fantasize about writing songs when suddenly some asshole with old Lubya Dubya bumper stickers all over the back of his truck swerved in front of her and she had to jam on the brakes.

"Damn those Bush lovers! I'm not ready for heaven yet." The Dubya driver sped up and Joy accelerated back to the speed limit.

"Well, let me tell you *mi cuento*, hon. Nineteen ninety-nine I was in my last year of middle school. I was one of the weird kids. I wasn't *gorda* like I am now, but just kind of quiet, *tranquila*. I actually looked a little like you might have at age thirteen. I was nervous about going to high school, but also kind of looking forward to it. I thought it would be different, maybe meet some other kids like me." Now some tears pricked Joy's eyes. Her voice altered and she spoke as if she was back in middle school.

"I was in social studies, second period. We were watching some kind of educational program. All of a sudden, they interrupted with a news bulletin about the high school where we were going that fall. Kids had been shot. The teacher could have turned off the TV, but she didn't. A few kids were crying. Some of them had older brothers or sisters there. I think one kid's dad was a teacher there. We must have watched for half an hour. Finally the teacher turned it off. They wouldn't let us go home. So we had to go through the whole of the rest of the day just waiting, telling the other kids what we'd seen on TV. None of the teachers said anything else, although they all looked sad and angry and upset that day. It felt weird, like maybe it was some kind of movie. It wasn't until I got home that I found out more about what happened. My dad was out of town, but my mom was lying on the sofa with a glass of wine, watching the TV."

Joy remembered that her mother had leapt up, knocked over the wine glass, and run across the room to give her a hug. It was so uncharacteristic that Joy just stood there. While her mom sobbed, Joy looked over her shoulder at the screen: thirteen dead, including the shooters, who turned out to be two students at the school; the kid hanging out the window, desperately trying to get away from whatever had gone on inside; the hysterical girl, sobbing about how one of the shooters had almost shot her but killed the kid next to her instead; the girl who had been praying to God and Jesus and he shot her, too; and the teacher who bled to death as kids who'd never taken CPR, much less trauma surgery, tried to help him. These scenes were played over and over and over again on the television, and years later, Joy could still see them in her mind.

Lucy didn't know what to say. Columbine happened on April 20 (Hitler's birthday) in 1999, the same time of year as Waco and Oklahoma City. Lucy was only seven then, and her parents didn't have a TV. But she must have gone to a friend's house after school and seen the news there. It was when she'd talked with her parents that night about Columbine that her mother had told her the story of Luby's restaurant. These two stories were probably the foundation for Lucy's pilgrimage years later.

She paid attention to all the killings after that, especially the big horror, September 11 2001. It was her mother's birthday, and Lucy awoke happy because they were going horseback riding after school that day. But when she went out to the kitchen, her parents looked really grim. They had heard the news on a Christian radio station. They sent her off to school, and they went to their jobs. But Lucy didn't get to go riding that day after school. Instead they'd gone to church and prayed for all the souls who'd lost their lives. Lucy knew it was selfish to think of the horse she didn't get to ride, and she prayed as strongly as the rest of them, especially for the kids who'd been on the airplanes. They would never get to go horseback riding or do anything else on earth, although surely they'd gone to heaven.

That night Lucy had a dream, one that she would remember the rest of her life. She was riding a flying horse, Pegasus, from Greek mythology. She got to the plane as it headed towards the two towers. She landed on the wing and the door opened. The parents of the kids stood there and pushed their kids towards the horse. There wasn't room for the parents, but they smiled bravely as the horse lifted off. The children looked up to the clouds and never saw the plane hit the towers. She awoke with tears but got up and drew the flying horse, herself clutching the mane, and three beautiful little kids holding on to one another with the horse's tail streaming out behind. She had made another picture of them landing in a beautiful meadow beside a brook and the children's relatives waiting with their arms outstretched.

Lucy told Joy about her 9/11 dream and they both agreed that it would have been great to have a whole herd of Pegasus horses save everyone from the airplanes. They imagined horses saving all the kids at Columbine. Mustangs, the descendants of Hidalgo, ran all the way from Blackwater Mountain in Oklahoma to get to Littleton, just in the nick of time, and rescued all the kids before they were shot. And the teacher didn't die either. They imagined a herd of buffalos stampeding into the high school, the beasts whirling through the library, as Joy suggested, trampling the shooters, then fleeing through the cafeteria and ending up on the football field.

Or maybe, Lucy suggested, the school nurse saves the lives of the two teenagers by reviving them after the buffalos knock them over. And later on with incredible help from various therapists they put these kids back together again. Joy looked at her skeptically but played along. "And then everyone in Littleton emptied their homes of guns and weapons, and the Lockheed Company turned their weapon-making facility into a renewable energy factory. And no one died that day. And Columbine was just a fairy story two boys wrote for their creative writing class." Lucy's and Joy's eyes shone with tears. A horn blasted. "Watch your driving, lady," a man in a red sports car yelled out an open window, as Joy's jeep veered into the left lane. He accelerated and she swerved back to the right. She noted his old bumper stickers as he sped off: "What's Our Oil doing Under Their Sand?" "Cheney IS a Dick."

Joy laughed. She was glad she hadn't sideswiped that driver. She hadn't voted in either of the elections where Bush and Cheney had won, as she was too young for the first, and too drunk in Mexico for the second. But she'd occasionally read the papers and agreed that Cheney was a dick.

"Well, Lucy, we're almost here. I haven't seen my mom in ten years. She's not going to recognize me. She's going to think you're me." Joy realized she really needed to pee. It was never good to meet a long lost relative with a full bladder. They pulled off the highway and found a Taco Bell. When Joy came out of the stall, she said, "Lucy, put on this necklace my mom gave me and this hat. I've kept them all these years. I left home wearing them. I want to play a joke on my mom. To break the ice, so to speak."

Joy was incredibly nervous. She went back into the stall to pee again. She came out and dumped the contents of her purse on the counter to find her breath spray and lipstick. She recognized her good luck in finding Lucy. If Lucy hadn't been with her, she might have just kept on driving all the way to Montana. Joy looked at herself in the bathroom mirror. She saw a fat girl with sad eyes and thought of the Shawn Mullins song about the unsmiling LA girl. Joy smiled, and she did look prettier. Okay, she thought, if Lucy can go on a pilgrimage all by herself praying for people killed by sickos, I can go see my poor dying mother and not completely freak out.

Joy joined Lucy back in the jeep. "OKAY, *muchacha, vámonos.*" And she woman-handled the vehicle out of the parking lot with as much bravado as a macho Vietnam Vet on a chopped down Harley.

Chapter 16

"Sweet Jesus, those women are…beautiful." Trevor — muscular, short, with a completely shaved head — had been thinking of saying something derogatory. But the women's presence had forced a different "b" word out of him. He and the other two men, Emile and Mack, had found an observation point behind a hillock to watch the dancers in one direction and the veterans in the other. The men wore dark clothing and night vision glasses so technologically advanced they appeared no thicker than sunglasses. If anyone had been watching them, they might have thought it strange for men to be wearing sunglasses at night. But more likely they would have sensed their hostility and gotten the hell away.

They *were* scary men; the worst of the worst from Abu Ghraib. The famous photos picked up by the media were like schoolyard bullying compared to what these contractors had done. There were no photos of their atrocities. That would have been completely unprofessional. And there were only a few witnesses to their brutalities, for all the prisoners they had "interviewed" were dead. The witnesses included two former guards, both of whom remained alive and were part of the group of wounded veterans. The men from Abu Ghraib had tried to recruit these men to their current employer but they refused.

These vets who'd served in Abu Ghraib wanted nothing more to do with torture. They wanted help with the PTSD they had acquired from participating in violence, and they wanted to do something decent with the rest of their lives. The contractors from Abu Ghraib had then tried to kill them in Iraq. Shit happened over there. "Stuff," their boss, Donald Rumsfeld, had said. But it was really "shit." And shit could happen over here, too, in America.

A third witness was Bill, who hadn't participated in the violence, but on special assignment, he had observed it, gotten the contractors kicked out of their jobs, and, unbelievably (to them), gotten them arrested. It had taken a while, but they'd been released and were now employed again by a company, ready to fulfill a deadly contract. Luke was going to get Bill, and Trevor, Emile and Mack were going to take care of the other two vets in the campground. And then, as a bonus, there would be women.

Trevor looked at his companions. Mack was over six feet tall, extremely lean, very strong, with short graying hair. His face resembled that of a prehistoric lizard with cold perceptive eyes. He had huge hands and feet, and his arms were long in relation to his torso. If the Guinness book of records was into measuring the length of penises, Mack might have won that distinction. He'd used it a lot too, on women, men and even on animals. Right now Mack's appendage rested comfortably along his inner thigh, waiting, like the rest of him.

Emile was about average height and build. With cornflower blue eyes and naturally blonde curly hair, his face was so sweet and appealing he could gain the trust of anyone. Emile's first sexual experience at age seven with a fifteen-year-old babysitter had introduced him to the world of inappropriate sexual behavior, eventually leading him to become a serial rapist and porn actor. He'd spent much of his youth in Europe where his father was career Army and he often sprinkled his language with French and Spanish.

Trevor let out a large fart.

"*Merde, pendejo,*" Emile said, but in a whisper.

Trevor snorted. He loved irritating Emile, who was just too pretty, although his appearance was damn helpful at times. Trevor, shorter than average with an acne scarred face and no neck, knew that he and Mack frightened most people. Tonight, Emile's attractiveness — and his dancing ability — would be useful to get close to the dancers below. While Emile and Trevor distracted the troupe, Mack would knock off the vets as they pissed in the dunes or once they fell asleep. The two Indian men looked strong but they were old. Then before getting the women, they'd have to deal with the guitar players. They were just musicians, easily overpowered. "Let's wait until those flamencos have drunk a bit more. Then, Angel Face, while we get us some vets, you're goin' dancin'."

"Sounds good, *hijo de puta*, I do feel like dancing." Emile leered at Trevor. "I'm going to get the video ready. This will be something I'll want to watch again and again. Maybe even sell it." He wished it had been safe to make videos of what they'd done in Iraq. There was a big market for torture and death footage. When this gig was done, Emile was going back to the porn industry, but this time he was going to produce the films, and he'd only perform in the ones he wanted to star in. *Dancing with Death in the Dunes* would be a great *entrée* to his snuff film career.

* * *

George had dismissed all the Secret Service agents. His wife still wasn't home. Sitting out in the yard facing northeast, he decided to call his dad. George pictured his father looking out his backyard to the ocean. He knew that George senior loved his property in Maine, as much as George junior loved his home in Texas. One couldn't imagine two more different places. And in many ways the two men were as different as the two states. But they had each found the physical space that suited who they were. And they had found that level of maturity between parent and adult child where neither tries to convince the other of his or her own "rightness" but respects, and even sometimes celebrates, their differences. George found himself hoping for one of those miraculous conversations one can have with a parent later in life, after many years of strife. He punched in the Kennebunkport number, but after a few rings the answering machine clicked on. Too bad, George thought, Dad must be out on the boat. George knew that his dad had an emergency phone and radio, but he never had the cell turned on when he was out on the ocean. That was fine; the old man deserved some peace and quiet after dealing with all those kids, his wife, the CIA, and his presidency.

George walked northeast away from his home, frowning when he noticed a ladder up against a tree. "Damn it. Must have been left outside by one of those tree-hugging landscapers." Angrily, he grabbed the ladder, but just as he pulled it away, he looked up and saw how the solid branches ascended almost like steps as far as he could see.

It was the most enticing tree-climbing invitation he'd ever received. George leaned the ladder back against the trunk and started climbing. When he reached the top of the ladder, he wrapped his fingers around one of the branches, which felt to him remarkably like a person's strong arm. The fingers of his other hand went around another branch, and feeling an incredible surge of life, George pulled himself off the ladder and placed his feet on lower branches. He wished he wasn't wearing cowboy boots. He sat on the first convenient branch and pulled them off, and along with his socks, threw them to the ground. Then he resumed climbing.

George was about fifty feet up when he found a branch that looked like a perfect seat. Another branch was conveniently positioned to support his back, and another exactly where his feet fit comfortably. He sat down and relaxed. He felt wonderful. How had he not known about this tree? He thought about that great Stones song, *You Can't Always Get What You Want*. George chuckled and wished he'd used their lyrics in some speeches.

He closed his eyes. It was much cooler inside the tree branches than it had been on the grass. He listened to the leaves rustling and the birds singing. Then he heard another song, very faint: "*You can get...*" Could the tree be echoing his song? He listened closer: "*You can get...anything you want.*" No, it *was* different, or maybe someone had mixed up the lyrics. He did that with words all the time. He hoped the tree wasn't mocking him. Then the song came on stronger, and he knew it was someone else singing, and the person had all the words right for this song:

> *You can get anything you want at Alice's Restaurant.*
> *You can get anything you want at Alice's Restaurant.*

Walk right in it's around the back,
Just a half a mile from the railroad track.
You can get anything you want at Alice's Restaurant.

George turned towards the voice. And he almost fell out of the tree when he saw her sitting so close to him on another branch! The woman was in her sixties, and her name tag read Alice. Holding a menu in her hands, she smiled and looked at George directly. Tentatively, he smiled back. He had the same feeling that he'd had when he'd seen his wife's face in Mother Nature in that dream a few months ago. How did women do that? He never saw that similarity in men's faces.

Alice sang again, *"You can get anything you want at Alice's Restaurant."*

George decided to enter into the spirit of her offer. He knew what he wanted most of all at this point in his life. Forgiveness. Forgiveness from all his fellow Americans who hated him. Could he ask for that at this restaurant?

"Forgiveness. That's what I want."

"It's on the menu here. We've got just about everything. You just have to ask."

He took the menu from Alice and scanned the First Course:

- Stolen 2000 Election with Supreme Court Sauce and Floridian Fakery
- On the Lookout for Reasons (any Reasons) to Invade Iraq and Humiliate Saddam
- Disdain of 2001 Democratic and International Warnings about Al-Queda and Osama
- Too Much Summer Vacation 2001

"That's not fair. Everyone needs a vacation. I didn't know Al-Queda was about to strike."

"Just keep reading, please, George. You need to review everything before you get to Forgiveness."

- Misuse of September 11 2001 Patriotism as an Excuse to Invade Iraq
- Architect Abuse of Others Before and During the First Term
- Not Believing Scientists on Global Warming
- Using Orwellian Language to Mis-describe Programs like the Clean Air Act and the Healthy Forest Initiatives
- Putting Oil and Power before People's Lives
- Invading Iraq Knowing that the Rationale was Trumped Up
- No Weapons of Mass Destruction
- No Imminent Threat
- No Nuclear Capability
- Stolen 2004 Election with Ohio You-Can-Fool-People-Twice Manipulation
- Hundreds of Thousands of People Dead and Wounded in Iraq

George looked at Alice. "I don't like this. Nothing here seems very good. Also, I don't see Forgiveness anywhere."

"You're right. Those dishes aren't too tasty but that's what you have to start with." Alice looked at him sadly and thought of all those young men she'd known who were sent off to Vietnam. She thought of all those young men and women who had been sent to Iraq. Many of them would never eat in her restaurant, and it was because of this man. It was hard to allow him in her place, but she never turned anyone away.

"Why don't you check out the next page?" she suggested.

George had that look on his face he'd had when reading the *My Pet Goat* book in the minutes after he'd been informed of the planes hitting the World Trade Towers. He examined the second page entitled "Second Course Offerings: A Reckoning."

- Suffering
- Taking a Moral Inventory

- More Suffering
- Apologizing
- Making Amends Where One Can
- Redemption

And way down on the bottom:

- Forgiveness Possible

"There's not very much on this page." He looked peeved. Only the last couple of items seemed appealing.

"No, George, there's plenty there. But you have to start with the first item, and take them in order."

He regarded Alice. She looked tired, and a little overweight. Still, he could see that she'd probably been a very beautiful woman years ago. Now her hair was graying and wispy around her face. She had circles under her eyes and lines in her forehead and radiating from her mouth. Her body resembled an apple covered with a faded dress, the hem of which sagged. Her hands were red and without any rings. She wore running shoes, but her ankles looked too puffy to actually permit running.

"This is what serving does to you, sir. It's okay. It's what I wanted to do with my life."

Then she smiled. "But I'm glad I was beautiful when I was younger." Her eyes sparkled, and as she straightened up, her figure transformed from an apple to an hourglass. And in the tree, surrounded by leaves and branches with the wind in her hair and her now richly-flowing silky gown outlining her body, she suddenly looked like the most desirable woman in the entire universe.

George stared with new interest, a wolf-like look on his face.

Alice stood balanced on a branch, and with her hand on one hip, she sang very slowly, very sexily, "You…can…get…anything…you…want…at…Alice's…Restaurant…."

Then she abruptly drew back. "Except Alice!"

She began to laugh. And suddenly George felt as horribly humiliated as when people laughed at him with his misstatement of "Fool me once, shame on you; fool me twice, shame on you...er me...er us...." But it wasn't that kind of laugh. It was a kind laugh, and before long he joined her.

George had a sudden memory of a girl he'd dated in high school. She had probably been the most unusual and interesting person he'd ever dated. She was physically very attractive. He'd hoped to at least get some French kissing that one night out with her, maybe more. But her personality had been so strong, and the conversation so unusual and intellectual, he couldn't bring himself to touch her, and he never asked her out again. But she had gotten into his unconsciousness, and she was actually the start of his recognition that women could be equal to men. It was one of the main things that he disagreed on with those chauvinistic Saudis. Their attitudes towards women were completely senseless. Why couldn't all the oil in the world have been found in Scandinavia, or Canada, or Australia or even Rwanda, where he'd heard that the new constitution required half the members of the government be women?

He realized these were really original thoughts. George wasn't used to thinking this way. He wished he'd found this tree when he'd been in office. He would have climbed it often. Alice nodded. "Trees do have a lot to offer. Women have a lot to offer. My restaurant has a lot to offer. Well, sir, back to the menu. Shall we start with 'Taking a moral inventory?'" She had a pen and pad in hand.

"Yes, it's a very good place to start," George answered, and they both settled back on their respective branches and began working together, as two American equals.

* * *

Darrell and Bill waited quite a while before they asked the waitress to check on Lucy. When she returned and told them that no one was in the restroom, they knew that Lucy had taken off.

"Goddamnit!" cried Bill, striking his fist against the table.

"Don't say that, you, you, you...." Darrell tried to contain himself.

"Unbeliever? Blasphemer? Antichrist? Yeah, that's me, the Antichrist." Bill actually knew a lot about the Rapture besides reading that *Left Behind* book, as there'd been a couple of fellow soldiers who believed in it, and he used to argue with them occasionally. "Actually I'm not the Antichrist. But I am Jewish. Even better for you. Go ahead and make my day and try to convert me. Then let's go to Jerusalem and rebuild the temple."

Darrell was astonished. There weren't that many Jews in Killeen. He could start with Bill and maybe this journey would provide him other opportunities to bring Jews to Jesus and yes, ultimately to Jerusalem. Lord Jesus, please, help me, Darrell thought to himself and then said to Bill, "The Jewish people have always believed that a Messiah would come and he did. It was Jesus, who came to save us all."

They were waiting in line to pay. The person at the counter was a trainee and didn't seem to know how to use the register. Bill realized he was going to have to listen to Darrell, who was looking at him with such sincerity that Bill almost felt sorry for him. Bill didn't feel like arguing anymore. He just wanted to get going and find Lucy. However, he decided to let this Christian give a Jew his most persuasive conversion speech. They were going to have to wait there anyway until the clerk figured out how to do her job.

"Will you pray with me?" Darrell took out his Bible from his daypack and flipped to the Old Testament. No need to go to the gospels straight away. He didn't want to alienate this Jew, who actually could be the Antichrist. Darrell felt goose bumps, tears in his eyes, and a sense of premonition. Oh, Lord, if this was the Antichrist, and he, Darrell, managed to convert him, the Rapture might happen right then and there. Then he frowned. Maybe Bill was just an ordinary Jew. No matter, it would be fine to get one.

Bill snapped his fingers in front of Darrell's face. "Darrell, snap out of it. You had that Rapture look on your face!" Bill had seen that look before, a cross between the universal dreaminess of praying and the utmost smugness, condescension, and exclusivity in some of the so-called interfaith gatherings back in Iraq. Thankfully, in Iraq they'd had this terrific chaplain who'd dampened down any major evangelizing. Converting people was so misguided. Bill was far from being a devout Jew, but he liked that aspect of Judaism, that they didn't want any converts. They just wanted people whose maternal ancestors were Jewish all the way back for almost six thousand years. Why couldn't Christians, and Muslims, for that matter, leave everyone else alone like the Jews did?

There were still five people in line before them. Bill decided just to play along. "You know, Darrell, I would just love it if I could believe that Jesus was the Messiah. But look at how messed up the world is. As messed up as it was before Jesus. He's had a long time to make things right. I just don't think he's gotten here yet. And why should it be a *he* anyway?"

Darrell regarded Bill with horror. A woman? Impossible. How could a man think like that? Darrell knew that women had been in the military, but he thought that was really wrong. Women belonged at home, cooking and caring for children. He started to answer, but Bill interrupted.

"Listen, we've got to find Lucy. I know she's headed to Littleton." Bill had considered splitting from Darrell, but figured he knew more about her plans and if God really was on the side of Born Agains, he'd be more likely to find Lucy with Darrell's help. A few minutes later, their bill finally paid, they trotted out to the parking lot. Their plan to find Lucy was a good one, but when they went out to the motorcycles, one had a flat tire and the other wouldn't start. They couldn't find a mechanic open and by the time they got the bikes fixed the next day and made it up to Littleton, Lucy was gone.

Chapter 17

Judith was still working on her jokes. She found a lot of humor in the hospital routines and had an appreciative audience. The nurses loved coming into her room. She also kept singing, which was good physical and mental therapy. Ben and Joseph had found a keyboard for the piano-playing visitors who wanted to accompany her. They played hymns, tunes from musicals, rock and roll, rhythm and blues, hip-hop, and rap.

One of the occupational therapists further inspired her with stories of others without limbs. One was a mother without arms who could change her baby's diaper with her feet, and in her adapted van could pull up to McDonalds drive-thrus and purchase Happy Meals, extending money to surprised cashiers and then deftly collecting bags of food with her toes. Another was the teenager with stubs for arms and legs who could play football. Judith could hardly believe this but the therapist insisted it was true. If a teenager without limbs could play football, and a mother without arms could care for a baby, then a woman without any limbs or sight could tell jokes and sing before an audience.

Judith was glad she'd had some sexual experiences before losing her limbs and glad that Joseph knew her before the explosion. She wondered if Joseph would continue to desire her. She took inspiration from a woman who had been born with little "flipper" arms and legs. To some she was hideous, especially when she became pregnant (in the old fashioned way, not by artificial insemination in a doctor's office). But to her sculptor friend, she was just as beautiful as any other expectant mother. He created a statue of her and placed it in London's Trafalgar Square. The white marble sculpture of a hugely-pregnant woman with the flipper arms and legs caused a hullabaloo: some people felt it was ugly; others believed that the statue repre-sented courage, dignity and empowerment. If a statue could precip-itate such an uproar, what kind of response would she — a living, joking, singing, limbless blind veteran — cause? Judith knew that "the public" might react quite differently from her family and the nurses.

Judith was glad they'd put the statue of the pregnant flipper woman in a public place. Maybe when someone constructed the memorial to the Iraq War veterans, as surely someone would, they'd put a disabled person like her in the memorial. Not terrified as when she was wounded, but triumphant after rehabilitation. That damn IED may have taken her limbs and sight, but Iraq hadn't taken away her ability to entertain other people.

Judith, Joseph, Ben and Amy made plans to go to a concert. Judith had been out to a few church services, where she'd been welcomed. The concert would be different, with a big crowd of people she didn't know. Not that she could see them, but she anticipated stares: a black blind woman with no arms and legs being pushed by a red-faced, perspiring white guy, flanked by a black man on one side and a tall Vietnamese woman on the other.

They were going to see John Prine and Mary Chapin Carpenter. Joseph loved John's songs, and Amy had said Mary wrote music inspired by angels. Maybe Willie Nelson, Lyle Lovett, or Robert Earle Keane would show up. Or Eliza Gilkysin, Bonnie Raitt, or Michelle Shocked. Anything was possible in Texas. Well, once the lights went out, everyone would be focused on the stage. And if she was ever going to appear on stage herself, then Judith was going to have to get used to being in public.

Dressed in her best with dramatic makeup and braided hair woven with flowers, Judith looked like an Oscar nominee as she arrived at the concert hall in a limousine driven by Joseph's friend. They'd had the option of a Hummer, but Judith and Joseph nixed that idea quickly. Ben and Joseph helped Judith into her wheelchair, and then leaving her and Amy outside the concert hall, went to get the tickets.

Amy and Judith waited by a huge urn of flowers which Judith identified by their scent. Judith listened as vehicles disgorged their occupants and Amy described the women's gowns as if she were Hollywood's Mr Blackwell. They were laughing when Judith heard a Hummer. It had a distinctive engine sound that she'd never forget. Amy told her it was bright yellow. Then she described the people who emerged from it. A large white man opened the back door for two women expensively dressed with big hair, rings on every finger, huge bracelets, necklaces, and earrings and makeup slathered on their faces. Laughing raucously, the men stayed with the vehicle as the giggling women walked closer to Judith and Amy. They overheard the women's Texan-accented conversation.

"And she got so much money in the divorce, it was just unbelievable, Betty Sue. Somehow he forgot to change his will. So when he shot himself, she got even more money."

The other woman, who had huge frosted Texas hair, touched the forearm of her friend and laughed. "She's set for life now. Too bad we lost the best cleaning lady we ever had, but I always like it when a woman gets money that way!"

Betty Sue teetered on her high heels. "Yeah, Tammy, those soldiers are so stupid."

"Ben and Joseph will be back soon, Judith," Amy whispered. Horns blew. The men who'd been driving didn't make any move to park the Hummer. It was as if they wanted to be seen with their huge vehicle. They'd lit cigars and Judith made a face when the smoke wafted in her direction. She asked Amy to move her upwind.

Tammy and Betty Sue continued to talk loudly. "Yeah that stupid husband signed up for the Guard. Then he got sent to Iraq and nothing happened to him, but he got disability for PPD or whatever. Said he couldn't work but he was faking it. And now he's dead and his wife's got all the money."

Judith was beginning to boil. "What's wrong with those women, Amy?"

Amy looked at them, their men and the vehicle, and said, "Well, besides owning a Hummer plastered with Lubya Dubyas bumper stickers...."

"Lubya Dubya! I should have known. I hate that bumper sticker. Wheel me to those women now, Amy," Judith ordered. "Please."

"This is not good," hissed Amy, but she wheeled Judith closer to the other women. Judith drew herself up. "Hello, ladies, I couldn't help but overhear you, and I wanted to let you know that it's PTSD, not PPD. Post Traumatic Stress Disorder. And it's real. No one's faking it."

The women looked down at Judith. Her dress was artfully arranged but a person would have to have a pretty poor imagination not to see that she didn't have any arms and legs, and an even poorer imagination not to realize where the limbs had probably been lost. These women, either because they were drunk, or just limited, didn't seem to have much imagination. "What would you know about it? You're probably faking your injuries, too," Tammy said, and chuckled, which made Betty Sue giggle, too.

Judith felt an incredible surge of anger. Just a few inches away from the women, she began to rock in her seat. Then all at once she launched herself into them.

Tammy shrieked as she was hit, and as she fell over she took down Betty Sue. A thrashing pile of bodies, legs, flimsy high-heeled shoes and ringed fingers flailed. As Judith lay on the heap of thrashing women, she started shouting lines from the old Monty Python movie. "I'm not dead yet. I'll bite your arms and legs off with my mouth."

The women's husbands ran over and started pulling the women up. Amy was trying to help Judith, who was still shouting. "I am a decorated Iraq War veteran, and I lost my legs and arms and eyes over there, and I've got goddamned Post Traumatic Stress Disorder, and so did that poor soldier you're bad mouthing, you goddamned fucking bitches."

By this time, Joseph and Ben had returned, and with Amy's help, they lifted Judith back into the wheelchair. Restrained by their male companions, Betty Sue sobbed, but Tammy kept yelling and jabbed her stubby bejeweled finger at Judith. "I'm going to sue your ass." A security guard arrived. Tammy screamed at the guard, "Did you see what she did to me?"

Judith now sat calmly and quietly in her wheelchair.

The young uniformed man hadn't seen the incident and he was trying to figure out how a person with no arms and legs could attack anyone. He'd just seen the pile of bodies on the ground and figured one of the able-bodied women had pulled the other woman out of her wheelchair, or maybe she'd fallen out. The guard hated this part of the job. He wished his supervisor was there. Crap, he was going to have to sort it out by himself.

The women's husbands were also confused as to what happened, but they knew without a doubt that the woman in the wheelchair was an Iraq War vet.

Ben took charge. He flipped out his district attorney's badge and stood in his best courtroom posture. "Let's get the story straight, ladies," he said, looking directly at the flailing women. "My sister is a decorated Iraq War vet, and as you can see she is completely disabled from injuries received in service to our country." Ben was sure Judith was at least half responsible for what had happened here. This was the fierce little sister who would take on any challenge and when younger beat the shit out of bullies. He cleared his throat. "So I think we need to all calm down, go our separate ways, and enjoy this fine concert."

The Hummer husbands nodded and led their wives away. Tammy kept yelling, "Don't touch me. She's a faker and she's ruined my hair." One of the husbands yelled over his shoulder at Judith and her companions, "Sorry to have bothered you folks."

Once they left, Judith beamed at her brother, whose back was turned towards the Hummer people. He was laughing so hard his shoulders shook. "You know, Judith, I want to high five you so bad." He high-fived Amy instead.

"Yeah, that's the thing I most miss, brother," Judith said. "That IED took away my ability to high five...but not to do the low dive!"

And they laughed. This was going to be a great concert. Judith sat up straight; the others straightened too, as if they were going down the red carpet to the Oscars. The foursome enjoyed what turned out to be one of the best events of their lives. And Judith had her first public performance. She thought it came off pretty well.

* * *

While Judith and the others were enjoying the concert in Dallas, at the Colorado campground the guitar players strummed the last few notes of the *soleá*. It was a song of sadness, but the sort one could recover from with help and time, unlike the never-ending grief of a *siguiriya*. Breathing heavily with the exertion of the dance and the altitude, the dancers stretched and then reached for shawls and jackets. They slipped on their shoes. As one guitarist put his guitar away, a woman approached him and gave him a kiss. He smoothed back her hair and she gently brushed his cheek with the back of her fingers. *"Cara mia, bella Lydie,"* he whispered. Married over thirty years ago, they were in their fifties and were the "mom and pop" of *Las Brujas Buenas*. Their daughter, Lupe, moved towards them. She was one of the most accomplished dancers, although this young woman would get even better as she matured, because this was not ballet: it was flamenco.

"Buenas noches. Heard your music. Lovely," said a very attractive curly-haired man who had appeared out of the darkness. *"Con mucho gusto, mi nombre es Emile,"* he continued as he shook the guitarist's hand and let his eyes rest on Lupe. When he touched the hand of the guitarist's wife, though, Lydie felt evil flow through his palm to hers. Emile was looking at Lupe. He had dismissed her mother as an old woman, so he didn't see her face as she stifled a gasp. Lydie hadn't sensed such evil in years, but a childhood in Franco's Spain had sensitized her and she was suddenly alert to danger. She stepped back. She needed to observe this man very carefully.

Meanwhile Lupe, who was too preoccupied by Emile's good looks to register that he might be anything less than angelic, took a step closer to him. He smiled at her, took her hand as if to shake it, and then drew it to his lips and kissed her wrist. She blushed; no one had ever done that to her. Her mother silently hissed and folded her arms across her chest. While the other guitarist continued to play, Lupe's father offered Emile a glass of wine.

Emile tipped back the rosé and handed the empty glass to the father. "*Quieres bailer*, Lupe? Would you like to dance?" Emile held up his arms.

The young woman now felt emboldened. She hadn't really had much experience with men as two of the male dancers were gay, and two were attached to two (or sometimes three) other women. The rest of the dancers were female.

"*Por supuesto, sí.* Of course, yes." Lupe took Emile's hands and they improvised a graceful dance around the fire. The father clapped *palmas*. The other guitar player concentrated on his music. Entranced, the dancers watched the young couple twirl around the fire. Curly-haired Emile with the face of an angel and slender Lupe with her long black hair streaming past her hips were dancers from a dream. Emile wore combat boots, but he was very graceful, and although dancing closely, he didn't step on Lupe's bare feet.

Only Lydie was not mesmerized. She continued to feel evil emanating from the man who danced with her daughter. She moved closer to the "*Brujas Buenas*" van where she knew there was a nine-millimeter handgun under the front seat. Lupe's father had taught her to shoot when she was a girl in northern Spain, and although she'd never fired at anyone, she'd had to aim at men, and she knew she could shoot, and shoot to kill, if necessary. "*Je suis prêt*," she whispered. It was an ancestors' motto. "I am ready." Unnoticed by the group, Lydie placed the gun into one of her coat pockets, and watching Emile, she stood in the shadows.

At the nearby campsite the two Indian men had the vets in a circle. One man beat the drum and the other sang a prayer. Seventeen vets and the young boy made twenty people around this fire. The Indian with the fat braid had invited the men to participate in a sweat lodge once the prayer was complete. A couple of vets had done sweat lodge ceremonies, but the rest had never had that experience. When the prayer was over, sixteen of the men entered the sweat lodge and one vet remained outside to bring in hot stones. Inside the sweat lodge, the boy circled the group and offered the vets water. The other Indian continued to drum and to sing a prayer outside. He didn't notice a man approaching.

Mack silently crept closer to the lone veteran outside the sweat lodge. He was one of the two men they wanted to kill. Juan, the vet without a foot and missing most of his arm, must be in the sweat lodge, he thought. The vet moving stones into the tent had limbs but Jeff's face was a nightmare of fused skin grafts, and his mind was mostly shattered with psychosis.

Trevor and Mack were responsible for the vets' injuries after they had blown the whistle and accused the contractors of torturing Iraqi prisoners. When Trevor had the opportunity, he had thrown a grenade at Juan, and laughed as the man's foot went in one direction and his arm in another. Jeff had witnessed the attack and tried to stop Trevor, but Mack had held him back and forced him to watch his friend suffer. Then they'd thrown gasoline on his face and lit him up like a firecracker. When the medics arrived, they'd found two men screaming in agony. Trevor and Mack had vanished from the scene. Neither of the wounded men knew they'd each been blamed for the other's injuries until they woke up a few days later. They tried to describe their assailants (who they suspected were the contractors), but it had been dark and all they could say for sure was they were Americans.

Months later, Juan and Jeff had found each other in a VA psych ward. They'd become good friends and stayed together after that hospitalization. However, they would get drunk in between admissions and end up fighting in their paranoia. They always apologized once sober, but the roller coaster of sobriety, remorse, drunkenness, accusations, fighting, jailing, and psych admissions became the central story of their lives. When drinking they would talk about finding and killing the two contractors who had ruined their lives, but when sober they realized they didn't have the resources. They had no idea that Trevor and Mack had been looking for *them*, and in the spirit of the sweat lodge, they weren't thinking of the torturers at all.

Trevor, meanwhile, had almost reached the flamenco guitarist. When the action happened, it happened very fast. Trevor smashed the guitarist on the side of his head, tossing the guitar aside, and pulling out a gun which he aimed at the remaining dancers. Emile whipped Lupe around so his arm was across her neck, choking her, and his body hard against her back.

"No one move," Emile said. "There's two guys we want, forever, and…" He squeezed Lupe's breasts roughly. "…her, for a while." He grinned. "No one move, and no one else gets hurt." This was a lie. As long as the two vets died they didn't care whether others died too. While Emile pulled Lupe towards the Hummer, Trevor held a gun on the dancers.

As the flamencos were being attacked, Mack smashed a rock on Jeff's head while he bent over the pot outside the sweat lodge. As he fell to the ground, the Indian beating the drum stopped and began to approach Mack, but Mack pulled out a gun and aimed it at the fallen veteran. The drummer stopped moving. He was only mildly surprised at this turn of events. He'd seen plenty of fights and had broken up a few. This evil man would make a mistake.

Holding the gun on Jeff, and watching the elderly Indian, Mack began pulling pins out of the ground and the sweat lodge collapsed over the men inside. He hoped they'd suffocate, but to be sure they died, he planned to set the sweat lodge on fire. Mack grinned thinking about the horror of their deaths.

He had just tossed accelerant onto the sweat lodge when a stone came flying through the air. It hit his temple, and knocked him to the ground. The elderly Indian drummer moved quickly and attacked Mack from behind with a blood-curdling shriek. Jeff, who had come to, maneuvered his body and tripped Mack just at the right moment so that he fell face first into the fire.

Back at the flamenco camp Emile, dragging Lupe, and Trevor, holding his gun on the remaining flamencos, were retreating from the dancers towards the sweat lodge. It sounded like Mack needed assistance. Emile wanted to fuck the woman so badly he was almost ready to do her right then and there. He was glad he had the video going and he could enjoy watching this scene later. Just then he heard a click, and felt cold gun metal on his neck. Another gun was aimed at Trevor. One of the flamencas, who'd gone to bed, had returned with a weapon when she'd heard the commotion, and signaled by Lydie, she had been ready too.

"Let her go, now," said a deep feminine voice.

Emile hesitated. The gun pushed more firmly against his head. Sex or death? He knew he couldn't have sex fast enough, although this whole scene was forcing him closer and closer to climax. If he didn't die, this was going to be a great video.

"Sure, *es muy feo*, she's pretty ugly, anyway."

And he pushed Lupe hard in the direction of the fire, hoping she'd get burned. Emile was just turning to attack the person holding the gun when he was whacked on his head. Howling, he fell to his hands and knees, blood streaming down his face. He didn't look so pretty anymore. The person holding the gun kicked him in the head with her boot, and he fell over on his side. She gave him one last vicious kick in the groin. He shrieked, and then she shot him in his leg.

"OWWWWW!! Why did you do that?"

Lupe's father and the other dancers subdued Trevor as Emile howled.

With the help of the Indian drummer, the vets had escaped from the sweat lodge and overcome Mack. Trevor and Mack were soon tied up, lying face down in the dirt. Emile was sobbing in a fetal position and holding his hands over his leg. The camp host had heard the commotion and called the state troopers. Everyone could hear the sirens getting louder and could see lights flashing in the distance. The Indians, the wounded vets and the flamencas stood around their captives. The vets looked terrible but they felt terrific. They had survived an attempt on their lives, and at least for that moment, they no longer felt crazy or disabled. This had been a *great* sweat lodge.

Near the other fire Lupe's father and mother enveloped their daughter in a hug. She was sobbing. Lydie still held the gun on Emile, who moaned and swore. Lupe wanted her mother to shoot Emile again, but the state police had just arrived and Lydie didn't want to be arrested.

A few minutes later one officer was attending to the bleeding man while the other heard what had happened from the people standing. Everyone explained that the men had attacked them and that one man had been shot while trying to kidnap and rape the young woman. The troopers asked the two women and the Indian man to accompany them to the Alamosa police station for a statement and offered to take them to hospital afterwards. They declined the latter, not wanting to be anywhere near Emile, who had been whisked off in an ambulance. The state troopers ran identification on Mack, Trevor and Emile and were pleased to get a number of hits, including some that would involve the FBI.

The next day *Las Brujas Buenas* drove off towards New Mexico. The Indians and most of the vets waved goodbye. But the two friends, Jeff and Juan, decided to go along with the flamenco group as protection. Lupe's mother was happy to have them. She nicknamed the amputee Corazón, and the mangled face vet she called Bravo. They would do something decent with the rest of their lives.

* * *

Joy's childhood home looked worn out, with peeling paint, pots of dead plants, and a weedy lawn. An old picture of an Easter bunny appeared in one window, and a Halloween pumpkin in another. No one answered the door. Joy peered through one of the windows but didn't see anyone. She did hear the TV. She knocked again. Finally they heard footsteps. She trembled as the door opened.

"Can I help you?" A slight barefoot woman in a bathrobe with hair pulled back in a bun looked at them. The screen door remained between them, locked from the inside.

"Mom? It's me. Joy."

The woman put her hand up to her face and looked closer through the screen door. The young woman who stood before her didn't look anything like the child who'd left home all those years ago. But the voice was the same. "Joy? Joy? Is that really you?"

The older woman fumbled with the lock on the screen door and finally got it open. Lucy stood back while the two hugged each other. It was a genuine hug. Both were crying. Tears swelled up in Lucy's eyes. She thought of her parents back in Killeen and hoped they weren't worrying about her. She was going to have to send them a postcard: "Hi Mom and Dad, doing great. Met lots of..." What should she say? "...very unusual people?" "...Christians?" "...people I could save?"

"Mom, this is Lucy. I gave her a ride. She wanted to come to Littleton." Joy didn't say anything more, but her mom seemed to understand. She gave Lucy a hug which brought even more tears to Lucy's eyes. She pulled the young women inside and closed the screen door leaving the inner door open. A warm wind blew in the scent of cut grass from the neighbors' yard and flushed the stale air out the back. Joy's mother pulled her daughter down on the sofa and held her hand as Joy told her story.

Later that evening before their meal, Lucy asked to say a prayer. "Thank you, Lord, for all you have given us. We are so grateful." She paused. She didn't know what else to say except, "Amen."

* * *

George and Alice talked in the tree for a long time. They had gone through the first and second courses and George felt like taking a break. He wished he had a good cigar, but Alice indicated that this was definitely a non-smoking restaurant. "How about dessert?" He loved a good pie, and he thought maybe Alice would indulge him because he had consumed everything on the menu. It was hard to swallow it all. Some of it he had almost forgotten.

Brushing her hair back from her face, Alice looked at George. "You know, we do have a dessert menu. Just desserts, nothing else. Are you sure you're ready for this?" She peered at him.

"Sure, I'll take any dessert."

"Coming right up, sir, your just desserts."

Alice pulled out a list that included the names Cindy Sheehan, Celeste Zappala, and Jean Prewitt, as well as those of other mothers and fathers who'd lost children in Iraq. She handed it to George and then unrolled another long list with names of the war injured including Peter Damon, the wounded soldier in Michael Moore's movie *Fahrenheit 911*.

"Oh, God, not them." The former president put his head in his hands.

"Yes, them," Alice said. "You know, if every president who sends men and women into war had to face each parent or loved one left behind, and face all the wounded, he or she might think really, really hard about whether the war was worth it." Alice held the list in front of George's face.

She continued. "What if there had been a draft when you started the Iraq War? And your daughters had been sent? And one came home in a flag-draped casket and the other returned without limbs and her beautiful face horribly disfigured?"

Alice suddenly felt flooded with rage. She had worked many years on controlling her anger, finding it a very useful emotion to acknowledge internally, but a very negative emotion to manifest to others. She tossed the second list to George and then she dropped down to another branch, doing a Cirque du Soliel move quite grace-fully in her long skirt and without revealing her legs above mid calf. She then hung upside down from her knees and let her beautiful arms dangle. When Alice flipped herself up, her ribbon was gone, and her hair flowed like a lion's mane around her flushed face. Her eyes sparkled. The angry emotions were transformed. Six inches from his face, Alice looked directly into George's eyes. And he didn't shift them, as he had so many times before.

"Just put yourself in their places, George. Be a father who has lost a child in this war. Maybe you *did* think the Iraq War was justified. Maybe you *did* believe this war was part of the war against terror. But we've just gone through the first and second courses and you've acknowledged to me that this was not true." Alice said the last words very slowly.

George clutched the lists of just desserts. Tears welled up in his eyes and a few fell down his face. He was very familiar with the first name on the first list. He thought back to the summer of 2005 when Cindy Sheehan had camped down the road from his ranch, refusing to leave until he came out and talked with her about her son, Casey, who had lost his life the year before in Iraq. He *had* met with her briefly shortly after her son had died, but she had become embittered as more information came out over the following year, and finally she had demanded another meeting, which he refused. From then on she campaigned against the war, leading to her camp just down the road from George's ranch. Many people had joined her in Crawford, and with little else in the news, Camp Casey had become a big story. And when the news kept showing him mountain biking while other young soldiers were getting blown up in Baghdad, George had not known what to do. The Architect, dealing with his own accusers, couldn't fully participate in a Cindy smear campaign. But there were plenty of others ready to criticize Cindy, and they tried. It didn't really stick, though, as most people were sympathetic to a parent who had lost a child, especially when the parent feels, strongly, that someone is to blame. It wasn't an act of nature, or a horrible, unpreventable disease, or even a car accident that had killed Casey. It was an unjustified, totally elective war, and George started that war.

"Why didn't you just go out and meet with her?" Alice asked.

"You know, my wife asked me the same question. Laura even volunteered to go out and talk with her. I wouldn't let her go, and I couldn't go either. I just couldn't face her anger. I might have gotten angry myself."

Alice sat back. "That's bull."

He examined the lists in his hands. "You want to know the honest truth? Cindy Sheehan was the beginning of realizing that I might have been wrong. No one knew that while I was riding around on my bicycle, I was thinking how I should have done things differently. But I didn't know what to do." George put his head back in his hands and cried some more.

Alice saw that he truly seemed remorseful. Maybe George really didn't know what to do in 2005 when things started go bad in Iraq and his popularity began to slide. She'd seen remorse in others who'd visited her restaurant. They had also done terrible things, although not on the scale that this man had. The first thing Alice tried to teach them was just to sit and think, and figure out what *not* to do first. For many, prison would be the next step. She wasn't sure if this man was going to go to prison. Maybe. Maybe not. But when you're a public figure and you've made a Huge Horrible Mistake, and you realize it internally, how do you acknowledge it externally? And how do you get everyone else around you to help you make amends? Using the analogy of one of those huge oil tankers, once you've decided you're going in the wrong direction, it takes a long time to turn even slightly, much less completely around.

"Well, George, here we are now. You can't change what happened in the past, but you can look at it honestly, and you can change what happens in the future to some degree. Cindy, Celeste, Jean, and all those other mothers, fathers, grandparents, children, and other loved ones of the dead and wounded are still out there. You can still go talk with them."

George thought back to his experience in the hospital talking with the soldier and his family. That had actually gone better than he'd thought. They had listened to him, even that Jezebel sister. And the family had forgiven him. The soldier who'd lost his limbs had forgiven him. Was it possible that others would forgive him? Were there any precedents amongst other presidents? Hey, that sounded good; maybe he could use that in a speech someday. Precedents amongst presidents.

He wondered if any other presidents had started unnecessary wars. Well, Kennedy had with Vietnam, but then he got assassinated, and while many had loved him before he died, almost everyone loved him afterwards. Could he get himself assassinated? No, even if he did, now he was an ex-president. That really wouldn't do anything for his posterity. Kill himself? Interestingly, no president had ever suicided. Why was that? Other executives committed suicide after abysmal failures. His mind returned to apologies and forgiveness. He was a Christian, and as such he knew that more than half the New Testament had to do with forgiveness. Christians would forgive him, and if he understood other religions correctly, non-Christians would forgive him, too. Jews had Rosh Hashanah and Yom Kippur, and Buddhists had Compassion. He didn't know what the Muslims had, but they probably had something on forgiveness, except for those damned fundamentalists who started this whole thing.

"That's not really true." Alice stared at him, crossing her arms over her chest. "Who was Saddam's ally in the 1990s? Who supported the Saudis through most of the twentieth century? Whose entire economy is built around oil, and didn't care much about conservation or renewable energy? Yes, those 9/11 killers were cowardly murderers, and they were all Muslims, most of them from Saudi Arabia. But would you brand all Christians as barbarians for the acts of Timothy McVey or Eric Rudolph?"

Alice gazed at George sympathetically. It was hard to learn new things in your mid-sixties. But he was an ex-president. He still wielded incredible power and could do something to repair this Huge Horrible Mess he'd inflicted on America.

"Put yourself into the shoes of the mothers and fathers who lost their children in Iraq, or in the shoes of a parent who's lost a soldier to suicide."

George shuddered. He couldn't imagine that.

Alice changed the subject, seemingly. "Did you ever read *Madame Bovary*?"

"No, ma'am, that was one of those books that I'm sure I was supposed to read in high school or college. My wife probably read it." He looked at his bare feet and thought about his wife and how good she was.

"One of the lessons of *Madame Bovary* is about hubris, pretense, and how much harm you can cause by doing something you know nothing about. In this story there was a man who believed he could treat the clubfoot of a young boy, although the man knew nothing about surgery, and the boy could walk. He didn't need anything done to his foot. It was the man's vanity, and pompous self-importance, that made him operate on this youngster. The leg looked straight for a few days, but the inevitable infection affected the wound, gangrene set in, and the boy would have lost his life if a proper surgeon hadn't intervened and saved him, albeit now without a foot and unable to walk. "

The analogy went over his head. "Don't you get it?" Alice asked. "Both Iraq and the United States have gangrene now. You screwed around with something that you didn't know anything about. I'm not sure who's going to come in and 'save the day,' but you can take responsibility for your part, here and there. You can do something to keep the gangrene from spreading and killing us all."

George looked surprised. There? In Iraq? She had to be kidding. It was going to be hard enough to do something here. There were thousands of families of the dead and there were even more families of the wounded in the United States. This was going to be utterly impossible. He rubbed his forehead and his eyes.

Alice spoke again. "It's not impossible. You just need to concentrate on it, to the exclusion of everything else. Stop fundraising. Stop going to parties. How about exercising with wounded vets instead of celebrities? Look at all the AA literature again. Even though you gave up drinking, a lot of people think you're just a 'dry drunk,' that you never really accepted AA in your heart, especially the part about making amends. And read your Bible and other great literature like *Madame Bovary*. Do you still have that list Mother Nature and the librarian gave you?"

"How do you know about that?" George snapped.

"Women know about a lot of things," Alice said, stretching up to the branch above her and easing out her back. The conversation with this man had enlivened her and she really did look beautiful, even though he couldn't figure out how old she was.

"It doesn't matter how old I am," she said. "Just think about what I've said and what we talked about. You can take the menus with you. I'm thinking about retiring. This last war has really done me in. It's just a repeat of Vietnam. Although this time, people tried to prevent it before it started. That really was amazing. But you went ahead with it anyway, George."

Alice began singing to the tune of that old Bee Gees song, *I started a joke*. "You started a war, and set the whole world crying."

Tears welled up in her eyes. She didn't want to tell George, but she'd lost her only son in Vietnam, not long after that song by Arlo Guthrie immortalizing her came out. Alice had been a single mom but she'd kept her son in activities where he could interact with men. He had loved baseball and Cub Scouts. She'd wanted him to take piano; he liked music, however he'd told her, "Mom, if there's a war, scouts will prepare me better than piano lessons." Then there was a war, and maybe scouts had been helpful. He'd almost made it back. Five days before the end of his tour, his helicopter had been hit, and he'd lost his life in the crash. There'd been no badge for helicopter crash survival. Alice closed up her restaurant and wandered around India and Thailand with all the other hippies in the 1970s. It was a very mixed-up time with way too much hashish and too many men, but eventually she'd found a retreat in northern Thailand and slowly found herself. Alice returned to the United States and re-opened her restaurant, although it was quite different, and she was different. Along with nutritious tasty food, she served compassion, and often her customers, the regular ones, had compassion awakened in themselves.

This last customer, though, was her toughest. Unlike most of them, she'd see in the news what this man did or didn't do. He could never not be an ex-president. "I've got one more recommendation for your book list," Alice said. "*The Buddhist and the Terrorist* by Satish Kumar. And now we need to stop and say goodbye."

"Oh, sure." George took one last look at Alice. He knew he'd never see her again. He didn't know the words, but what he saw was a living Kwan Yin, a goddess of compassion. Wrinkled, tired, worn, but still beautiful and wise, way beyond any of those so-called advisors he'd had at the White House.

George reached out to shake her hand just as she reached hers towards him. A current passed through their fingers. She looked into his eyes, and he didn't avoid them as he often had with people who tried to look honestly at him. Endless compassion and truth were what he felt as he let go of her hand and climbed down the tree.

He didn't look up until he got to the bottom, and when he did, he couldn't see anything beyond leaves and branches. But he could hear her singing, *"You can get anything you want at Alice's restaurant...."*

Chapter 18

Joy's mom, Alma, had made a big breakfast for Lucy and Joy, who had surprisingly good appetites. After breakfast, Lucy asked if they could go to Columbine. Alma had visited there over the last ten years, and prayed mostly for Joy. She had gotten to know some of families of the victims over time. Maybe someone Alma had met would be there, and she'd be able to introduce Joy, the daughter she thought she'd lost.

It was Saturday and there weren't many people around Columbine High School. A memorial had recently been completed in adjacent Clement Park. Alma had helped fundraise for this in an effort to deal with her own sorrow. She'd had to go door-to-door requesting money from people in the community. Alma became stoic as she'd performed her task. She didn't get offended if people weren't interested. Surprisingly, some people who had reacted with indifference or hostility sent donations a few days or even weeks later. Alma learned patience, the greatest lesson of these years without Joy.

The three women stood at the memorial site overlooking the school. Some recently planted trees were still quite small, but Alma could see them twenty to forty years from now, when they'd provide good shade and beautiful fall leaves. Lucy knelt and began to recite the 23rd Psalm, *"The Lord is my shepherd, I shall not want...."*

Joy thought of a phrase from a Lucinda Williams song, *Repeat the 23rd Psalm*, and wondered where things might have gone wrong for Eric Harris and Dylan Klebold. How had they gone from happy toddlers to teenagers with weapons killing and wounding dozens and aiming to destroy the whole school? She had seen Michael Moore's movie, *Bowling for Columbine*, and she thought he'd figured out part of the puzzle. Littleton was the home of Lockheed, and many of the Columbine parents worked there producing "weapons of mass destruction." But there were other towns with weapons industries and they didn't have school shootings. It had to be something within the kids, maybe partly related to their families. The violent video games they watched incessantly. And the access to weapons. And the bullying. And the extreme anger of Eric, in particular, the leader of the two. The need to feel like a hero, albeit a dark one. Why hadn't he talked with anyone? Eric had written that he hoped a hundred kids didn't die. Who was on Eric's "live" list? And Dylan had told a kid not to go to school that day. They had some empathy. There was some ambivalence towards their planned violence.

What, if anything, could have tipped them away from their violent actions?

While Lucy prayed, Joy imagined the beginning of a conversation where things went right, instead of wrong: *"Mom and Dad, I feel really, really bad about school. Most of the other kids hate me. I wish they were dead."*

"Son, I'm sorry you feel this way. Let's talk." And as the dad talked with the son, the mom removed all the weapons from their home. These simple words and actions perhaps could have unraveled the tragedy before it happened.

Lucinda Williams' words about understanding where things went wrong were still running through Joy's mind as Lucy finished her prayer. She turned and noticed her mom talking to two men who must have arrived after Lucy had begun. Lucy was still kneeling, eyes closed, praying silently now. Jesus, Joy thought, she is one religious kid. She reminded Joy of all the Catholic parishioners in churches she'd visited in Mexico. She never found what she was looking for in those *iglesias*, but she liked going into them, dark cool respites from the maddening Mexican sunshine.

Alma interrupted Joy's reverie. "Joy, I'd like you to meet some friends."

"Hello," said the taller of the two men, "I'm Joel and this is Matthew." Both men reached their hands towards Joy. "We've met your mom here before and we're so glad to meet you."

Matthew added, "The prodigal daughter."

Alma looked a little embarrassed and Joel glanced at Matthew. Joy folded her arms across her ample chest. Another moment where things might go wrong.

"He wasn't meaning to be critical," Joel said.

"We're just so glad to meet you and know that you've returned to your mother," said Matthew.

Joy took a deep breath and looked at the placard with the names of the Columbine dead. Kids who didn't come home from school that day and would never come home. She looked at her mom, frail and trembling. Joy had never understood until that moment the power that children have over their parents. The power and the responsibility.

"*Con mucho gusto*. I'm very pleased to meet you, too." Joy unfolded her arms and shook hands with the two men. Lucy came over and she was introduced to the newcomers.

Alma explained that Joel and Matthew were Air Force Academy faculty. Joel, who was Jewish, was a professor of philosophy, and Matthew, a Baptist, was a biology teacher. Matthew had been one of the leaders of a faculty/student group called The Heathen Flight, which aggressively proselytized non-Born Again Christians and non-Christians with flyers for Mel Gibson's *Passion Play*, evangelical emails, and crosses placed on dorm doors. Students who wouldn't attend chapel after breakfast were escorted back to their dorms with chants dooming them to burn in hell.

Joel was one of the first faculty to protest against these discriminatory activities. He rarely attended synagogue services, but he often sat before a Torah which had survived the Nazis in Poland and had been brought to Colorado Springs Air Force Academy as a symbol of freedom. He'd seen the ugliness on the faces of the chanting evangelicals and the intimidated looks on the faces of the other cadets. It was the Nazis and the Jews all over again.

Joel and Matthew met one day when Joel loudly interrupted the chanting led by Matthew. Their argument almost came to blows, but another teacher intervened and this led to faculty meetings where the issues were discussed, often heatedly. At one point Joel realized that Matthew was trying to convert him, which was an absolutely ridiculous proposition. Joel burst out laughing, which prompted fervent praying by Matthew. That meeting was eventually adjourned because one man couldn't stop laughing and the other couldn't stop praying.

The next gathering held at the Columbine memorial was an inter-faith service for those faculty who wanted to attend. Columbine had been chosen as a place of common ground. Everyone, no matter their religious background, could relate to the victims and understand that there could be a universal compassionate response to suffering. This meeting was the beginning of transformation for this group, and eventually things changed at the Air Force Academy. Matthew and Joel, much to their surprise, became friends, and they visited Columbine regularly. On one of their visits they met Alma.

Joy could see that the three older people had really connected and were delighted to see her. She smiled at her mom, who appeared years younger as she smiled back. Lucy noticed a holy connection, a golden glowing web arcing between the two men and two women. "Thank you, Lord, you've heard my prayer." Lucy took a piece of paper out of her backpack, wrote something on it and pinned it to the message board where others had left notes. As they walked back to their cars, they looked up to the mountains and saw a rainbow stretching from Columbine towards Alma's home. This could have seemed cliché, however rainbows are common in the western states, and like shooting stars, can be interpreted as responses of hope from the universe. Which was just how Joel, Matthew, Alma, Lucy and Joy experienced that beautiful natural phenomenon.

Later that day, after dinner was finished, the three women sat in Alma's family room and Lucy talked about her pilgrimage to honor the dead. Lucy knew that everyone was going to die. Her favorite literary hero, Sophocles' Antigone, had said so twenty-five hundred years ago. But the question was how one died. The massacred didn't have a chance to choose. Their deaths came not from disease, natural phenomena, accidents, or old age but from someone, usually a he, deciding to kill other human beings.

Alma, a western history buff, described the Sand Creek, Colorado massacre of 1864. Occurring during the Civil War, this was not as well known as the 1890 Wounded Knee, South Dakota killing which happened at the end of the Indian Wars. But more people died in Sand Creek, and the crime was more heinous, if any massacre can be classified as worse than another. Six hundred Cheyenne and Arapahos, with their families, had camped by the Sand Creek, water that flowed into the Arkansas River in southeastern Colorado. These Indians had given up fighting and believed that they were under the protection of the US military. Chief Black Kettle had reported to Fort Lyon the previous day and was flying the white flag over his tribe's encampment. Colonel John Chivington had also reported to Fort Lyon and been told the Indians were peaceful. But Chivington hated Indians, and with seven hundred alcohol-fueled men, he descended upon the Indian families, who had few weapons. The heavily armed militia raped, mutilated, killed, and scalped at least two hundred Indians, most of them women and children. Some weeks later in Denver, Chivington, boasting of his accomplishment to an adoring crowd, brandished scalps of pubic hair.

Joy and Lucy imagined the horror of having your genitalia cut out of your body. "How could they do that?" Joy asked. "Beasts. Creatures from hell. *Diablos muy malcriados.*" Lucy murmured a prayer for the dead.

"I've sometimes wondered if any of those men regretted what they did," Alma said. "I want to think some of them did and in some way atoned for their horrible acts. But maybe they didn't. Maybe some military from the Sand Creek massacre killed more Indians at Wounded Knee twenty-six years later."

Then Alma explained about Wounded Knee. It was December 29 1890 and one Indian group, under their leader Big Foot, had agreed to surrender but still had their weapons. A struggle between an Indian and a soldier resulted in a gunshot which incited the military to fire. After the smoke cleared, one hundred fifty Indians and twenty-five soldiers lay dead. This was the last massacre of Indians by US soldiers. Perhaps the collective guilt of White America towards Indians had finally overflowed into awareness, and it was all the more poignant for some Americans when they learned that the movement which underlay Wounded Knee was basically spiritual. Called the Ghost Dance, Alma explained, this new religion, inspired by the visions of a Nevada Pauite, Wovoka, had swept the Plains Indians. The military didn't know what to do with people who ignored admonitions to behave like Christians. Wovoka advocated dancing (a form of prayer for the Indians), a return to all Native ways, and a complete renunciation of alcohol. Wovoka had preached that the earthworld would perish, but the Indians would be reborn into a new world of eternal existence, free from suffering.

Lucy was astonished as she heard Alma's words. This Pauite prophecy was very similar to the prediction of the Rapture. But the Rapture, as Lucy knew, had been prophesied originally by an Englishman, John Darby, half a century earlier. Could Wovaka have known about John Darby and the Rapture? It seemed unlikely. Hesitantly, she mentioned her thoughts to Alma and Joy.

Joy responded, "I read something about the collective unconsciousness from Carl Jung, a Swiss psychiatrist who lived in the early to mid 1900s. There's something in our minds that's pretty much all alike for all humans. It's not just Christian or Indian or anything else, it's human. It's the return to the garden, the return to home."

As Joy was speaking, Alma had moved to the desk in the corner and was tapping away at her computer. "Here's some of Wovoka's words," she said, "translated: *Jesus is now upon the earth. He appears like a cloud. The dead are still alive again.... When the time comes there will be no sickness and everyone will be young again.*"

Lucy sat back, dazed. Darby and Wovoka had lived at different times in completely different worlds, and Carl Jung had even lived later in another completely different world. She spoke a biblical passage she knew well, 1 Thessalonians 4:16-17: *"For the Lord himself will descend from heaven with a cry of command, with the archangel's call, and with the sound of the trumpet of God. And the dead in Christ will rise first; then we who are alive, who are left, shall be caught up together with them in the clouds to meet the Lord in the air; and so we shall always be with the Lord."*

The words hung in the air. No one said anything. Alma noticed how fatigued the others appeared. She felt tired herself. They hugged goodnight and Alma and Joy went to their bedrooms. Lucy stretched out on the sofa in the living room and drifted off to sleep.

Hours later she began to dream. An Indian man and a preacher stood nearby but appeared not to be aware of each other. The Indian began to dance and pray. The other man stood still and spoke in his own language. There was fire, and Lucy heard cries of people some distance away. An older woman came up to Lucy and took her by the hand and led her away from the two men. As they started to walk towards the crying people, the older woman gave Lucy an antique map of America. She opened it, but then woke up. Lucy could still feel the map's texture and see its warm light.

Lucy stretched and sat on the edge of the sofa. She thought about how far she'd traveled. On the wall she saw a *National Geographic* map of the United States. Where would she go next? Northwest to Ruby Ridge, Idaho where Randy Weaver and his family had shot it out with government authorities and a Federal Marshall and Randy's wife and son had died? Ruby Ridge had been one of the triggers for Waco and Waco had triggered Oklahoma City. Lucy remembered reading that Randy Weaver still spoke passionately about his hatred of the government at gun shows, but he couldn't own any firearms, due to his weapons-related convictions. Ruby Ridge seemed more like an old-fashioned gunfight. It didn't fit with the idea of her pilgrimage.

Alma had not shut her computer down. Lucy crossed the room and sat down at the desk. She googled "American massacres" and was discouraged to see so many entries. The worst school massacre in American history had happened in Bath, Michigan in 1927. Forty-five people, most of them children, had been killed in an explosion set by a local man. Lucy had never even heard of the Bath massacre. Would people forget the massacres of her own life eighty years into the future?

She looked at the map on the wall again. One of the school shootings had occurred in Red Lake, Minnesota. A disappointed, suicidal teenager had killed nine people and then himself. These shootings didn't get as much publicity as Columbine, but the deaths had a major effect on the community of mostly Ojibwa Indians. Lucy got up and walked over to the wall. She noticed that the source of the Mississippi was very near to Red Lake. She traced her finger down from northern Minnesota, past Iowa, Missouri, and Arkansas on the left, and Wisconsin, Illinois, Kentucky, and Tennessee on the right, ending with Louisiana cut in two pieces by the great river. Lucy had never seen the Mississippi but she remembered the day she'd first learned about it, as the name had a wonderful sound.

Lucy's finger ended in New Orleans. Poor old New Orleans. Lucy could remember the news scenes of this tragedy. She'd been thirteen years old, and her parents had borrowed a TV from the neighbors to watch the horrifying effects of Hurricane Katrina, which hit August 29 2005. The results were well known: the rich and middle class were evacuated, while the poor remained behind. Broken-down levees fell apart and up to twenty feet of water flooded almost the entire city. Few arrangements had been made to organize or evacuate the remaining people, many of whom overran the Superdome and Convention Center. Widespread looting occurred with thugs and gangs taking weapons and ammunition from stores. Anarchy raged outside — and inside — the shelters, with people robbed, raped, and shot. Hospitals filled with seriously ill fell apart as generators failed and supplies ran out. The first emergency teams were completely overwhelmed and exhausted and more help, organized and armed with guns, took several days to arrive, in spite of anguished pleas for assistance.

As the hurricane raged, the president went to a Republican Party fundraiser in California. His first speech regarding the response of the Federal Emergency Management Agency (FEMA) didn't make much sense. "Heck of a job, Brownie," he'd said, using the nickname of FEMA's director while the TV news anchors showed footage of the disaster and survivors begging for help; over a thousand people died and thousands more lost their homes and all their belongings. It didn't seem like America.

Some of the Katrina families had resettled in Killeen, and Lucy knew some of the kids. Many were still in shock, frightened for their future; others were bitter, having seen society fall apart. A few kids were scary, and Lucy generally stayed away from them. Lucy knew that New Orleans had been partially rebuilt, but the rip in society hadn't been healed. The aftermath of Katrina had affected too many people, and others like her could see the consequences of indifference and inaction, and the huge gulf between the rich and the poor.

Her parents, along with others in her church, had viewed the flooding of New Orleans as part of the prophecy of the world's end. Some of the Katrina survivors had joined Lucy's church. They'd previewed the end of the world in person and never wanted to go through it again. When the final tribulation came, they wanted to be raptured into Heaven and not be left behind again on a hellish earth.

Lucy wondered if Katrina's devastation was a man-made tragedy or part of the Revelations prophecy. She felt strongly that New Orleans had to be her final destination on her pilgrimage. As she looked at the map, she knew that it would be her last stop before she returned to Killeen. It would be a long walk from Littleton to Red Lake. Then there'd be a lengthy trip down the Mississippi. She didn't think that she could make it to Virginia Tech or the Amish school in Pennsylvania, but she'd pray for them, somewhere on the river. She wondered how she would travel, but she didn't worry. Lucy had gotten this far, and the Lord would help her.

After mailing what Lucy hoped was a reassuring postcard to her parents the next day, Joy drove Lucy beyond the Denver airport to the vast agricultural fields of eastern Colorado. Joy and her mother had tried to buy her a bus pass, good for two months, but Lucy had insisted that she wanted to walk. As Joy drove west towards home, she looked in the rearview mirror and saw Lucy give her a last wave. Joy nodded to her Virgin of Guadeloupe and sent a prayer from her heart for a safe journey for her friend. Lucy had promised to send a postcard when she got back to Killeen, which she thought would be late October. Joy had decided she would go looking for her if she hadn't heard anything by Halloween. But first she needed to spend some time with her mother.

Lucy would be okay. Somehow, just like Dorothy in *The Wizard of Oz*, people would help her. That's the way things happened for people who were on a mission from God.

* * *

As soon as the motorcycles were fixed, Darrell and Bill drove straight to the Columbine memorial, where Darrell got down on his knees and prayed for the dead and injured. Bill looked over the site and frowned. He imagined being a target for a shooter and shifted uneasily. He didn't know why those two students had killed all those kids and that teacher. He knew people who had much worse childhoods and they never tried to kill anyone.

Bill agreed with General Wes Clark who said, "If you want to play with guns, there's a place for you. It's called the Army." Bill had been one of those kids who liked to play with guns. He'd loved video games, too, like Eric and Dylan, but he'd never wanted to kill anyone, until he got to Iraq and realized he'd have to kill or be killed.

Bill noticed a bulletin board where people left condolences and quickly found Lucy's signed message: *Joy, Alma, and I are here with Joel and Matthew to pray for the victims and those still suffering.* Who were they? What was it about this girl? And where in the world was she now? Bill wondered why he was trying to find someone who obviously didn't want to be found. But if he gave up, then Darrell would eventually be the one who found her, and that would be unacceptable.

Bill felt like he'd been given a mission, and he'd never given up or failed any mission, except for shutting down those assholes from Abu Ghraib. But he hadn't known they were freed until Luke had attacked him in the barn. Bill swore silently, thinking about those torturers. They were as insane as these Columbine killers had been. "Hey, Darrell, there's a note here from Lucy. She was here with Joy, Alma, Joel, and Matthew. Do you have any idea who they are?"

Darrell thought for a few moments, shrugged and shook his head. There were churches all over the United States with believers. Probably folks from a local church, he thought, although Joel didn't sound Christian. Darrell wondered if he was a converted Jew. It dawned on him that maybe Lucy had done a conversion. Darrell felt joy spread through him as he considered this possibility. Lucy was really something. She would be a great wife. He just had to find her. "I don't know who they are. But I think she's going to Red Lake, Minnesota. Red Lake was the next school shooting that happened after Columbine."

"Okay, well, let's get some maps and head northeast. You aren't going without me, and I guess I'm not going without you," Bill replied.

"Let's roll, uh, uh…."

"It's okay. Just call me the Antichrist," said Bill. He looked at Darrell and smiled. "I'm not going to hurt you. You can even try to convert me. We have a thousand miles ahead of us. Do your best."

Darrell nodded. That was exactly what he was thinking.

Chapter 19

George was really tired after talking to Alice. Or maybe it was the tree climbing. His feet, now back in his boots, hurt. He had been unable to find his socks after he'd climbed down from the tree, and the rough leather was creating blisters on his heels. He felt the air pressure change and heard thunder as the storm broke. The rain started falling in hard drops before he made it home. He was soaked through in moments but then a few minutes later he happily eased his body into the hot water of his indoor spa.

George had closed his eyes when the skylight above him suddenly cracked. Pieces of plastic fell and a flood of cold water splashed down on his body. Before he could climb out of the tub, he was hit with yet more water and debris. "Jesus Christ. The goddamned skylight broke." George hauled himself out and grabbed a towel.

Water continued to pour in, and the bathroom soon looked like it had been hit by a hurricane. George shivered, and it was not just due to the temperature. Anything that reminded him of Hurricane Katrina brought back one of the most shameful memories of his presidency. He knew he'd really screwed up. He'd been in vacation mode and hadn't seen any reason to cancel that California fundraiser even when he knew people were suffering. And he'd really stuck his foot in his mouth joking around about the loss of Senator Trent Lott's second home and having a drink someday with his good buddy on a newly-built porch. Jesus, that was a dumb, insensitive thing to say. Why hadn't someone told him not to joke around? And he thought being funny was a good way to leaven...levitate...whatever that word was, to make people laugh. Katrina wasn't funny. But he couldn't think about that now. He had his own mess to worry about.

He put some towels down on the bathroom floor but they were immediately soaked. Water and debris continued to pour in from the roof. George roared with anger. Why was this happening? He felt disgusted and inadequate. Squelching through the wet carpet, he ran down the hallway to the living room to call for help. As he picked up the phone, George noticed that the television was on but without any sound. It was some kind of war movie. He punched in some numbers for the grounds manager, put the phone up to his ear, lay back on the couch and listened to the dial tone. An inane recorded voice began reciting endless options. Resigned, George closed his eyes and listened, waiting for the option to speak with a real human being.

Suddenly the sound of helicopters burst into the room. Startled, George opened his eyes. The sound boomed from the TV, but George was shocked by what was happening to his living room. The room was completely dark, with the exception of the light coming from the TV screen, and it was filling up with swirling dirty water. About a foot and a half high, the flood was soaking up through the cushions on the sofa. George tried to yell but couldn't hear himself over the din of the helicopters. He tried to stand, but he seemed stuck to the sofa, and when he looked he found that thick vines had entwined themselves around his lower legs. What the hell was going on?

The helicopter noise subsided and the screen showed a scene of American soldiers who had invaded the home of Iraqis and had several men handcuffed and kneeling with their faces on the floor. One man pleaded politely in perfect English, saying that he and the others were journalists. A soldier pointed his gun at the Iraqi and told him to "shut the fuck up." The journalist went silent. Even with his own misery swirling around him, George sneered at the cuffed Iraqi journalists with their perfect English. He identified with the American soldier. "Heh, heh, shut the fuck up. I wish I could have told our journalists to do the same. Shut the fuck up, Helen Thomas. And you, too, you goddamn Steven fucking Colbert." George wished some of those American soldiers were here with him in his flooded home. He wondered what movie he was watching. He was going to have to watch it again someday from the beginning once he got this mess cleaned up.

Suddenly the scene on the TV shifted to the back of a truck. The truck bed was full of something, but George couldn't make out what.

Then he realized: it was full of bodies. And they were moving. The *Night of the Living Dead* in Iraq? George was compelled to look. The bodies were alive, but they were piled up as if they were dead. Some of them on the bottom might die if they weren't unloaded soon. George had a sickening *deja vu* feeling, which he recognized from his one visit to the Holocaust museum. He retched but nothing came up.

George tried to turn his head away, but he found it as frozen as if he were wearing a neurosurgical "halo." He tried to close his eyes but they were jammed, pinned open, as if in some sort of opthamological gadget. Not to be able to move or even blink while watching the writhing bodies was utter torture.

The film fast-forwarded to the aftermath of the death of a platoon's most popular soldier. The film then went to slow motion as it depicted the never-ending grief suffered by his fellow soldiers and loved ones at home. This was an awful movie. George felt pure horror. Meanwhile, the water lapped higher, it was now up to his waist. He opened his mouth to scream.

"Even if you could scream, no one would hear you. You're all alone except for me and the soldiers of this movie. It's called *Gunner Palace*, by the way. It's a documentary of your Iraq War."

The deep voice had come from the left of the television set. George slightly moved his non-blinking eyes and was horrified to see that woman – Mother Nature. She swayed gently in a wicker basket suspended from the ceiling, her toes just touching the water, which was surprisingly clear underneath her. Her blue-green gown looked like it was made out of a waterfall glowing with lava light. If George hadn't been so scared, he might have glimpsed parts of her body through the water dress. Piled up above her neck, Mother Nature's hair was festooned with Mardi Gras beads. In the air beside her hovered a table with a cup of coffee and a beignet. On the cup George could see the words Café du Monde.

He understood that much French. If George hadn't gotten it before, he did now. Mother Nature had brought Katrina to Crawford.

The woman smiled. "How does this feel?"

George struggled to get free, but the vines held him tighter to the couch. The television set should have been submerged and shorted out, but somehow it kept rising with the floodwater and continued playing. It now showed a soldier talking about another soldier who had been killed. The television set advanced closer to George and got louder. The water was nearly up to his armpits.

Mother Nature kicked some of the water playfully at George. When the water left her foot it was clean, but by the time it hit George's face, it smelled like sewage, and some excrement plopped onto the crown of his head. He retched again and tears began to run down from his unblinking eyes. Unable to move any part of himself, George couldn't shake off the feces. The television set was now just a few feet from his face. On the screen, another American soldier had died.

Mother Nature, whose chair had moved closer as well, looked at the image of the dead soldier. She aimed the remote and paused on the man's face. "Yes, that man, if he'd lived, *might* have been one of the people to organize the evacuation of New Orleans. He *might* have countermanded the order of the white people who kept the brown people from leaving New Orleans on that Crescent City Connection Bridge into high and dry Gretna. But he wasn't there, because he was dead. He died in Iraq because of you, George. And other people died in New Orleans because of you." She looked at him directly. Only his head and neck were above the water line.

"DEAD. DEAD. DEAD," she boomed.

"Please, help me." The feces dripped down George's face into his mouth. He retched again. The program on the TV seemed to be stuck on an endless loop. One minute it was showing the writhing bodies in the truck and the next the killed American soldiers.

All at once George heard the sound of a dog. He moved his eyes slightly to the right. In spite of his deplorable situation, he felt amazed to see yet another person in the room, a man he'd never met before. Maybe this guy would rescue him.

The man, who looked like Beethoven, sat on an armchair that

floated on the other side of the TV. The poodle he held on his lap growled at George. "It's okay, Atwater, he won't hurt you," the man said in German-accented English.

"Beethoven? Is that you?" asked George, bewildered. Everything was so weird, somehow it didn't surprise him that Beethoven would appear with a poodle, near a waterfall-clothed Mother Nature, in his Crawford ranch home, which was now flooded as badly as New Orleans after Katrina.

"Beethoven? Ha! No! Don't you recognize me?" The man dressed in nineteenth-century clothing considered George with disdain. "No, why would you? You're an American, and from what I understand, you probably didn't take any philosophy classes in college or study the subject on your own." The man who looked like Beethoven frowned with that look that the people of mid-nineteenth century Frankfurt, Germany knew so well. The television conveniently switched to PBS and showed a tombstone which read "Arthur Schopenhauer." The man on the sofa nodded. "That's me."

Who in the heck is Arthur Schopenhauer? thought George. He cursed himself once again for having goofed off in college...and afterwards. And what was this guy doing here in his living room with Mother Nature?

Arthur was thinking the same thing. The nineteenth-century man was well aware that he had died, and although he knew his work would live on, he himself should have returned to the undistinguishable "Will" where he'd been before birth. What was he doing sitting on a sofa with one of his beloved dogs, who was also long since dead, near a gorgeous woman barely clothed in a waterfall and some American guy who seemed destined for drowning? Arthur frowned. This was really going to take some thought.

Mother Nature laughed. "You guys! You just kill me! No one knows everything. Not even one of the most brave independent-thinking brilliant minds that ever lived."

George looked at her hopefully.

"No, not you, mister," she said icily. "I was talking about Arthur here, the man who looks like Beethoven. However, not even he knows everything."

Now both men glared at her. The dog, though, wasn't barking or growling anymore. He was grinning, as dogs sometimes do, and he thumped his tail at the woman in the swinging basket chair.

Arthur frowned. "Atwater, cease."

"Oh, he likes me, Arthur. Almost all animals like me. Most humans do, too, at least some of the time. You do, too, Arthur. You wrote beautifully about nature." She seemed to change, briefly becoming the lovely Elisabet Ney, the artist who had sculpted a bust of Arthur in the year before he died, and who had given him a glimpse of real female beauty: physical, emotional, intellectual and creative. She gave Arthur one more brilliant smile as Elisabet and then transformed back to her Mother Nature form, splashing water with her toes and tossing her Mardi Gras-bead-festooned hair as she swung in the hanging chair.

Arthur was fascinated by this experience of being brought back to life. He was going to have to revise his work, as he hadn't believed in reincarnation before, and except for Elisabet, whom he met at the very end of his life, he hadn't believed that women could be as intelligent and creative as men. "Madame, I'd like to speak more with you about this experience. I may need to revise my philosophy."

George spoke up. "Uh, you know, it's great that you two are enjoying some kind of reminiscences and philosophical discussion, but I'm up to my neck in dirty water, and I am so damn sick of watching the same poor soldier dying on that goddamned TV set. Could you PLEASE help me?" George sobbed as he spoke. More sewage slid into his mouth. He retched, spat, and retched some more.

Arthur considered that all his views on suffering were surely confirmed by the man on the sofa. Mother Nature looked at George and thought the same; however, she also thought of rebirth and regeneration.

She snapped her fingers. As if someone had pulled a giant plug in a huge bathtub, the water began to recede. After the last gurgle disappeared, the vines vanished and the television screen finally went blank. The halo and eye gadget were gone too. George was still covered in smelly muck. He remained still, his only movements his breathing and his blinking eyes.

"What did you learn this afternoon, George?" Mother Nature asked softly as she rocked gently in her wicker chair.

In spite of everything George had just endured, he wanted to say something sarcastic like, "That I should get a different roofing company," but he knew she could bring back the flood, the vines, the torture gadgets and that god-awful *Gunner Palace* with another snap of her fingers.

"In the words of Benjamin Franklin," he replied, "'an ounce of prevention is worth a pound of cure' – and a lot cheaper too. We couldn't have prevented a hurricane, but we could have prevented the damage and we could have saved most of the lost lives."

His body suddenly relaxed and George was able to wipe the shit away from his face. He stretched his arms and legs. In spite of the stench, George felt wonderful. Absence of pain and being able to move were amazing sensations.

"Where are you going to get the money for all that prevention?" Mother Nature continued to sway in her chair and sipped her coffee. Arthur patted Atwater, who grinned, tongue hanging out, and thumped his tail.

"I'm not in office anymore." George looked exasperated and felt annoyed. "I can't do anything now." He cricked his neck and popped his knuckles. Damn, it felt good to move again. He'd never understood that immobility was a form of torture. If he'd still been in office he would have had to get that struck off the list of allowable interrogation techniques.

Mother Nature started to respond but Arthur looked at her and an invisible current seemed to pass between them. "Madame, may I speak here?" She nodded and folded her legs in a lotus position.

Arthur removed Atwater from his lap, rose from his armchair and paced slowly in front of the besmirched man on the sofa. His mind was flooded with new knowledge. "You certainly can do something virtuous. You don't need all this, for example," he said as he gestured to the room, and rooms beyond. "Your daughters are grown up; they have jobs. Your wife, a former librarian, would be quite happy getting all her books from the public library. You two could build a small home in a corner of your ranch and be perfectly happy. You can donate the rest of your assets and property as a veterans' recuperation home. All wounded vets from the wars when you were president can stay here. You can invite them into your humble home, ask for their stories, and their forgiveness. Meanwhile, they can enjoy swimming in your pool, catching your fish, and taking turns tooling around on your ATV and riding on your ten-speed, the one you rode around with Lance."

Arthur had bequeathed almost all his assets to wounded impoverished veterans of the Prussian War, and he was proud to suggest this same plan to a man who evidently had far more wealth than Arthur had ever known. But he was wondering how he knew all these biographical details about this other man. Arthur glanced at Mother Nature and she winked at him to continue. He went on, talking with confidence. Being reincarnated was quite illuminating.

"You could set a good example to everyone else who made vast sums of money during your regime. Shame them into donating their ill-gotten gains to help wounded veterans and repair the infrastructure to prevent tragedies such as Katrina..." (He wondered who she was—he'd known a few wild Katrinas in his day) "...You could also try to reduce the national debt, which I believe you thrust your nation into during your term. You could be the president remembered for his attempts to make amends for his mistakes. The Prodigal President." The nineteenth-century man looked at the twenty-first century man and spoke more softly. "Compassion, sir, the greatest of virtues, that makes all suffering bearable. And you, sir, have the power to invoke it."

Mother Nature looked at Arthur with respect. She knew that he regarded philosophical study, the arts and music, and most importantly, compassion for one's fellow humans, as the greatest of virtues, the virtues that made up for all of life's inevitable suffering. Could suffering elicit compassion from George?

George, meanwhile, was recalling the words "compassionate conservative" from his first presidential campaign. He had really believed this about himself then. He still believed that he was basically a compassionate man. "Well, I'd have to talk to my wife about donating our ranch to the VA. That would be quite a sacrifice."

But George already knew what Laura would say. She was a decent person and very loyal to him. She'd lived in a little one-room apartment in Fort Worth when she'd been a librarian before they had married, and before that she'd grown up in a modest home in west Texas. She'd still have their home in Dallas. Texas had a law of eminent domain. No matter what, one's home could not be taken by the government. But a home, or a ranch, could be *given* to the government. There was no law against gifts, especially from a president to the people.

Mother Nature smiled. "And when you aren't listening to wounded veterans and the families of the dead, you might be reading. I suggest you add to your list some of the extraordinary essays written by Arthur. His works are in all the libraries."

Arthur had been sure his work would last for at least a thousand years and was not surprised at all to learn that his books could be easily found two hundred years after he wrote them. "I'll be happy to give you signed copies, George. Perhaps first, you'd care to clean up."

George stood up. He approached the others to shake their hands, his Texas good manners resurfacing. But when they made faces, George shrugged and staggered towards the kitchen. Over his shoulder he said, "Send me your books, Arthur. Sorry I missed them earlier in life."

"I will." Arthur turned to Mother Nature and said, "Better late than never."

As George disappeared up the stairs, Mother Nature and Arthur remained in the living room, with Atwater licking Mother Nature's bare feet. A bowl of figs appeared between them, and they began to eat as they talked. Mother Nature reverted her appearance back to that of the charming Elisabet Ney, and Arthur felt more relaxed than he'd ever been in his last life. He would definitely have to revise some of his essays, particularly that one on women.

* * *

The next morning when Maria and Charlie learned what had happened in their absence, they were astonished—and relieved that the others were unhurt in the fight against the Abu Ghraibs, as they called the brutes who had attacked the vets and the flamencas. However, the women were worried about Lucy, a seventeen-year-old girl traveling by herself around the United States. They had no idea whether she had allowed Bill to escort her, but knowing how determined she was, they doubted it. But if she had let Bill accompany her, perhaps both of them would be in danger, if other Abu Ghraibs were after Bill. Maria and Charlie knew that Lucy believed that God would protect her, but they wondered if a belief in God would be enough against those from Abu Ghraib? They decided that two women bikers would even the odds.

Maria and Charlie headed east from Great Sands, aiming for Nebraska, where they hoped to find Lucy. If they didn't find her there, then it would be a fast ride to Red Lake, Minnesota. Maria and Charlie had never been to western Nebraska before; they didn't know anyone who had. It was one of the great empty places in the country. They accelerated their motorcycle up to eighty miles per hour. They only slowed down to ask if anyone had seen a young, slim teen with straight light brown hair walking along the road.

As Maria and Charlie searched for Lucy in Nebraska, Bill and Darrell were looking elsewhere. The men decided that Lucy had gotten a ride out of Littleton with those folks mentioned on the memorial board and wondered if she'd stop at Wounded Knee, South Dakota before going on to Red Lake. Although Darrell said Lucy had never gone there before, their church had a mission in Wounded Knee, and some of the men built houses there every summer. As it was also the site of another massacre, Lucy might include it on her pilgrimage. Wounded Knee was the home of the poorest Indian tribe in the United States. People were mistrustful of outsiders — and to some degree, also of themselves — as they'd basically had a civil war in the 1970s between the tribal government and the self-named traditionals. The fighting was brought to national attention when some FBI agents called in were killed.

Looking around after their arrival, Bill knew Wounded Knee wouldn't be the easiest place to be white, and with Darrell it was going to be even harder. Ninety percent of the locals were Native, and many of them looked at the two white men with suspicion. Darrell looked like some kind of cop, and Bill knew he looked ex-military; he couldn't help that.

Darrell scanned the area for a church and was surprised to see a few. He pulled out his Bible and started to read. A few passersby gave them wide berth.

Bill groaned and thought to himself, They'll think we're missionaries, Mormons on their mission. He'd never been accused of being a missionary. "With all due respect, Darrell, please stop reading the Bible. Let's get a drink." Darrell looked askance at him but followed him into a poorly lit bar. A neon sign behind the bartender showed Indians celebrating over the dead body of a yellow-haired man. Everyone — a couple of dozen men — stared at them. Not a good sign, Bill thought. But he knew how to behave in hostile territory. Custer's Last Stand couldn't be any worse than Iraq.

"A longneck." The bartender didn't say anything but he pulled the cap off a beer and slid it to Bill.

"A Dr Pepper, please." The bartender gave Darrell a dirty look and then a can of the soft fizzy drink.

Bill took a long pull off his beer and wiped his mouth with the back of his hand. Darrell popped the top on the can, which sounded very loud in the silence of the bar. But nothing happened. The other drinkers went back to their conversations and Bill and Darrell relaxed.

Later that day they visited the site of the Wounded Knee massacre, but Lucy wasn't there and no one seemed to have seen her. They got out the map and looked at the route to Red Lake. In the southwest corner of Minnesota, directly on the route to Red Lake, they noticed a place called Pipestone where the red rock of peace pipes was chipped out of the earth. All the Indian tribes from miles around regarded it as a place of peace, and remarkably no battles had been fought there for over a thousand years. Darrell and Bill agreed that this unique place was where Lucy might go. It was late in the day and they were tired. Looking at the map again, Darrell suggested nearby Custer State Park to stay overnight and Bill shrugged in agreement.

* * *

Judith was ready to leave the hospital. Her body was stronger and she was able to use her arm stumps and torso muscles to get into her wheelchair, take a shower, and even get dressed if her clothing was hung properly. Nothing was easy, but each time she swore that something was just too ridiculous and impossible, she thought of the injured Iraqis who had no rehab and few resources. She wondered how they survived. Probably just barely, even though she was sure their families helped them the best they could. Just like her family helped her.

Families and friends could be a source of irritation, however. Joseph and Ben had argued about where Judith would go after she left the hospital. Judith had listened for a while, then interrupted them. "Guys, guys, guys. I know I can't live by myself, but I can't live with either of you either."

They had both looked shocked.

"But I'm your brother...."

"But I want to marry you...."

"I'm going to go stay with Grandma in New Orleans." Judith knew she wouldn't have made it this far without the help of these two men who loved her. But they loved her too much. Too much love and help was smothering. Judith's grandmother had always been very relaxed, and Judith wanted to be with someone like that. She also knew that her grandmother needed some help from her and Judith wanted to be a helper instead of just a recipient of help.

"Grandma is so angry at Bush," she'd explained, "I'm going to have to work on calming her down. I've got to persuade her to put away her anti-Bush voodoo display. I agree that Dubya royally screwed us, but he's got to live with his actions the rest of his life. Might as well pray for him and get Grandma to start praying for him."

The men knew they were defeated. On the day of her departure, Joseph helped Judith into the wheelchair and Ben picked up the suitcases. As they headed down the hallway, Judith sang a peace song *a capella*. On the elevator the other riders, doctors and nurses, chimed in, and when the door opened on the first floor, it was as if a heavenly hospital choir was giving Judith a holy send off into the world.

* * *

Lucy was lost. She'd stopped to get some water at a farmhouse, and after the elderly farmer had heard her story, she had offered Lucy an old bicycle. Full of food, Lucy had happily ridden off, but she'd lost her bearings. She stopped and looked at the sky. The sun was setting so she knew which way was west. She was trying to go northeast to Minnesota. Unfortunately the road was going northwest to Wyoming. She hadn't seen any cars for hours. What was she doing out here in western Nebraska? She felt very lonely and wished that Maria and Charlie were there. Even Bill and Darrell would have been okay. Lucy pulled out her Bible, lay down on the grass, and thought about Jesus. She knew he'd been alone in the wilderness as an adult but she wondered about the years when he was a teenager. No one knew where he was during that time. Maybe he'd traveled around like her. Previously she'd thought the notion blasphemous, but now, sitting alone by the side of the road, she wondered what the chances were that Jesus had married and had children. She doubted it. Jesus never had sex, for one thing. Lucy blushed, recalling details of her high school sex education class. She wondered why she was thinking of sex at all, and Bill and Darrell appeared in her mind. Later, Lucy fell asleep with thoughts of Jesus and what it might have been like, if she'd lived two thousand years ago and met Jesus when he was seventeen.

"Are you sure you want to do this?" Jesus asked Lucy.

Lucy looked back at him shyly. "Yes. Don't you?"

"I do. But I don't really know what to do." They sat beside a stream on a bed of moss under a tree. It was summer and the sun was setting. A rough pony tethered nearby ate grass. Otherwise they were alone. "I don't know either."

They kissed, and kissed a lot more. Soon there was a tumble of hands and cheeks and shoulders and hips and thighs and hardness and wetness and then, rapture.

Sometime later they rested in each other's arms, and they fell asleep.

Lucy woke up to millions and millions of brilliant stars overhead. It was the most beautiful night she'd ever seen. She still had the glorious feeling of sleeping in the arms of a beloved. But as she recalled her dream, shock as quick as an electric current surged through her body, and she sat up. Sleeping with Jesus? Kissing Jesus? Making love with Jesus? No. That wasn't right. Lucy blushed and felt terribly ashamed. She looked around for her Bible. It wasn't right to have dreamed of Jesus that way. But she could still feel the wonder of the whole experience. Oh, Lord, she prayed. And that's what she continued to do, under all those bright twinkling stars in western Nebraska.

* * *

"We're sorry, sirs, for this inconvenience. We didn't understand your security clearances. Those individuals who injured you must be apprehended. We have warrants out for their arrests."

Trevor, Mack, and Emile tried not to look too satisfied, but inside they felt incredibly lucky. They didn't know which of their bosses had secured their release, but someone very powerful had helped them and had Luke released too. He would soon join them. Southern Colorado was full of prisons and they easily could have ended up in the Florence Super Max. They knew that other ex-military had been imprisoned for Abu Ghraib. But it would not be them, not today. And they were going to make sure they were never caught again.

It was a bright shining Colorado day with just a little bit of snow on the mountaintops. Emile was on crutches, but his injury was healing and he was surging with feelings of revenge. He knew they had to find Bill and the other veterans, then he'd track down that bitch who shot him and fuck her daughter to death before killing the mother. Luke soon pulled up in a Hummer. He compared injuries with Emile; he had revenge on his mind as well. He'd help them kill Bill and then he'd get the other man and Lucy. The Hummer's black paint was chipped and the bumpers were dented, but the four men were satisfied with the vehicle. They weren't going incognito anymore. The men from Abu Ghraib put on their shades, grinned and piled in.

They headed out of town with the CD player turned up as loud as it could go, singing along to lyrics about a pimp having a bad day. Their contacts had told them that Bill and Darrell were likely heading to the Black Hills or Wounded Knee, so that's the direction they drove. They'd found a suitcase full of money on the floor of the rear seats, and they'd been told there would be ten times that much waiting for them in Las Vegas when they finished the mission. There were other people much higher in rank who wanted Bill and the other vets killed.

The Hummer roared north on I-25. They almost clipped a few Toyotas and Hondas, but those nimble cars were lucky that day and nothing happened to them or their passengers. One of the Honda drivers swore at the Hummer. "Goddamn Hummer. Wasteful, selfish Hummer drivers think they're hot stuff until they run out of gas."

And that's just what happened a couple of hours later, on a lonely stretch of highway in Wyoming. "Fuck! Fuck! Fuck!" screamed Emile as they got out of the vehicle.

"Can't you think of something more original to say?" Trevor replied evenly. Since Luke had been injured and separated from the others, Trevor had taken over leadership of the group. He slipped into meditation mode. Breathe in. Breathe out. Screaming and swearing was not going to make gasoline appear. Trevor had never understood the compassion part of Buddhism, but otherwise, he thought it was a very realistic religion. Life was full of suffering and attachments just made you suffer more. This *bastard* was way too attached and he was making everyone suffer. Trevor thumped Emile on the arm. Hard.

Emile whipped out his gun and aimed it at a fence post twenty feet away. He shot a series of holes from the top to the bottom. Every shot pierced the post straight down the middle. He looked satisfied. And he stopped swearing.

"Okay, we can wait for someone to come by, or one of us can walk up the road." Trevor looked at his map. "Looks like there should be a town about five miles ahead."

He decided to go himself. He really couldn't stand Emile and needed to get away from him for a while. Trevor blamed Emile for their troubles from Abu Ghraib. He got too excited and killed that prisoner when unknowns happened to be observing. And one of those unknowns was Bill. That had been their unraveling. Trevor looked at Emile and thought, I'm going to kill him too, once we've taken care of Bill. He folded up the map and began walking north.

Trevor had their only credit card, the car keys and the cell phone. He wouldn't put it past the others to take off without him. Breathe in. Breathe out. Buddhism, which he'd superficially learned about in a prison program, was great. Bill suffering first. Then Emile suffering. *Adiós* to attachment to their lives. Trevor already felt much better.

Chapter 20

George's home was a complete mess. Some of the gross green mold that had taken over the homes in New Orleans was growing on his furniture and on the floor. He couldn't believe how fast it had appeared.

After showering in the girls' bathroom and changing into some clean clothes, he'd brushed his teeth and swished mouthwash several times, but he couldn't get rid of the taste of feces. He retched and squirted half the tube of Crest into his mouth. Finally, feeling fresher, he returned to the living room.

Here he noticed that floodwater had damaged the photos of him with other world leaders. All his greatest moments were now covered in crud. Suddenly panicked, he thought of Saddam Hussein's pistol. George ran to his study, looked in his desk drawer and groaned. The pistol had been submerged too. "Shit."

George looked for something to clean the gun, but everything was covered in green mold. He took off his clean shirt and frantically rubbed the weapon, his most coveted possession from his days as president. He believed this was the very weapon Saddam had brandished when planning to assassinate George's father.

George finally got the exterior clean, but he could see more mold in the gun barrel. Maybe if he fired it, he'd clear it out. George found the bullets he'd had made especially for this pistol and loaded them. Then he went over to one of the windows, now broken from the flood, and aimed at a big oak tree in the backyard. The feeling of power that came with handling a gun surged through his body. This is what he'd always wanted to do as a kid: fire a gun from his own home. George closed one eye and pulled the trigger. Nothing happened. The gun had jammed. "Shit."

He knew to be careful with a jammed weapon, as it could misfire if not handled correctly. He thought he knew how to open guns, but there must have been something different about Iraqi weapons, or maybe that devil, Saddam, had put some special tricky device on his pistol — because when George opened the barrel to take out the bullets, the misfired bullet exited and slammed into his big toe on the same foot that had been injured by the chainsaw.

"YOWWWWWWWW!"

His yelling could probably be heard for a quarter of a mile, and sure enough, some Secret Service agents came running. They found the former president, shirtless, lying on his side and bleeding from his right foot — it had almost healed! — still clutching Saddam's pistol in his hand.

"What happened, sir?"

"Goddamned Katrina wrecked my house and Saddam finally shot a Bush. YOWWWWWW!"

The agents looked around at the suddenly spotless home. Katrina had happened years ago and there were no hurricanes in Crawford. One agent rapidly bound up George's bleeding foot and the other spoke urgently into his cell phone.

An hour later George was sitting on a gurney in an emergency room at Fort Hood. A woman in a white coat approached him. "How are you, sir?" She looked professional and concerned.

"I'm feeling much better." George smiled, a bit wanly. His foot had been cleaned. He'd been told that the end of his toe couldn't be re-attached, but as he was full of morphine, he didn't care. This was the best he'd felt in years. Morphine was a lot better than alcohol and some of that other stuff he'd used.

"I have a few questions for you. We're doing a survey." She pulled out a clipboard. "Could you tell me what's meaningful in your life? I have a few options for selection, or you could just tell me." She looked at him expectantly.

Was he hallucinating? She appeared to work there, with her white coat, glasses, and official hospital badge. George looked around. Where was the Secret Service when you needed them? What's meaningful in life was the kind of question he could really get into trouble over. On the other hand, he was feeling good; he wanted to answer this question. "Well, my wife and my daughters. They are number one, all three of them. Kind of like the trinity. Heh, heh, heh," he chuckled, imaging the three of them in place of God, the Son and the Holy Ghost. That made a lot more sense to him, even though one part of him knew that it was blasphemy to think so. "Let's see what other choices you have here." He looked at the list.

"Higher power. Yep."

"God. Yeah."

"Prayer. Sure."

He paused. Prayer, that was a good one. It surely had worked to help him with that goddamned flood. Well, Mother Nature-damned flood. Crap. Who had caused it? God? Mother Nature? That Arthur Beethoven guy? Global warming? He shook his head. He must be out of his mind to be considering global warming.

George looked at the rest of the list. It didn't have "home" as a choice, but he knew that's what he'd circle. Home, his blessed home. He loved being there. He suddenly had an overwhelming wish that he'd lost the second presidential campaign. He still would have had his time as a president, but he wouldn't have had to deal with Iraq and been made to look so bad over Katrina. He could have simply stayed on his ranch, cutting brush, fishing for bass and riding his bicycle.

Fucking Saddam. Fucking Katrina. Fucking Osama. The morphine was starting to fade. He looked at his foot, which was starting to hurt. Now he'd have his own daily reminder of Saddam. Fuck.

"What about patriotism? What about love of our country? Our Constitution? Of all the ideals behind Lady Liberty?" The voice of the woman in the white coat pierced George's consciousness.

George examined her again. She looked different. Her clothing seemed to have changed into clouds and her badge had become a smooth pond which reflected his face back to him like a mirror. The image shocked him. He was haggard, like a man in his nineties or like one of those poor concentration camp victims found alive, barely, at the end of World War II. Or maybe one of those Guantánamo prisoners after days of hunger strikes. The pain in his foot advanced with a vengeance and he felt like he was being devoured by a ravenous animal. He looked again at the woman's face and felt horrified. It was her, again. Mother Nature.

She pulled up a wheelchair and sat in it. She brought her face very close to George's and whispered to him. "I might seem like your worst nightmare, but really I'm your best hope. Although you may not understand this, I have your eternal interests at heart."

Mother Nature pushed a couple of buttons on the morphine drip, and George sighed with relief. She continued. "Morphine is wonderful stuff, isn't it? Comes from nature. Everything good ultimately comes from nature, my friend." As the morphine kicked in, George felt more hopeful. Mother Nature had never called him friend.

"I'm not surprised that you mentioned your family and thought of your home. And I'm sure you feel that way about God, too. But you didn't mention your country. That's a bit strange, I think." She paused. "Or that seven-pound bass, which you said in 2005 was the high point of your presidency thus far."

George cringed. Other men might have said the same during an extremely stressful period. It was a moment of pure joy to catch a decent-sized fish in a place one least expected to catch one, an act that resonated with all men's ancestral memories of hunting for food, and also resonated with Jesus and his fishes. George didn't articulate this at the time he'd answered that question, but if he had, it would have made him seem less foolish.

Mother Nature put her hand up. "Yes, it would have been good to explain the metaphor and satisfaction of catching that bass. But you just aren't an Abraham Lincoln, or a George Washington, or a Mahatma Gandhi, or a Nelson Mandela. You never should have been President of the United States. You weren't a public servant. You didn't put the good of the people before everything else. You're just an ordinary guy, at heart. But unfortunately for everyone else, you became the president, with access to immense power, but without any sense of the responsibility that should have accompanied that power."

The morphine held steady on George's foot but the rest of him was feeling lower than the proverbial snake's belly.

"Yes, I like that image. You look like you do feel lower than a snake's belly," Mother Nature said with a strong Texas accent. Now she was wearing a pair of hand-tooled leather boots with images of desert flowers, some tight sexy jeans and a be-ribboned rodeo shirt. A few snakes appeared at her feet and slithered up the gurney. George saw them and screamed. If he'd looked, he would have seen that they were just bull snakes, the type that eat vermin. But his eyes were squeezed shut against the horror. George's screams filled the emergency room. Nurses and agents ran into his room, and when they whipped open the curtains, what they saw was a man thrashing about in his bed yelling about snakes. A cocktail of lorazepam and haloperidol sedated him into oblivion.

Hours later, when an orderly came to clean the room, he was surprised to find a few snake skins. He shrugged, picked them up and took them home for his grandchildren's amusement.

* * *

Like Lucy, Maria and Charlie also slept under beautiful western Nebraska stars, beside a river in a state park. They'd talked about Lucy and hoped she was okay. Maria had known her for a long time and knew what a genuinely unique person she was. Even with her idiotic Rapture ideas, Lucy was a real seeker who wanted to understand the world and maybe make it better with her strange, wonderful pilgrimage. Charlie admired what she saw as the patriotism in Lucy's pilgrimage. Dozens of Charlie's ancestors had fought for America, all the way back to the Revolutionary War. But she realized there were other ways to love one's country, other ways to protect it, and other ways to make it better. Maybe Lucy was onto something. They would find her, and help her accomplish her mission. Then Charlie would figure out her own next mission.

Just before pulling out of the campsite the next morning, they read a sign that told the story of how the Platte River flowing from northwest Nebraska to Fort Laramie, Wyoming had been one of the main routes west for settlers. But it had also been Sioux country, the land of Crazy Horse, and a vortex of clashes between the European immigrants and the Indian tribes. The immigrants had been like a little stream at first, just a few people heading west, but then the stream enlarged, spilled over its banks, and destroyed grassland habitat for the buffalo. The immigrants brought diseases that killed the Indians and guns that killed the buffalo. And then the stream became a raging river of soldiers, traders, miners and settlers who eventually overwhelmed the tribes.

Maria considered the death and destruction of these people and animals more than a century ago. She and Charlie could ride free anywhere. They did not have to fear being speared or captured or forced to become some a soldier's or settler's wife. She knew there must have been some lesbians back then. *Gracias a la Virgen*, she thought, that she and Charlie lived in these days. With all its faults this was still the best time in American history to be a woman.

The women headed up to the Niobrara River and followed it for the rest of the day. This was a truly beautiful river. While ninety-five percent of Nebraska was cultivated, these grasslands around the river were as wild as they'd ever been, their source of nourishment underground streams. The native grasses of Niobrara were one of the subtle wonders of the earth. As Maria contemplated the natural beauty, Charlie thought about the warriors who'd fought on the Plains. She imagined what it must have been like to ride a horse through this beautiful country. It wasn't bad on a motorcycle, but on horseback, it would have really been something. And not just riding for fun, but riding to hunt for buffalo and riding against enemies. That would have been the way to be a warrior, Charlie thought. Like the American Special Forces soldiers in Afghanistan who rode horses in the early part of the war. Charlie had been jealous of them. The

Special Forces were one reason she'd joined the military, hoping they'd change the rules, even though women were not allowed in that elite group. Nevertheless, Charlie had been a warrior.

Warriors were different than soldiers, she decided. Warriors implied something mythic, fighting for a cause. Fighting for one's home and one's people. Soldiers took orders and grumbled. Warriors sucked up hardship and asked for more. Soldiers dreamed of their pensions. Warriors dreamed of winning great battles. Charlie knew that a lot of her fellow soldiers were really warriors. But they'd mostly been treated like common soldiers. She gunned the engine, making Maria hold on tighter.

Eventually they saw signs for a rodeo, all ages and all amateurs, in Laramie, Wyoming. They pushed on and reached Laramie later in the day. They were tired and figured it was time to splurge on a hotel. They found a simple place. The old woman at the desk, Pretty Woman, her name tag read, had an ancient, walnut face, but her body appeared strong with no extra flesh. She looked over the two young women and didn't say much, just gave them the room keys after they handed over some cash.

Pretty Woman figured they were gay. She'd seen women like them on that Ellen Degeneres show. Gays, especially lesbians, irritated Pretty Woman. That show irritated her too, but she watched it. She sighed and looked at the cracked clock on the wall. Almost time for the "Degenerate Show," as she called it. After watching this vile show, and once her relief showed up, she'd go to the rodeo. Her daughter was riding in it, as were a few cousins, and she wanted to see if they were going to land on their asses. She'd have her video camera handy to record them making fools of themselves.

A hundred miles down the highway from where Pretty Woman was shaking her head as she watched Ellen hug her attractive female guests, the men from Abu Ghraib had found gasoline and had managed to put extra fuel into jerry cans without killing or hurting anyone. Emile had wanted to punch out the attendant just on principle, but the other men had prevented him. They needed to keep going without any further incidents. They had argued over which route to take too. Trevor had wanted to keep to the main roads. The other three wanted to take back roads. Trevor finally pulled out his gun and said, "We're going to Laramie. It's the biggest place around here. Any one of our targets might be there." The man with the gun and the keys prevailed.

* * *

Judith easily adjusted to staying with her grandmother, who lived in a new home built by a church. When Judith had first arrived, Abbie had described her anti-Bush shrine in detail. She had brushed some items across her granddaughter's cheeks, and when Judith felt the pinheads in the Bush doll's knees, she convinced her grandmother to remove them. Abbie had arthritic knees and Judith felt this was just bad karma. While she couldn't get her grandmother to dismantle the shrine, Abbie did agree to add figures of Mary, mother of Jesus, positive female images that might change the energy directed towards Bush. Persuasion of a more angelic sort.

Judith missed Joseph, but she was glad she hadn't given in to his marriage proposal. She could relax with her grandmother in a way that she couldn't yet around Joseph. In a way, he'd been too helpful. She did miss sex, but sometimes she just wanted to be touched. Her grandmother didn't care what they did when he visited, but Judith felt awkward with Joseph in her grandmother's home. The romantic magic of the rehab hospital had faded.

One weekend while Ben and Joseph were visiting, they found themselves watching comedies on TV and trying to figure out why certain things made people laugh. Some of the jokes were racist, and since Joseph was the only white person present, he had to represent all whites. He had a hard time doing that. There were tens of thousands of different white groups, and how could he represent all of them? Judith, Ben and Abbie laughed at Joseph, as blacks had been lumped together in America for hundreds of years and it was only fair for whitie to have his turn. But they agreed there was some humor that they all could laugh at, and they enjoyed Chris Rock, Ellen Degeneres, Jon Stewart, and Whoopi Goldberg.

Judith listened carefully to what made them laugh and pretty soon she was ready to try out some jokes for them. They howled with laughter, especially when she made fun of herself. They fell silent, however, when she told them that she really wanted to go public, at a local comedy club.

"Judith, no one is going to laugh at you," Ben said. " I can't believe you're still thinking about doing this. You're going to have to see that shrink again."

"You laughed. And I've had enough of shrinks. I need laughter."

"You can't see the audience to judge their reaction," offered Joseph.

"Don't matter. I can hear them. And anything that needs seeing, you and Ben can describe it to me."

Abbie looked at Judith carefully and then said, "Yes. Yes. YES! That's a great idea. And I hope all those damn idiots who voted for Bush, especially the second time, are sitting in the audience. They'll see that even though the damn fools sent my beautiful granddaughter to Iraq, and only half of her comes back, she's still kicking. Yes, I like that idea. I'll help you, dear, if these men won't."

They argued for hours, but Ben and Joseph couldn't overcome the two women.

The manager of the local comedy club took a bit more convincing, but Judith was persistent. She said she'd do it for free, even give her tips to him. When that didn't work, she threatened to go to the newspaper with a story of discrimination towards blacks, vets, the disabled, and women. (Judith thought about adding "lesbians" to the list, but the manager had already met her boyfriend, and she just couldn't pull that off.) The manager finally relented and scheduled her for Thursday, when hardly anyone would be in the club.

On opening night, no one in the audience except her family and the manager knew her true state of disability. Joseph pushed Judith

— who was wearing fake arms and legs — on stage in a wheelchair. "Break a prosthesis, baby," he whispered before he left. Judith wore sunglasses, like Stevie Wonder, and was dressed up like the Statue of Liberty with folds of cloth draped over her arms.

"Whatchu lookin' at?" Judith spoke with an ignorant accent. She didn't feel nervous at all. She actually felt like she imagined Whoopi Goldberg felt on Broadway. She faced the audience and looked stern. Her family had said there were more men than women, that the audience was racially mixed, and a few looked like veterans. She'd know when she connected: when they started laughing.

"Ain't you evuh seen no black Lady Liberty?"

A couple of people laughed.

"Or is it a black Lady Liberty with sunglasses? I got these shades on 'cause Ah'm blind. So Ah's a blind, black Lady Liberty. Ah am the ultimate patriot. If Justice can be blind, so can Liberty. Uh, huh, uh, huh." She bobbed her head right and left, and licked her lower lip with her tongue. "So pretend we got deese two blind ladies leading our country. The blind leading da blind, so to speak. What we got then?" She paused. "We got a goddamned bunch of rascals runnin' things. And Ah am talkin' about 2000 to 2008. That Reverend Jessie Jackson had it right before that 2000 'lection. He tol' the country to 'Staaaaaaaayyy ooooooooouuuuuuuuuuut of the bushes.'"

Judith repeated this. "Stay out of the bushes. But did we listen? Did we listen?" She lifted her chin to the audience. She wished she still had arms and legs and could stand with her hands on hips.

"Heck no!" someone shouted from the audience.

Judith smiled. She'd connected with someone besides her family.

"So Lady Liberty and Justice, we's blind. Maybe we were watching too much TV or spendin' time at Disneyworld, but we was not payin' 'tension in Florida dat fall of twooooooooo thousand. No, we was not. So dat bitch, Katherine Harris, kept all those good people from voting, or threw 'way der votes, and then that goddamned Sue-preeme Court voted five to four to put that damn Bush in de White House." She paused. "Along with his damn Dick."

Everyone laughed.

Judith had thought a long time about Katherine and those Supreme Court justices who had sided with the Republican Party in the infamous court case awarding the 2000 presidential election to Bush rather than Gore, who'd won the popular vote. Scalia, Thomas, Rhenquist, O'Conner, and Kennedy. In Judith's opinion, there would be a special place in hell for them, along with Bush, Cheney, Wolfowitz, Rice, Rumsfield, Feith, and Rove. They'd all be roasting without arms, legs, and sight. But they'd be able to hear one another scream as they kept getting blown up over and over and over again, just as she had, in horrible, excruciating pain for the rest of their lives.

"So while Ah was at Disneyworld, long with mah frien' Justice, the country was starting its long flush down the toilet." Judith realized no one was laughing. She needed to get back into that humor groove. Just thinking about the people who were really responsible for her injuries brought back bitterness. This was going to be harder than she thought. "So, folks, we have gone down the toilet, and it is one smelly, ugly place."

Judith changed her accent to standard Midwest. "Some people think the great USA stands now for Ugly Shitty Assholes, thanks to the Bush that was in the White House and all the Bush lovers he brought with him." Judith squinted towards the audience. "Anyone out there vote for Bush in either election?"

There was silence.

"Yeah, I doubt anyone would admit it now. But even with stealing the election both times, about half of Americans thought he was the right man to lead our country."

Okay, she knew it was time for the funny part. "So, in 2000 either you didn't vote, or you voted for Gore or Nader. Or maybe Buchanan, but I doubt that."

That got a laugh.

"And Kerry in 2004. So you all were patriots. I want someone to come up and shake my hand. And I like really firm handshakes."

A young man in the front row stood up. He looked old enough to have voted in 2004 but probably not 2000. "I'll volunteer, ma'am."

"So, what's your name?"

"I'm Jerry."

"Jerry? Like Jerry Seinfeld? You trying to take over my job here?" Everyone laughed, including Jerry.

Judith shook her head. "Okay, Jerry, before you shake my hand, let me ask you what kind of work you do?"

"I'm a student, over at the law school."

"Ha. You goin' be a lawyer? Ha, ha, ha, ha...."

The student started laughing too, as did the audience.

"You not crazy, are you?" Judith looked in his direction with fake suspicion.

Jerry looked back at her. He'd actually had a psychiatric evaluation after both parents died in a car accident, caused by a drunk driver. He'd been told he was totally sane, just overwhelmed with grief. "No, I'm actually certifiably sane. A doctor told me that a few years ago."

"Well, you sound like a patriot to me, then. Going to law school to right the wrongs of the world, and put all those criminals behind bars. So let me shake your hand. You shake it good and tight, friend."

Jerry almost tripped getting on the stage. Everyone laughed and he bowed. He came up to her, grasped her right hand and shook it vigorously. Judith would have loved to see the looks on the audience's faces as her whole arm came off in Jerry's hand.

He looked shocked to find her arm suspended in the air. He'd been studying personal injury law, and he realized how easily he, or anyone, could be sued. But Judith burst out laughing, and then the audience did. Jerry just stood there with the arm.

Judith pretended to get stern again. "Look what you did! You took my arm off. I thought you were a patriot. Were you one of those secret Bush voters? Maybe you even voted for him twice. He already took my real arm off and now you've got my fake one."

Judith turned towards the audience. "Could I get some help up here please? Could someone get my arm back from Jerry and put it back on me?" Ben and Joseph waited to see if anyone from the audience would volunteer.

Jerry looked at the arm, which was from a store mannequin. Suddenly he knew that she must have lost her limb in Iraq. She must be a vet. He looked at the other limbs and realized they were fake too. And maybe she was really blind. Jerry was a member of United for Peace and Justice and had marched in all the DC protests against the war. A big reason for going to law school was to gain tools to fight the bastards who started unnecessary wars. Protesting could only go so far. He'd wondered if soldiers could sue the government for injuries they received in war. He thought there was something in the law that prevented this. But what if the war was found to be fraudulently planned and conducted? Just like other frauds that caused injuries. Lawyers had taken on the automobile industry. Asbestos companies. Cigarette manufacturers. No one had taken on the instigators of a war, but maybe it was possible. Jerry was lost in these thoughts when he suddenly saw Ben's face looming before him.

"Could you PLEASE give me my sister's arm so I can put it back on her!" Ben demanded. Jerry looked at him. The audience was howling.

"Sure, sorry. Here's her arm." Jerry blushed but smiled. He gave the arm to Ben, who tried to put it back, but it fell off. Jerry tried to help, and abruptly one of the legs clattered to the floor.

Ben sprung back in fake terror and Judith also looked horrified. "Jerry! What have you done now? You weren't content with taking off one arm? You gotta have a leg too? Now I know for sure you voted for that Bush and his damn Dick." Judith appeared steamed. She turned to her brother for help. "Ben, just give Jerry all my limbs. That Bush took them once before, and this Bush voter can have them again." Ben removed Judith's other arm and leg and loaded Jerry up, so he looked like he was carrying firewood. Ben glared at Jerry who smiled sheepishly. Judith said, "You in a big mess now, Jerry."

Jerry stared at the limbs and then at Judith, who appeared regal in her green gown and pointed crown in spite of her limblessness. She growled, "Come on, I'll fight you even though you got all my legs and arms. And unlike that guy in the Monty Python movie, I can't even see you. It don't matter though. I'll bite you. Or fall on you and squish you to death. And I got my brother and my boyfriend to help me. And if we need any more help I got my grandma here, too!"

"And me too!" someone yelled from the audience. Abbie and another older woman stood up and waved their canes at Jerry. The audience laughed and cheered the two defiant women.

The manager nodded his head, grudgingly. He would have to revise the schedule. And he wasn't taking any of this woman's money; she'd earned it. Maybe she was going to make it. A standup comedian who couldn't stand up. Someone who could read the audience but couldn't see. Someone who should make you cry but was making you laugh instead. Now that was really bold.

* * *

George really looked forward to a good night's sleep after his day at the hospital. He wished his wife was back from her trip: cuddling with her would help him settle down to sleep. Luckily, the flood hadn't gotten into the bathroom cabinet, so all his bottles of sleeping pills were intact. As he opened the cabinet, he had a shocking glimpse of himself in the mirror. He looked even worse now than he had in the hospital when he'd seen his face in Mother Nature's phony badge. As he considered which pill to take, he had an unwelcome memory of pills and seniors.

One day back in the fall of 2005 he'd made the mistake of going to a seniors center to show the old folks how great the new Medicare Part D benefit would be. While the cameras rolled, George and an elderly vet sat down at a computer to see how it worked. The senior had a list of sixteen medications. The first computer hadn't functioned at all, then the senior couldn't find his glasses, and, once he found them, he couldn't work the keyboard. Finally George entered the man's numbers and came up with the plans in which he could enroll. But each plan only listed the number of medications covered, not the specific medications. There didn't seem to be any way to check which meds were under which plans.

Finally someone found a book that explained each plan in detail. It took an hour to cross list medications and plans. Then the senior complained that he had very difficult-to-treat diabetes, hypertension and depression, and his doctors were always changing his medications. Would he have to change plans each time his doctors changed his meds? And why didn't any of the plans want to pay for the Valium that he'd been taking for forty years to deal with his PTSD from World War II? He was ninety years old and he couldn't give it up now. Whenever he tried, he couldn't sleep and ended up in the hospital, at an average cost of eight hundred dollars per day. Valium cost about ten cents a day. "Your taxes at work," the senior said to the camera.

The Valium exclusion didn't make sense to George, but when he viewed the program later, the videographer explained that Congress (George was relieved they'd blamed Congress instead of him) had decided that seniors took far too many tranquilizers and that the government wasn't going to pay for those dope drugs. Medical professionals had protested the exclusion, but the Republican majority in Congress had pushed through this rule. George had been made to look like an idiot, and the World War II vet came off like a class act.

George had the best health insurance available. Even if he didn't have it, he'd always had plenty of money for excellent medical care and medications. He would never have to deal with Medicare forms, formularies, and denials. He hoped whatever pill he took now would banish the memory of the veteran and Medicare Part D from his mind and make him look better in the morning. He examined all the bottles and decided on a little purple pill. It looked like a little purple heart, and he briefly thought of all the Purple Hearts recently generated. Far too many, he sighed. May they all rest in peace. George swallowed the purple heart and lay down on his bed.

George was soon in dreamland, this time a desert wasteland. He wore pajamas, quite unsuitable for the rocky, harsh landscape. Men on horseback were riding fast towards him.

"You goddamned idiot, get over here!" a reassuringly American voice yelled at him. George turned and ran, wincing, towards the rocky cover. He was barefoot.

"What the fuck were you doing out there? Don't you know that those Afghanis can shoot from miles away?" The powerfully-built man in fatigues looked at the man in pajamas with disdain and pity. "Name's Pat. What's yours?"

"George."

"Okay, George, let's hope they don't see us, and we'll live another day. I'm going to call in their location and maybe we'll see them blown to bits."

Pat fiddled with the radio and spoke some numbers. The horseback riders thundered towards them. In his pajamas, George shivered beside the strong military man, who looked familiar. All of sudden, awareness hit. It was Pat Tillman, the pro football player who'd volunteered after 9/11. The man who'd given up a multi-million-dollar contract to fight for America. A genuine hero.

"Pat, hello. Pat, uh, uh, thank you." George stumbled over his words. "You are one of our heroes."

Pat got off the radio and looked at the other man skeptically. He started to laugh, and suddenly, hell broke loose. The rock hiding their position blew up, pieces flying everywhere. One chunk hit Pat in his torso, then another blew off an arm, then something went through his head. It was all over in seconds. The hero was destroyed, lying all over the place, in bloody bits. George was just thinking that the men on horseback couldn't possibly have done this when he heard an American bomber and saw it speeding off to the west. He looked in horror at the bloody pieces of his companion. Suddenly the torso sat up, and the mutilated head, several feet away, shook itself and said, "That sucks. Can you believe it? Friendly fire! Goddamn idiots. Now I've only got half a brain and no arm. Do you think I could play football now? Is there a handicapped professional league for former soldiers? Shit. I don't even care about that anymore. I'd planned to run for Congress when I returned. That vet from Georgia did it after he lost three limbs in Vietnam. I can do it, too, if I can just put my head back on my body. Help me out, will yah?"

George just stared at him with an open mouth.

"George, you said?" Pat looked at him a little more closely. "GEORGE! Of course I know you. My commander-in-chief, the jerk who started the Iraq War on faulty intelligence and trumped-up data to fit your insane fantasies of power and control. And diverted resources away from Afghanistan and our real enemies."

George backed away.

"No, you can't leave me, now, George. And because this is a dream, I know everything you did after I died. You turned me into a hero as advertising for your goddamn war. And this was after I told everyone my views about Iraq. That it was a complete lie."

Pat rocked his head, gently, in his remaining arm. "I was a soldier and I loved America, so I did my job. But you used me, and you lied to my family. You are the sickest bastard I've ever met and I hope you rot in hell. I might look like hell, but I'm headed to heaven."

And with that, the injured man disappeared in a mist that swirled skyward and left George behind, alone in Afghanistan.

"No, don't leave me. HELLLLLLLLLLLLLLPPPPPPPPP!" And he was still screaming when the Afghanis descended upon him and cut him up into little pieces.

Chapter 21

Lucy sat near the river and watched the water swirl downstream and thought about her dream. She had eaten a granola bar and had some lemonade to drink. She didn't know that some scholars and people of faith believed that Mary Magdalene and Jesus had been wife and husband. Lucy had never read *The Da Vinci Code* or *The Jesus Papers* or other books that described Mary's power as being so threatening to the men who surrounded Jesus, that after Jesus' death, these men transformed Mary into a prostitute. Too grief stricken to fight back, Mary didn't have the strength to challenge these very determined men who would change the course of history with the religion that came from Jesus' teaching.

It was as if Mary was a lovely garden, ravaged by these men like a multitude of hurricanes. Remnants of the garden survived, but were so small and fragile, they were almost imperceptible. A "Gospel of Mary" existed — a German scholar by the name of Dr Carl Reinhardt unearthed evidence in Cairo in 1896 — and had it not been disregarded early on, the New Testament would consist of "the gospels according to Matthew, Mark, Luke, John *and* Mary." Surely that was what Jesus would have intended.

Lucy also didn't know that many believed that Jesus and Mary had had a daughter during Jesus' missing years. Perhaps she'd been left in her birthplace and raised by kind people until Mary returned after Jesus' death. This little girl survived to have children, and Jesus and Mary's grandchildren and their descendents spread throughout the world. Just as Mohammed's genes multiplied through his daughters, so Jesus' proliferated through his daughter. Perhaps Lucy was even a descendent of Jesus and Mary. Almost anything was possible. If she had known these stories, Lucy might have understood her dream better. As it was, she wouldn't forget what she'd dreamed, and someday she'd discuss it with someone who would help her understand its significance.

Lucy turned on her small radio for some music. She could only find one station and just caught the words "Antigone Rising" before she heard their female voices. Antigone was one of Lucy's favorite literary heroes who she'd learned about in her high school English class. She, along with Joan of Arc, was amongst the few women mentioned in literature or in history who had great courage. Joan of Arc and Antigone had both been condemned to death, although Antigone had taken matters into her own hands and hung herself in a cave. Antigone had stated, very matter of factly, "Everyone will die," but hers was a wrongful death. Antigone had died too soon, Lucy recalled thinking, like all those people killed in the massacres. Antigone should have had a child with her beloved Haemon, and their descendents should have lived. Just as all those people killed in Waco, Oklahoma City, Columbine and all those other places should have lived, too. At least Antigone did live on in Sophocles' play and again in the songs of Antigone Rising. Perhaps those other people who had died too would live again in stories or songs.

Kind of grunge rock, Antigone Rising was not the style of music that Lucy usually listened to. Maybe Maria would have liked it. Charlie would definitely have enjoyed it. Lucy realized again how much she missed them. It was really lonely in western Nebraska. She felt like she needed to get moving. She decided to pretend to be Antigone fleeing her home, but a different Antigone, one who would not end her life in a cave all alone. Antigone wouldn't have had a bicycle. Over two thousand years ago, Antigone would have had a horse. Assuming they let women ride horses in ancient Greece.

Imagining a horse made Lucy think about where she would go to find Maria and Charlie. Maybe the Crazy Horse Monument in South Dakota. Joy had told her all about the revered Indian chief riding an enormous horse and the Polish sculptor whose vision, time and money had begun the monument in his honor. Joy had advised Lucy to forget the four faces of presidents at Mount Rushmore, which she'd described as a tourist-crammed patriotic Disneyland. Joy had said that this horse under Crazy Horse was so enormous and powerful, it could have saved the passengers on the doomed 9/11 airplanes or swooped in and rescued the Columbine kids too.

That horse was inspiring but too big for Lucy's imagination that day. Lucy loved the American rider, Frank Hopkins, played in the movie by dreamy Viggo Mortensen, and she loved his horse, Hidalgo, even more. As she rode north, she imagined herself as Antigone on Hidalgo, a mustang ridden by an American cowboy whose mother was Indian and whose father was Anglo. He rode Hidalgo in a deathly cross-country horse race in Saudi Arabia, against pampered horses ridden by even more pampered, arrogant Saudis who had complete disdain for an American half-breed on a mustang. As the cowboy had insisted, however, American Indians were just as much "people of the horse" as the Saudis, and he went on to prove it by winning the race.

Lucy identified with Jazira, a young Saudi girl in the movie. Jazira had the right spirit. Not all Saudis were bad. Even some of the competitors in the race had been decent. Lucy imagined she was some combination of Mary, Antigone and Jazira riding Hidalgo accompanied by Haemon, Frank and Jesus. She traveled north alone, but no longer lonely.

* * *

"This is great, isn't it, Charlie?" asked Maria. She wore a cowgirl hat, a revealing shirt with "Laramie Rodeo Queen" across her breasts, and extremely tight low cut jeans which displayed a rose tattoo on her lower back. As the two women walked the aisles to find their seats, every man and most women looked at Maria. Charlie was dressed a little more conservatively, but she also attracted stares with her short spiked hair. They found seats in front of several young men, and Maria gave them a beautiful smile before she sat down. She had checked out this maneuver in the hotel room mirror, so she knew she was just a centimeter on the right side of decency. Each time she moved, the guys behind her sighed. They couldn't help but look at the rose tattoo as it fluttered just above the top of her jeans.

Charlie had a Semper Fi tattoo visible on her upper back above the neckline of her tight-fitting cotton shirt. One of the men sitting behind her noticed the Marine insignia, nudged his buddy and pointed. Zach, a Jarhead who'd been in Iraq, had only recently gotten out and was a little nervous in crowds. A rodeo, if they'd had them over there, was the sort of place Iraqis would have sent a suicide bomber. But Zach always loved horses, and his little sister was in the barrel racing competition, so he'd forced himself to overcome his anxiety to see her compete. Zach had the same Semper Fi tattoo on his left arm. He leaned over so that his mouth was next to Charlie's ear. When Charlie quickly turned to see who was speaking, he pulled up the sleeve of his T-shirt. Charlie acknowledged him and they talked quietly under the noise of the crowd. She introduced him to Maria, and he named his companions. Soon they were all laughing and Zach started to relax.

Pretty Woman sat nearby and saw those lesbians talking with the young men. She spat out some sunflower seed shells and looked at the young people more closely. She knew those young men and liked them. She thought it was a shame those girls were gay. She blamed that Ellen Degeneres for glamorizing female homosexuality. Pretty Woman spat out some more shells.

Her eyes swept through the crowd. She picked out all the people she knew, seeing a few couples who shouldn't have been together, as one or the other was married to someone else. Then she spotted some other men — three of them, standing close together — who made the hairs on the back of her neck rise up. She could sense auras and these men gave off the ugliest waves she'd felt in a long time. A wave of putrification rolled towards her across the crowd, magnitudes of evil compared to Ellen. Pretty Woman saw the men scan the audience and then watched their eyes stop on the two lesbians. She realized they wanted to brutalize these two women. Pretty Woman wondered if it was a sexual thing, if these women had rejected them. Possibly, but it felt like something worse.

She tapped the shoulders of two young hulking men in the row before her. They were her nephews, defensive players on the Laramie Mustangs varsity football team. "Nephews, we got a situation here. See those men over there by the bullpen?"

The young men nodded.

"And see those attractive young women sitting over there by Zach and his brother?"

"Yep," they said at the same time. They'd noticed the good-looking newcomers and had thought about moving closer, but knew their aunt would disapprove.

"I think those men are going to do something bad to those women. Gotta watch them. Gotta help them, when the time comes."

Pretty Woman's nephews loved her. She'd been the one who'd cared for them when their parents were passed out from drinking, which was pretty much every day of their childhood. She'd been at every football game they'd played; she was more important to them than their coach, which was saying a lot.

"Sure, Auntie, whatever you say."

Trevor scanned the crowd. He was glad to find the two women, but only as a means to locate Bill. In Trevor's mind, the women were unimportant. He knew, however, that Emile would have other ideas. He'd want to treat those women like he did the Iraqi prisoners, for his own enjoyment rather than a means to get information about Bill's whereabouts. Trevor would have to restrain Emile, at least until the women gave him what he wanted. Then Emile could satiate his desires. Trevor wished Emile was more professional, but in this business there were all kinds. You had to "run what you brung," or in Rummy's words, "use the Army you have, not the one you wished for."

Trevor spoke to the other men. "When they go pee. That's when we get them. They probably know where that asshole Bill is." The Hummer was parked nearby. They'd hustle the women into the vehicle and take them somewhere to torture information out of them. And then kill them. It was a plan. It would work as well as anything they'd done in Iraq.

Chapter 22

"Charlie, I've gotta go to the little girls' room. Wanna come with me?" Maria stood up and stretched. All the young men, and a few old ones behind her, sighed. One man's wife hit her husband with her pocketbook. Charlie sensed the commotion behind them. She turned and scowled, only half seriously. The men looked at her respectfully. After all, she was a Marine. "Yeah, I'll go with you."

The three men from Abu Ghraib watched Maria and Charlie moving towards the restrooms. Pretty Woman had spilled her sunflower seeds and her nephews were distracted by rodeo riders, so when they looked back across the arena, the two parties of interest had vanished. Pretty Woman told her nephews to spread out to find the men and she got up and walked quickly towards the restroom, most likely where the women were headed.

The restroom had a separate exit and entrance. There was a long line outside the entrance but Maria and Charlie weren't in it. Pretty Women surmised they might have gone in the exit when someone came out, and she did the same. The room was packed. Pretty Woman looked under the doors of stalls for the fancy flower leather-tooled boots she recalled them wearing. She'd made it all the way to the stall closest to the entrance and was about to give up hope of finding them, when she looked back towards the exit and saw Maria and Charlie heading out of the restroom. Pretty Woman tried to follow them, but a young mother with a double stroller, twins and two other children, spilled a huge diaper bag and Pretty Woman was stuck.

Unfortunately for Maria and Charlie, the three men were waiting for them outside the exit. They acted as if they were jealous, slightly drunk boyfriends and grabbed the women's arms as they came out. Underneath draped jackets, Luke and Mack shoved small handguns into the women's backs. Luke's gun on Maria poked the center of her rose tattoo. If Charlie had been alone she would have tried something, but the leer on Luke's face and the gun in Maria's back convinced her to bide her time.

The men quickly escorted the women to the Hummer where Emile, with his injured leg, was waiting in the front passenger seat. Mack jumped in the driver's seat. The others pushed Maria and Charlie into the back on the floor of the Hummer. Their cheeks pressed flat on the cold metal floor, they couldn't see out and no one could see in through the darkened windows. As Luke and Trevor gagged and tied Maria and Charlie to each other, backwards, with duct tape, Mack maneuvered the Hummer out of the parking lot.

Out of breath, Pretty Woman arrived on the scene seconds after her nephews, who had seen the men put the women into the Hummer and noted the license plate before it roared through the exit. They excitedly relayed the numbers and letters to their aunt as they all piled into their pickup. The nephews' truck looked pretty beat up, but they had worked on the engine, and in a cross-country race their pickup probably could beat a Hummer. "Better gas mileage, too, Auntie," one boasted as the other revved the engine, skidding onto the highway.

In the Hummer, the men in the back seat rested their boots on the women's bodies and Trevor began speaking. "We want that guy Bill. You know who I'm talking about. You were with them, and you know where he's going."

Maria knew these were the most dangerous men she'd ever seen, but Charlie was not intimidated. She shrugged. She couldn't speak with the gag. Her shrug earned her a hard jab in the ribs. She grunted, but she'd tensed and she was satisfied that nothing had broken.

"You know where he's going. He and that other idiot, that Jesus freak. They're after that girl. Why, I don't know. She doesn't look like much to me. I woulda thought they'd be after you two. But you wouldn't want them, would you?" Trevor regarded them with disdain. "You're lesbos, right?" He sneered revoltingly and jabbed Charlie again. "I want you to start thinking and start thinking out loud. Otherwise you're going to find my friend here taking your girlfriend's clothes off and you're going to see her raped in every possible way, while we keep driving up this highway." And to emphasize this possibility, he drew out a knife and waved it menacingly in front of Charlie's face.

Charlie couldn't see Maria, but she could feel her girlfriend's fear. Okay, she thought, I'm going to have to think and act pretty quick here. She looked around the interior of the Hummer. She'd been in plenty of these in Iraq and knew they had all sorts of storage areas and hand grips. She figured if she could do something to get the vehicle to wreck while they were still on the main road, there was a good chance that she and Maria would not be injured, bound together on the floor. She noted that none of the men, including the driver, were wearing their safety belts. Idiots.

Charlie shrugged and crossed her eyes down towards her gag. Trevor cut through the duct tape near her ear and then ripped it savagely off her face. She didn't wince even though it hurt like hell. She licked her lips, felt grateful for having a sexy singing voice, and then started to sing lyrics to the Stones song, *You Can't Always Get What You Want*. She knew these lines by heart. It must have been intuition that made Charlie sing that particular song, because these guys dug the Stones.

Mack, at the wheel, started to swerve the Hummer in time to the song. Charlie sang the refrain again and Mack turned the wheel like he was a downhill ski racer. That gave Charlie the opportunity to ground her body between the metal struts and throw her legs around to kick Trevor in the groin. As he fell over, screaming, the other man lunged at Charlie, but she was ready for him and gave him such a hard kick with her flowery boots that he slammed down, hitting his head on the metal floor, knocked out cold. Mack, glancing in the rearview mirror and whipping his head around as he drove, couldn't believe what had just happened. In spite of his injured leg, Emile was about to throw himself on the women. If Mack had been any smarter, he would have pulled over, dealt with the women who were still tied-up, and helped his friends. But he wasn't very smart and he was enraged.

Pretty Woman and her nephews followed on the highway a few hundred yards back. They'd seen the Hummer sway rhythmically and figured the other driver was just having a little thrill. They were amazed to see the Hummer cross the yellow line, then cross back, just before it would have smashed into a semi, then veer off the side of road and crash in a deep ditch against a fence. The nephew driving slammed on his brakes and drove off the road. They jumped out and ran over to the Hummer.

Maria and Charlie, lying on the floor braced against each other, had survived the wreck without any injuries, although their wrists were chafed and bleeding. The four men didn't fare so well. In agony, Trevor gripped his groin with one hand and braced his broken collarbone, which had snapped during the accident, with the other. Luke was still unconscious from Charlie's kick. Mack and Emile had been thrown against the smashed windscreen and were covered in blood. Neither was badly injured but Emile's face would never look so pretty again, especially after the local general surgeon stitched him up.

Pretty Woman and her nephews ignored the injured men and helped free the two tied-up women. Pretty Woman never gave a thought to their sexuality. It was completely irrelevant. Using a Swiss Army knife, one nephew cut through the duct tape and the other ripped up his T-shirt to make bandages for their wrists. Another vehicle had stopped, and before long the state police and ambulances arrived.

Pretty Woman and her nephews attested to the kidnapping. The men, three of them now on gurneys attended by paramedics, didn't say anything, but they knew they now wanted to kill Maria and Charlie as badly as they wanted to kill Bill. And once they'd dealt with that threesome, they'd come back to kill those interfering Indians.

As Charlie walked away from the immobilized men, she sang the Stones song softly, changing the words, "...*sometimes, you fuckers, you geeeettttttt what you deseeeeeeeeeeeerrrrrrrrrrrve."*

* * *

Hundreds of miles away, the men in the New Orleans Disabled American Veteran (DAV) group were furious. They'd heard that there was a comedian making fun of injured veterans. One of them had a son who followed standup comedy, and he said the vet spouted stuff like: "It's hard to be a standup comedian when you don't have any legs." When his dad, an alcoholic Vietnam vet who'd lost a couple of friends in the war and later several more to suicide and prison, heard this while they ate breakfast at home, he leapt across the table and pinioned his son between the refrigerator and the counter top. His wife had to hit her husband a few times with a flyswatter to get him to let his son go. The dad apologized and the son, backing out of the kitchen, told his dad he didn't know more than he'd said.

When the vet brought this up in the DAV group, another man said his cousin had heard of the show, too. "It's just not right. Just like Nam, that Raqui war never should 'a happened. Goddamn Bush and Cheney. All them people kilt, ours and theirs. And all them wounded. There's not 'nough programs to treat them. And now someone makin' fun of wounded vets? What kind of damned world do we live in?"

Another vet opened a tattered copy of a New Orleans tabloid. He flipped to the back pages, pausing to look at some young ladies with extremely large breasts.

"Don't you get 'stracted now. Find out when that jerk is workin' next. We gonna show up and show that idiot the business."

They found the ad for the "In Your Face Live Comedy Club: The Standup Comedian Who Can't Stand Up" and agreed to attend the show. The volunteer psychologist who sat in on the group suggested they have the same rules as in the DAV meetings: no weapons, no fisticuffs, no name calling, and no alcohol or drug use. He asked if they'd mind if he showed up, too.

"Yeah, you can come, doc. You use some of your fancy words on that asshole."

A couple of days later, the men had paid the entry fee and sat at small tables in the In Your Face. No one brought weapons, but some of them were intoxicated. A few wore military attire. They sat stone-faced through the first act, a young gay Catholic man suffering through the dilemma of wanting to be a priest. The Vatican had proclaimed homosexuality to be a major sin, an invincible barrier to priesthood. In his act the gay priest wannabe pretended to give Communion and spoke his innermost thoughts as imaginary men came through the line. Some of it was funny, but in a sad sweet way, the psychologist thought. He wondered if he should talk to the young man after the show and perhaps recommend psychotherapy.

The doc mentioned this to one of the oldest vets, Ted, who had fought in both Korea and Vietnam. Ted shook his head. "Naw, don't talk to him. That's why he's here, doc, using humor to deal with his conflict. I thought you told us to do that." Ted struck a pose the psychologist often used, right hand to chin with right elbow resting on left hand and said, "Humor is one of the mature defenses."

The psychologist smiled at this older man, who'd taught him so much. Actually the whole group had taught him more than most of his formal doctoral program. Maybe tonight would be another lesson.

The scattered applause for the young man died and the manager leapt on the stage. "And now, ladies and gentlemen, our newest star, one of our classiest acts, the standup comedian who can't stand up!"

Ben wheeled Judith onto the stage. For this show, she'd dispensed with the artificial legs, but fake arms filled the sleeves of an Astros jacket. "Yep, this is me. The standup comedian who can't stand up. And believe me, I'd like to stand up for this audience. I'm told there's a lot of military decorations out there." Judith paused. "Are those real, ya'll?"

"Damn straight, they are," a deep voice replied.

"Well, thank you, sir. Could I have a little help? Someone who knows how to salute?"

One of the younger vets bounded up on the stage. "Yes, ma'am, I can salute for you." And he demonstrated his best salute. "I'm salutin' now, ma'am."

"Audience, you tell me. Did he look like the president on the Abraham Lincoln that great day in May of 2003? Does he look Navy? Does he look like he helped accomplish that mission?"

A few guffaws from the audience.

"No, I'm not Navy, ma'am. I'm Army. I was a cook." He'd been trained as a cook, but one day when his group was short of soldiers, after a few had been killed and injured, he was ordered to go out with the platoon. He'd had to shoot at a family, and he'd seen a little kid bloody, not moving, as the family screamed in terror and rage. He still wasn't sure if he'd fired the fatal shot. But in his nightmares he was the murderer.

"Here. You help me, son. As you can tell, I ain't got no legs. Well, maybe you can't tell." Judith looked mischievous. "Could be sittin' on 'em, like some yoga queen. Can you look down there and see if you can find 'em?"

The young man hesitated. It appeared that she really didn't have any legs and he'd have to get very close to her to make sure. Also, in spite of his big talk when they'd first heard about this act, if she didn't have any legs, then it didn't really matter where she'd lost them. Maybe she'd been in a car accident or had that flesh-eating bacteria he'd heard about.

Judith sensed the young man's confusion. "You go sit down now, son. Thank you for your service." Judith pulled herself erect, and even though she couldn't salute, she gave that "superior officer" look she could imitate so well. The young man saluted, turned off the stage and sat down in his seat. Judith continued. "Anyone else want to help me?"

The psychologist considered going up. But he wasn't a vet. And he had enough sensitivity to know that's what this evening was about. He had his cell phone in hand, ready to call 911 if necessary. A psychologist was very good for certain situations, but police were better for others.

Ted realized as soon as he saw Judith wheeled onto the stage that she was a military veteran and she'd been severely injured in the war. He'd spent enough time in rehab himself to recognize other wounded vets. He decided to sit the thing out and see which one of these fools was so dense he couldn't figure it out. Jesus, he thought, this woman has balls. He decided that he was going to shake her hand after the show. But looking at them more carefully, he realized they were fake.

At Judith's invitation, another vet walked onstage. He went straight for Judith's hand. Maybe he thought it was real. Maybe he just wanted some female contact, even if on stage, surrounded by fifty other people. He grasped and off it came. Ben had fixed the limbs so the hands easily detached. The man looked shocked.

"Now see what you done? Jesus Christ! You took my hand. Give it back now. I need that sucker," Judith cried loudly.

The vet tried to stuff the hand under the end of her sleeve. His lip quivered. He began to cry, audibly.

Judith heard him and began to softly hum. At first only the vet with her hand could hear her. She hummed a bit louder, and then the others heard her voice. A few joined in as she began to sing the words of *Fix You*, a favorite song with this generation. Judith wished she had arms to put around this soldier's shoulders. All she had was her voice.

Amy slipped up on stage and hugged the young, sobbing soldier. Ben had the proudest look on his face. Nothing in the courtroom could beat this. The psychologist beamed. He liked that Coldplay song. He put his cell phone away. He wasn't going to need it tonight.

* * *

George was reading a work of literary fiction, *Saturday*. He hadn't tried much literature, besides what the librarian and Mother Nature had given him, since a few summers before when he'd read Camus' *The Stranger*. But his wife had given him *Saturday*, saying that this

British author, Ian McEwan, was considered to be one of the best living writers of the English language. In this book one of his main characters, a London neurosurgeon, was sympathetic to the Iraq War. Laura hadn't read the book, but she thought that George would like this viewpoint in a work of literature.

George was having a hard time as there were some incredibly long sentences and lots of poetry—although the car accident between the neurosurgeon in his Mercedes and some thugs in their beater, and the squash court battle between the two doctors, were pretty entertaining. But when he got to the argument between the doctor and his young adult poet daughter, George started to squirm. The daughter argued forcefully against the war and explained her participation in a huge protest that took place a few weeks before it began, on Saturday (hence the title), February 15 2003. George vaguely recalled some demonstrations, but as he didn't read papers then or watch the news, he didn't know the extent of the protests. He was shocked to read that there had been a huge protest in London that day, the biggest peace demonstration the world had ever seen. He snorted. Just the stupid kind of thing that poets would be involved in. He thought that Laura must have been tricked into getting this anti-war book, and he tossed *Saturday* on his wife's pillow.

Looking at her side of the bed, he sighed. She was at a yoga retreat. She'd started yoga after the re-election, perhaps her way of dealing with the stress of being First Lady. He thought it was kooky but Laura had told him that many Republican ladies had started taking yoga.

Thinking of his wife and yoga, he fell asleep without any pills and found himself in a beautiful Texas meadow blooming with bluebonnets and red paintbrush flowers. He felt a soft breeze and heard an old show tune, something from a Shirley Temple movie. Then he saw a little girl skipping through the flowers, occasionally turning in circles, and laughing. How pretty, he thought. She walked towards him, smiled, spun in a circle, curtsied and held out some flowers.

"Thank you, young lady." He accepted the flowers and sat down on the ground, "crisscross, applesauce," as his daughters used to say.

"Do you like these flowers, Georgie?"

She twirled again. When she stopped, he looked closely at her face — and his jaw slackened. "Robin? Is it you?"

"Of course it's me, silly." The little girl smiled and danced, just as she used to all those years ago.

George was shocked, but full of joy to see his little sister. She'd had leukemia, and in the 1950s there was no treatment for that illness. A happily playing child one week became a pale, bedridden youngster the next, and the following week, she was dead. Something died in his family when his beloved little sister disappeared, and no one ever spoke about her again.

"Georgie, let's play." Robin took his hands and he got up and they danced in a circle. He was the size and age he'd been then, just a few years older than her, a big brother who loved her more than anyone in the world. They danced and sang old Shirley Temple songs, and the sun shone, the breeze blew, the birds twittered and he felt pure love. They found a beautiful patch of bluebonnets and lay down in them, head to head, with their arms flung out, feeling the earth and laughing like summer angels.

George was still laughing with his little sister as he awoke, but his face was wet. He was truly crying on God's shoulder now. Thoughts tumbled through his mind. How his mother seemed to change after Robin's death. How he changed. How so much of what happened in his life since then went back to that horrible time of loss for his family. Why didn't they talk about his little sister?

He wanted to think more about his dream, but he was flooded by the memories of that sad time in his family. George put his face in his hands and cried. Back then no one talked much about people who had died, particularly children. At least not in WASP families. His mom had the other kids to raise. His dad had his job. George turned into a boy disconnected from healing, a young man who just wanted to party, and later, an addicted mature man headed for an early grave. He knew his wife and Jesus had saved him from that fate, but now, remembering Robin, he also knew there was something more to come.

"How about other little kids, George?"

Jarred from his reverie, he opened his eyes and groaned. There she was again, Mother Nature, seated in his favorite chair and dressed as a doctor in a white coat with glasses on her nose. She twirled a stethoscope. "Do you know how many kids they've estimated have died in Iraq due to your war?"

No, of course he didn't. He hated it when she asked him these questions.

She walked over to the bed and looked down at him. "Yes, all those older brothers, mothers and other relatives grieve just like you and your mother grieved all those years ago. And they're going to keep grieving their loved ones. That's what wars do." She paused. "Besides death from bombs and guns, there's depleted uranium and other chemicals that cause cancers, George. Lots of leukemia in children. What are you going to do about all those cancers in all those children?"

Mother Nature was surely the worst nightmare of them all. And he knew she was going to keep coming back. "Fundraise for cancer research?"

She nodded. "A start. But you've also got to do what you can to clean up the mess you've made in the Middle East. Like Jimmy Carter building those Habitat for Humanity houses, you need to go to Iraq and personally lead the cleanup of depleted uranium. Just think of Robin and what she would have wanted. Maybe your mom could go with you and help with the cleanup." Thinking of Barbara Bush in a hazmat suit in Baghdad, Mother Nature smiled wryly. She folded her hands together at her chest in a namaste, bowed to George and vanished.

George tried to recapture Robin's laughter and her hands in his as they danced in the bluebonnets. But his vision morphed into a vision of another little girl, in Baghdad, dying of the same leukemia. Wards of little girls. He sat up, put his feet over the side of the bed, and held his head in his hands. He couldn't imagine his mom in Iraq cleaning things up (how in the heck, he wondered, do you clean up depleted uranium?) but maybe once he told her of his dream, his mom would want to do something big in memory of Robin, and for all those other little kids and their families. Yes, she would help him and God would help them both.

George was interrupted from his thoughts by a loud knocking outside the door to the garden.

"Okay, okay, hold your horses, I'll be there in a minute." He grabbed a bathrobe and walked towards the noise. When he opened the door, he was surprised to see Dick, who pushed his way in and pointed to a chair. George sat.

Dick put his hands on his hips and snarled. "Let me get straight to the point. We've been monitoring your dreaming and we are really disturbed about last night's dream."

"Monitoring my dreams? How can you do that? That's not fair. That's not right," George sputtered, and he rose from the chair. Dick gave his nasty smile again and pushed George back down with a poke of his finger. "We had to do it. It was for your own good and the good of our country." He emphasized the word "our." "Besides, you know we've been monitoring other people's dreams for years, ever since we figured out the technology."

Dick grinned. It was so elegant. Spike an opponent's drink. Induce a headache, the worst headache ever. Have an ambulance ready to take the victim to a specific ER with an MRI. Sedate the patient with memory-erasing Versed. Insert the nanochip. Give an analgesic. Awaken victim. Headache gone. Brain tumor and aneurysm ruled out. Patient leaves happily without knowing anything about the inserted nanochip. Dick and his cronies hadn't even considered the courts, much less Congress, on this procedure. Monitoring dreams was so much more elegant than simple spying, telephone taps or checking computer records. Recording the unconscious was *real* spying.

George looked appalled. He thought he'd recalled all his visits to the hospital but maybe this had happened when he had his colonoscopy. That's when Dick must have orchestrated this outrageous procedure on him, the president.

The scientists had told Dick that if George ever dreamt of his beloved little sister, then they better watch out. Robin would awaken compassion within George, and when that occurred, it would be as if a giant tsunami had hit his brain. Who knew what he would do? Their worst fear all along was that George would tell the truth, all the truth, nothing but the truth. They knew that George really believed in God, and that was the weak link for keeping the lid on the truth. The truth about the fraudulent elections. The truth about the missed opportunities to prevent 9/11. The truth about the feigned intelligence that triggered the Iraq War. And the truth about all the greedy business deals made at the horrific expense of average Americans. Names. Dates. Meetings. Memos. George sometimes acted dumb, but he wasn't stupid. He had gone to Yale and Harvard and had gotten his average grades honestly. The power of truth from an awakened president would change everything. Dick shuddered thinking about it.

Unfortunately there wasn't a photographer in the room to record this historical tipping point. George, with his day old stubble, stale breath, mussed up hair, and bare feet, glared at Dick, who was clean shaven, elegantly coifed and wearing an expensive suit with shiny black shoes. It was as if the old-fashioned, freedom-loving, truth-telling American was standing up to the greedy capitalistic empire-building American. Suddenly George got up and pushed Dick hard in the middle of his chest with his finger. Dick dropped to a footstool.

"You didn't mind when they tried to impeach me, Dick. And when that failed, you tried to get me to resign. You wanted to be the president all along." George paused. "Hell, you *were* the president all along. I saw those crappy, insulting *Nation* magazine fake family Christmas photos: you're the Big Daddy of the house, Condi's at the piano, Rummy and the Architect are chuckling by the fireplace, and

I'm your stupid ventriloquist doll. I bet you laughed your ass off when you saw that back in 2005. Because you knew that's the way it really was."

The two men stared at each other like two bull elephants. Dick tried to stand up to calm his former boss. But George pushed the other man back down. In spite of his ratty bathrobe and dishevelment, he looked presidential. "No, you shut up now, Dick. You aren't going to control my memoirs or my memories or my dreams. I'm going to write and speak the truth about what happened. And I'm going to spend the rest of my life trying to make amends for what I did wrong. You leave. Leave right now. And don't ever return."

Dick stood up, his face flushed with fury. If anyone had witnessed this exchange they might have thought of Satan. But George just held his gaze, as others had done with the evil one. Speaking the truth really had power over evil, George realized. The suited man cowered and backed out of the room.

George walked over to the table with his Bible. He picked it up and turned to the Kings chapter. He knew there was something in there that might help him. He thought about those days when he'd felt so sure he was right about so many things, including those wiretaps on American citizens. It had seemed right at the time; it had seemed clear that he needed control of any information out there to fight terror. Some Americans had agreed with him, and it seemed pathetic to have to get permission from a judge, especially someone who'd been appointed by a Democrat.

But now, knowing they'd put something in *his* brain to monitor *his* dreams, he felt complete outrage. He felt violated as a human being. A song came into his head. It was a song his daughters had liked, maybe because they felt under such scrutiny at the White House, which *was* a crummy place to be a rebellious teenager. He would have absolutely *hated* being an adolescent in the White House.

George sang *Every Breath You Take* tunelessly and got a word wrong, but finally understood the lyrics, and why his daughters had liked this Sting tune so much.

Still singing, he walked into the next room and was shocked to see Dick there, fiddling with the plugs in the wall. "What are you doing? I told you to leave."

Dick looked up. He had an iPod in his ears and couldn't seem to hear what the other man said. His body twisted in an odd fashion and his head dipped like a bobble doll in a grotesque dance.

George strode up to him and ripped a cord out of the socket.

Dick looked really offended and took the plugs of the iPod out of his ears. "What did you do that for? I was listening to Johnny Cash's *Ring of Fire*." Of course, he had also been making sure the spy devices in the living room were still functional.

"OUT! OUT!" George shoved his former best friend towards the French doors. "LEAVE NOW. And don't EVER come back."

Dick put his iPod back into his ears and did a little dance wiggling his bottom. He sashayed out the door and mouthed the words, "We're not done, Dubya." Dick left the door open and continued dancing down the driveway to his car. He pranced as if he didn't have a concern in the world. He knew he'd keep George in court for years with lawyers who would just delay and delay. That's what lawyers were for. And he had plenty of money to pay them. In spite of the stock market collapse, Dick had made so much money in the past ten years he was never going to have to work again. This dream monitoring was great stuff. He was going to make even MORE money with that technology. He started chuckling and then sang along with *Ring of Fire*.

But instead of the word "fire," he heard the word "liar." Dick shook his head. That wasn't right. He tried to sing the correct lyrics, but the words kept coming out wrong, like some thingamajig had been placed in the singing part of *his* brain. A song gone crazy. Dick whimpered. It was as if the famous country singer had turned his truth-seeking eye on the lying-est liar who ever lived and wasn't going to leave off tormenting him until Dick was forced to acknowledge his own lies, if to no one else but himself.

As Dick staggered down the driveway and had a sudden vision of himself in a ring of fire, he screamed, "I am not America's biggest goddamn liar."

* * *

The local police later found Dick's car off the road in a ditch. Dick was kneeling on the ground outside the car, yelling and sobbing about Johnny Cash and burning in hell. When they put him in the police vehicle, he repeatedly shouted, "I WON'T TALK TO EVIL."

He had no identification on him and looked so disheveled they hadn't recognized him. The police officers were relieved to drop their raving passenger off at the local hospital. "Another whacko for Waco," one officer chuckled to the other. They knew he'd end up in the state mental hospital in Austin, where most of the acutely agitated psychotic patients were sent, or perhaps in a locked padded room at Fort Hood. Either way, they figured it would be weeks before this crazy was released.

Meanwhile, George had opened a phone book and was looking up neurosurgeons. He'd try Dallas first. They had to have someone who'd know how to get this thingamajig out of his head. He hoped that the doctor had voted for him, like that neurosurgeon in *Saturday* must have voted for Blair. He sighed as he flipped through the pages. It was going to be a long day. But he felt enormous satisfaction in having kicked Dick out of his house, and having stated out loud his plan for truth and honesty. He *was* the decider. And this time he'd decided on the truth.

Chapter 23

If there had been a spy plane following the travelers, it could have taken the following photos: in northwest Nebraska Lucy riding her bicycle towards Crazy Horse; Bill and Darrell on their motorcycles driving there from Wounded Knee, South Dakota; and Maria and Charlie heading towards the Black Hills. The skies were sunny over all parties and there were few vehicles on the roads they traveled. Even Lucy was making good time, speeding downhill on a state highway.

Many Americans didn't know it, but Crazy Horse had become an American pilgrimage site which celebrated rebellion, freedom, and nature, fundamental aspects of the spirit of America. Henry Thoreau, Ralph Waldo Emerson, Harriet Beecher Stowe, and Samuel Clemens might have recognized it as such. And Abraham Lincoln and George Washington, if they could have escaped their presidential rocky cliffs and the bounds of history, might have enjoyed a horseback ride around the monument with the Indian chief whose acts of valor had inspired it. The Black Hills of South Dakota were the wild heart of North America. Like Mount Kailas in Tibet or Uluru in Australia, the Black Hills served as a spiritual source for North Americans. Many thought it would have been better to have nothing manmade in the Black Hills, but once Six Grandfathers, the Lakota name for Mount Rushmore, was desecrated, the only way forward was to have an even bigger monument to Crazy Horse. Lucy and the others were being drawn there for renewal and replenishment before the next stage of their journey.

Bill and Darrell arrived at Crazy Horse first. It was August, right after the Sturgis motorcycle rally, and they found the parking lot filled with bikes, mostly Harleys, accompanied by leather-clad, rough-looking people. But they all appeared very respectful, as if they'd finally found the right sanctuary for their spiritual beliefs. However, this was America, and to get to the outdoor viewing area, visitors were first channeled through a huge gift shop. It was full of more Indian-themed items than most gift shops in America, but there was also plenty of plastic non-Indian American kitsch.

Bill detested gift shops, especially this one, which he saw as utterly antithetical to the spirit of Crazy Horse. He led Darrell through the aisles as if the items on the shelves were invisible. No sooner had they passed through the doors at the back when the men stopped dumbfounded. They stared at the enormous statue of the man and horse carved in the mountaintop surrounded by forest.

Bill felt peaceful. This was the America that he yearned for. This was part of what he'd tried to stand for in Iraq. The complete opposite of the horrors of Abu Ghraib. Strength. Beauty. Nature. Spirit. The sacred aspects of America. He nodded. This was the right place to be and somehow the spirit of Crazy Horse would lead them to Lucy.

Darrell had somewhat different thoughts. This place was pagan. The horse was like something from the Apocalypse. It seemed an ungodly place, except for the gift shop, where he felt safe. Darrell shivered. All those leather-clad, tattooed, nose-pierced motorcycle freaks made him nervous. He fingered the cross at his neck and remembered that Jesus was with him wherever he found himself. Then he noticed one leather-clad man with a huge picture of Jesus on the back of his coat, and his companion with a Virgin of Guadeloupe embossed in her leather jacket. He breathed a sigh of relief. "Where more than one is gathered in my name...."

Bill wanted to walk around the monument, but visitors were restricted to the buildings, except for the first full weekend in June when they could walk to the top. Bill didn't really want to go there. He would rather have circumnavigated Crazy Horse through the wooded trails he imagined below. Although it was not allowed, some people slipped by the security guards and were able to walk peacefully in the forest. But it was really too late in the day to try such a hike.

They decided to camp in nearby Custer State Park. Bill didn't think much of the name. It should have been called Crazy Horse, he thought. But Darrell felt relieved to leave the sinister Crazy Horse and go to Custer. Darrell had always thought that Custer looked like Jesus, and of course they'd both been martyred.

No matter the name, anyone would agree on the park's beauty. Huge granite rocks protruded from remnants of ancient glacial scrapes out of the ground and out of the lakes, as if from Avalon. With deep shades of green, grey and brown, glinting with clear streams and lakes, the park was a jewel of the Black Hills.

Driving through Custer, they glimpsed a buffalo in the forest shade, exposed by its steaming breath in a shaft of sunlight. Even Darrell seemed to feel the beast's power, but he also felt afraid; these strong animals could bowl a person over and quickly trample the life out of him. They watched the buffalo breathe in silence for a few minutes. Then they continued on to the campground.

Later that evening, settled near beautiful Sylvan Lake, the men sat before a campfire and observed the granite boulders emerging from the water's surface. In spite of the number of people camping in the forest, the place was peaceful. Sylvan Lake inspired quiet, and the campers weren't noisy, as in some other campgrounds. Bill thought of his ancestors around similar fires, thousands of years ago, elsewhere on the earth. He figured everyone came from some kind of tribe, and in a place like Sylvan, anyone with the right spirit could be an Indian.

* * *

Maria and Charlie exceeded the speed limit almost the whole day, but the state troopers had been elsewhere and the women arrived at Crazy Horse Memorial just as it was closing. They looked around but didn't see anyone they knew. Another couple in the parking lot, two gay men on bikes, told them about a nearby place to camp, Custer State Park, and gave them directions.

Later, as Charlie and Maria entered the park, they drove less than the ten mph limit out of respect for people taking after-dinner walks.

They noticed a campfire with two men. Suddenly one of the men whooped and hollered and then jumped up and ran towards them. Maria and Charlie looked at each other. "Shit," they said at the same time. How did those guys get out of that Laramie jail so quickly and get up here? Charlie was just pulling a weapon out of her bag when the man shouted, "Maria. Charlie. It's me, Bill."

Maria was off the motorcycle instantly and within moments was giving Bill a big hug. Once she released him, he embraced Charlie and then told them where to park their bike. When the smiling women looked in Darrell's direction, he merely nodded; he didn't trust lesbians.

Charlie and Maria related their story of the four men from Abu Ghraib in Laramie. Bill was shocked to hear that they had been released from jails in Colorado, and he felt furious that they'd come dangerously close to killing Maria and Charlie. The men were imprisoned again now, but he knew they'd never stop looking for him, and the others he had befriended. Bill was going to have to deal with them some day, whether it was in court or on the battlefield. At least he could relax that night. He fell asleep looking up at the stars, hoping that Lucy was looking at the same night sky.

* * *

Lucy had fallen asleep looking at the stars. She was in the Buffalo Gap Grasslands, fifty miles south of Custer State Park. In August the nights were equal in length to the days, and she woke up the next morning after a very deep sleep. Lucy had a good feeling about South Dakota and the Black Hills. She planned to stop in nearby Hot Springs and find a church. It was Sunday and she felt the need for a service. She was hoping to pray and sing hymns with people who felt the way she did about life.

Hot Springs was the right place for Lucy. It had been a spiritual place for the Indians, and the white settlers had felt that presence and built churches in the region reflecting their own religious beliefs. It had at least twenty-eight churches: Baptist, Lutheran, Episcopalian, Church of Christ, Latter Day Saints, Catholic, Presbyterian, Greek Orthodox, Methodist, Unity, and a few non-denominational Christian churches. There were no synagogues, Buddhist temples, or mosques. She would have had to go to Rapid City for those. But with a population of only about five thousand people, there was space for everyone, Christian or not, to attend church.

Lucy arrived mid morning. She hoped for a church where she'd find the Born Again who believed in the Rapture, but she knew all Christians believed in Jesus, and that's what she really needed. She saw a Latter Day Saints church with people filing through the front door. She pulled her bicycle up to the side of the church where she figured it would be safe. She ran her hands through her hair, as she knew she was a bit disheveled from the bike ride. Lucy entered the church, got a drink at a water fountain, and sat down in one of the back pews. She opened up the worn Bible, closed her eyes and prayed silently. It felt so good to be among other believers.

When she opened her eyes she saw that a young man, nicely dressed in a suit, had seated himself next to her. She smiled slightly at him, and he smiled back. The minister asked all to rise and sing *Rock of Ages*, originally a Jewish song. This particular congregation had gained some Jewish converts and the minister liked the song. He *was* a believer in the Rapture and felt proud of converting a few Jews to help fulfill the prophecy. Every Jew counted, even those in little Hot Springs, South Dakota. He'd given their names to the National Rapture Database. The minister figured that the Lord would know when the final number was reached, but in the meantime it was proper that someone tallied this in a computer.

Lucy hadn't gotten a service sheet, and the nice young man showed her which hymns were next. She thought about her parents. She needed to send them a postcard from Hot Springs and tell them she was doing well, in the company of other believers. That was certainly true this morning. And as she listened to the minister, she realized she'd found other people who believed in the Rapture also.

She relaxed as she took in the familiar words: "And those who believe and follow the holy words of Jesus Christ shall be raptured into heaven on the day of reckoning. And those who don't believe, will remain on earth which will become hell, filled with plagues, hurricanes, floods, hot winds, drought, and death."

The minister thundered as he said these words. It was easy to imagine the inevitability of the prophecy, although if one looked outside, Hot Springs, South Dakota appeared just a peaceful ordinary American town.

When the service was over, the young man asked Lucy if she'd like to have some lemonade. She agreed and they went into the fellowship hall. He introduced himself as Sam Brown. He handed her a cup and she drank it without stopping. He laughed and got her another. "You must have been thirsty. It does get hot in there. No air conditioning. We don't really need it here in South Dakota. Although with global warming, it's going to get hot here too." He said this very matter-of-factly. Global warming was an inevitable process predicted by the Bible. Lucy believed the same.

She looked over her paper cup at him. He was probably her age. "Do you go to school here?" she finally asked.

He looked a little embarrassed. "Yes, I have one more year of high school. I'm eighteen though."

Lucy smiled at him. "I'm seventeen but I finished high school last December down in Killeen, Texas."

Sam asked Lucy, "How'd you get to South Dakota?" They had moved outside now and stood near the parking lot. Lucy pointed at her bicycle. Sam was impressed. She didn't look that strong and he wondered how she had ridden all that distance. An older couple approached Sam, who turned to them and said, "Mom and Dad, Lucy has come all the way from Texas. Lucy, I'd like you to meet my parents."

The older folks smiled politely and shook her hand. Sam's mom lingered longer. "Lucy, please join us for lunch. We would be glad to have you."

Lucy smiled at the family. "Sure, I'd like that. I'd like that a lot."

They put Lucy's bicycle in the back of their four-door pickup and in a short time arrived at a one-story ranch home set off a dirt road, surrounded by a barbwire fence. Some cattle and a couple of horses grazed in a grassy lot beside the driveway. A retriever ran out from behind the house to greet them. Everyone got out and the dog jumped up and licked their faces. Lucy laughed. She hadn't been kissed by a dog in a long time.

Lucy helped Sam's mother set the table and put out some casseroles. Sam's father said a prayer of thanks, and they began to eat. Lucy didn't say much. She knew that some families were quiet when eating, and others spoke a lot, arguing with food flying out of their mouths. This family seemed like the quiet kind. After they'd eaten, the parents said that they had lived their whole lives in South Dakota. They had gone on a few vacations to Florida and some medical missions in Honduras where Sam had learned Spanish. Lucy was a bit surprised to meet a Spanish-speaking Anglo family in South Dakota but realized that there were Spanish speakers all over America. She told them a little bit about her pilgrimage, saying that she was almost halfway done, her next stop Red Lake, Minnesota.

Sam considered her thoughtfully. He had a summer job bagging at a grocery store, but he had Sundays and Mondays off. "Dad, could I borrow the truck and take Lucy up to Custer this afternoon? That's on the way, Lucy, to where you want to go."

His mom and dad looked at each other and nodded at the same time. American families weren't all like the *American Psycho Freddy Texas Chainsaw Massacre Blue Velvet American Beauty* families depicted in Hollywood. In spite of their Rapture beliefs and trader-miner-settler-rancher ancestors, the Browns had made an effort to understand the history of the area and learn what happened to the local Indians. There wasn't anything the Browns could do to change over a hundred years of history, but they could learn about Crazy Horse, Sitting Bull, and Black Elk, and they felt the same awe the Indians felt each time they ventured into the Black Hills, or, as the Indians called it, Sa Papa. And like most other families anywhere, they were nice.

From bookshelves behind him, Sam picked up a favorite book, Mari Santos' *Crazy Horse*, to take with them up to Custer. If there had been some kind of emotional meter for how much he loved the area, he would have scored near the top. Sam's ancestors had been in South Dakota for five generations. This was a puny amount of time in contrast to the Sioux or the Cheyenne or the Crows. However, it was a long time to be in one place compared to most other Americans, who moved frequently and often didn't seem tied to one landscape.

Sam often thought about North America before people arrived some twelve thousand years earlier. It must have been incredible, with herds of mammoths, saber tooth tigers, buffalo and huge bears, as well as millions of wolves and eagles. He was glad that these latter animals had survived, but he wished he could have seen mammoths. When he'd read *Jurassic Park*, he had thought it was a great book, but he'd rather have resurrected mammoths than dinosaurs.

As Sam drove with Lucy to Custer, he told her about his thoughts on mammoths and they imagined seeing them out the window. "There's a herd over there. A real big one, some smaller adults and a couple of babies." They recalled what they knew about elephants and imagined mammoths behaving as North American native elephants.

It was mid-afternoon when they got to Custer. Sam drove to Sylvan Lake. He told Lucy that his parents had brought him there since he was a baby and he'd done his first rock climbing on the huge granite rocks protruding from the forest around the lake. He pointed out an enormous rock in the middle of the lake which he'd swum out to every summer since he'd learned to swim. In spite of the cars and people, this was still a special, sacred place to him. He imagined it as it was two hundred years ago with no one there except a few Indians.

"Lucy," he said, "I wish this place hadn't been called Custer State Park. Maybe Black Buffalo or White Buffalo State Park. Or Crazy Horse State Park."

"Or how about Mammoth State Park?" Lucy said.

They both laughed.

Sam sighed. He knew there were plenty of people who wanted to remember Custer as a hero, even though others thought he was the devil. And the statues of the presidents on a sacred mountain in the Black Hills was a huge effrontery to the Indians. But just as the Spanish had built their churches over sacred Aztec sites, blasting US presidents' faces into Mount Rushmore was to make sure that the Indians knew who was in charge of the country.

"That's why the Crazy Horse Monument is so necessary," Sam explained as they slowly drove around the lake. "He was a hero, and people need heroes. And heroes get statues. And big heroes get big statues. Even though I don't think Crazy Horse would have wanted a statue. He would have wanted the land returned to his people." He looked around. "The park should be renamed Crazy Horse."

Lucy recalled something that Alma had mentioned. "I think this place should be renamed White Buffalo Woman Park. This is so peaceful. From what I've heard, this place has her spirit."

Sam looked at her. "You're right. Replacing 'Crazy Horse' for 'Custer' would just make other people mad. And that's not what this place is about."

They observed the lake with its irregular edges and dark green water, smooth except for occasional insects bouncing off the water's surface. Gently sloping banks interspersed with massive granite boulders and soft pine trees surrounded the water. But their reverie was interrupted by the appearance of a massive RV. "Yuck. A modern day mammoth," Lucy said. An enormous invader, the recreational vehicle seemed out of place next to ancient Sylvan Lake. Sam shrugged and they looked back at the lake in a effort to ignore the monster.

The couple in the RV felt so relieved to be in the Black Hills. The beautiful Black Hills were a refuge, an oasis, after the endless monotony of Wyoming's dry plains. They had traveled all the way from San Francisco and hadn't seen anything so beautiful since Lake Tahoe. The driver stopped the vehicle and turned off the ignition. He glanced at his partner and sighed. The other man gazed at him, smiled and patted his arm. Then he got up, stretched and punched his arm up the air, shouting, "Yabadaba Doo! And I love you!" And he kissed him.

Neither man had been in the Black Hills before. Now they knew why the Indians revered it so much. Admittedly, Jackson Hole was pretty, but they'd had a devil of a time maneuvering their RV through that town, and they'd gotten a lot of dirty looks from the locals. They couldn't figure out if it was because of the RV or because they were obviously gay, or the California license plates. After that movie *Brokeback Mountain* lots of gays visited Wyoming, but even with their money they weren't really welcome. There was still a lot of homophobia out there in middle America.

Charlie and Maria noticed the RV as soon as it pulled in and nodded at the couple when they descended from the vehicle. The women weren't too thrilled about the RV, but these men seemed friendly, a nice gay couple. Charlie approached the men. "Hey guys, where are you from?"

The older man, the driver with the mustache, said, "San Francisco. So glad to be here. My name's Gary and this is my partner, Ronny."

Charlie smiled. "I'm Charlie and this is my partner, Maria." Maria walked over and shook their hands. They all smiled and relaxed. The Black Hills would be different from Jackson Hole or Laramie. They went back to the fire where Darrell and Bill were talking. After introductions, the six people stood there, looking at the flames and occasionally towards the peaceful lake. It was easy to imagine the scene without cars, trucks, or RVs, just small groups of people near glowing fires with smoke floating skyward and the smell of cooking food. All feeling the magic of Sa Papa.

Bill listened to the chatter of the foursome. Each couple seemed very compatible, and there was a physical and spiritual intimacy between the two women and the two newcomers that he could sense. He knew Darrell felt it, too, but Darrell was obviously uncomfortable with this group. Bill figured it was hard for him to see two lesbian women together, but two gay men would be an even greater sin. Bill knew that line from the Old Testament in Leviticus: "*Thou shalt not lie with mankind as womankind; it is an abomination.*"

Bill missed the kind of intimacy the two couples shared. He'd had it briefly with a few women, but he had really felt the long term possibility of it with Lucy. Just as he started to feel sorry for himself, Bill saw her. He thought he must have conjured her out of his deep longing. But after a minute he knew she was real and he got up and began to run.

When Lucy saw Bill coming toward her, her first thought was relief. Then she felt confused, as something else that had nothing to do with her spiritual journey overcame her. By this time, Darrell had started running too, a bit behind Bill.

Sam stood back. Lucy had told him about the two men, and it was easy to see which one was Bill and which was Darrell. Darrell looked similar to guys from church, but Bill looked like a soldier. And the two beautiful women at the campfire must be Maria and Charlie. And the other guys, who were they? They didn't look like they were from South Dakota. Well, this would be interesting, he thought to himself.

Lucy hugged Bill, and then they looked at each other awkwardly. Bill turned to Sam, who explained that he'd brought Lucy to Sylvan Lake. Darrell had approached by then, but Lucy was standing so near Bill it would have seemed aggressive to push him away, and Darrell could only look at her. The three young men and Lucy walked back to the group around the campfire, and after many more hugs and exultations, they caught up on what had happened to one another.

Later, keeping an eye on Lucy, who was now talking animatedly with Darrell, Bill pulled Maria and Charlie aside and grilled them on what had happened with the guys from Abu Ghraib, especially regarding where they thought the men might be. Bill just didn't think they were going to stay jailed. They had too many accomplices, and Bill knew how badly those men wanted to kill him, and probably now, the three women and Darrell as well. He examined Darrell, sitting close to Lucy and looking at her with adoration, and felt a stab of jealousy. Maybe he wouldn't mind if the Abu Ghraibs got Darrell. But that was an evil thought and he dismissed it immediately.

By the next morning, decisions had been made. Looking at the map, the next logical place to stop would be Pipestone, Minnesota. Lucy had wanted to keep riding her bicycle, but the summer was getting on and the trip would take too long. Besides, she'd had enough of traveling alone, at least for now. She would ride in the RV with Ronny and Gary, who had enthusiastically volunteered as transportation and company for this leg of the young woman's pilgrimage. They were going all the way to Itaska, the source of the Mississippi, so they could take her to Red Lake. Bill felt bad about not telling Ronny and Gary the entire story of the Abu Ghraibs, but then the men might not have offered to help Lucy. The others would ride their motorcycles, shadowing the RV all the way.

Sam really wanted to go with them, but he had to get back to his parents and his job. Lucy promised to write, and he left feeling thrilled that he'd introduced himself to her. You never knew who you might meet in church, he thought.

When it was time to leave, Darrell's motorcycle wouldn't start, and when inquiries confirmed that it would cost more to fix than it was worth, he decided to let it go and ride in the RV with Lucy. Bill was aggravated but couldn't do anything about this turn of events. He had to watch Lucy and Darrell chat in the back while Gary drove and Ronny rode shotgun.

Ronny knew all the show tunes, and he sang songs from *Guys and Dolls, South Pacific, The Sound of Music, Fiddler on the Roof, West Side Story* and *The Wizard of Oz* as they drove east. Darrell monopolized Lucy but later in the day, he agreed to ride the motorcycle when Bill said he needed a rest. Lucy had joined in the singing so Bill sat quietly with his arms folded, listening and shifting his eyes between the others and the landscape outside the windows. Bill had traveled in all kinds of vehicles but had never been in a huge RV before. Really all he knew about RVs was from comedies like *Meet the Fockers* with Robert De Niro and Dustin Hoffman or *RV* with Robin Williams. Luxurious RVs sure were comfortable, especially when he thought back to the Bradleys and Hummers in Iraq, but Bill wondered if an RV was the right way to see America. Maybe it was for some. Maybe it was America: a huge gas-guzzling home moving along endless highways, the interior decorated with photos of both living and deceased family members and pets, as well as handmade crocheted doilies, and little swaying signs: *"Mi casa es tu casa"* and *"Your mother doesn't live here, so pick up your goddamned socks right now!"*

Ronny's enthusiastic singing got old after a while. Bill would have liked to put on some Phish and Jackson Browne and drive the RV himself. He looked out the window and waved to Maria and Charlie, who were passing on the left. He must have felt safe in this big homey box with this strange collection of people, for he fell asleep.

Bill found himself in a garden, a miraculous, light-filled garden. Glowing flowers, bushes, and trees that he'd never seen before surrounded him. The sound of a stream filtered through the forest like music. He was dressed in his military gear and he held a rifle in his hands. He didn't sense any danger, but that didn't mean there wasn't any. He walked towards the sound and found the stream, about twenty feet wide and very clear. Bill could see round hand-sized stones through the pure water.

Bill sat down, took off his boots and put his feet in the stream. Just as coolness covered his feet, he saw Lucy on the other bank. She looked very sad. He got up to go towards her, but he could only move in slow motion. The stream, previously so beautiful and inviting, had gone murky, with green algal streamers curling around his ankles. He was midstream before he realized that he'd left his gun back on the bank. He wanted to turn and get it, but he didn't want to lose sight of Lucy, who seemed to be receding into the forest. He then realized some kind of net had been thrown over her and she was being dragged away. The Abu Ghraibs appeared, and they laughed at Bill. He tried to reach the other side of the stream, but with each step, he was being pulled down by the algae, which had become as strong as thick rope. As his head disappeared beneath the rapidly deepening water he heard Lucy's scream and he knew what the men were going to do to her.

Bill woke with a start. The RV was still moving and Ronny was singing *Miracle of Miracles* from *Fiddler on the Roof.* Lucy was safe. Everything seemed the same, but Bill knew without a doubt that the men from Abu Ghraib were free and they were coming to get him and his friends. He was going to have to get some guns. He doubted that these San Francisco gays had any weapons. He wasn't sure about the laws in South Dakota or Minnesota but he figured there were lots of guns to be had. There were guns all over America.

Bill walked up to the front of the RV, catching the rail as Gary moved into the passing lane and then swung back. "Hey, guys."

"Took a nice nap, Bill? Isn't it comfortable back there?" Ronny asked.

Bill felt irritated and overwhelmed at the same time. It would probably be hard to make these guys understand the danger that was out there. Anyone who hadn't been a soldier didn't really get it, how quickly things could go bad when the enemy was determined to kill you. "Ronny, I've got to ask you and Gary whether you have any guns."

Ronny and Gary both turned around to look at him, Ronny with great alarm. "We don't have any guns, Bill. Why would we need any? I mean this is the Wild West, and a lot of people here hate gays, RVs and people from California, but I don't think they'd want to shoot us."

Bill cleared his throat. He now felt embarrassed that he'd downplayed the danger of the men from Abu Ghraib. He was going to have to explain everything that had happened. So he went through the whole story in detail, the recent story of the other vets and the bad guys from Abu Ghraib, and their pursuit, now expanded to include Lucy, Darrell, Maria, and Charlie. And, if those guys found them, the list would also include Gary and Ronny.

Ronny gasped with each new detail, but Gary looked serious. "I get the picture, Bill. I might be a faggott, but I served in 'Nam and I know how to shoot. I actually do have a rifle with some ammo in the back."

Ronny gasped again. "We've gotta a gun, Gary?"

Gary patted his arm. "Yep. Sorry I didn't tell you, Ronny. Didn't want to alarm you. But I wasn't going to venture out into America without bringing my rifle."

Bill and Gary talked about what they would need and that they'd have to stay in one place for a few days for the background checks. They looked on the map and saw Sioux Falls up ahead. They knew it would have gun shops and, if not, a flea market where they could buy weapons. Charlie would agree with the plan. With Bill, Gary, and Charlie, they'd have a chance against the bad guys. Unless they'd recruited reinforcements. Or had superior weapons. Bill felt on alert. They had a plan and with weapons, could overcome the Abu Ghraibs and hopefully deal with them once and for all.

* * *

Judith and Joseph had reconciled. She'd had enough time apart and her desire for him had returned in full force. It was memories of the pleasure they'd shared that had saved her from the bleakness which engulfed her mind on seemingly random occasions. Abbie told the two lovers she would spend the weekend with a cousin and they should just enjoy themselves. And they did.

Breathing heavily, her heart racing, Judith lay on the bed, her body relaxing and flooding with hormones of love. Stretched out next to her, Joseph stroked her belly after he helped Judith turn her back to him. Her bottom rested in the curve of his waist. He snuggled closer so they lay together like two spoons, albeit one considerably shorter than the other. He kissed her neck and continued his caresses.

"Joey," she murmured. She'd started calling him this recently. Joseph was a bit too formal and fatherly. If she'd been a cat, she would have purred. She was so glad the IED hadn't hit her abdomen. For one thing, she'd be dead, but even in the odd chance she'd survived, her torso would be horribly scarred, and she wouldn't be able to feel the wonderful sensation of having her belly softly stroked round and round, as Joseph was doing.

Sometime later, as they lay side by side, Judith said, "Joey, I'm thinking about going to Crawford."

"Crawford, Texas? Jesus, Judith! Are you sure?"

"Yeah. Dubya will be there. Maybe he'll come and catch my act."

Joseph thought about it and then started laughing as he envisioned President Bush at a comedy club, the butt of Judith's jokes. Judith joined in and soon they were howling with laughter. "Yeah, you'll have to be ready with a video camera to take pictures of him when he sees me and understands what he did to me. And later you'll have to describe his face to me."

Judith could still feel her absent limbs. The docs had called it phantom pain, although sometimes it wasn't pain she felt, but more of a phantom presence. And she still dreamed of herself whole, without any disability. She had tremendous regret. However, the loss of her limbs and her sight had become her shtick. Getting people to react and laugh was now part of what she lived for, besides Joey. And the other part, of which neither was yet aware, would be the baby that was just starting to form in her belly.

"Yeah, let's do a show in Crawford. Maybe I'll get some other vets, 'Rack Rats,' and we'll do an all vet comedy show. Actually, let's invite Dubya. Maybe he'll show up thinking it's a photo-op with vets. He'll come all puffed up and then end up deflated."

"But he has to laugh, Judith. Otherwise you won't have done your job."

They kept laughing. They had an image of the former president, as a deflated puffball, leaking dust out of his goofy grin every time he wheezed a laugh. It could happen. Anything was possible.

* * *

"But George, honey, that just doesn't sound possible. No one could have put something into your brain. I mean, there isn't anything like that. No one can monitor someone else's dreams, or nightmares for that matter. Besides, when would they have done that? Why wouldn't you remember going for surgery?" Laura stood beside George. "Let me look at your head and see if I can find anything."

She examined him and everything looked fine. She pursed her lips. Maybe she'd have to cut back on yoga or watching chick-flicks with friends or their daughters when they visited. Laura was tired of Crawford. But she knew that George still liked their ranch. He cut brush and whacked weeds even when there were no journalists watching.

"Laura, I know something's happened to me and I have to do something about it. I can't talk with anybody about it except for you. And Barney." They both smiled. A good dog was really far more valuable than dozens of advisors. George was lucky enough to have a good wife and a good dog.

"Well, let's see what the doctor says on Tuesday. I think I made the right choice in that board certified neurosurgeon." George didn't tell Laura, but the doctor was also a board certified psychiatrist, the only doctor so dually certified in America. A registered Republican, too. This fact relieved George's anxiety about making the appointment secretly. Former presidents were supposed to have all doctors vetted by the Secret Service and get all their care through armed services hospitals. But if the Secret Service knew about this doctor, then Dick would find out and would stop him from seeing Dr Raintree.

George suffered the humiliation of knowing that someone could spy on his dreams for the next two nights. But once he got that damn thingamajig out of his brain, he'd find out who besides Dick had done this devilish deed. George wanted to chop them up, *Texas Chainsaw Massacre*-style. Or at least sue them for millions. That would get Dick where it really counted. George wondered if they had imminent domain in Maryland. He'd really like Dick to lose his fancy new home with its exclusive no-fly zone over his property. George couldn't believe he'd trusted Dick and mumbled one of Dick's favorite statements: "One percent chance of aggression requires a pre-emptive strike." *Requires*. Why had he ever gone along with Dick? Why hadn't he listened to his dad and a few others and tried diplomacy? It was too late now. At this point, all he could think of was getting this damn thing out of his head. Domestic surveillance *had* gone too far. It *was* against nature and it was un-American. He suddenly thought of the American Civil Liberties Union, the ACLU. He realized, especially in this matter, that they actually had the best lawyers. He shook his head. That would shock everyone: George W Bush calling the ACLU and asking for help. He jerked his head again and wished he could just rip the thingamajig out with his bare hands. It was going to be torture to wait two more days.

Laura had given him a pamphlet to read on "nightmare rehearsal" as a cure for nightmares. It sounded flakey and a bit frightening. George wondered why anyone would want to rehearse a nightmare. But he'd taken the information because his wife had given it to him. The brochure suggested that while awake, you review the details of the nightmare. Then you should imagine something very different that changes the outcome so that it is no longer frightening. Perhaps, George fantasized, Mother Nature could appear with small animals, instead of snakes as she had in the hospital, and be friendly and kind.

It was hard to imagine Mother Nature as anything other than a vengeful, hateful, powerful goddess. He didn't know much about nature and didn't really get the concept of wilderness. Wetlands, for example. To George, wetlands were just mosquito-infested swamps, something to drain and then erect houses or businesses on. He certainly didn't understand the concept of wetlands as nature's lungs, or kidneys as someone he'd probably fired had once described them. It just didn't make sense.

Maybe he could imagine Mother Nature from the mother angle. Admittedly, he had complicated relations with his own mother, but then so did many men. Like the Queen of England, Barbara Bush was formidable. She still tried to boss him around occasionally. But he could now sympathize more with his mother since his dream about Robin.

So George started to think of Mother Nature as a mother. Someone who takes care of you when you're hurt or sick. Someone who helps you solve your problems and learn necessary skills, like swimming, riding a bicycle, or reading. Someone who tells you you're the most loved person in the whole world. Someone who hugs you, sings you lullabies and rocks you to sleep. His mother had done all those things.

Hmmm, George thought. Maybe Mother Nature could help him with that thingamajig in his brain. She wouldn't like humans tampering with dreams, a fundamental process of nature. The brochure on nightmare rehearsal said that peoples who live more closely with nature revere dreams. George mused that he hadn't had many dreams before he left office. Or, if he had, he hadn't thought they were of any importance.

As George slept that night, he found himself at the most beautiful state park in Texas, Enchanted Rock. The huge granite monolith loomed over him like a gentle giant, and George felt ashamed of his previous plan to blast his face into the rocks. He soaked in the essence of the enchantment: gnarled expanses of rock, Texan oaks, bluebonnets in grassy knolls, and gentle sweet streams running haphazardly, though beautifully, through the forest around the edges of the granite giant.

George then noticed Mother Nature seated on a large boulder underneath a wide oak tree. She wore a dress made of living Texas wildflowers: bluebonnets, fire flowers, and daisies. Her long wavy light brown hair swirled around her gown. And she did look gentle—the first time he'd ever seen her sweetness. She smiled at him. "Is this what you were hoping for?"

George smiled back in relief. "Yes. You look uh…uh…uh…." His words failed him. For maybe the millionth time in his life he wished he were eloquent.

Mother Nature patted the rock and he sat beside her. He looked again at the dress made up of Lady Bird Johnson's wildflowers. Some women in Texas would pay millions for such a dress.

Mother Nature laughed. "It's not for sale. And no one could find this anywhere, although some men see this in some women when they're in a place like Enchanted Rock. Actually, some women see this in some women, and some men see this in some men, but I don't want to confuse you, George. This is one of my favorite dresses and I wouldn't be wearing it or meeting you here in this lovely place if you hadn't thought of me as a helpful kind mother. Not an adversary or someone to ignore, which in some ways is even worse. You can't dismiss Mother Nature."

George felt tears in his eyes. She took his hand and stroked it. The gentle pressure felt exactly as holding his mother's hand had when he'd been a small child. "I miss Robin so much. She was so sweet. And my mother loved her, too." He started sobbing. Mother Nature continued to stroke his hand. "You can't imagine how terrible it is to have someone you love sicken and die a few weeks later. Just disappear, and then have no one talk about her, as if she never existed."

Mother Nature could imagine. She was Mother Nature after all. Death was part of life. Many modern day humans, especially in places like America, didn't seem to understand this fundamental fact with their clean drinking water, modern medicines and technology. George's sister had died before treatments were available for childhood leukemia. However, Robin would have died sometime of something else and millions of years of witnessing the deaths of loved ones had given mourning humans the resources to recover.

"What could you do to bring your sister's spirit alive? What can you do to bring alive the spirits of those who've died in your Iraq War?"

George stopped crying. The prayer from Ecclesiastics appeared in his mind. There was a time for everything. He wished his family hadn't been so WASPy and uptight, that they'd been more like the Mexicans he'd known, who acknowledged their terrible grief.

He still didn't understand how unresolved childhood grief could lead to war (perhaps he should have read Norman Mailer's *The Castle in the Forest* about Adolf Hitler's youth), but he wondered how different everything would have been between him and his mother, and maybe between him and the world's people, if his family had simply talked about Robin and remembered her.

"Your grief can still be resolved, son. Better late than never. I agree with Jesus, Buddha and the others. It's never too late. I think you know what you have to do about the victims of the Iraq War. And about what you can do for natural resources, like wetlands. A clean environment prevents cancer. Spend more time in nature, spend more time talking to people who love nature, and more time reading literature and scientific reports about nature. Watch Al Gore's movie *An Inconvenient Truth.* You could even invite him to watch it with you in Crawford. I bet he'd come."

George felt very strange at the idea of watching *that* movie on his own ultrasupraplasma television set in his own living room, seated next to Al Gore.

She smiled at him. "Anything is possible, George, if you imagine it. Al would accept the invitation, I think. I also highly recommend *Earth in the Balance,* if you'd like yet another good book to read. Two thumbs up. Five stars. And my own personal mark for excellence: a triple rainbow."

Mother Nature caused a rainbow to appear in the sky and it stunned George with its unexpected beauty. "Spend more time here at Enchanted Rock. Watch that Gore movie. Read the book. Keep praying. You can do the right thing. People are very forgiving. I don't know if I'd call myself forgiving, but as much as I'm destructive, I'm also regenerative. Life *is* stronger than death, George."

Mother Nature stood up and stretched. The wildflowers in her dress moved gracefully. She bent over to give George a hug and whispered in his ear, "They don't know anything about our meeting or conversation. It really is NOT nice to fool Mother Nature. But you do need to get that thingamajig out of your brain. You'll like Dr

Raintree. She'll know what to do." At this, Mother Nature folded her hands at her chest in a namaste, bowed towards George and melted into a nearby field of wildflowers.

Chapter 24

They were able to buy guns in Sioux City in just over twenty-four hours. They ended up with an arsenal. Each picked out several of their own favorite weapons and a number of grenades. Ronny had been a baseball pitcher in high school, and since then he had helped out with the local Little League. He could throw far, fast, and accurately. Bill had played all sorts of sports too, and he had experience with grenades. Gary hadn't fired a gun in years, but the gun store brought back memories of Vietnam, where he'd been a good shot. Darrell had done some hunting, and he selected a rifle with a small cross engraved on the stock.

Lucy was the only one completely unfamiliar with firearms; she felt dread when she looked at the guns in the gun shop. This wasn't part of her pilgrimage. This was part of the problem. Guns killed people. She was shocked when she saw Maria pick up a rifle and pretend to aim it. Maria said she used to go deer and duck hunting with her father and brothers. She hadn't fired a gun in years, but like swimming and riding a bicycle, once a person knew how to handle a gun, he or she never completely forgot this skill.

Later that day, with Lucy watching apprehensively, Maria pointed her rifle at some empty beer cans on fence posts some miles outside of Sioux City. She aimed and fired three times. Three beer cans exploded in succession. Lucy flinched with each shot, but Charlie said, admiringly, "You go, girl." Charlie had had no idea that her girlfriend knew how to fire a gun. The others also gave shouts of encouragement as they shot off more cans from the fence posts. Bill was especially pleased and relieved to see the marksmanship, and thought maybe they did have a chance.

Lucy walked away from the group and sat down next to a large rock. She could see for miles in all directions, and her thoughts expanded to fit the space. She'd started out wanting this to be a pilgrimage to understand violence, pray for the dead, and to deepen her religious beliefs. And here she was with a group of people, half of them homosexual, all of them with weapons, and none of them interested in religion, except Darrell, who, along with Lucy, was the only true believer in Jesus Christ.

Lucy thought of David, the biblical David, who'd been just a kid, a shepherd boy who spent all his time slinging rocks and hitting targets while he watched the family's sheep. He must have only been about twelve or thirteen when the Philistines and their monstrous leader, Goliath, decided they wanted to destroy David's people, who were too frightened to fight. But David had the confidence of youth and knew how accurate he could be with a rock. He, of course, had never aimed at a person. But he had killed a sheep one day by hitting it squarely in the forehead. This was an accident and he'd gotten in trouble for his misbehavior. However, the incident had taught him the power of rocks, and after that he'd killed a few lions and bears and gained his father's admiration. So David believed that a rock could bring down a human, when aimed at the right place and slung with the right power. If David hadn't tried, or hadn't succeeded, the people of Israel would have been enslaved by the Philistines and might have disappeared. Lucy knew that David's story was one of the key stories of the Old Testament and she knew that the Jewish nation of Israel had to exist for the prophecy of the Rapture to come true. And all this would have vanished if one person hadn't tried something that seemed impossible. Lucy read from her Bible young David's words to Goliath, Samuel 17: *"You come to me with a sword and with a spear and with a javelin; but I come to you in the name of the Lord of hosts, the God of the armies of Israel, whom you have defied."*

Lucy closed her Bible and walked down to the nearby river. She carefully picked up five stones, just like David did thousands of years ago. She hadn't gone hunting with her family. She hadn't been a soldier. She hadn't even played softball. But she had thrust that knife into Luke's shoulder and she knew she could probably throw rocks at someone if they were trying to kill her. Lucy liked the feel of the rocks, smooth river stones.

"Penny for your thoughts."

Lucy turned around and saw Bill. She said, "They're worth a bit more than a penny."

He joined her in looking at the river and listening to the branches rubbing against one another in the wind. Lucy sat down and put the five stones in her lap. She wore a faded denim dress, and the damp stones weighed the fabric down so it stretched over her thighs. Bill couldn't help but look there. Stones. Her thighs. The dress. The sounds of the river. He knew he would do anything for this young woman, even if she wouldn't have him.

"I was thinking about David," Lucy said.

Bill groaned. Who in the hell was David? Some other guy from her church?

"You know, David, from the Bible."

Bill smiled. "David, sure, the young guy with stones who slew the bad guy when no one else would take him on." He knew the Old Testament from preparation for his bar mitzvah, although he hadn't touched a Bible since age thirteen. Of course he'd heard David's story again from the military chaplains. But the story came to mean something different to him in Iraq. He'd see young boys or men throwing stones at the Hummers and he eventually realized that he and the other Americans were the Philistines and the Iraqis were the Davids. Understanding this had made him feel sick. He'd never told anyone about his reinterpretation of David and Goliath. Seeing Lucy with the stones made him wonder if she was going to act as David had. "Are you going to do a David?" That was funny, Bill thought, and he laughed.

Lucy looked at him strangely, then angrily. "Anyone can be a David, even a girl. Except for that monster in the barn who was going to kill us, I've never hurt anyone. You don't know what I'm capable of."

"Sorry, Lucy. Don't be mad. We know what the Philistines would have done to the Jews if David hadn't been there to kill that monster, Goliath." Bill picked up a stone from the riverbed. He aimed and skipped it across the water almost to the other side. "The Jews would have been crushed. Maimed. Raped. Killed. Children sold into slavery. Extinguished. No more Jews. I wouldn't be here right now. Jesus wouldn't have lived and there wouldn't be any chance of his return as the Messiah."

Lucy thought for a while. "One kid. Just one young, small teenager saved them all." She glanced at Bill. "And it was because he fought against the impossible."

Bill gazed at Lucy. "That's right, Lucy. Sometimes you do have to fight."

Someone had once told her that many Jewish parents named their sons David, and this must have been the reason why. Lucy felt her doubt sweep away. She knew why these people were here. All of them wanted to help her and wanted to stop the Abu Ghraibs from hurting other Americans. However none of them wanted to lose their lives. She didn't know whether she could throw stones aiming to kill someone, but she decided she'd keep them and fill her small pack with more stones. And she'd practice throwing with a few tips from the others. Lucy was fitter and physically a lot stronger than she'd been some months ago, and now, just in the last hour or so, she'd become stronger yet again.

* * *

Bill's intuition was correct. The guys from Abu Ghraib had gotten out of the jail in Laramie. Only one call had been necessary. One of the jailers didn't question anything. The other jailer, an Iraq veteran, was more skeptical. But he didn't have much power in Iraq, or in Laramie, for that matter, and when he was told to release the four men, he simply did as he was told. The men said nothing as they took their belongings. They were especially happy to see the Hummer keys. They put on their baseball caps and sunglasses before they walked outside. A few prisoners watched them walk out the gate. "Mean motherfuckers. Ain't never seen such badasses."

The four men, bandaged up from their injuries when the Hummer wrecked, still looked formidable and they were furious. This was the third time they'd been thwarted. Trevor spoke on the cell phone as soon as they got outside the jail. The voice on the other end of the line ripped them with sarcasm. "You assholes haven't been able to get a few crazy vets, three women and a couple of religious nuts? You were supposed to have taken care of them weeks ago. Your payment's down to a hundred apiece."

"Wait, we were supposed to get—"

"Shut up. Get it done by the end of the week, and you'll have two hundred thousand each when you get to Vegas." The call ended abruptly.

Trevor was livid. Two days to find those fuckers. The men checked out the Hummer. Nothing had been touched inside. Thank God for the second and fourth amendments. All the weapons and ammunition were there. The vehicle was tanked up and they still had the extra jerry cans of fuel. They drove out of the parking lot, spraying gravel on the guards, and sped out of town. No one said anything for the first eighty miles. Then Luke said, "They seem to be on some kind of Indian thing. That girl was going to Red Lake, Minnesota."

Emile suggested, "Let's cut them off before they get there. Perhaps a shootout would be good. No *problema* there. We'll give them one." He examined their tourist map of South Dakota and Minnesota. Something caught his eye. "Pipestone."

"Pipestone?"

"Yeah, what's that?" Luke asked.

Emile read off the map: "Pipestone is the origin of stone used by the Indians for centuries for making their pipes, traditionally used in peace-making ceremonies. Native Americans have traveled to Pipestone or traded goods for pipes made from this sacred stone for thousands of years."

Trevor finally spoke: "That's where they'll go, and that's where we'll go. No peace for the wicked." They all laughed as they crossed out of Wyoming into South Dakota. Luke placed a call to their handler to explain their destination. The man grunted his approval. No place was off limits to the men from Abu Ghraib.

* * *

Joseph pushed Judith in her wheelchair down the main street of Crawford. They looked at the buildings, trying to find a suitable place for her act. They got the impression that most businesses were either pro or contra Bush. "We Lubya Dubya" said some signs, whereas others stated, "Support our Troops: Impeach the President." Feelings for or against the former president still ran strong in Crawford.

Crawford didn't have a theater, not even a movie theater. It did have churches, however, and one of them might be the best choice for a performance. Judith and Joseph decided to try the Baptist churches first, as they'd been raised Baptist. Judith really wanted George and Laura to attend their show, so once they'd secured the location, they'd put up notices in the Lubya stores.

Even if the Bushes didn't show up, maybe they'd catch her show at SMU in Dallas. Judith knew that Southern Methodist University, white and Christian as it seemed, actually had a long tradition of intellectual independence. A good friend of her grandmother's had told her about a Father Albert Achilles Taliaferro, a former Episcopalian minister, who in the 1980s and 90s, held non-denominational church services in an SMU auditorium. His church was attended by some of the most spiritually progressive people in Texas, including Willie Nelson. And in the evening, another enlightened man taught packed classes on the presence of the Goddess in all the world's religions. There were countless other examples. Judith's show would be welcome at SMU, and as a member of an audience, so would the former president, if he chose to attend.

Later that day Judith got permission from the Sunrise Baptist Church for her show the next evening. After a celebratory dinner back at the motel, Joseph did some channel surfing and hit the Comedy Channel. Judith listened to the comedians' voices, the audience's reaction and the words that made her laugh. She and Joseph observed how much laughter came from what one could hear, versus what one could see *and* hear. It depended on the comic. Most monologues were just as funny to the blind, but acts like Rowan Atkinson's Mr Bean depended on seeing his strange behavior and others' reactions to his antics.

Unfortunately for Judith, the comedy show ended and a slapstick John Candy movie began. But Joseph had some DVDs of standup comedians for when the Comedy Channel failed. Robin Williams. Whoopi Goldberg. Jerry Seinfeld. Margaret Cho. Billy Crystal. Sarah Silverman. *The Aristocrats.* Joseph groaned when he saw that one. Miguel from work must have slipped it in with the other DVDs.

"How about *The Aristocrats*, Judith?"

"No way, Joseph. Throw it away. That's sick and disgusting."

"But it made people laugh, Judith, when they really needed to laugh. Maybe you could try a version on stage."

While in Iraq, Judith had seen part of this film about the worst dirty joke ever told. The joke, told over and over again by various standup entertainers, was so appalling Judith couldn't make herself watch the movie through to the end. Prior to this film, veteran standup comedians only did this joke late at night when audiences were fired up and plastered. Supposedly this was Johnny Carson's favorite joke (amongst his fellow comics), but it didn't come to the attention of most Americans until 2005 when they saw *The Aristocrats.*

Strangely, the film had been inspired by 9/11. In the immediate aftermath of the tragedy, comedians had nothing to say and audiences didn't feel like laughing. At a Comedy Central Friar's Club roast of Hugh Hefner, comedian Gilbert Gottfried was loudly booed for an attempt at humor involving airplanes: "Sorry I'm late, but my plane had a connection with the Empire State Building." The only way he could think of to recover was to tell the aristocrats joke even though this was prime time. He accomplished what all comics hope to achieve: in the face of horrible reality, he made people laugh. Gil had completely cracked up this tough audience and broken through the 9/11 grief barrier. Humor, even sick humor, was another way to defy the twenty-first century terrorists just as Charlie Chaplin had defied Hitler and the Nazis.

"Yeah, right, Joey, I could just imagine myself doing my version of the Motherfucking Cocksucking family in a Baptist church."

Joseph winced. He'd never heard Judith use those words.

"But my aristocrats version would be inspired from that photo in *The Nation*. You know, the one with a happy American family in the living room at Christmas. Condi on the piano. Laura in the background. Donald listening and Dubya as a ventriloquist doll held by Dick." Judith looked subdued. She'd had that page ripped from the magazine up on a wall next to her cot in Iraq. Someone kept tearing it down, but with every new issue of *The Nation* sent by her grandmother, she'd put that photo right back up again. "Yeah, I guess I could tell a really good aristocrats joke. There was this family in Iraq and this other family in *The Nation* and...."

"Judith. Stop. Please." Joseph was about to laugh but Judith had tears running down her face. "Oh, Judith." Joseph held her until she stopped crying. He wiped her nose after she blew it on a tissue.

"What's sicker, Joey? The aristocrats joke or the Iraq War?"

Joseph looked at the stumps of her limbs and where her eyes used to be. "The war, Judith. There's nothing sicker than an unnecessary war."

Some moments passed. Joseph wasn't sure whether Judith was going to cry again. She surprised him when she broke into a smile. "So, I guess if they get sick of looking at me and hearing about the war, I'll just start in on an aristocrats joke. Sarah Silverman did pretty well with her version. Now she's got her own show on Comedy Central. I want one too. Wacky Wounded Warriors. What do you think? Is America ready for us?" Joseph hugged her and she continued talking. "Okay. I'm not going to tell an aristocrats joke. Especially in a Baptist church. It *is* sick. Not the church, but the joke!

But if I ever get to meet Sarah or Whoopi...." Joseph tossed *The Aristocrats* DVD in the garbage and they ended up laughing with Robin Williams for the next few hours.

The next evening Judith seemed nervous. Joseph fussed around, trying to calm her. "Do you want to go over your material, honey? I could pretend to be Dubya, or some other drunk redneck, and heckle you a little." He stood behind her and kissed her on the neck.

She giggled but pulled away from him. "Naw, I think I'll just wing it tonight. I'll use some of my old stuff and a few new ideas."

A couple of hours later, Joseph wheeled Judith out on the stage and left her there in a pool of light. She had on all her cosmetic prostheses, loosely attached to her stumps. Facing the crowd, Judith raised her chin to Joseph, his cue to shine a spotlight over the crowd, slowly moving it over their faces so he could see who was there. Now she wasn't sure if she wanted the former president to be there or not. To have the man ultimately responsible for her injuries in front of her, to have him listen to her story and see what she had become could be too much. Joseph would tell her if he was there with a "Yea," and if not, then a "Nay." It seemed right to use words from a courtroom. Judith had come to terms with her new life, but justice hadn't yet been served.

"Nay."

Oh well, on with the show, Judith thought and she started. "Hey, ya'll. I guess I'm like everyone else. Come to Crawford, Texas, hoping to see former President Bush. Not that I could see him, of course, because I'm blind." She moved her head from side to side, exaggerating the movement. "Or maybe shake his hand, but I can't do that because I don't have any hands." And she shrugged hard and her fake arms fell to the floor.

A few gasps of surprise came from the audience.

"Or maybe I'd just ask him why he sent us to Iraq when he knew there weren't any goddamned weapons of mass destruction. Just a pathetic dictator writing romance novels. Yeah, romance novels. Bet you didn't know that. Saddam wanted to be the next Danielle Steel.

Instead of outing Valerie Plame Wilson, Karl and Dick should have sent her to Iraq to have a little *tête-à-tête* with Saddam. He might have told her that he'd do *anything* for a publisher and worldwide distribution. Including abdicate. And then we wouldn't have had this stupid war and I'd be up here with my eyes and arms and legs, doing some kind of Ms Bean Three Stooges slapstick comedy. That damn dictator Saddam, asshole that he was, was no more of a threat to the United States than a no-limb, blind vet is a threat to Mr Bush. I'd really like to kick his ass. Bush, I mean. But I can't do that cause I ain't got no legs."

And Judith moved her torso and the fake legs fell to the floor.

The audience seemed stunned. They had come expecting some humor or at least inspiration. It was a comedy show in a church, after all. People started to look at each other, and a few in the back rose and tried to leave quietly.

Joseph said something to Judith.

"Hey, ya'll in the back. Please don't leave. Hear me out. You'll probably never meet someone like me ever again. Maybe you think I should just have stayed in that rehab hospital. Sure would have been more comfortable for me. More comfortable for you, too. Numbed with drugs, listening to TV all day long and let them take care of me, like some big baby. But I didn't do that. And you didn't stay home tonight. We're all here now." She paused. The people in the back had sat down and everyone was listening.

"And right now, I'm feeling pretty pissed off that President Bush didn't come to my show. Probably sitting up there in his ranch. Maybe he's reading Camus' *Stranger* again, trying to figure out the meaning of life. Or maybe he's watching baseball. Those Texas Rangers are playing tonight, ain't they?"

Someone from the crowd called out, "Yes, they are, ma'am."

"Thank you, son, your momma raised you right. Yeah, folks, I used to *love* baseball. Catching, pitching, running, hitting, sliding, winning. I was pretty damn good. I like those Rangers too. Maybe the only thing Bush and I have in common. 'Course I can't see 'em no more. Neither Bush nor the Rangers. But thank God for radio. I can still hear. And, most important, I still got my 'magination. Magi Nation, folks. It's all any of us got when you think about it. And mine is stronger these days, 'cause I ain't got much else left. So I'm just gonna 'magine our former president right here. Right here in this room. And I'm gonna talk to him, and he's gonna just shut up and listen, and then when he leaves here he's gonna use some of *his* Magi Nation to help put us back together again. Too late for me, as far as my limbs and eyes are concerned. I ain't no Humpty Dumpty. But it ain't too late for our country, the United States of America. Not everyone can be a comedian like me. Not everyone's got a great family like me. But that man, George W Bush, can go *sit* with wounded vets and the families of the dead. He can *listen* to their problems, and he can *help* them in ways only *they* know best. Sit. Listen. Help. The war wounded and families of the dead."

She paused. Joseph gave her a drink through a bended straw. No one tried to leave now. Judith had captured them. Even Joseph was impressed. This wasn't going to be comedy tonight. It was going to be tragedy, but it would be inspirational. He looked around the church and saw images of Jesus and the American flag. Magi Nation. That was another name for America. A twist in the O Henry "Gift of the Magi" story. Americans had given their lives and limbs, and the former president could give his pride, but instead of losing, he'd get something back of even more value. And so would everybody else.

* * *

George didn't slip in to see the show. He didn't know about it, although his staff did. A Secret Service agent attended in order to see if there was a threat to the former president. It was soon apparent that this limbless blind vet was no menace. It dawned on him that Judith was one of the most patriotic and inspiring speakers he'd ever heard. And he'd heard many eloquent speeches in his career. He wished the former president were there. As the agent drove back to the ranch after the show, he knew he'd write a report of "minimal threat" about Judith and her entourage. He wished he could sit down with his boss and tell him about the show. But he didn't have that kind of rapport with the man. It would be unlikely that George would ever hear of Judith. A shame, he thought.

George *was* oblivious to what was going on in Crawford that night. He rarely thought about the town closest to his ranch. He was glad he had some supporters there but he knew there was a large contingent of anti-Bushites including writers of that offensive local newspaper, *The Lonestar Iconoclast*.

That night, however, he wasn't watching his beloved baseball. Instead, to distract himself from thinking about the implications of his recent dreams, he was reading biographies on George Washington and Abraham Lincoln, the greatest presidents. He was determined to be remembered as great, too, even though it might take a hundred years for George W Bush to be recognized as the "father of democracy" in the Middle East. George read that lots of people hadn't liked Washington in his day, and even more people had disliked Abraham Lincoln.

George fell asleep in the chair with his book in his hands. When he woke in dreamland, he saw, striding towards him, none other than George Washington and Abraham Lincoln. George rose from his chair with his hand outstretched. But they kept talking to each other and walked right past the forty-third president as if he was nothing.

George felt shocked and then angry. He turned and called out to them. Suddenly, his arms were grabbed from behind and plastic cuffs were snapped on his wrists. He was kneed and fell to the ground. His ankles were bound and someone slapped duct tape over his mouth, shutting off his screams. All went dark as another piece of tape covered his eyes. Plugs were shoved in his ears and more duct tape applied. Someone kicked him in the back and the thigh. He pissed on himself. He got kicked again, began to throw up, and with his mouth covered in duct tape, had to re-swallow the vomit.

What the hell was happening? If only Washington and Lincoln

would turn around, they'd surely save him. Before he could wonder again why they were ignoring him, he felt someone pulling down his pants and underpants. Was he going to be raped? He struggled furiously but was held down, and then he felt a needle jab into his buttocks — and he sank into oblivion.

Hours later George came to. There was a horrible stench in the air. He still had the covers on his eyes and ears but he was breathing through his mouth, and he soon realized his hands and feet were no longer bound. He pulled off the eye tape. It hurt like hell as the tape ripped off his eyebrows. When he saw where he was, he whimpered.

George was in a concrete cell lying on the floor. No windows. No furniture. A hole in the floor in one corner and a plastic bucket of water in the other. A door. It was cold. He was wearing some sort of long dress made out of rough dirty beige fabric. No underwear. He felt his genitals through the fabric and sighed with relief. All there. His whole body ached except for his anus. Thank God Almighty they hadn't raped him.

He had no idea how much time had passed. He needed to piss. That's what the hole in the floor was for. He crawled over, and kneeling, peed into it, splashing some urine back onto his garment. Then he crawled to the bucket and took a long drink of water. It tasted strange, kind of metallic. Desalinized water. Oh, hell, was he in the Middle East? Had he been rendered? "Oh, God, why did you do this to me?" George crumpled to the floor in a fetal position.

"Yes, this is hell. You aren't in America anymore." It was an American voice, kind of old-fashioned sounding. Thank the Lord, George thought. Maybe he wasn't in the Middle East. Maybe he was just in some sort of US Army desert training camp in one of the coalition countries. He opened his eyes. And felt relief. It was Abraham Lincoln.

"President Lincoln. What an honor!" George stumbled to his feet. He felt ashamed to be wearing a dress meeting Abraham Lincoln, but what the heck, who cared? Honest Abe was here to get him out of this hellhole. One president helping another. George reached his hand towards the other man. "I'm President George W Bush. The forty-third president. From 2000 to 2008."

Lincoln didn't hold out his hand. He stared at George with a stern, sad look on his face. "I know who you are. We all know who you are. We watch over all the presidents."

"Well then, let's get out of here, and find me some other clothes. I don't usually wear dresses, heh, heh."

The gangly but dignified man looked at George. "You can't leave here. You've been rendered. I don't know if this is Egypt or Saudi Arabia or Bulgaria or maybe Iraq. It's definitely not America. And by the look of the clothing and how dry the air is, it's not Guantánamo."

George was beginning to wish it was Guantánamo. He'd actually have a chance there with American servicemen and women who would surely recognize him.

"No one knows where you are. The men who snatched you dumped you with some Russians, who brought you to a border. And by the smell of things you were brought here by camel."

"What did I do to deserve this? I don't belong here. Take me back to America."

"I can't take you anywhere. I've been dead for one hundred and fifty years. And even if I could, it seems right that you're here in this hideous place. You've done some terrible, terrible things to our country, including sending innocent men, and a few women, to places like this instead of treating them the way human beings should be treated, even, or especially, if they're imprisoned."

"But I'm an American. And I'm a president. I can't be treated this way. People are going to be looking for me." He started sobbing.

"You're right. You are an American. But presidents aren't kings. No one is above the law."

Washington suddenly appeared beside Lincoln. "As Benjamin Franklin said, 'What goes around comes around.'"

"No, I don't think Benjamin Franklin said that," responded Lincoln.

"Yes he did. I heard him say it at a dinner party."

"Well, I agree he said a multitude of witticisms, but...."

The forty-third president looked from one to the other. They weren't paying attention to him at all.

"GODDAMN IT! LISTEN TO ME! I'M A PRESIDENT, JUST LIKE YOU!"

The other two men looked at George and shook their heads. Lincoln spoke: "No sir, you are not anything like us. None of the presidents approve of what you've done. Not even Nixon. He actually learned something from the Vietnam War and Watergate. The Iraq War IS the worst war that's ever been inflicted on our country and the world. We aren't sure of the future of the United States. And the mistreatment of prisoners is one of the most heinous, barbarous atrocities ever committed by the United States of America. Why did you think you could get away with it? And don't blame it on Dick Cheney, who is a dick, by the way, as you say it in this century. So here you are, just like those you imprisoned. And here you'll stay. Everything, *everything*, done in the name of the United States to prisoners in US custody will be done to you, sir. Including maybe at the end, they'll...."

"Waterboard me?" George shrieked, recalling his missed opportunities to outlaw that barbaric practice.

The first and sixteenth presidents exchanged glances. "Possibly," Lincoln said, "but what I was going to say was that maybe at the end they'll take you to the Hague."

"The Hague? No, not that place. Make them take me to Guantánamo. Please." George pleaded and screamed as the other presidents faded out. However, he saw they'd left behind copies of the Constitution and the Bill of Rights, tattered but readable. He clutched the sacred documents to his heart and folded back into a fetal position on the concrete floor. Then he sobbed himself to sleep.

Chapter 25

Bill thought they had a fifty-fifty chance of making it out of Pipestone alive. There were more of them than there was of the enemy. And most of them knew how to shoot. They were glad they had real weapons. Tampons weren't going to work on the men from Abu Ghraib. Bill didn't know when the enemies would show up. He just knew that they would — and soon. He'd had a call from a buddy in the Justice Department, an internal affairs guy who was monitoring those who kept releasing the Abu Ghraibs. Bill felt terrible that he'd brought trouble to Pipestone, a place that had always meant peace to Native Americans. But he didn't know what else to do. He wondered if the horrors of Iraq would keep spreading like a deadly malignancy across America.

Bill, Charlie and Gary had assessed the park and noted the rock outcroppings that could be used for protection. They avoided a wide gouge in the earth in which a couple of Indian men, sitting on scaffolding above murky water, patiently chipped away at a rocky wall. The sacred red rock of Pipestone was said to be composed of the blood of people who'd sacrificed themselves many years ago. The Indians used this rock to carve peace pipes, precious to all Indian tribes and symbolic of the circle of life which must continue in spite of bloodshed. Bill feared there would be more blood added to the soil here, and some day other men might be chipping out his own blood from rocks.

Seeking solitude, Lucy walked the paths through the small forest around Pipestone. The stones in her pockets and pack felt reassuring, but she was very worried. She wanted to suggest to Bill that they should just all disband and perhaps the pursuers would never find them. But she knew that Bill would only remind her that the Abu Ghraibs would be after him forever and anyone associated with him would also be in eternal danger. He'd say it was better to face them here and end it once and for all.

* * *

The men in the Humvee made it to Pipestone later that evening. Emile was ready to go blasting in. It had been a long trip and they had made him sit in the backseat, jammed in with all the supplies. Sitting there made him feel like a little kid again, and he hated that feeling more than anything. They had also played classic rock music that made him want to tear his eyeballs out of his head. The other three didn't realize how angry Emile was until they arrived at the fake frontier fort in town and he spewed filthy words for several minutes. Trevor was glad he'd locked up the ammunition.

"Hell, you look like shit, Emile. Go take a walk and calm the fuck down. I want you at your best when we kill Bill and those other freaks," said Trevor.

He lit a cigarette, took a drag, and inspected the enraged Emile. The four had come a long way together, but after this deal, Trevor would part ways with Angel Face. He wasn't sure about the other two. Luke and Mack didn't annoy him anywhere near as much as Emile did. Trevor planned on taking the Hummer too, no matter what else happened. It was going to be his ticket out of this shitty deal. He stamped out the cigarette. "An hour. Rest. Food. Then show time."

* * *

Lucy sat down in the indention of a large curved boulder on which other people must have rested for thousands of years. She removed her sandals. Resting her back against the curve of the boulder, she felt its comfort. She could hear a stream flowing through the rocky crags of the forest. A slight breeze lifted her hair away from her face. She sat quietly and breathed. Soon the Lord entered her and she felt the power of Pipestone, too. She remembered a song, *Circle of Light*, from Walela, three Native American women with the voices of angels. Lucy had learned it for a school memorial service for a student who'd died in a car accident. She'd seen the lyrics and thought the use of the word "soles" in one particular line must be a typo for "souls." But the director had said soles of one's feet *were* connected with one's soul. He mentioned two of writer Kurt Vonnegut's most beloved characters who sat, facing one another on the floor, soles to soles and soul to soul. Soles of the feet could connect you with another person, but soles of feet also connect one with the soul of the earth.

Lucy looked at her own bare feet on the boulder, and sliding down the rock's surface, she moved her feet to the earth and squeezed the dirt with her toes. The spirit moved between her body and the earth and back again. And all at once she knew what she wanted to do. Walk. Walk away from Pipestone and the violence that would erupt. Maybe it was right for Bill and the others to remain, but a violent shootout was not part of her dream and journey. She wanted to walk away. But she didn't want to desert those who'd helped her.

Just then Bill appeared and told Lucy he'd found the perfect spot for her. It was up a ravine. If the Abu Ghraibs retreated in that direction she'd be in a perfect position to use her rocks. Bill didn't say so, but she'd also be sheltered, could easily retreat herself and it was extremely unlikely that the assailants would end up there. Lucy followed Bill, who then left her on a sloping boulder above a dry creek bed. She had faith that the Abu Ghraibs would be subdued; she'd stay to help, if needed, but then she'd be on her way.

A short distance away some horses nickered. A young, handsome long-haired Indian man tended them. He'd dreamed several times of a young girl, with brown hair, singing and walking north. Looking towards the ravine, there she was on the boulder where he often sat. Hank had told his dream to his spiritual leader, and she'd given her blessing for him to leave and take two horses when the time came. Now the time was here. He marveled at the predictive power of his dream. With supplies waiting, he lost no time in gathering them up and telling his younger brother of his intention to leave.

Hank had picked out the two horses he wanted. A red one for himself, and a sacred blue horse, a gentle mare, for the girl. The red could be as fiery as the color, except when Hank was mounted. The blue horse was quite rare but he'd been given permission to take this horse on his journey. He placed a couple of saddles and leather bags with sleeping quilts on the horses' backs. He swung up on the red horse, leading the other, and trotted towards the young woman. His brother swung up on a white pony bareback and trotted after the other horses.

Lucy heard the horses coming up behind her. She turned to look at them, and the sight awed her. Three horses. A young man on a red. A younger boy on a white, and a riderless blue horse. All set against a beautiful lush green background with the sun setting and the Indians' long black hair and manes and tails of the horses waving like flags in the wind.

"You're going north, aren't you?" Hank said.

Lucy brushed back her hair. The teens' black hair was longer than hers. The blue horse nuzzled against her face. She put her hand up to stroke the mare. "I have to finish something here first but then I'm headed to Red Lake, and then to Itaska." Lucy hadn't known that for certain until she said it. But, yes, she was going to Itaska, the source of the Mississippi.

"I'm Hank." He slid off the horse and held out his hand. Lucy shook it, feeling his spirit go through to her arm, neck and out the top of her head. The young man felt it, too. "My dreams told me you'd be here. This horse is for you for the journey."

Hank didn't know where these dreams came from, but people had told him it was a great gift. He'd read about Black Elk, who'd also had this dreaming gift, and also loved horses. Hank had ridden horses all over Minnesota and had gone on several memorial rides north in winter. Summer was a much easier time to ride, and he knew plenty of places they could stop on the way.

Lucy touched the blue horse's face again and the horse nuzzled her. "I love horses, Hank, but I need to walk. My soles have to be connected with the earth."

Hank understood and said, "Horses' and humans' soles, same

thing. When you ride a horse that's meant for you, your soul goes through the horse's soul and into the earth. And we can walk sometimes, if you like."

Lucy hadn't touched a horse since Texas. The magic of animals, and this animal in particular, reached out to her. Hank and his younger brother stood by their horses, manes, tails, and human hair mingling in the wind. Minutes passed while they breathed together without speaking. Lucy hugged the blue horse's neck. The mare nuzzled back with her head. Lucy looked down at her bare feet next to the horse's hoof. Both were connected to the earth.

"My friends need some help," Lucy said.

Briefly, Lucy told them her story, emphasizing the dangerousness of the men in the Hummer. The two Indians grinned at each other. "No problem, missy. We're on tribal land here. The Feds have no jurisdiction. We know about Abu Ghraib. Reminded us of the way our own ancestors were treated. If those guys possess weapons on our land, then they are going to find themselves locked up for a long time. And, they don't know this, but we've also outlawed any vehicle that gets below ten miles per gallon on the rez. Part of our fight against global warming. So we'll confiscate the Hummer, too." Hank smiled. "Exceptions for any vehicles registered to Natives. Although some of them have switched over to ethanol. Better in the vehicles than in Indians." He laughed. "This *is* Indian country." Hank and his brother whooped, parodying themselves. Then the younger boy cantered off with the most important message he'd ever delivered in his life thus far.

Lucy hoped her plea would get through. She didn't want any more carnage. She opened her backpack and dumped the stones on the ground. Hank told her that the tribal police would handle this and there'd be no violence. Lucy wanted to believe him but she insisted that they wait just in case her stones were needed. Hank nodded and squatted back on his heels. When the young woman was ready, then he'd fulfill the promise of his dream and Lucy would return to hers.

* * *

Hank's brother told his father and uncle what Lucy had told him and they contacted the tribal police who went to talk with Bill and the others in the campground. Bill gave them background on the dangerous men from Abu Ghraib, and Maria and Charlie told the police what had happened in Colorado and Wyoming. The well-armed group set up a roadblock just inside the Pipestone boundaries. It was an excellent location for the tribal police, but a very disadvantaged position for those approaching the park.

Meanwhile, another group was tailing the Hummer full of the Abu Ghraib men. It was the vets from Colorado. The jailer from Laramie had communicated with those in Colorado Springs and had tracked down the vets, still camped near the Great Sand Dunes. When they learned that the Abu Ghraibs had been released from Colorado Springs and Laramie jails, they knew Bill and the others would be in trouble. The vets were warriors, after all, and even if they had only half their bodies and impaired minds, they still knew how to fight. So with the two elderly Indian men and their grandson, the vets had traveled as fast as they could from Colorado. The jailer in Laramie, a practical man, had put a navigation device on the Hummer. He communicated coordinates to the vets who caught up to the vehicle in South Dakota. They discreetly tailed the Hummer into Minnesota, waiting for the right moment to intervene.

In the Hummer, Emile, Trevor, Luke and Mack were anticipating an easy hit on Bill and his comrades. They figured they'd catch the group totally unaware. Trevor was already fantasizing of how, afterwards, he'd get rid of Emile and take his share of the payoff. So he was shocked when he drove over a hill and all the Hummer tires blew out. Swearing about the sharps he could see on the highway, he wrestled the vehicle to a stop. Emile, seated in the back, had whipped out his gun, and confused by the sudden turn of events, fired his weapon. The bullet ricocheted through the interior and ended up hitting Luke in his arm. Luke shoved open the door, and staggered away from the Hummer, screaming. Then they all heard an amplified voice. "We've got you surrounded. All of you, get out of the vehicle with your hands up."

Shocked by this turn of events, Trevor surveyed the scene, still in the driver's seat, one hand on a sawed-off shotgun. In the twilight he saw ten vehicles and at least twenty Indians with rifles all pointed at him and the Hummer. He cursed. What was it with this guy Bill that people helped him so readily? He wished he'd killed that fucker in Iraq.

That was when they all heard the engines of other vehicles approaching the Hummer from behind. The Indians groaned and tensed up. Trevor, Emile and Mack smiled and felt hopeful. Even Luke momentarily forgot his bleeding arm. Their higher up contact must have come through and sent reinforcements.

The tribal police aimed their rifles above the Hummer towards the highway. Then the motley motorcade rode over the hill and fanned out on the sides of the road. As they piled out of their vehicles, the tribal police saw the elderly Indian men and a child. They relaxed. The newcomers were reinforcements for their side. The Abu Ghraibs weren't going anywhere except death or jail.

Trevor, looking in his rearview and side mirrors, was stunned. He knew it was over for him, at least for that day. He yelled out, "I'm going to put down my weapon. Don't fire." He dropped the shotgun and opened the Hummer door.

"Step away from the vehicle. Lie down on the ground. Face down."

Trevor did what he was told.

"You in the back, get out of the vehicle. Slowly. No weapons. Hands up."

Mack got out with his hands up and lay down beside Luke, who groaned. His arm hurt like hell and he felt completely humiliated. It could get worse. The Indians didn't know how crazy Emile was. A puddle of blood formed underneath Luke's body.

"Your friend could die if you don't get out of the vehicle like we said."

Emile could see Luke through the open door. He was of a mind to shoot him and Mack and Trevor and then shoot anyone else he could before he was shot to death. But he didn't really want to end his life in Pipestone.

He reluctantly placed his weapon on the floor, eased out of the Hummer and held his arms up in the air. Emile looked at all the Indians with their rifles pointed at him and turned his head around to look at the vets behind him. At least this was a worthy surrender. Unlike that situation in Colorado when they'd been overcome by women dancers. He lay down on the ground, slowly, after pointing his ass in the direction of the Indians. Almost as soon as he hit the ground, he felt his hands jerked around behind him, and a voice said, "You have the right to remain silent."

He didn't hear the rest. The voice was female. Humiliated again by a woman. How in damnation had that happened? He wished to hell he was back in Iraq where the women knew their place. If he hadn't been bound he would have turned around and ripped the woman's clothing off and raped her as he strangled her. He recognized other female voices among the people attending to the injured Luke.

A few hours later the Abu Ghraibs found themselves in a very secure tribal jail cell. These guys weren't leaving the lockup this time. A smart prosecutor was already in the process of gathering information from a variety of sources and finding a trail of extremely serious charges all over the west, to add to the original accusations from Iraq. The jailed Abu Ghraibs knew they'd failed in their mission when a scruffy-looking public defender informed them he was now their lawyer. They were completely screwed.

Bill, Charlie and the others had resisted giving up their weapons to the tribal police but they finally agreed with the intervention of the other vets and the two elderly Indian men. They could have been incarcerated as well, for bringing weapons onto tribal land and especially into Pipestone, but the police used their common sense and the attestation of the Indians from Colorado. Bill and his friends still didn't quite believe that the Abu Ghraibs would stay locked up until they were informed that the prisoners had no money. Their powerful backers had vanished. The Abu Ghraibs weren't going anywhere but to a courtroom and then to prison.

Bill and his group were extremely relieved that it ended peacefully. A shootout at the OK Corral was fine for the movies, but a real gun battle, with screams, crying, swearing, sobbing for mothers, blood, shit, guts, brains, and sudden death for some and agonizing deaths for others, was absolutely hideous. And Pipestone would have been desecrated.

Charlie was the only one who regretted there was no battle. She had looked forward to firing weapons against an enemy again and prevailing in the shootout. She really was quite an aggressive woman.

At some point, Bill and Maria realized they hadn't seen Lucy for hours. They were shocked that they'd forgotten about her. When they went to the ravine she was gone. They had thought their problems were over, but now they had a whole new one to solve.

* * *

Dr Raintree's office didn't look exceptional from the outside. It was in an upscale part of Dallas, not too far from the SMU campus. Crepe myrtles, lilacs, lush clipped grass, and some shade trees framed the doorway to the small one-story building. At the entry a fountain trickled delicate soothing sounds. Inside, the décor was Asian and as George and his wife entered the office, Laura wondered if a feng shui expert had been consulted. Laura had a passionate interest in Myanmar and other Asian cultures, and the ambience of the doctor's office instantly appealed to her. Between the bamboo floor, rugs with designs from nature, soothing art, and another flowing fountain, the doctor's office felt very balanced. Laura relaxed; she felt confident this was the right place for George.

A middle-aged woman with a kind but business-like expression greeted the couple. She showed no obvious sign of recognition as she handed George some forms to fill out. He planned to pay directly for services, as he had for the preliminary X-rays and blood tests that Dr Raintree had requested, so he ignored the insurance forms. He was relieved not to have to deal with bureaucracy. He filled out the part of the form asking him for his goals for treatment. He first wrote "get thingamagig out of head" and then "rid self of nightmares." After some more thought, he added "leave legacy of love and admiration." He already felt a bit better just writing those words.

Soon the secretary bid him to follow her. George kissed his wife. Perhaps he had a premonition that he was going on a long journey and wasn't sure when or how he would return. He had the same look on his face as he waved to reporters just before striding across the lawn to a waiting helicopter. He automatically raised his arm and gave his beauty-queen wave. However, Laura was already absorbed in the newest issue of *O, The Oprah Magazine,* and as the secretary walked ahead of him, it wasn't clear to whom he was waving.

They walked down a hall to the last door on the left. It was open and the secretary indicated that he should enter. George took a couple of steps forward but then stood in wonderment. The color scheme was mostly green with some browns, blues, and purples. A small fountain trickled underneath a large window which overlooked a delicate Japanese garden. George felt as though he stood on the threshold of a peaceful forest glade.

Dr Raintree blended in with the décor and he didn't seem to see her initially. She rose from her chair and walked over to greet him. His first impression of her was that she appeared to be a woman who lived in the woods, felt very comfortable there, and was completely independent. He glanced at her left hand. No ring on the fourth finger. No rings at all. He looked up at her remarkable face, her very large dark eyes and sensuous lips. Her skin was darker than the Mexicans who worked on his ranch, and her eyes looked like the Vietnamese hairdresser he visited every week. She shook his hand firmly but gently as she introduced herself and asked him to sit down. She took a seat away from her desk, such that they were both seated at two points of a triangle with the fountain and Japanese garden forming the third point.

"Tell me why you're here," she said kindly.

George, who hadn't expected to be treated so gently, felt tears prick his eyes and then flow down his cheeks. Dr Raintree didn't seem surprised. She remained silent as she listened to his sobs and the trickling fountain. Eventually she gave him a box of Kleenex. George took a few tissues and blew his nose. "I, well, I've got this thingamajig inside my head. They can see my dreams. And I'm having terrible nightmares. It's been going on for months. I've even thought about drinking again, but I know that's just going to make things worse. Can you help me? Can you get this thingamajig out of my head? It's bugging the hell out of me."

"Tell me more about your dreams."

And so he told her about the zombies from Iraq, Mother Nature, Arthur, scary Nic, Pat Tillison, his dead little sister and of being rendered followed by the refusal of the two greatest presidents to help him. Then he began to sob again, and he continued for a long time.

When he was able to speak again, she asked a number of other questions which he answered. She then looked at some X-ray reports.

"Can you help me, doc?"

She smiled at him. "Yes, I can. First, let me tell you, you don't have any thingamajig in your brain. Everything looks fine on the X-rays and other testing. But your dreams tell me that you've got something serious going on with your soul, and that's going to take some real hard work in this office, but even harder work outside of here. You haven't tried psychotherapy before. This really is a sacred place, in some ways like a church, or a synagogue or a mosque. Here anyone can gain understanding of him or herself and change, as long as you enter the realm of honest inquiry and compassion towards yourself. We'll see what happens."

She asked him to keep a dream journal, to write down every detail of what he remembered at night, and to return twice weekly for the next six weeks. She told him she thought he'd get better, if he responded as other people did.

"Who would have thought? Dubya doing therapy." He smirked but tears still pricked his eyes.

She smiled and indicated that the time was up for that day.

After George left, Dr Raintree looked at her garden. He was the last patient of the day. She had a lot to think about. She'd treated him like any other initial patient, but she knew he was different than her other patients. She took her Koran from a drawer and began to read, paraphrasing some of the words:

> God promises you her forgiveness and bounties.
> And God careth for all and She knoweth all things.
> She granteth wisdom to whom She pleaseth;
> And she to whom wisdom is granted receiveth
> Indeed a benefit overflowing;
> But none will grasp the Message
> But women and men of understanding.

She read the note at the bottom of the page which further described the meaning of this passage. "*No kind or generous act ever ruined anyone.*" She looked up at the wall nearby where this phrase was depicted in calligraphic Arabic, so skillfully that the words were disguised in the art. This man would never know she was Muslim and that she hadn't voted for him either time. While she was a registered Republican, she'd stopped voting that way after Regan's first term. However, she could separate out aspects of her life, so she could work with almost anyone who entered her office. Unlike many other patients, though, her work with this man could have historic repercussions, so she'd have to draw from her deepest sources of strength. She prayed again in Arabic, put on a CD of spiritual music from all the world's great religions, and began to dictate her notes.

* * *

Before the Crawford show, unbeknownst to anyone except herself,

Judith had teetered on the edge of a deep depression, an enormous gaping hole of despair, something so ancient, so deep, dark and horrifying, that she felt she'd never emerge if she fell in. She had reasons to be depressed, remembering all those things she could no longer do, like running, walking, dancing, playing the piano, kicking, throwing a ball, swimming, riding a bicycle, writing, typing, painting, cooking, holding a child, riding a horse, or hiking in the mountains. The list was endless.

And she couldn't see either, so that eliminated even more possibilities for joy.

But something about that evening, being there in the hometown of the former president, and feeling furious that Bush didn't show, drew her away from the edge of the abyss. She wasn't going to fall into that horrible dark place. She wasn't going to disappear and be forgotten. She was going to turn around and walk (in her mind she could still walk) back towards life. She was going to do everything she could to show others the truth through Comedy and Tragedy. People responded to both. It was part of their nature. And she would eventually get that man, George W Bush, who'd been the cause of her losses, to understand what he'd done. And then she'd get him to apologize to her and all those others he'd wronged. And then she'd inspire him to make amends for his actions. Judith really believed that Bush was a religious man. She didn't think it was just political bullshit, as her brother and grandmother said. And if the former president truly heard God, then God would tell him what he needed to do now, in his retirement. God and Judith would work together. Judith was a believer and she, too, heard God.

One of her friends, a Unitarian, had come to see her in the hospital and sung that old song, *What a Friend we Have in Jesus*. She first sang it through the old way, and then sang it through with new words:

What a friend we have in Jesus; what a friend in Esther too.
What a friend we have in Buddha, and a prophet lives in you....

The song with revised lyrics included all sorts of friends from history and imagination and had comforted Judith immensely. Even Mohammed could be a friend. Just don't draw any pictures of him, she thought. Respect and inclusion. She had considered changing the words of other songs, like *Onward Christian Soldiers* rewritten as *Let's Fight Global Warming*. Keep the melody, but change the words and include everyone.

She and Joseph planned to continue on tour. She had enough money from her disability benefits and could check into any VA hospital if she needed medical care. Her brother had said he could contribute to her expenses, too. Joseph had quit his job to help Judith. They were all on a mission from God.

* * *

Hank and Lucy had watched the tribal police arrest the men from Abu Ghraib. Lucy felt as though she'd been holding her breath for hours and sighed with relief. She looked at the stones near her feet and realized that she wasn't a David. "I'm ready to go now," she said to Hank. He held the reins of the blue horse as Lucy mounted. She sank back in the saddle and felt the horse shift beneath her weight. She nodded at Hank, who gently kicked his horse and they set off. The sun was setting as the two young people trotted north, their souls connected to the earth through the clip-clopping of the horses' hooves.

The journey north flowed like a dream. The young Indian man knew people along the way who helped take care of their horses and gave them places to stay. The horses had great endurance and could go up to fifty miles a day. Often they used dirt trails that Hank knew from his previous journeys. It was almost possible to imagine themselves two centuries before during the North American Age of the Horse.

As they rode, Lucy and Hank talked about whether having horses was worth everything else that came with the Europeans. This discussion had come up many times in countless Indian gatherings over generations. People who loved horses were willing to risk almost anything else to have them, even something as horrible as smallpox, one of the worst European exports. Horses. To look at. To care for. To ride. To hunt better. To raid better. To make war better. To have fun, riding fast. To visit a beloved more easily and more often. And to rest with a trusted horse at the end of a day. Horses brought out the full glory of the Indians, as the animals had done for people the world over. Hank, who'd never seen smallpox, but knew horses well, couldn't imagine a world without them. Lucy had always loved horses. She had a model horse collection as a kid, and she had been thrilled to have riding lessons. It had been horses in her and Joy's imagining that had saved all the 9/11 and Columbine innocents from death. Lucy couldn't picture a world without horses either.

Hank and Lucy agreed that the Age of Cars and Oil had diminished the mysterious power of horses. Horses didn't fit in with modern roads and vehicles. Hank hoped the Age of Oil would end and people would return to riding as well as bicycling and walking. It would become the Age of Horses, Bikes and Feet.

They also talked about Lucy's pilgrimage to pray for the dead. Hank thought this was a very worthwhile endeavor. He'd gone on spiritual retreats before, but with the exception of rides with other Indians to commemorate Wounded Knee, they'd only been for a few days. He'd never heard of a pilgrimage around the central part of the United States, but he liked the idea and was glad to help Lucy fulfill her dream.

Hank's gentleness had an effect on Lucy. He didn't pray with her as Darrell had, or argue with her as Bill had, or admire her as Sam had. Hank listened quietly and at different points on the journey, he told her his beliefs, handed down from thousands of years of religious traditions. What he said felt no less sacred than anything Lucy had experienced in church or in reading the Bible. She hadn't really acknowledged it, but she was changing. She never spoke to him of the Rapture. They did speak of the violence that shattered Red Lake.

On March 21 2005, in a Red Lake community of mostly Ojibwan, a young teenager, Jeffrey Weise, who was anguished beyond reason, had taken his family's weapons and turned them first on his grandfather, then on schoolmates and teachers, and finally on himself. Ten people died that day, seven were injured and a whole community suffered shock. This story didn't receive as much coverage as the Columbine shootings. Perhaps white America still wasn't that interested in Indian America. Maybe because the numbers of dead were lower, and the Iraq War and politics were more on peoples' minds by that time. Possibly the public was getting desensitized to school shootings. But Lucy had read every detail she could find about this story, and in her mind it was as horrible and senseless as the others.

It was soon after Labor Day when Hank and Lucy arrived in Red Lake. They rode in mid-afternoon and went to the trailer home of Hank's aunt, where there was pasture for the horses. Later the two sat on the grass and looked at the enormous expanse of Red Lake. Low, bluish clouds overhead reflected in the water. It would soon rain. The lake was so wide, and the clouds were so low, they felt like they were in a water sandwich. They smelled like horses but in a good way.

Hank responded to Lucy's unasked question. "I didn't know him, or any of the other people hurt or killed that day. But I know one of the drummers who prayed for everyone afterwards; he gave a Bemidji prayer for all the suffering and for healing that eventually comes, to some." He reached into a bag he was carrying and took out a few grains of rice, offering them in the four directions, saying something in Ojibwa Chippewa. The wind blew the grains away, although a few grains fell in Lucy's hair.

Lucy thought of a prayer, but somehow it didn't apply. The long horseback ride with all the quiet greenery of Minnesota, after the parched journey from Texas, had changed something fundamental in her soul. Feeling a beautiful animal moving beneath her as they traveled over land revered by generations of people who knew nothing about Christianity or Jesus or the Rapture, had opened up a larger picture in her mind — a first glimpse of a worldview that was both holy and large enough to contain all kinds of beliefs.

She realized she was never going to understand how another person could take a gun and kill innocent people. All she could see was that their beliefs caused more grief, which gave others reasons to do other acts of violence that caused even more grief. Cycles of grief and revenge could go on forever, although this hadn't happened here in America yet. Maybe the country wasn't old enough, or perhaps people had advanced enough to not give in to perpetual mass violence.

Lucy and Hank sat quietly in the grass until it began to rain. Then they ran to the trailer and an elderly woman opened the door. Hank left Lucy with her and said he would return in the morning. He had other people to see and Lucy would be in good hands with his Aunt Sarah.

After a long hot shower and a simple meal of heated-up canned ravioli, Lucy was shown a bunk bed. Sarah said she'd stay up to watch Jon Stewart's *The Daily Show*. She told Lucy the show wasn't as funny in 2009 as it had been the previous eight years, but there was always something ridiculous going on in the world to inspire comedians to make people laugh. Lucy had never heard of Jon Stewart's show and she fell asleep before it started.

Later that night she had a long dream. She was traveling by horseback, over the same land she'd just crossed, but there were no roads, no automobiles, no trucks, and no trains. No oil. Just horses. Was it in the eighteenth or nineteenth century? Or was it sometime in the future, the twenty-second century? Lucy was traveling by herself but she wasn't feeling worried. She rode over a hill and suddenly saw hundreds, maybe thousands of buffalo. In astonishment, the horse stopped. If it was the past, this was before the buffalos' near extinction. Or if it was the future, the buffalo were back, stronger than ever. Lucy looked behind her and was startled to see four men riding on horseback coming up fast. She began to feel frightened and knew these were the horrifying men from Abu Ghraib. They would kill her if they got the chance. Her horse sensed her fright and began at once to gallop down the hill straight into the buffalo herd.

In real life a horse charging into a group of buffalo could have one of two results. The buffalo could scatter and stampede off in any direction, or one or more buffalo could charge, and a rider and horse would be gored and crushed into the ground. But in Lucy's dream she and her horse were enfolded into the herd and magically became like female buffalo protected by the enraged males. As she looked back, she saw the biggest buffalos charge the four evil men and trample them to death.

It was morning and Lucy got up and told the old lady, who was sitting in the kitchen, of her dream. Sarah nodded. This was a very good dream. It was a White Buffalo Woman dream, she told the young woman. Sarah gave Lucy a cup of tea and told her that she would soon assist her on the last leg of the journey, starting at the source of the Mississippi, not very far from Red Lake. Lucy looked at the older woman. This fit in terms of her pilgrimage and altered beliefs: to go from the source of the great Mississippi that divided the United States down to the mouth of the river in the Gulf of Mexico. She wasn't thinking of the practical difficulties of such a journey, only the spiritual qualities, which made perfect sense.

"That's right," the older woman said. "You can start by canoe, just a few feet from the very beginning of that great river. We'll get things sorted out for you. I like your dream a lot. If you're traveling with the buffalo, you're going to be safe. And those bad guys are gone, or going to be goners pretty soon. 'See ya, suckers. *Hasta la vista*, babies.'" She grinned and laughed. Living alone, she watched lots of cable TV and movies and she mostly loved the ones where the underdogs prevailed. Pretty soon Lucy was laughing at all the great lines that Sarah recalled, one right after another, complete with accents.

"My name is Inigno Montoya. You kilt my father. Prepare to die."

"Remember the Alamo!"

"It's a good day to die."

"Go ahead. Make my day."

"What we have here is a failure to communicate."

Lucy finished laughing and took the older woman's hand. "Can I say a prayer?"

"But honey, we've just been praying."

They laughed again, so hard they cried. Eventually they stopped and sat in silence until Sarah said, "Let's go to the school. I knew Jeff's grandfather and his girlfriend was one of my friends. That was a terrible day. We knew they didn't get along well. But no one thought Jeff would kill people. I'll take you. It's Saturday. No one will be there. Then when we get back we'll look over my gear and I'll outfit you for the Mississippi. Let me call Hank."

Hank met the two women at the school. He'd brought his drumming friend and the four of them sat and prayed by the memorial site. Lucy said the same prayer she'd said at Columbine and Hank and Sarah sang a song for the dead as Hank's friend drummed. They ended with a prayer for safe journeys, both for the dead and the living.

Hank gave Lucy a token woven from the horses' manes and told her to tie it on her life vest before she went down the Mississippi. It would help her. Lucy thanked him and realized she had nothing to give him. But Hank disagreed. "Yes, you have given me something. You gave me a journey from my dream. That's a first." He grinned at her. "But it's not going to be the last. I'll have other dreams and other journeys. Thank you for this one."

They hugged each other and Hank left.

The young woman and the old woman looked at each other. "To the garage!" Sarah said.

Chapter 26

George didn't have any dreams for the next few nights. He was immensely relieved as he didn't think he could go through any more torture. He examined himself in a floor-to-ceiling mirror. He looked damn good, even in pajamas. He didn't want to review his night-mares and imagine changing them as Laura had suggested, and he hadn't written anything down in the journal given to him by Dr Raintree. Just talking with her and her reassurance that he didn't have a thingamajig in his brain seemed enough. As he lay in bed that night, he reviewed his favorite memories as in a slide show, enhanced with patriotic music, applause and cheers from adoring crowds. The colors, sounds and smells were vivid, and his pride was enormous as he drifted off to sleep.

George soon found himself on a ship, the SS Abraham. Wearing the flight suit of a Navy aviator with helmet in hand, he and the co-pilot grinned and waved to the huge crowd of sailors who yelled and clapped before a big sign they'd erected: MISSION ACCOMPLISHED. Landing a small plane on the naval destroyer was an expensive, potentially disastrous stunt, but this is what George wanted, and the Navy had complied. After all, he was the commander-in-chief. Pumped up by the successful landing, he spoke exultantly of the invasion of Baghdad and the toppling of Saddam.

George finished his speech and the music suddenly screeched to a halt. The applause died. The sailors turned to ashes and George was all alone. The formerly magnificent Navy cruiser transformed into a huge old rusted oil tanker. It smelled of diesel and cracked painted signs indicated Libyan registration. The sun disappeared, and fog and wind enveloped the ship. Ocean spray hit the deck and in no time George was drenched. His uniform became faded and ripped. He looked down and saw blood run down one of his thighs.

"What the hell?"

He felt a great sense of doom. Something horrible was behind him. Something that was going to get him. Something that he feared more than anything else in the world. He didn't want to turn around but he found his body slowly revolving. He wanted to jump into the heaving ocean. He wanted a bolt of lightening to come from the sky. He wanted the deck to give way beneath him and allow him to fall into the oily depths below. He wanted anything but to see what awaited him. But his body turned and there he was.

Osama. Osama bin Ladin. The Most Wanted Terrorist in the Whole World. Right there. Ten feet away. George's fear grew monstrous. Osama gazed calmly at George. He wore the garb of a mountain man from Afghanistan, although he carried not a gun but a Koran. A neutral observer might have said Osama looked more like a prophet than a terrorist. But to George, Osama appeared as the Antichrist.

George found in his hands a small, well-thumbed Bible. It was an older version from the 1940s, much like one his father carried in World War II. George thrust it out towards Osama, like someone warding off a menacing vampire.

Osama looked bemused. He opened his Koran and began to read, in English. He knew much of the Koran by heart in Arabic, but he needed to read the passages in English so this man might understand. *"And verily the Hour will come: there can be no doubt about it, or about the fact that God will raise up all who are in the graves. Yet there is among men such a one as disputes about God, without knowledge, without guidance, and without a Book of Enlightenment. Disdainfully bending his side, in order to lead men astray from the Path of God: for him there is disgrace in this life, and on the Day of Judgment we shall make him taste the penalty of burning fire."*

The wind had picked up and it started to rain. More ocean water washed over the decks, and the ship heaved so that George had to grasp a ladder to keep from being swept overboard. Osama stood unaffected by the dangerous tilt of the tanker.

George wanted to say the Lord's Prayer, which he knew by heart, but his fingers flipped to Revelation 11 (17-19), and he repeated the words of the twenty-four elders: *"We give thanks to thee, Lord God Almighty, who art and who wast, that thou hast taken thy great power and begun to reign. The nations raged, but thy wrath came, and the time for the dead to be judged, for rewarding thy servants, the prophets and saints, and those who fear thy name, both small and great, for destroying the destroyers of the earth."*

Osama gazed at George with puzzlement. "That's a great prophecy for *you*. *You* are who they're talking about. Not us."

Holding the Bible, George felt righteousness overcome his fear. "What are you talking about? *You* destroyed the Twin Towers and killed all those innocent people! *You* and your jihadists, radical Islamists, *you* are the destroyers and God will destroy *you*."

Osama smiled back at him. "Ah, so you're admitting Saddam Hussein was not the mastermind behind September 11? Kind of a bad mistake to make. Your Iraq War sure has…" Osama switched to a west Texas accent, "…riled up a lot of folks in mah neck of the woods, er, desert. For that, I'd like to offer you my eternal gratitude." He bowed slightly.

This infuriated George. "Saddam was just as much of a menace as you were. Are. Whatever. And now they have democracy over there in Iraq, and all those other countries are going to have it, too. And a hundred years from now, I'll be remembered as the Father of Middle Eastern Democracy."

Osama began laughing. "You are a fool. A complete idiot. They don't have democracy in Iraq. They've got civil war. A civil war that's already worse than your own Civil War. We're talking Sunnis versus Shias," he sneered, "not Rebs versus Yankees." Osama paced the deck. "You've got insurgency all over Afghanistan. You've got religious jihadists all over the Middle East who revere me. A hundred years from now, *my name*, Osama bin Ladin, will be remembered, and yours will just be a pathetic footnote, except when they refer to the beginning of the decline of America. You bankrupted your country for an unnecessary war. And you never caught me. Islam, the true form, Wahabism, will rule most of the Middle East for another thousand years, thanks to me and thanks to the great Sayyid Qutb. He learned so much from the heathens of Greeley, Colorado."

George looked puzzled. "Sayyid Qutb? Who in the heck is that? Another terrorist?"

Osama narrowed his eyes scornfully. "He's the greatest Islamic prophet since Mohammed himself. Wrote all his beliefs in a book, *Milestones*. Cliff Notes summary for you: Qutb called for worldwide Islamic revolution, subjugation of all non-Muslim people and institutions, and universal imposition of Sharia. He's now in heaven. Tragically he was hanged by that traitor of all traitors, Gamal Ebdel Nasser, in 1966."

George held his Bible up as if to ward off the words of the other man, but remained speechless.

Osama continued. "You know, I've heard of your Rapture beliefs. Why don't you know anything about Sayyid Qutb? Too busy making money? Too busy exercising? Too busy using up oil and petroleum?" Osama smiled. George shivered.

"Yes, and thanks for your addiction to oil. You and your kind need our oil more than we do. In our country we can return to the way things were a hundred years ago, or fourteen hundred years ago. You can't. You *will* be destroyed. Our God is more powerful than your God."

George was stunned. Somehow all of this sounded like a prophecy from Revelations. But it was coming out of the mouth of this evil, vile terrorist who'd plagued his life for years.

Osama regarded him slyly. "Want to convert?"

This infuriated George. He thrust his Bible again towards the robed man and began saying the Lord's Prayer, "*Our Father, who art in heaven....*"

Osama interrupted him. "I didn't think so. But if you change your mind, let me know. We'll take any sincere converts to Islam. We've converted lots of Christians. And there will be a lot more. I remember one of your short stories from the 1970s when oil was scarce and gasoline was expensive and hard to get. People who ran out of gas soon realized that the only way to get their cars to go was to get out, get down on their knees and pray to Mecca. Pray sincerely to Mecca and Mohammed. Great prophetic story. I can just see it now. It will be gridlock, as your citizens tumble out of their mini-vans, Suburbans and Humvees, and fall to the ground, facing east, and praying as hard as they can to Mecca for oil and gasoline. Praying and then converting to Islam."

The tanker suddenly tipped, and George, drenched, tattered and bleeding, began sliding to the edge of the deck.

"Pray! Pray to God!" Osama shouted as George fell overboard. He could still hear Osama yelling as the cold waters closed over his head.

"Lord Jesus Christ!" George woke with a start and sat up, his breath and heartbeat rapid. He was covered in sweat and freezing cold. "Lord, Lord, Lord, save me please. Please save me, Jesus." Trembling, he noticed the dream journal book and picked up the pen lying beside it. Writing the dream was all he could think to do.

* * *

Sarah had often canoed the Mississippi, once the whole way, as Lucy was about to do. She loved every section of the river, especially the beginning at Lake Itaska. It was best to arrive very early in the morning, before the tourists showed up. She would pray where the lake met the river, the mysterious source of something that eventually became much bigger than one could ever imagine. Then she would walk carefully across the mouth of the river. It looked like she was walking on water. However, as you got closer, you could see stepping stones just under the water's surface. They were slippery, though, and it was easy to fall in. It had been years since that had happened to Sarah.

After her walk across the water she'd slip her loaded canoe a few feet away where the Mississippi was several feet wide and clear of rocks. Then she'd glide over clear water through a green tunnel of trees. Each time she did this, it felt like she was being reborn. This experience was spiritual for Sarah, and she hoped it would be for Lucy, too.

At ninety, Sarah knew she was nearing the end of her long life. She'd been born in 1919 and had been sent to the Indian School in Carlisle, Pennsylvania with her brothers and sisters. None of them had made it home, as they'd been taken by pneumonia or tuberculosis. Something had been wrong with her, too. For years she scarcely said a word, just did her work silently at the lodge at Lake Itaska. But the lake and the river had healed her over time. And in her last thirty odd years she'd reunited with other Natives in horseback pilgrimages. Horses and canoes had brought her back to life.

Working in the garage with Lucy, Sarah wondered if the young woman was strong enough to do this trip. Did she know anything about rivers and canoes?

"Sure. I went to some church camps and Girl Scouts. Haven't done it for a few years, but it'll come back, I think," Lucy replied.

Methodically, the two women picked out all the gear Lucy would need. She could pack ten days worth of meals before she'd need to stop, but she'd need clean water to drink long before she ran out of food. It was possible to purify water from the northern part of the river but the tablets couldn't deal with all the chemicals and agricultural toxins further downstream. Water would be the limiting resource on this expedition. But Sarah knew state campgrounds and other places to stop for water. And people along the river would help Lucy, too.

Lucy wanted to be home by November at the latest. It would be getting colder, and, in spite of the postcards, her parents would be worried by then. They might worry even more once they were reunited and she told them that she no longer believed in the Rapture. She still loved Jesus, but she also loved the people she'd met, none of whom believed in the Rapture. This belief had been crumbling during the whole journey, but the trip on horseback had dissolved any last remnants. She still believed in an afterlife, but now she understood that it was available to everyone. All persons' souls lived on, not just those who were Born Again.

From her journey through the heart of America, Lucy had come to embrace the idea that the earth was precious. The natural environment sustained people and had to be protected, otherwise people weren't going to survive. Lucy felt ashamed of her prior beliefs: that the earth's resources could be depleted and destroyed, and then be renewed only for the chosen few. Seeing America's people and its land had opened her eyes to reality. The Rapture just didn't make any sense, and Lucy now realized that it was a shockingly dangerous idea. She knew there were other Christian churches and even other religions. Maybe there was another one for her. She'd have to search. She couldn't stay in Killeen. Maybe she'd move to Austin. Her high school grades were good enough to get into UT, and one of her teachers had told her she could get a scholarship, if she kept her grades up. Lucy wasn't sure what subject she'd study. The remainder of her journey and her dreams would guide her.

The next day at Lake Itaska, Sarah bid her good luck and said a prayer in Ojibwa as Lucy got into the canoe. She waved goodbye and the current took Lucy downstream. It was a beautiful September day. Sarah loved that the white people called this type of day "Indian Summer" as it was the most lovely time of the year. Gorgeous and without bugs. Sarah prayed again, then pulled out her phone. She called friends who lived along the river and asked them to watch for a slim brunette in a green canoe. Prayers were good; so were cell phones.

* * *

Bill, Maria and Charlie sat in a bar in Minneapolis. They felt a bit out of place, as this was one of those dark wood, old money bars, but it was quiet, and they weren't bothering anyone. It had taken ten days to sort out everything in Pipestone. They'd sped up to Red Lake as soon as they were released but hadn't found Lucy and no one they talked with had seen her either. The men from Abu Ghraib were still in jail, Bill had been informed. There had been a few calls to try to force their release, but the Indians wouldn't budge, especially after they'd heard the full story from Bill. The Indians worked all their connections to get the charges documented until these dangerous men could be transported to a higher security prison while they awaited their trials. The charges were so serious, there was no bail.

Bill felt relieved about the Abu Ghraibs but felt despondent about Lucy. He knew she'd gone north, probably to Red Lake, but then where would she go? Ronny and Gary had driven around in their RV looking for her, but after a week they'd stopped the search and were on their way home to San Francisco. Red Lake was it. That was the last place on the list. The three discussed the possibilities. The Amish school in Pennsylvania? Virginia Tech? Frustrated, Bill got up and went out to the parking lot to look at the Mississippi River. He'd done some canoeing in Ohio and really loved rivers. In Baghdad, he'd thought about canoeing on the Euphrates, but that would have been a very bad idea. That river was filled with blood and he didn't want his added to it. Maybe the Mississippi had blood in it, too, but not as much as the Euphrates.

Bill felt terribly alone. While Maria and Charlie had finished their coffee, he walked to the river, picked up a few stones and skipped them on the water. He recalled the stones that Lucy had held. He was glad she hadn't had to use them. Some people didn't need to deal violently with evil, although he had certainly appreciated her knifing Luke. But basically she was dealing with evil in another way by doing her pilgrimage. He threw a few more stones as hard as he could and they reached the other side. He aimed for a large rock painted with numbers indicating the height of the river. After a few tries, he hit the numbers. He wondered if way back he was related to the David who slew Goliath. It was possible. Anything was possible. Even finding Lucy. Bill returned to the bar and just as he sat down, his phone rang. It was one of the vets.

"Got some information for you, Bill. Lucy's going down the

Mississippi. The veteran grapevine. My cousin called her daughter's boyfriend who knows a kid who…." When Bill got off the phone and related the information, Maria excitedly said, "Sure, that sounds right. Lucy loves water. She's good in a canoe, too. We went to Girl Scout camp in Oklahoma a few summers."

Charlie heard the love in Maria's voice and felt jealous. When Bill was outside looking at the river, they'd argued over whether they should just leave Lucy to her journey or continue looking for her. Charlie had become unsure again about Maria's friendship with Lucy and had asked her many times if Maria had ever hooked up with her. Maria insisted that they hadn't and that she herself hadn't even realized she was attracted to women until she met Charlie. That made Charlie feel a bit better and she quit talking about Lucy as a rival. Although the feelings hadn't completely dissipated. Without the adrenaline and focus of a fight, her suspicions and irritability had resurfaced. However, she decided to pretend this was a military mission and act like a professional to find the target.

Bill sensed the love in Maria's voice, too. He was glad Lucy had such a good friend and he felt that it would be easier to find her if all three of them were looking. However, he'd find her even if he had to do it alone. He had dreamed about Lucy and even dreamt of their children. He was only twenty-three, but this was the woman he wanted to spend the rest of his life with. He needed to make sure he found Lucy before Darrell did.

As they pulled out maps and tried to figure out where they might find her, Bill idly wondered where Darrell was. The tribal police had let Darrell go before the others for some unknown reason. He'd said he was going back to Texas to wait for Lucy in Killeen, but Bill thought he was lying and had probably traveled to Red Lake on his own. Bill got up and paced while Maria and Charlie continued to study the maps.

Meanwhile, Darrell was enroute to Texas in an Amtrack train and he was thinking about Lucy, and praying for her. He'd been frantic when he first realized that she'd disappeared. When he learned that she'd gone off willingly on a horse with a young man, he was bewildered. For several days he'd hitchhiked southern Minnesota and even went up to Red Lake but didn't find Lucy or get any response from God, as he had hoped. Darrell finally decided to return to Killeen. He prayed that the Lord would protect Lucy and bring her back unharmed to their church. In the meantime, he would tell her parents what she'd been doing, and together they'd figure out what to do. When she arrived in Killeen, he and her parents would be ready. They'd welcome her back to the church, he'd marry her, and everything would be fine.

* * *

If Lucy had known what she was really taking on, perhaps she wouldn't have started the trip down the Mississippi. To get to the Gulf of Mexico, she'd have to travel 2,552 miles, go through twenty-nine locks, traverse dangerous rocky St Anthony Falls in Minneapolis, make her way through treacherous currents near St Louis, and avoid being crushed or swamped by enormous barges. The trip could take as long as six months, but had been done by other canoeists in as little as a hundred days.

September, with water at the lowest level, was probably the easiest month for a canoe to navigate the river, and Lucy got lucky with several weeks of Indian summer weather. She found quiet camping sites and fresh clean water every night. She saw deer, coyote and even some eagles. As she went further south, larger boats appeared, but nothing she encountered was too threatening or too difficult until she arrived in Minneapolis.

In Minneapolis she found the rocks of St Anthony Falls. These were impassable so she would have to portage. Walking down the little trails alongside the rapids, she started to transport her belongings down to where the water was calm again. She soon met a couple of students doing a school project on the river. They helped her, and she treated them to a meal with some of the money Sarah had given her. The students were impressed with her journey. They were glad it was them she'd met, they told Lucy, because there were thugs along the river. She nodded; she knew that. However, she felt protected on the river journey, and if she ran into trouble, God would help her, as he had before.

Sarah's calls would also help her. The older women knew folks in Hannibal, Missouri, Natchez, Mississippi, and Venice, Louisiana, last stop before the Gulf. Sarah's friend in Venice had agreed to return the canoe to Sarah the following May on her annual trip to Minnesota. This friend had also agreed to help Lucy get back home to Killeen. Sarah hoped Lucy didn't run into anyone who wanted to harm her, but she'd have to leave that to the Great Spirit. She also hoped she'd get her canoe back, as she wanted to be buried in it. But if she didn't, well, so be it. It was Sarah's time to give her belongings to other people and she was glad Lucy had the canoe.

Meanwhile, Bill, Maria, and Charlie had decided to split up. Bill would go north along the Mississippi and Maria and Charlie would travel south. They would drive on The Great River Road and ask if anyone had seen her in places where Lucy might stop. Once one of them found her, they planned to call the other party to join them.

Bill stayed in the bar, on his third drink, brooding, after the women departed. He sensed a bigger purpose to Lucy's journey than simply prayers for the victims of past violence. Bill didn't know exactly what it was, but in his mind he linked Lucy and her journey to the Iraq War. The homegrown killers *were* terrible, but what they did was dwarfed by the war, which, after Vietnam, was the most colossal American tragedy ever. Lucy had told him the numbers, and Bill remembered: George Hennard, 24; David Koresch, 75; Timothy McVey, 168; Dylan Klebold and Eric Harris, 13; Jeff Weise, 9; Charles Carl Roberts IV, 5; Seuing-Hui Cho, 32. And he had another number he'd never forget: 2,986, the number of people killed in America by Al-Queda and Osama on September 11 2001. Bill had 2,986 tattooed on his upper arm underneath a Lady Liberty. He closed his eyes and saw all these names and numbers as if lit up on a scoreboard.

As he had his fourth drink, Bill pondered the numbers for the Iraq War. He hadn't seen the most recent figures, but he knew it was close to 5,000 US dead and over 100,000 – some said over a million – Iraqis. Those numbers should have the names of George W Bush and Dick Cheney next to them. It was probably treason to think of Bush and Cheney on the same list as Koresh and McVey, not to mention Osama, but they were the ones who had caused those deaths, so they belonged next to those numbers. An unnecessary war was just as evil as anything executed by terrorists and by the deranged. Innocent people had still been killed. And it wasn't just the war dead that Bill considered as he had his fifth drink. He was feeling a buzz now. It was the injured, the physically wounded and emotionally impaired, like himself. Bill still had nightmares about what he'd seen and done. He didn't think his nightmares would ever cease, but the cost to him, he thought as he used his eyes to look at his hands and his legs (the human body truly was a miracle), was tiny compared to the enormous cost to other vets who'd lost parts of their bodies and brains. And what about all the Iraqis who'd been grievously injured? There must be millions. And all the Iraqis with PTSD. Bush and Cheney would go down as being the worst mass murderers of the twenty-first century. Bill felt sure of this.

Bill imagined meeting Dubya and having a very long talk with his former commander-in-chief. Bill didn't know how such a meeting would ever be arranged. But he saw himself speaking with the man, explaining what happened to him and others over there, and asking him why in the hell he'd started that goddamned war, and demanding that Dubya spend the rest of his life doing what he could to improve the lives of the wounded and help the families of the dead.

Bill realized that he was teetering. He needed to focus on something positive. Lucy. Helping Lucy. That might help him make up for the people he'd killed. At least he hadn't killed any children. Well, he hadn't killed any kids himself, but there had been incidents involving kids, and the horrific sounds of dying kids screaming was never far from his mind, especially as he slept. He knew that plenty of other soldiers had killed kids, either by accident, or in terror, fearing that it was either "them or us." Many of those deaths had been carried out by Humvee and Bradley drivers. Bill knew those drivers would be messed up for the rest of their lives. Didn't the assholes who started this war understand that the trauma of war torments soldiers forever? And continues into the next generation and the one after that? Did they ever consider that at all? Probably not. Bill knew that not one of those fuckers had ever served as a front line soldier in battle. Not Dubya. Not Dick Cheney. Not Wolfowitz. Not Rumsfeld. Definitely not Condi.

Bill was really drunk and was considering ordering a sixth drink when he looked up at the TV above the bar and noticed the ticker tape on CNN: 4,839 US war dead; 32,678 wounded; 200,000 estimated Iraqis dead. They never listed the Iraqi wounded. And no one ever listed the numbers of the psychologically damaged on either side.

"Is there a hotel nearby?" Bill mumbled to the bartender as he put two twenties on the bar. He didn't want to drink himself into oblivion. Then he wouldn't be any damn good to Lucy or anyone else. He retained enough clarity to know he'd have a hard enough time walking fifty feet, much less driving all over Minnesota.

"Yeah, right next door. Decent place."

"Thanks, I owe you one."

"No, sir. It's actually us who owe you one." Bill wore an Army cap and in his sleeveless shirt, anyone could see his tattoos. The bartender made sure Bill got to the front desk of the hotel and then returned to his job at the bar. He hadn't planned to serve the obviously drunk vet any more drinks; if Bill hadn't asked about a hotel, the bartender was going to ask for his keys, or call the cops if Bill tried to ride off. The bartender didn't want any deaths on his hands, especially another Iraq War vet.

* * *

Neither Bill nor Maria or Charlie had ever followed a river. These days, how many Americans could say they had? There were some who had journeyed parts of rivers, but only a small percentage of modern day Americans who had gone down any rivers all the way. The Rio Grande is navigable by kayak almost all the way from its source. The Mississippi is too, by canoe or kayak. But most people didn't have the time or the inclination. Highways are quicker; and people who want to know more about river life can just stay home and "visit" a river on the nature channels or on the internet.

As Bill drove north along highway 169 and Maria and Charlie went south along highway 61, they all fell in love with the Mississippi. Being on motorcycles it was easy to imagine journeying alongside a river on horseback, or on foot as people would have done a thousand or ten thousand years ago. However, they didn't find Lucy.

Bill felt very discouraged by the time he got to Brainerd. He stopped at a bridge overlooking the river. He realized the road ahead veered away from the river, and on his motorcycle, he'd be out of view of the river for miles. This was going to be harder than he had thought. He looked upstream first, then crossed the highway and looked downstream. No sign of Lucy. Bill decided to travel as fast as he could to the next crossing he could see on the map. He hoped he didn't miss Lucy in between the two bridges.

Meanwhile, Maria and Charlie had found an extremely beautiful part of the river south of Minneapolis near Red Wing. The Richard J Dorer Memorial State Forest had gorgeous places to picnic. They had their priorities straight. They asked about Lucy at every opportunity. Then they found a secluded spot, parked the motorcycle, retrieved a sturdy blanket, ran off into the woods and made love. There weren't many bugs in mid-September, and hunting season hadn't started. It would have been humiliating and probably dangerous to be found by men with guns. But they were lucky.

They got as far as Winona and then, looking at the map, realized there was something wrong with Iowa. In that state there were roads leading to small towns along the river, like legs on a centipede, but they couldn't find a road that followed the river, as there had been so far in Minnesota. Tracing the Mississippi with their fingers, they saw that Wisconsin and Illinois had the same problem as Iowa. The road shadowing the Mississippi didn't seem to pick up again until Hannibal, Missouri. Maria and Charlie wondered who decided not to put a continuous road along the river in those states. There were roads, of course, but they were all just local. Maria and Charlie had gotten used to the stretched-out highways of the west with hundred-mile views, and had been enchanted by the river road. They had anticipated such a road all the way to New Orleans.

They decided to stay overnight in Winona. It was a liberal town where people didn't seem shocked by the sight of two women holding hands. They had toned themselves down a bit, wearing baggier clothing. Maria had her hair pulled back and Charlie was letting her hair grow longer and had decided to stop dying it blonde. Her real hair color was a mousy brown. They wore no makeup and had friendlier smiles.

The next morning after a late breakfast Charlie stayed behind at the campground while Maria walked to a mall to shop. Since they hit Winona, the refrain from an old Tom Petty song, *Refugee*, had been going through Charlie's mind. She sat by the river at a picnic table under the shade of an oak. It was very relaxing to watch the water flow by and hear the sounds of children having fun in a nearby playground. So different from Iraq...well, at least her experience in Iraq. Kids probably used to have fun in Iraq and maybe they would in the future.

She began writing some words that could become song lyrics. She couldn't tell if her words were any good, as she'd never tried writing before. But it felt good to write things down.

> *No longer lonely, no longer blue*
> *I've got you, baby, you've got me too*
> *Can't forget what I've seen, can't forget what I've done*
> *That part of me's fucked, that part's come undone*

But I can set it aside, 'cause I've got you, babe
Right by my side, right by my side
Winona, gotta own her, Mississippi to the east
Plains to the west, here we feel the best,
Sure better than that damn Iraq
Sure better than that damn Iraq

Charlie knew it needed some work, but as she looked at her words and watched the Mississippi, she realized how relaxed she felt in Winona. She knew they'd find Lucy. It was just a matter of time. And then there'd be more fun and games getting that girl back to Texas. But eventually, things would settle down, and then where would Charlie and Maria find a home? This might be a good place. Minnesota seemed a lot friendlier to lesbian couples than Texas.

* * *

Joseph and Ben channel surfed one night sitting in a hotel room while Judith listened. They hit Comedy Central and Judith listened to Jon Stewart's *The Daily Show*. It had been broadcast for thirteen years and was still one of the most popular comedy news shows. For many viewers, Jon's show was how they got the daily news. Many considered him the most trusted man in America. His sarcasm, satire, and impish interviews of newsmakers were just the right answer to the insanity that had descended upon the country since the 2000 election.

Judith realized, as she heard Jon joke around with a guest, that she wanted to be on the show too. She would have to think hard to find some jokes that got him. Before she'd been injured and blinded, she'd read one of his books, a parody of American history. She recalled the pages about the Supreme Court justices. In this book, the justices were all naked and the reader was supposed to match robes from the opposite page to clothe them and make them decent again. The photos were really shocking. Undignified. Ugly. Upsetting.

Maybe that was the point, Judith thought. At least five of the justices had been "indecent" in their votes for the Republicans in 2000, which stopped the vote counting in Florida and gave Bush the presidency, even though more Americans had voted for Gore. Judith thought Jon should have put Katherine Harris, Florida's then secretary of state who corrupted the election process to favor Republicans, on the same page with her own indecent naked body.

The naked bodies, of course, were those of others matched for race, sex, age, and general body type. Those bodies really didn't look too good, Judith recalled. Her body had looked beautiful before the accident.

Later that evening she sat naked in the bathroom in her wheelchair and waited for Joey to return with a fresh towel. She wondered what she looked like now. She'd gained some weight, and the extra weight could only go to her breasts, abdomen, and butt. Joseph had told her she was still beautiful, and when she was with him she felt that way. He told her that she looked like one of those hand-sized European mother goddess figures from thousands of years ago. Very round goddesses without arms or legs and often without eyes, they were comforting and reassuring to behold, and perhaps in the time they were revered, to actually hold. With Joey's encouragement, Judith thought of herself as an old-fashioned goddess.

Maybe that was how she should approach a hypothetical interview with Jon Stewart. How would Jon deal with a goddess? He was married to a lovely woman, so he was used to living with one. All women could be goddesses, just as all men could be gods. "The god/goddess in me salutes the god/goddess in you." Judith sighed. She wished she could do the beautiful namaste salaam, with two hands folded together at the heart. She could still bow her head and upper body, although she had to be careful so she didn't tip forward. Although that could get a laugh. Jon would have to pick her up and put her back in her chair. She wondered if he was strong enough. It would be fun to be picked up by Jon and put back in her chair on national TV. Judith would have to practice falling out of her wheelchair so she wouldn't get hurt. She would definitely have to do her own stunt work. There weren't too many body doubles out there who looked like her.

Maybe Judith could get him in on the joke, and before he picked her up, Jon could strip off his jacket showing a sleeveless Superman T-shirt and muscular arms which Judith hoped he had underneath his news anchor attire. Maybe Jon could do a little preening first, showing his biceps to the audience. And then do some preparation squats like a grunting Olympic bench presser. Could a medium-size middle-aged Jewish man pick up a round African American female limbless veteran goddess? She weighed about a hundred pounds without her arms and legs. And she knew that firefighters had to carry people of equal weight up sand hills to pass their exams. Maybe she'd mention this to Jon, and if he was the type who had always fantasized about being a firefighter, perhaps it would get him all fired up and he'd be able to lift her, *no problema*, and put her back in her wheelchair. Then maybe next she'd have a Janet Jackson wardrobe malfunction. Could the audience (and sponsors) handle a semi-naked limbless blind vet? Could Jon? It could be embarrassing or it could be pretty funny, to pick someone up, realize that her clothing had come apart, and try to figure out what to do next. Judith was pretty sure that Jon could improvise. And Judith could keep talking, casually mentioning that she was an embodiment of the Goddess, that breasts were totally natural, and thank Goddess that the explosion had left her with them. Too bad she wouldn't see the audience reaction, but she'd hear it, and that would be enough.

Judith was going to have to try this skit out with Joseph. She knew he could pick her up. But he weighed close to 200 lbs, worked out daily, and lifted her many times a day.

Later, during a commercial, she turned to him. "Hey, Joey. How strong do you think Jon Stewart is?"

"Why do you ask?"

"I'm just thinking something over. Do you think he's stronger than Colbert?" Judith giggled, imagining Jon and Steven fighting over the privilege of picking her up off the floor on national TV.

"What's so funny?" asked Ben.

Now Joseph was laughing too, as if he'd latched on to her thought waves and knew exactly what she was conspiring. "Jon may not be stronger, but in picking you up he'd prove he's more patriotic than Steven." They spent the rest of the evening talking and laughing about which talk show hosts were more manly and who'd be better at improvising when a blind limbless vet had a wardrobe malfunction.

* * *

"And that was the end. I was in freezing water up to my neck, drowning, and that asshole, Osama, was cursing me." George finished speaking. He trembled. It was as terrifying to recall the nightmare as it had been to experience it. Osama still hadn't been caught, and the humiliation and horror of the dream brought home how much George feared this man. As bad as the Mother Nature and zombie dreams had been, or even the terrifying one about God, they were nothing compared to the Osama nightmare. The incarnation of the Devil, Hitler, Stalin, Pol Pot and Idi Amin all rolled up together in the persona of Usama bin Muhammad bin Awad bin Ladin.

Dr Raintree looked at George thoughtfully. "You know, in dreams the characters can be who they are. But on another level, all the characters in a dream…." She paused. "You may not like to hear this, but all the characters in a dream are aspects of yourself. The shadow side, so to speak."

George was horrified, then angry. "I am nothing, NOTHING, like that evil monster." He got up and walked around the room. He thought about leaving. How could she say that? He sat back down in his chair.

Dr Raintree continued. "What do you believe many Muslims in the world think about you? And many Europeans and others who declined to join in the war against Iraq? And for that matter, how many Americans view you as being almost as bad as Osama?"

George felt so angry he couldn't speak. He clutched the arms of his chair.

Dr Raintree said softly, "Dying from a bomb or a bullet feels pretty much the same, I imagine, whether you're in New York City or Baghdad. And if you're lying on a stretcher in a hospital emergency room, with half your body destroyed, it would be the same experience whether you're an American or an Iraqi." She paused again.

"It's also interesting that your subconscious puts the confrontation between you two on an oil tanker, a very old one in very poor repair, falling apart into the ocean, and you're the one falling into the cold waves. Osama seems to be unaffected. What do you think that means?"

George curled his lips under his teeth and appeared chagrined and petulant. He'd been told many times that most of the oil used in the United States came here on tankers from around the world.

"Oil." He shuddered. He'd actually read a summary of *The End of Oil*. And he had mentioned the "C" word, conservation, in his 2006 State of the Union address. But no one seemed to listen, and he hadn't repeated that word, mostly because he didn't really believe in it. George had never had an environmental perspective. Just as he couldn't really imagine a non-Christian perspective, he just didn't imagine life from anyone else's point of view. And until recently he'd never recalled his dreams the way he did now. Dreams and imagination. What in the hell was happening to him?

Dr Raintree looked at George. She didn't know what was going through his mind, but it seemed to be something profound, perhaps a breakthrough. That didn't happen often, but in her office she'd witnessed other patients' moments of enlightenment. This would be a really good thing for George, if that was what was happening to him. And although ethically she could really only consider his health, she also thought a breakthrough for this patient would be good for the country. Perhaps even good for the world. She breathed steadily and watched.

George cleared his throat and said, "The Age of Oil is over. It's finished. Goddamn." He put his head in his hands. "And those bastards over there don't need oil. They *can* live like they did a hundred years ago. But we can't. We need oil. We can't live without it." He hit his fist into the palm of his left hand several times.

Dr Raintree said gently, "We could live without oil, but a lot of things would have to change. Many people think of our need for oil as an addiction, George. What do you think?"

George really thought of oil as an absolute necessity, but he used to think that way about alcohol, and he'd given that up with Laura's help. She'd made him understand the consequences of drinking. But admitting an addiction to oil? What could he, one man, do? It was as if the whole country would have to admit an addiction to oil.

George glared at Dr Raintree. "The detox would be a killer. And recovery even more of a bitch. Excuse me." He looked embarrassed but then saw on her desk an *AA Big Book*. "Guess someone would have to write an OA, Oil Anonymous, Big Book. Heh, heh."

"Perhaps you could write it, George."

"Me, write a book dealing with oil addiction? That would be crazy. That would be like going on tour with Al Gore. I mean, I know my dad and Bill Clinton worked together on the Asian tsunami, but me, writing about oil and global warming, that's impossible."

George was feeling worse. "I thought therapy was supposed to help me feel better. And get this thing out of my brain."

Dr. Raintree was not surprised to see that George had reverted back to believing that there was some kind of chip in his head. "We can get the 'thingamajig' as you call it, out of your brain, I believe, but it is going to require as much effort as you put into quitting drinking. Probably more."

George decided to change the subject. "Osama even tried to convert me to Islam."

Dr Raintree pondered him. She still hadn't mentioned that she was a Muslim herself, an American Muslim who attended a liberal congregation, but a Muslim nonetheless. This wasn't the time to bring this up, however.

"Tell me more."

Chapter 27

After Lucy made it past St Anthony Falls and traveled further down the Mississippi, she set up camp and while watching the river flow, recalled her river journey thus far. Lake Itaska's green tunnel had given way to a broad river which hadn't been too difficult to manage. Then there had been a tricky part, where the river braided through trees and small islands, but she'd eventually found her way. Except for the falls, she'd had no challenges. She had plenty of supplies and it wasn't hard to find clean water along the route. There had been no rain and the weather was kind to her; it was neither too hot nor too cold. The solitude was the best part. She hadn't been alone since Nebraska, and her journey called for time for reflection.

As she thought back over her travels, she could see a pattern emerging. The Jewish lawyers. The nuns. Maria and Charlie. Kenzo, Jesus, Bill and the other Iraq War vets. Darrell. The Abu Ghraib horrors. Joy. Sam. Ronny and Gary. Hank and his horses. Sarah and her canoe.

Lucy had gone on this journey to pray for the dead, but she'd found the living.

According to her church, all these people, except Darrell, would be left behind to suffer the hell on earth after the Rapture. And according to the prophecy, the idyllic scene before her eyes would be destroyed and recreated just for the chosen few. Lucy winced as she recalled the preacher's words.

She realized paradise could be here on earth now with nonbelievers. Even if the Rapture was real, Lucy wanted to be left behind with her new friends on earth.

She was thinking about this the next day as she glided past Winona, and Maria spotted her. She and Charlie had been watching from a grassy slope by the Mississippi.

Lucy wasn't surprised to see them. She'd had a premonition she'd see someone she knew. Lucy paddled the canoe towards the shore and got out with open arms. She hugged Maria, who was jumping up and down and yelling in greeting. She hugged Charlie, too. She felt surprisingly happy to see Maria's lover.

Later Maria called Bill, leaving a message on his cell to say they'd found Lucy and they would wait for him in Winona. Later yet, Charlie announced, "We're thinking about staying here, Lucy. This place is nice. Restful. Green. There's a VA in Minneapolis and a smaller clinic in Rochester. I know I'm going to need their help." Charlie had a pile of money in a bank account. It was enough to get started.

"I can get a job and once I get residency, maybe I'll go to college and get a nursing degree," Maria said. "Maybe Charlie will go to college, too."

Charlie wasn't sure about that. She liked action, something physical. "Maybe. What about you, Lucy? What are you going to do?"

"I'm going down the Mississippi. All the way to the Gulf."

"In the canoe?" Charlie asked.

"Yeah, in the canoe."

"What about Bill? You know he's going to want to go *contigo*, with you, *chica*," said Maria.

Lucy looked down at her bare feet. "I don't know. I've really liked being alone. Something's happened to me. I... I...." She stopped and some tears pricked her eyes. "I don't believe in the Rapture anymore."

"Hallelujah!" Charlie cheered, and Maria gave Lucy a hug.

Lucy kept talking, her voice wavering a bit. "I thought I was special. That all the people who believed in the Rapture were special. But we aren't. We aren't any better than anyone else. And the destruction of the earth, as part of the Rapture prophecy, is about killing people, just like David Koresch or Timothy McVey."

"Or Bush and Cheney," Charlie added.

"Yeah, them, too," Lucy said.

That evening Bill found the three striking women seated around a blazing fire in the campground. But he only had eyes for Lucy, who looked luminous. She didn't look like a teenager who needed protection anymore. The light that he'd seen flickering in her was now more like an Olympic flame, something that would never be extinguished.

He wondered what had happened to her since she'd left the group in Pipestone. Bill was going to have to wait to find out. After greetings and small talk, he hugged each of them, but Lucy pulled away from him quickly and said she was tired and needed to sleep. He watched her retreat to her tent. He stayed up for a long time gazing into the fire and at the stars above. He had no idea what he was going to do tomorrow, or the next day, or the rest of his life. But it had to be with Lucy. She didn't need him anymore. But he needed her.

* * *

Judith didn't know how you got on *The Daily Show*. Her brother had encouraged her to send a letter describing her act. That didn't get any response. As they toured around Texas, Oklahoma, Nebraska and Kansas, they watched Jon Stewart interview senators, congressmen and women, Hollywood stars, and authors. Journalist Michael Weisskopf with his *Blood Brothers* book made it, but they didn't see any wounded veterans interviewed. Ben and Joseph started writing a book about Judith as they thought that might be a good way to get on the show. They wrote up Judith's comedy skits and audience reactions, interspersed with memories of her childhood, youth, service in Iraq, her injury and recovery. However, the writing was slow going. They'd never written a book before and they hadn't realized how hard it would be. But they kept working at it. At least they had a title: *Blue Voice in Red States: A Blind Limbless Vet Takes Center Stage*.

Judith had come up with her stage name, Blue, as they toured the red states. She liked the name Blue, the universal nickname for the home plate baseball umpire. Blue had the final word at home plate. Not even the baseball commissioner could overrule her. And at least while she was on stage, Judith, Blue, would have the final word, even in these red states.

Ben faxed a book chapter to Jon Stewart. Again, no response. They tried Steven Colbert. No response from him either. Ben suggested that maybe these guys didn't want to be upstaged by a vet or another comedian. While they traveled in the car, they listened to Al Franken, now a Senator from Minnesota. He was damn funny. Joseph thought that maybe radio would be a better way to get publicity. So they sent information about Judith to all the *Air America* talk show hosts. None of them responded. But finally, one night, they got a fax from Amy Goodman. She was touring the midwest and would be in Lincoln, Nebraska. Could they meet her at the college radio station for an interview? Amy would also try to put Judith on TV, if possible. Judith, Joseph, and Ben were ecstatic. "Amy Goodman. Wow!" cried Ben.

"Eat your hearts out, Jon, Steven, and *Air America*," Joseph said to Ben as Judith laughed. He knew she'd be happy to give them interviews later, if asked, but she was thrilled to give Amy the scoop.

* * *

Lucy agreed to let Bill accompany her, but she didn't want him in the same boat. She liked being alone in her canoe, and with all the stuff, it would have been a tight fit. Bill knew how to kayak, and after selling his motorcycle, he got a kayak with enough room to store his belongings, which didn't amount to much.

Bill told Charlie and Maria that he'd turn on his cell phone for an hour or so at dusk, a good rendezvous time. As Lucy and Bill launched their boats into the river, Maria and Charlie waved them off and wished them luck. They weren't too sure about the future of this couple. Bill sure seemed interested but Lucy was so young, still forging her own identity, and she seemed lukewarm towards Bill.

The two women were surprised she'd agreed to his company. Maybe the experience at St Anthony's Falls had made her realize she was vulnerable. Maybe it was Bill's story of God and the helicopter, which he'd told the night before.

A man is marooned on an island. He prays for help from God and soon a helicopter arrives. The man waves the helicopter away, saying he'll wait for God to come save him. A fishing boat shows up and he waves it away, saying God will save him. A Zodiac motor-powered raft shows up and he declines their help as well, again saying that God will save him. Days pass, he dies, and ends up in heaven where he angrily questions God. "Why didn't you save me?" And God responds, "I did try to save you. I sent you a helicopter, a fishing boat and a raft. I can appear in any form at any time when needed. Human beings just need to understand that." As the man gnashed his teeth, God reassured him he'd have another chance in his next life.

Lucy had smiled when she heard this story, although she didn't agree with the reincarnation part. Maybe she figured God had sent her Bill. At any rate, she agreed to his company for the time being.

It was fortunate that Bill and Lucy weren't in the same boat. They argued before they went around the first bend. "The channel is over here to the left, Bill," Lucy had called out.

Bill yelled at her, "No, it's not. It's in the middle."

Bill had more clearance in his kayak than Lucy had in her more heavily laden canoe, but Lucy was riverwise, and on that bend Bill ended up caught on a sandbar. Lucy, sailing past him, looked backwards when she heard him swear. She turned her canoe around and paddled back to where he was struggling to get dislodged. Bare chested, dressed in his kayak skirt, trying to balance between the kayak and the sandbar, he looked ridiculous. Lucy laughed. She didn't say it, but she was thinking, I told you so.

As soon as Bill pushed off the sandbar and hopped back in his kayak, Lucy turned her canoe and glided south with the current. Bill soon caught up to her. He was stronger and his kayak was more maneuverable. Paddling in silence for several hours, they surprised many herons and even a few pelicans which, squawking, flapped out of the river. Once they saw a bald eagle dip into the water and emerge with a huge fish.

"Too bad we can't do that for dinner, Lucy," Bill yelled.

She felt more relaxed now. She still wasn't convinced it was a good idea to have Bill with her, but he did seem to know how to kayak. After his mishap with the sandbar, he hadn't argued with her anymore about the best channel. And he hadn't run aground again.

A few hours later they pulled up to rest on a small island and hauled the boats on shore. Noticing signs of beaver, Lucy told Bill she'd seen the animal one evening near a stream that emptied into the Mississippi. "I watched that beaver gnaw on a tree for two hours, until the tree finally came down," Lucy began. "And then it dragged the tree over to its dam and started gnawing on it again. Can you imagine how sore your jaw would be if you were gnawing on a tree for hours?"

"Beavers have a lot of tenacity," Bill said. He paused a moment and then, turning to look at Lucy, added, "So do humans."

Lucy smiled at him. Bill still had his shirt off, and in the warm sun, he looked really handsome. Lucy felt something she hadn't felt since the day she rode the motorcycle with him. She wanted to touch him. She moved closer. Just then, out of the corner of her eye she noticed a group of canoes coming around the bend. She drew back and said, "We've got company."

Bill swore. Lucy composed herself. As they waved to the group of senior citizens in their armada of canoes, she wondered what was happening. A few days ago she didn't even want this guy with her. Now she wanted to touch him, to feel his skin against her.

She shook her head. "Let's get going, Bill. Maybe if we catch up to those people, we could camp with them."

Bill groaned. This was *exactly* the opposite of what he was thinking. He did not want to spend their first night on the river with a bunch of senior citizen chaperones. Would he ever get a chance to be alone with Lucy? He pulled his kayak into the water and angrily paddled off. This time he was in the lead. They seemed to lose the cheerful group and stopped for the night on a perfect island. However, a few hours later the evidently super-fit senior citizens pulled up to the same island. They proved to be excruciatingly social.

Over the next few days as they traveled down the river, Lucy acknowledged her feelings for Bill, at least to herself. She'd never fallen in love with anyone, so she wasn't sure if this was love or not. Or True Love, like she'd read about. She was still a Christian and Bill would always be Jewish, even if he said he was lapsed. These thoughts were confusing to her. She didn't see how she could fall in love with someone who wasn't Christian, so she kept her thoughts to herself. With women, Bill wasn't aggressive, and even though he was falling more deeply in love with Lucy every day they spent on the river, he decided to act like a brother. He didn't want to frighten her away.

Lucy and Bill developed a rhythm as they paddled south. Indian summer stretched on into October. They met up mostly with older people who didn't have to worry about school schedules and with a couple of families with home schooled (or rather boat schooled) children. Bill imagined doing the same with Lucy and their future children.

Bill and Lucy camped on sandbars that emerged from the river. They got so used to life on the river, it was a shock to go into towns now and then for supplies. The smell of oil and the sounds of vehicles assaulted their re-tuned senses. So-called civilization was anything but, and they stayed away from towns as much as possible, keeping with the music of the river.

They talked at night about their life experiences. Lucy didn't know much about Jews, and although Bill didn't really want to talk about the religion of his youth, as he considered it, he told her about Judaism. As Lucy listened she understood how unlikely it was to expect thousands of Jews to convert to Christianity, especially Rapture-believing Christianity. How many Jews had converted to Christianity in the last hundred and fifty years? Bill himself only knew two such men, and he said it was because they'd fallen in love with Catholics whose families had demanded the men's religious conversions before they could marry their daughters. He didn't mention it to Lucy, but he'd heard that those marriages had ended in divorce and the men had returned to Judaism.

The sounds of the river soothed the two young people. Bill began to sleep better, although he would still occasionally suffer a recurrent nightmare from an experience in Iraq. As hellish as Abu Ghraib had been, another incident had been far worse. In the horrendous heat of the summer, sweat pouring down their faces and bodies, he and his platoon had been driving through some dry, brown village with narrow streets, guns at the ready. A hundred yards away, a group of children ran out in the road. Sitting in the front passenger seat, Bill yelled at the driver to stop, but the soldier just pressed his foot on the accelerator, heading straight for the young, disheveled kids standing in the street holding something in their hands. Then the little suicide bombers exploded. The bomb had detonated before the Americans hit the kids and it didn't disable their vehicle or injure the soldiers. But it killed some of the children and wounded the rest, who were injured even more badly when the Hummer ran over them and kept driving. The soldiers' curses and screams mingled with those of the injured and the bystanders. The nightmares always ended with Bill screaming and tears streaking down his face.

One night Bill woke, trembling and sweating from the familiar nightmare. He cursed and got out of his sleeping bag. He looked at Lucy, who was sleeping peacefully. He walked to the river and put his feet in the water. It felt cool. The sounds of nature and the presence of the young woman nearby made him feel better. The world wasn't all just the dry desolate horror of Iraq and Abu Ghraib.

Bill recalled something from a German literature class he took his last year of high school. The teacher had the group tackle Goethe's *Faust*, in English and in German. He'd had to start with the Cliff notes to get the story straight, but then he'd read the English version and parts of the enchanting German original. Until now, sitting at the edge of the river, he'd never really understood Goethe's "eternal feminine" as a savior of humankind. In the story it was God, Mary Mother of Jesus, and Gretchen, the soul of the real woman who had fallen in love with Dr Faustus, that had saved the man. He wished he'd understood this in high school. He'd have to track down that high school teacher and tell him that he finally understood Goethe – and the point of any great literature. It helps you live. It was just as helpful as religion. Maybe more.

Bill wished these forces of nature, love and literature could bring back those Iraqi kids. He knew he couldn't bring the dead back to life, but he could help some others, maybe kids that had been injured by the war. He knew Vietnam vets had done this in Vietnam years after their war had ended. Those kids and the vets would live to experience the good of the world, not just the suffering. Mulling these thoughts, Bill eventually returned to his sleeping bag, and after glancing at Lucy, he fell asleep. He had no more nightmares that night, and never dreamed that particular one again.

He didn't wake until he heard the sound of water boiling. Later, as they drank their coffee by the water's edge, Bill told Lucy about Goethe's *Dr Faustus* and Gretchen. Lucy had never heard of the story. She frowned when Bill told her that Gretchen's love for Dr Faustus had resulted in her own untimely death, and the deaths of her brother and mother as well. Dr Faustus didn't value Gretchen's love until after she was dead. Lucy didn't think it was such a great story. Bill thought of arguing with her, but instead asked her what great work of literature appealed to her.

"*Antigone*. That's the story for me. Out of everything I read in high school, that's what stands out. Antigone stood up to the king and everyone else because she believed in the authority of a higher power, even though she knew that belief and the action she took as a result of it would result in her death." Lucy frowned. "I guess she had to die, too, like Gretchen, to make her point."

"Just like Jesus," Bill replied.

They watched the river.

"Maybe to have a great effect on others, you have to die young after doing something heroic," Lucy offered, but then she looked at Bill, who had acted heroically with the suicidal vets, and later against the men from Abu Ghraib. She knew she didn't want him to die young. He should continue to be a hero and live a long life. She thought of someone else. "But then there's Nelson Mandela. He's a great hero and he's a very old man."

Bill looked back at Lucy. He was trying to think of a woman who'd been a hero and lived a long life. He thought of Joan of Arc, but she died young. Florence Nightingale? He wondered how long she lived. She symbolized all the amazing nursing care wounded soldiers received. Then it occurred to him that lots of people were heroes. They just weren't remembered because no one had written about them.

Things were getting too serious. Lucy splashed water at Bill. And he returned a volley of water. They were soon soaking wet and laughing in the sunshine, calling themselves names from the world's great literature. They soon shifted into film heroes.

"Superman!"

"Wonder Woman!"

"Spiderman!"

"Glenda the Good Witch!"

"Barney!"

"Barney? That stupid purple dinosaur? Barney's not a great hero," Lucy said.

Bill splashed more water at Lucy and answered, "He was to me. I loved Barney when I was a kid. He was a friendly dinosaur. I even took him to Iraq with me."

Bill could see Lucy's nipples through her white shirt. He wanted to kiss her. He moved closer.

"He didn't come home with you, did he, Bill?" Lucy asked quietly.

Bill hesitated. "No, I lost him over there."

Lucy lifted her hand, as if to stroke Bill's cheek. Then she looked up.

"Company."

Bill groaned. It was another cheerful group of senior citizens coming down the river. It suddenly dawned on Bill that a story about a beloved stuffed animal had moved Lucy to almost touch him. Just a story. A last gift from Barney.

Later that day, Lucy and Bill narrowly avoided a submerged tree trunk. "That was close, Bill. We have to pay more attention, otherwise we're going to need help from Superman."

"Or Gretchen."

"Or Barney."

Lucy smiled and Bill wished they were on shore, but she paddled away from him, and he had to push hard to catch up.

Days later, they reached the Missouri River, close to Hannibal, the childhood home of Samuel Clemens, better know as Mark Twain. Bill had read most of Twain's books either as a boy or in high school, and he wanted to push on to Hannibal. But Lucy was tired and so instead they stopped at the nearest island, Zeigler. They could check out Hannibal the next day. As they set up camp that afternoon, they saw more riverboat traffic, including paddleboats with tourists coming up the Mississippi to see the fall colors. The air had gotten a bit nippy at night but the weather was still beautiful during the day.

Hannibal turned out to be a disappointment, as it had been turned into a tame tourist town. Bill was pretty sure that Samuel Clemens would have hated what had happened to his boyhood town. If he'd been alive, Bill figured that Sam probably would have written something quite funny about the kitchy place it had become. However, he'd likely be genuinely pleased that people still enjoyed his stories and still traveled the Mississippi.

Watching the river later that day, Lucy asked Bill if he knew whether Mark Twain had ever been a soldier. Bill told her that young Samuel Clemens hadn't actually served in the big war of his day, the Civil War. He was from Missouri, a territory at the time of the Civil War, and he briefly joined a hastily organized militia. But after possibly killing a man who may or may not have been a Yankee, Sam decided that war was not for him. He fled to Nevada where his brother lived and eventually went on to California where he wrote so eloquently about jumping frogs. If he'd stayed with the militia, perhaps he would have died in the Civil War, and then there would have been no Mark Twain, no Tom Sawyer, no Huckleberry Finn, and a huge piece of American imaginative literature would be missing.

Bill knew some people might have said Sam Clemens was a coward, but in Bill's mind, the great writer was a hero. Bill recalled his teacher saying that creative imaginative literature was just as important to the survival and soul of a nation as its soldiers. Bill hadn't believed it at the time, but he did now. He wondered what inspiring works of literature would never exist because future authors died in Iraq. On the other hand, he knew that great books would probably emerge from the conflict in Iraq. Without war, there would have been no *Illiad*, no *War and Peace*, no *All Quiet on the Western Front*, and for that matter, no Bible or Koran either.

Lucy seemed especially quiet and thoughtful after visiting Hannibal. She'd told Bill that she'd wanted to pray for the dead of September 11 2001 in Hannibal. However, like Bill, she felt the town was Disney America, not the beautiful from-sea-to-shining-sea America she'd come to love in the last few months. She realized that a place of natural beauty by the river would be more appropriate. Bill listened. He had something to tell her, but it wasn't quite the right time. "We'll find the right place for you, Lucy. I have a strong feeling about that."

As they paddled south the next day, they noticed beautiful limestone cliffs to the east with occasional waterfalls cascading into the Mississippi. They'd heard about the mound culture of Indians and Bill said that the biggest mound ever found was coming up in Cahokia, Illinois. He'd read that Cahokia had been the biggest city north of Mesoamerica until surpassed by Philadelphia around 1800. Its population had collapsed well before most of the Europeans arrived, because of diseases the very first explorers brought and overuse of the land by the Cahokians themselves. Their mounds had survived, however, and the largest one was turned into a national monument in recognition of the people who'd lived there before the modern day Americans. People who probably thought their empire would go on forever, like the Romans, the Mayans, and the British. Actually, like the Americans, Bill thought. Perhaps, he mused, some future archeologists would name a national monument to the United States of America. He idly wondered what it would look like. Maybe New York City or Washington DC, although those cities might be underwater. Las Vegas, Nevada. Bill smiled. That would be perfect as a monument. Probably be preserved forever in the desert.

Bill and Lucy pulled their boats up to a rocky shore and tied them off. Bill wanted to sit with Lucy by the river and hold her hand as he told her more about himself, but Lucy was tired and she went to sleep right after dinner.

The next day she had her energy back and following a trail up the bluff, they set off towards Cahokia. Eventually, they got a ride from a retired teacher in a pickup truck. "Yep, the mound builders," he lectured as they traveled. "They didn't have rocks here like in Egypt or Mexico, but they had earth. And they had people. Maybe they were slaves or compelled to work by the priests. Those Cahokians had a lot of power in their day. At the top of the big mound they could see the Mississippi pretty clearly in both directions. The Indians traveled up that river all the way to Minnesota and back down to the Gulf."

The old man looked at the two young people. "I like what you're doing. I never tried that myself. Except just a couple of trips on riverboats for a day or two. Can't swim, like I imagine you folks can."

The teacher let them out at the entrance to the monument. It was the middle of the week and the place seemed deserted. Lucy and Bill paid the admission fee and walked in silence to the top of the mound. They hadn't walked such a distance in a while, so they were breathing hard by the time they got there. Then they turned around to look at the panorama and tried to imagine what the mound builders would have seen. The lights of St Louis were visible at night, but during the day, the view looked pretty much as the Cahokians would have seen it a thousand years before. Lucy told Bill about Mrs Weiskopf and *The New Yorker* map and suggested Cahokia should have been on the map. Looking east they imagined a map of the United States over the curve of the earth and talked about September 11 2001. They imagined Shanksville, the Pentagon and Manhattan as they'd been at dawn that day, and then what those places looked like by noon. Bill knew this was the right time to tell Lucy his story.

"Lucy, I went to all of those places before I signed up. I wanted to know, as best I could, why I was going into the Army. I went to Manhattan first, then DC and then Shanksville. This was 2004. Spring break my freshman year in college. I was reading the *Iliad* and stuff about World War II, and of course I'd followed everything in the news since 9/11. I liked college but the other students were just into their iPods, MySpace, football, and beer. No one really talked about Afghanistan or Iraq. So when everyone else went off to party for spring break, I decided to visit the 9/11 sites."

Bill paused. He was thinking mostly about Flight 93 and Shanksville, Pennsylvania. When it was initially hijacked, the people on that airplane were probably terrified but were thinking that their flight would end up peacefully on a third world tarmac as had most other hijacked flights prior to 9/11. But then they'd learned via cell phones about other planes crashing straight into the World Trade Center Towers and the Pentagon. They knew their hijackers had turned the plane and were headed back east. The passengers and crew didn't know which target their hijackers wanted to hit, but they knew they were going to die, too, and take the lives of other Americans if they didn't do something. Some of them may have thought they could land the plane safely, if only they could wrest it back from the hijackers. This was the most heroic deed he'd ever heard of, something out of Homer's epics. Bill still got chills down his back and tears in his eyes when he thought about the people on Flight 93 who'd fought back.

"Yeah, Lucy, Shanksville. It was peaceful there. Kind of like here.

I spent a few hours there, and then I hitchhiked back to college. I withdrew and signed up for the Army the next day. I told them I wanted to go to Afghanistan, but they sent me to Iraq. And except for a few periods of leave, I stayed there from 2005 until January this year. Got out just in time for a Super Bowl Sunday party with some of my old college buddies. They were still drinking. I didn't have anything in common with them, and after I got into a fight, I ended up in the VA hospital, eventually transferred to the Houston VA. That's where I met up with those suicidal screwed-up vets."

Lucy took Bill's hand. It was the first time she had touched him since that brief hug in Winona. It was as if a current of electricity flowed between them, but more cosmic, something from the stars, the genesis of love. It didn't burn them, just drew them closer. Then, high on the mound built over a thousand years ago by a long gone people, Lucy and Bill had their first kiss. They'd thought so much about other people who disappeared in an instant, but now all they were thinking about was love. Death could arrive in an instant, but so could love. And love had arrived. Death was busy somewhere else. And as Bill kept kissing Lucy, he realized he hadn't even had to mention Barney again.

* * *

"This is Amy Goodman reporting from the University of Nebraska, Lincoln. I have with me today Judith Brown, a decorated Army veteran of the Iraq War. She was severely wounded in the war but has become a comedian, a sit-down comedian because she can't stand up due to her injuries. Judith, please tell me how you became a comedian."

"Amy, I've always made people laugh. You know, kind of Whoopi Goldberg-like. A combination of physical humor and wit. As you can see, I can't do physical humor anymore, but I've got more wit than Jerry Seinfeld, Chris Rock, and Robin Williams combined. And they've got twelve limbs between them."

For a few moments there was silence.

"It's okay, Amy, you can laugh."

There was silence until Judith laughed. "It's really okay, Amy, to laugh. Although, come to think of it, I don't think I've ever heard you laugh. I'm going to have a hard time being a comedian if no one laughs. Okay, forget the jokes, for now. Back to the accident. The last thing I remember I was holding the steering wheel and had one foot on the accelerator and the other on the clutch of the Humvee. The last thing I saw was a family running across the street. They were frightened but also defiant. Then blackness, pain, screams. It seemed to go on forever, but the medic and another soldier got to me and saved me. Next thing I knew, I was in a hospital in Germany, and they told me I'd been there for a week."

"When did this happen, Judith?"

"Almost two years ago. Ramadan, 2007. I stayed in Germany for a month. I was too unstable to be moved. But then I finally got transported and spent most of that year at Walter Reed. They did what they could, but I couldn't use all the contraptions they wanted to fit on me. And I didn't speak. I could hear them, but I couldn't communicate. I was a hopeless case. They thought I was permanently, severely brain damaged. And maybe I was, but I think I was just in shock over losing half my body and my eyesight. They finally sent me back to Texas so I could be close to my family, and thanks to them, I ended up in a rehab hospital instead of a warehouse for medical vegetables. My family insisted on rehab. I was pretty much a Million Dollar Baby by the time I got there. Now I'm a two million dollar comedian."

"Do you mean that's how much money was spent on your medical care?"

"Yep. Your tax dollars at work. But all I was before the Texas rehab was a lump on a bed. An expensive lump."

"So how did you go from being a lump to a comedian?"

"Amy, I have the greatest family in the world, and I was lucky enough to have a wonderful man who knew me and loved me before the accident. And they all stuck with me, even though half of me was gone. I don't mean to say that the doctors and nurses didn't do anything. They did everything for me. If I still had knees I'd get down on them and praise them to the highest. And if I still had hands, I'd fold them at my chest and pray twice a day for all the healers who helped me. From the medics who saved my life in Iraq all the way through to the staff at the VA hospitals where I check in every now and then: THANK YOU!"

"Judith, at this point there are close to 40,000 injured Iraq War American vets. I don't think I've heard of anyone quite like you. A quadruple amputee blind comedian."

"Amy, I am a wonder woman. Yes, I am. And I'm going to let you and all your listeners in on a secret. I'm going to be a mother, too."

There was silence.

"That's right, Amy. That means I've had sex recently and I really enjoyed it and so did my fiancé."

Amy Goodman usually didn't talk about sex. "Sex and the disabled" was a topic not usually discussed anywhere in the media. "How...."

"Now, Amy, I'm not going to go into any details. We are, after all, on *Democracy Now* not FOX! Let's just say, thank God, thank Goddess, I didn't have any pelvic injuries, like some other poor soldiers. And our baby is due in April next year. Now let me tell a joke. Did you hear the one about a man and his mother and his mother-in-law and his sister and his wife and his wife's sister? They were...."

"Judith, we need to break to announce the local station where *Democracy Now* is being broadcast. We'll be back in a minute."

* * *

George kept reporting his dreams to Dr Raintree. One day he told her that he was certain that the thingamajig was gone. "Yeah, doc, I had the most wonderful dream. I was in the White House. I was still the president and I couldn't sleep so I got up and walked to the Oval

Office. I just wanted to sit there in the chair behind the desk. But when I got there I found Dick in the chair. Sitting in my chair. I was wearing my pajamas, and Dick was wearing a hunting outfit. He was grinning and spinning my chair around. Then he stopped and put his feet up on the desk and tilted the chair back. His boots were muddy. He laughed, said he was in charge and always had been. Something was bugging me behind my ear. I reached around, and it was like the biggest zit you ever saw. Dick had tipped his chair back and was still laughing, so he didn't see when I turned around and popped it and this golf-ball-size thing flew out from my fingers, hit him right in the chest, and he fell over backwards. Then I saw smoke and fire and the floor opened up underneath him and he disappeared, shrieking into hell. The floor closed up and I was left standing there with the smell and smoke of brimstone still in the air."

George grinned. "And you know how I felt? I felt reborn. I felt healthier, happier and more sure of myself than I've felt in a long time. That thingamajig was gone. And so was Dick. He really was a dick."

Dr Raintree had to smile. Too bad this was a private counseling session and she wasn't Jon Stewart or Larry King. George looked ten years younger. Her work with him had come to a turning point. And his work was just beginning.

"So, doc, I got that thingamajig out of my head, and I'm really grateful to you. I think I know what I have to do next. But it's going to be so hard. I might have to work harder than I did when I was president. And I'm kind of an old man now. I hope we still have a country for old men. Heh, heh."

Dr Raintree was not sidetracked by the mention of the Coen brothers' movie. "Your wife will help you, George. Think of Robin and Mother Nature from your last dream. Think of the soldier and his family in the VA hospital. Be led by your dreams, not pushed by your problems."

Dr Raintree had gotten that last line from a fortune cookie. Wisdom, she'd learned, could be found in the oddest places. George and the doctor looked at each other for a few moments and listened to the sound of the fountain. Finally George cleared his throat. "I think this will be my last session for a while. I'm going to do some fishing with an old friend and then you'll see what I do next."

She nodded. What he did with the rest of his life was up to him. She knew she'd done her best possible work with him, but she wouldn't know for sure if he'd changed until she read about it in the papers and saw him on the TV talk shows. She didn't think he'd come back to her office. No one would probably ever know about their work unless he brought it up. Maybe he would mention it in his memoirs. The first president to undergo psychotherapy. She smiled. Maybe he'd become a spokesperson for psychotherapy. Anything was possible. Another good line from a fortune cookie.

Autumn

Chapter 28

Lucy and Bill had made their way down the huge mound. They both felt like Moses after his encounter with God. However, they weren't bringing down any commandments, just love. Camping under the bluffs by the river that night, there was more kissing, but Bill knew that Lucy would want to be married before consummating their love. He was ready to return to Hannibal the next day and get married in a cute church by a nineteenth-century-look-alike preacher or paddle quickly to Memphis and be wed by an Elvis impersonator in Graceland. Or find a ferry boat captain to marry them.

"Lucy, I'd like to marry you. As soon as possible," he whispered.

Lucy looked at this man she'd been kissing for the past hour. She'd never kissed anyone for more than a few seconds. Her whole body was tingling. This was the first time she'd really felt like a woman. She knew now why, for many, just saying "no" was impossible. If Lucy didn't have such strong religious beliefs, she'd no longer be a virgin. And she'd be perfectly happy.

She smiled back at Bill. "I'd like to marry you, too."

That was settled. The next step was to find out where to get married and by whom. So maybe it was being in love, which is a sort of delirium, that almost killed them the next day.

They'd been playing a game on the river where one would pull ahead, then the other would catch up. As soon as they touched each other's boat, they'd have to stop and kiss or hold hands or touch in some way. It was a most enjoyable way to go down a river. But they weren't paying enough attention to their surroundings, and as the day went on and they got closer to St Louis, the river traffic increased. Unbeknownst to them, the local river currents were tricky, too, and at some point Lucy's canoe tipped over and out she went into the river.

It was dusk and Bill was paddling ahead of her. He heard her scream before he saw what happened. He tried to get to her, but the currents pushed him away. How could things change so quickly? He cursed and yelled for Lucy, who was screaming and struggling. He knew she wasn't wearing a life jacket. He could see it floating downstream along with other belongings in their waterproof containers.

Suddenly Bill saw a life preserver attached to a rope appear in front of Lucy. She grabbed it and was pulled towards a small boat that seemed to have materialized out of nowhere. Strong arms lifted her out of the water. Bill managed to maneuver his kayak near the boat and someone threw a line to him. "I'll tow you in," a man yelled. "My wife's in another boat. She'll try to get your canoe and stuff."

Lucy was shivering with the cold and shock. She had seen death there in the water. But love had held her up and kept her from getting muscle cramps or being sucked down into a whirlpool. And it must have been love that directed the savior's boat. The captain gave Lucy a blanket and offered her some hot tea. "I was lucky to see you. Name's Mark."

"Thank you. Thank you." That was all Lucy could say.

"This is why we carry life preservers and why I practice throwing them every Sunday. I do that instead of going to church. You're the fifth person I've saved from drowning," Mark was pretty proud to tell her. "And, young lady, you should have been wearing your life jacket."

Lucy was feeling better physically. "You're right." She'd worn it almost every day, but somehow, falling in love had made her forget to put it on. Bill! Where was Bill? "BILL!"

"I'm here, Lucy. Being towed. I'm here."

They soon arrived on the east side of the Mississippi River at a small dock where the river couple kept their boats. Released from the tow rope, Bill paddled over to some steps and made his way across the dock to the boat where Lucy sat huddled on a bench. He ran over and hugged her for a long time.

Mark interrupted, saying, "Alright already, we've got to get her some dry clothing and she might like to have a nice warm bath. Here's Emily, coming up in the other boat."

Bill and Mark could see that there was no canoe. A couple of Lucy's bags sat on the deck. When Emily got close she said she'd grabbed what she could see but the canoe had disappeared. Lucy started to cry. The canoe didn't belong to her, and she wondered how she was going to finish her journey. Emily told her not to worry about it now. "Warm bath. Dry clothes. Hot food. A good night's sleep. We'll talk about it in the morning." Emily took Lucy towards a small building they owned and Mark helped Bill unload his kayak and pull it up on the dock. The building was mostly for storage and repairs but it had some cots and extra sleeping bags, a small kitchen and bathroom. It would be a bit snug for four people but better than sleeping on the boat, especially after the day's near tragedy.

The next morning, Mark and Bill were outside on the dock early and the conversation turned to Mark's boat. Bill thought it looked very familiar but he couldn't place it.

"It's a modified Swift boat, Bill."

"A Swift boat? You're kidding, right?"

"No, I'm former Navy. Vietnam Vet. And a Kerry supporter, I'll have you know." He looked at Bill. "You didn't vote for that bastard, Bush, did you?"

Bill smiled. "It's none of your business who I voted for."

"Yeah, you don't look old enough to have voted in 2000. Actually, you don't look old enough to have voted in 2004 either."

"That was my first election to vote in. The year I volunteered. Army."

"Army. Ha! What's an Army vet doing on the Mississippi?"

"I'm Lucy's escort."

"Well, you didn't do much yesterday, did you?"

Bill looked really chagrined.

"It's okay, son. Those currents are tricky. People have died in there. That's why I practice all the time with my life preserver trick. Here, why don't we throw a few? I bet I can even teach an Army vet how to throw a life preserver."

"You're on, dude. Army beats Navy any day."

They threw the life preserver again and again, aiming at some buoys in the water. Bill caught on pretty quickly.

"You didn't vote for Bush did you?" Mark asked again.

"Of course not. I'm a liberal Jew from Cincinnati. I've never voted for any Republicans. Yet."

"I'm glad I rescued you. Even if you are Army. Let's go see how Lucy's doing."

* * *

It was time to return to New Orleans. Judith wanted to rest. She'd played out the comedy circuit. She couldn't be "on" anymore. She never did hear from Jon Stewart. But even if he'd called, she would have turned him down. She was too tired to make a trip to New York City and she wanted to see her Grandma Abbie. She loved that old lady. Judith had been in Iraq when Katrina hit, and she'd been incredibly worried when she realized her grandmother hadn't left the city. She'd ended up in the Super Dome with thousands of others and eventually had been evacuated to Houston. There she used her organizing skills from precinct work to help others. Even though her home had been condemned, Abbie's spirit never flagged regarding the future of New Orleans. However, when she heard of Marty's death and Judith's injuries within a few weeks of each other, Abbie suffered a profound depression. Eventually she pulled herself together so that she could focus on Judith, initially praying for her survival, and once Judith was back in the states, mobilizing every resource she could imagine to ensure the best treatment for her beloved granddaughter.

Judith and Joseph had one more show to do in Baton Rouge, but because Judith was so homesick, Joseph arranged for them to have a night with Abbie. They arrived at Abbie's home without Ben. He had had to return to Dallas as he had cases piling up. But a nephew out of school and out of work had volunteered to help Judith and in return, he'd have a place to live.

That night, Judith's grandmother prepared a feast. They ate cornbread, greens, fried chicken, gumbo, and some special pecan pie piled high with whipped cream. In respect to her doctor's admonitions, Abbie ate small portions, but this was no diet food. After dinner they moved into the living room.

Joseph couldn't help but marvel at the altar Abbie had erected around the TV set. It seemed to grow larger each time he saw it. Items were spread out on the TV and on the small table to one side of it and the set of shelves to the other, and even on a rug in front of the TV — Bush and Cheney memorabilia, defaced or altered in some way: mugs with a big W slashed through with red, a Cheney doll with a rifle shooting at a dangling bluebird of happiness, a Bush puppet, a T-shirt with a *Mad* magazine-style picture of Bush saying "Liar, Liar Pants Afire" and much more.

"I'm summoning suffering to those bastards," Abbie said proudly. "I am going to keep praying for their torment until they apologize and make amends for what they did. Even once that happens, and I know it's going to happen, Joseph, I'm going to keep my altar going."

Joseph looked at Abbie. "Do you really think Bush and Cheney would ever apologize?"

Abbie replied, "Bush says he's religious. Says God speaks to him. Maybe he'll see the light. But Dick Cheney? His salvation, I seriously doubt. But stranger things have happened. Maybe even old Dick Cheney will apologize for all the lies he told. And give back all the money he got. Maybe he'll do it from prison, trying to plea down his convictions."

They all laughed.

* * *

The day after his last appointment with Dr Raintree, George found himself on his property chopping wood. Whether he used an axe or a saw or a small chainsaw, the process of cutting wood felt so fundamentally good, he could have done it for at least an hour. He used to go for hours, but now, at age sixty-three, he grew tired sooner. He found the tree where he'd met Alice and sat down underneath it to drink some lemonade from a thermos. He wondered if he climbed the tree again, if he'd find Alice. Of all the strange people he'd met over the last six months, she was the most familiar, a mother who owned a restaurant and probably comforted more people in her life than most doctors or nurses. Thank God for women like Alice. Women like his wife and his daughters.

His wife really enjoyed not being the First Lady anymore. She could go to yoga with her friends without a big hoopla, just one car of Secret Service folks. Laura still supported libraries and visited schools but she could relax now. Didn't have to worry about being heckled. Not that she was heckled. But he was, almost everywhere he went, so they didn't go out together in public much anymore. And his daughters enjoyed not being First Children anymore. They'd put together a funny retirement video for his birthday in July. Mountain biking. Fishing. Chopping wood. Clearing brush. Napping in the hammock. Taking a vacation to Florida. Playing cards with old friends. Playing golf. Visiting his parents. Telling jokes. Taking them out to fancy restaurants for dinner. Making speeches for Republicans. Except for the last, all the sorts of things any well-off retired American might do.

George was going to have to talk first with his wife and daughters and tell them what he was really going to do with his retirement. Sure, he'd do some of the activities of any retired person. He couldn't keep his sobriety otherwise. But his family would be really surprised when he told them that he would spend most of his retirement with wounded veterans and the families of the dead.

His wife had told reporters when he turned sixty that he wasn't that introspective. That had been true then, but these last six months of suffering had made him profoundly contemplative.

George knew he hadn't suffered as the veterans and families of the dead had suffered, but for him, he'd suffered plenty, and he wanted to meet with others who could help him change. Dr Raintree had suggested a man who knew a lot about dreams, suffering and God. Bill Moyers would probably be very surprised to receive a call from George W Bush, but Bill was a very forgiving, thoughtful person and he'd likely respond to the former president's query.

George smiled. That was one of the great things about being an ex-president. You could just think of a person, and if that person was alive, you could contact him or her, and they'd usually at least speak with you, and probably agree to meet you. Almost *everyone* wanted to meet and talk with a president, even a former president. Even if the person hadn't voted for him. He'd call Moyers tomorrow. Now was the time to cut up some more branches. But he'd use the chainsaw instead of the axe. He could feel already sore muscles in his hands, arms and shoulders. George didn't want to hurt himself anymore.

* * *

Lucy's canoe was gone for good, and with it, most of their money. Bill had some disability funds he could tap into, maybe enough for them to complete the trip. Mark and Emily offered to take the young couple to Louisiana, and after a bit of discussion, they accepted. Lucy was extremely disappointed at losing Sarah's canoe. She found it hard to look at Bill. Kissing and talking about marriage had almost gotten her killed. Perhaps the phrase should be "love, rather than pride, goeth before a fall." She offered to help Emily with preparations for the trip but Emily had her routine down and suggested that Lucy rest. Lucy wandered a short distance upstream and sat in the sunshine. She wondered if she and Bill were meant for each other as Mark and Emily seemed to be.

Emily had known the young couple would be coming. She'd been dreaming of them for a few weeks. That was partly why her husband had been practicing daily his drill of throwing the lifesaver. She dreamed of a young woman with long hair about to drown and a young man unable to save her, followed by a journey with the two on their Swift boat.

It would be snug with four people but doable. The boat was pure luxury compared to the one Mark had served on in Vietnam in 1969. This one had a galley, bench seats which turned into beds, a head, an enclosed outdoor shower, comfortable fixed seats for trawling, and no one shooting at you. That was the best part.

"Did you know Kerry?" Bill asked Mark as they sat on the dock at dusk the night before their departure.

"No, I didn't. I didn't even know he'd been in a Swift boat until 2004. Well, maybe I did. Maybe he was in one of those newsletters they send out. But I didn't pay attention. Hell, I didn't pay attention to politics until that damned Iraq War started. Jesus. Fucking 'Nam all over again. I don't understand how any American could have supported the Iraq War after Vietnam. But does anybody but the Vietnam vets and their families remember 'Nam? Anyway it really pissed me off when I saw those damn Swift boat assholes criticizing Kerry. He served. He got wounded. Bush and Cheney did fuck all. So I formed a group of Kerry-supporting Swift boaters. We did what we could."

He finished his O'Douls and tossed the can in a bucket labeled "RECYCLE." "Yeah, we had a Swift boat 'Battleship' game."

"You mean the game kids play on a board with red and white plastic pegs?"

"Yeah, right," Mark said sarcastically. "No, real boats, out here on the water. We creamed their asses."

The two men laughed.

"You almost make me wish I'd joined the Navy."

"Yeah, Bill, you had a serious lapse of judgment when you went into the Army."

"I found out that I got seasick every time I was on a boat."

"Oh, you're one of those. Well, if you start to get sick on my boat, please spew over the side."

The conversation drifted to wars of the twentieth century and to wars of the past stretching all the way back to the first written records of battles in Egypt and then imagining the likely fights of their caveman ancestors.

"I wonder what other wars we'll have this century," Bill mused.

The Iraq War was still going on. Americans were still getting killed there. And plenty of Iraqis were still dying. The Taliban was keeping the war raging in Afghanistan. In Lebanon and Gaza, Hezbollah, Hamas and Israel were still at it. And there'd been skirmishes with Iran. Darfur and Sudan were still hellholes that no one really paid any attention to, as no Americans had died there.

"China? North Korea? Venezuela?"

"Venezuela?"

"Yeah. Maybe allied with Cuba."

"Canada?"

"No way!"

They sat quietly, listening to the sounds of the river.

"Could we go a whole century without a major war?" Bill asked. "Even half a century? Or maybe a quarter of a century?"

"Depends what you mean by 'we.' Do you mean 'we' as Americans? Or 'we' as Earthlings? The damn thing is, we had a chance at world peace after 9/11, if we Americans had just concentrated on Afghanistan. Everyone was with us. Most countries lost citizens on 9/11. It was the WORLD trade towers that got hit. Not the AMERICAN towers. We could have gotten rid of the Taliban, those shits. Found Osama. Tried that devil, put him in a very tiny cell on Rikers, and then started working on our goddamned foreign fossil fuel addiction and global warming, the real security problems."

Bill looked impressed. "Why aren't you running for office?"

The older man started laughing. "Because I am not insane. If I had to do all those things politicians do, I'd become a raging alcoholic and probably have to kill myself." He paused. "I've actually thought about it, Bill. I liked organizing the Swift boat group. And I used to be mayor of a little town. But there's so much bullshit to running things. Most people have to be like Machiavelli to run things. Are there any good politicians who've maintained their sanity and their morality?"

Bill didn't know but he said he hoped Obama would continue to be the good man that he seemed to be.

"Maybe you should run for something, Bill."

Bill laughed. "No way."

"What do you want to do, Bill?"

He looked at the river. "Beyond helping Lucy, I have no idea."

"You could go to college."

"Yeah, I know. I started, but dropped out to volunteer in the Army."

Mark, like so many others, had been drafted for Vietnam. He could have gone to Canada but when two friends were also drafted, he went with them to war. But they'd died and Mark had become a homeless alcoholic. Sad stories repeated over and over and over. Mark was glad that Bill looked like he was skipping years of needless suffering and going straight for a meaningful life. Bill had met his Emily in his twenties instead of his forties. "Well, we'll help you and Lucy. What's she going to do when you get to the end of your trip?"

"Don't know. I have no idea. But whatever it is, I'm going to do it with her."

"Let's drink on that. Give me another O'Douls. And, Bill, maybe you should have one too instead of that Bud."

"Okay, doc."

And the veterans of the two tragic American wars sat on the dock, listened to the river and the sounds of frogs, and thought about the past, the present and the future and wondered how it all would fit together.

* * *

George's talk with his wife and daughters went surprisingly well. They had tried to stay out of politics and had believed him on the reasons for the Iraq War, but now they were mostly concerned about seeing him relax and enjoy life. They liked being around him. He was a great dad and husband but he'd been insanely busy for so long. They only wondered if this new mission might take him away from them too much of the time, and stress him even more.

"Well, you could come with me," he said. "Just sometimes. And only if you want to. I'd like you to be with me on some of these visits. But you don't have to." He knew he'd have the company of the Secret Service. He was going to have them the rest of his life. He *was* afraid someone would try to kill him. There were lots of kooks out there. And many non-kooks who simply hated him.

Laura had given George a hug. "We'll come with you, dear, some of the time. Now, can I talk with you about maybe trying yoga?"

And that was it. With his family and God behind him, he could do anything. Next he would have to change his speeches. He had one scheduled in New Orleans the day after tomorrow. It was the usual Republican Party fundraiser. Tons more money would be raised for the local Republican Party and he'd get paid a hefty amount for appearing. But this time he would donate his fee to a local vets group building homes for disabled vets and to Habitat for Humanity.

Usually he talked about the fight on terror and his tax reductions, but this time George would pay tribute to what Jimmy Carter had done as an ex-president. George would then encourage all those wealthy Republicans to donate their time and money to help wounded veterans, the families of the dead, and any Katrina victims who still needed assistance.

"Let's go to the VA hospital and visit some vets tomorrow. Could you come with me, girls?" he asked later that day. He still called them girls even though they were close to thirty years old.

"Yeah, Dad, we'll go."

So that was how they spent the next day. The chief administrator of the hospital didn't even know the former president was there, until he got an excited call from a hospital nursing supervisor. President Bush had just shown up and said he wanted to visit some vets. An AA support group meeting was going on, and when George passed by and paused, the leader noticed him, and without missing a beat, asked him to join, if that was okay with the vets. The group members nodded their agreement and George and his daughters sat down in the circle. The Secret Service agents stood near the door.

Introductions went around and when it came to him, he said, "I'm George. I'm an alcoholic. I haven't drunk anything for the past twenty-three years." He actually had a longer history of abstinence than anyone there except the sixty-four-year-old psychologist group leader who had served in Vietnam and had been sober for thirty years.

After introductions were over, one of the young vets said, "I don't want to be disrespectful, sir, but why are you here?"

There was silence. Sixteen veterans, his two daughters, and the Secret Service agents looked at George. "I'm here to make amends, son. I've made some serious mistakes and I plan to spend the rest of my life making amends. I'm going to give a speech tomorrow night but I might as well practice here with you soldiers. It's hard to admit, but I was wrong about a lot of things to do with the Iraq War. And Katrina. And global warming. Probably some other things too, but I'll start with those."

* * *

The time with the vets went surprisingly well for George. Maybe it was because it was an AA group. They were very forgiving and very humble. They'd all made serious mistakes in their lives. Disappointed their parents. Shirked their responsibilities. Ignored or cheated on their spouses. Belittled or neglected their children. Drunk or gambled away their savings. Hurt or killed people in car accidents. Served years in jail or prison. To be truthful, none of them had ever started an unnecessary war, but to them, that was just a magnitude of difference. Besides, George came across as a regular guy, easy to talk with, and sincere in his belief in the Almighty.

However, when George arrived at the Republican fundraiser the next day, he froze. He truly wanted to say, "I was wrong. The Iraq War was wrong." But he just couldn't do it with all those nicely-dressed, wealthy Republicans sitting before him in the convention hall. He loved the cheers, the money, the adoration, and he knew that would all vanish if he started saying, "I was wrong." This was no AA group. Most of them weren't vets or recovering alcoholics, and, like most people, they wouldn't readily admit mistakes in public or in private.

After the speech George rode in the limousine back to the airport. His daughters faced him on the opposite seat. "Weren't you going to change your speech, Dad?" his eldest daughter asked.

"Just couldn't do it, honey. This is going to be harder than it seems. I don't really know how to change in public."

He thought back to the change he'd made at age forty when he stopped drinking and gave his life to Jesus. That had been hard enough but he'd been pretty much a private citizen then. Sure, his dad was head of the CIA, but the public didn't know the kids of the CIA directors. He was just a rich businessman who finally realized he was an alcoholic. But now he was an ex-president who'd made catastrophic mistakes which had killed a lot of people, left thousands more wounded, and even more people bitter and disappointed. And if he started talking this way with the one group of people who still genuinely liked him, they would hate him too. He wasn't sure he could give up the love. Maybe it was better to keep the changes private with small groups of vets first, then go public sometime in the future. Way off in the future.

Sitting in the limousine with his daughters, and still feeling the crowd's adoration, he wasn't thinking of any of his dreams or night-mares; it was almost as if he'd forgotten about Robin and Mother Nature and the zombies in the cave. Dreams had a way of fading during the day; however, like everyone else, George had to sleep.

* * *

Judith was tired and she wished Joseph had just cancelled the show, but they hadn't let anyone down yet and Abbie encouraged Judith to do it. There weren't many people in the audience; it was going to be a tough crowd. Maybe it just wasn't that funny to see and hear from a limbless, blind female vet. Maybe people would laugh more if she'd been a man. Most of the great comics were men. Well, at least she was black. That should help summon laughter. But she was a woman. Couldn't change that. Earlier in the day she'd thought about some of the women that made men laugh. Whoopi Goldberg. Tina Fey. Dolly Parton. Joseph had turned Judith on to Dolly Parton; otherwise she wouldn't have known the sweet saucy country music star could make people laugh. Judith had also listened to the DVD of The Blue Collar Guys, white guys who'd made a ton of money making jokes about average middle America white men, married or with girlfriends. Lots of henpecked, anti-gay, NASCAR-loving, TV-watching, beer-drinking, and football-viewing jokes. Joseph had told Judith that the audiences for the Blue Collar Guys were almost one hundred percent white. She was thinking about this when she started her monologue.

"I can't see you, but my manager tells me that half of youse is black and the other half white. You look like a chess board, out there."

A snicker or two.

"But that means you all are smart. Unlike those audiences for Jeff Foxworthy and the other Blue Collar Guys. Their audiences look like that oh-so nutritious white Wonder Bread. I can't believe they still sell that Kleenex food anymore. But someone buys it. Just like someone buys Jeff Foxworthy. Tonight, however, you've bought me. I sure am different from Jeff. Black, for one. Female for another. And no arms and legs and I can't see. Can't be like Jeff, no matter how hard I try. But I could be like Whoopi or Tina or Dolly, my favorite ladies of comedy, if only I had my legs and arms. My sight would be nice, too, but I'll start with limbs. So how about I go pay a visit to say, Dick's house, and see if he can help me get them back? I could have picked George's or Donald's or Paul's or even Condi's house, but I think Dick is the one to ask. The real decider. Him and that

Halliburton. Anybody here know how much money Dick and Halliburton made off the Iraq War?"

There was no answer.

"Millions for Dick. Billions for Halliburton. Yep, all that money for them. Cost to us: over four thousand Americans dead and over thirty thousand wounded. Hundreds of thousands of Iraqis dead and about the same number wounded. And three trillion dollars of our money spent. Charged up to ourselves, our kids and grandkids." She paused. "You ain't laughing."

Someone laughed.

"Thank you. I am a comedian. There's a joke in here somewhere. Okay, let's visit Dick."

Judith paused and then, turning her head left, said, "Knock, knock."

In a deeper voice and turning right with a snarled expression, she said, "Who's there?"

Left: "Judith Brown, Army veteran, purple heart."

Right: "No thank you, we don't want any."

Left: "Mr Cheney, I'm not selling anything. Just want to talk with you."

Right and back to snarling: "Okay, as long as I don't have to give you any money, I'll open the door."

Joseph made the sound of a door opening up. Then slamming shut. The audience laughed.

Left: "Now why did you do that, Mr Cheney?"

Judith, turning right again, contorted her face into a snarl with a look of terror.

There was more laughter from the audience.

Judith turned her face back towards the left: "I just want to talk with you, Mr Cheney. I've come all this way from New Orleans to Maryland. I would have helicoptered in, but I don't have the bucks for that, and besides you've got a no-fly zone over your property. You 'fraid someone's going to bomb you? Don't worry. Just get out that little gun you shot that old guy with and you should be fine."

Sound of the door opening up again.

"Thank you, Mr Cheney. See, I don't have anything to sell. And I ain't got any weapons."

"What do you want?"

"Why, I want my legs and arms back. I want my eyes back."

Slightly less snarling: "You need to go to a VA hospital."

"Naw, I already tried that. They couldn't give 'em back to me. But I know you have a lot of money and maybe you could help me and other vets with some things we need."

"So you do want money?"

"Everybody wants money, sir. But...." Judith sang a line from the Beatles' *Can't Buy Me Love*. "Yeah, I want money. But not for me, sir. You give money to some other vets and their families. And just give me some love."

Turning right again, she snarled. Somehow Dick Cheney and love just didn't go together. The door slammed shut again and he screeched, "Don't come back or I'll get you arrested."

Judith sang the Beatles' refrain at the top of her voice. A few moments after she finished the song, she exclaimed, "Dick really is a dick!"

Everyone laughed.

The thought passed through Judith's mind that she really would like to see Dick lying in the ruins of a shattered Humvee, his legs and arms gone, shrapnel in his face and chest, and screaming because he was blind. That might be the only way he would understand. Four, or was it five-deferment Dick? What an asshole.

"Humph, audience, that didn't work. Damn that Dick. Selfish bastard. Well, maybe it's 'cause he's a white guy from Wyoming. He don't like no black woman from Texas. Especially one who's got no limbs and no sight. Maybe I'll go visit Condi. She's nice and she's black. And I really like the way she plays the piano. And those clothes. Whoa, you go girl. Not that I can see what she's wearing now, but I used to love watching her on TV. Powerful. Attractive. Smart. Way cooler than Colin Powell. Too bad she didn't get 'lected to be the next president. But maybe she could help me."

"Knock, knock."

There was a piano at one end of the stage. The curtain opened, and Joseph, wearing a Condi-style wig, a silk jacket and high heels, glided across the stage and sat at the piano. He said, in a very cultured, intelligent-sounding female voice, "Who's there?"

"Condi, it's me. Judith."

"Are you here to play a duet with me?"

"Naw, I'm a singer."

"Well, come on in, dear. I'm in the living room, at the piano."

Joseph began to play some Rachmaninov. The manager appeared on stage and wheeled Judith over towards the piano. "Condi, can you play some blues? I like that classical music, but I'm more a blues singer."

Condi turned around and gasped.

"Yeah, now you can see why I don't play no piano. But don't worry, I can sing. I'm good." Judith bobbed her head. "How about a hymn? Yeah, that's something we could do together. How about *Praise God for Whom all Blessings Flow?*"

Shakily, Condi began to play the lovely hymn. The playing got stronger. Judith sang the traditional words through the first time. But then she changed the lyrics as Condi repeated the music.

> *Scorn Bush for all the deeds he's done*
> *My arms and legs are long gone*
> *And I am blind, as you see*
> *Thanks to you and yours, Condiiiiiiii.*

Condi tried to stop playing the piano but found she couldn't stop. Her fingers were as if anchored to the keys by invisible strings and she couldn't move from the piano seat. Judith continued, her voice getting stronger.

> *And you in your Armani suits*

And perfect hair, you look so fair
But you desired Bushhhhhh... (Judith stretched this out)
...hhhhh's war
and you're stuck here now,
can't me ignore.

Condi looked terrified, but kept playing the song. Her fingers couldn't seem to stop.

Judith sang louder.

You're kind of like OJ,
That murderer who got away
But he's now locked up for other trouble
and God will soon penetrate your bubble.

Judith sang the hymn with the same dignity that she would have sung a solo in church. In spite of her injuries and graceless clothing, she looked elegant. And the woman hunched at the piano appeared a haggard former shell of herself as she cringed, face contorted. Condi kept playing, not making a single mistake. However, her spirit appeared to be oozing out of her. Finally, collapsing over the piano, she wailed, "Oh, what a world. Who would have believed a little soldier like this could destroy my beautiful wickedness?"

Judith received a spontaneous standing ovation from the crowd. She bowed her head before them and sang *The Wizard of Oz* song, *Ding Dong! The Witch is Dead*. The crowd started singing with her and Joseph, acting as Condi, crawled from the piano to Judith's wheelchair and clutched at Judith's robes. Eventually, Joseph stood up, removed his wig, waved to the crowd and pushed Judith off the stage.

The next day, driving back to New Orleans, Judith told Joseph that she almost didn't have the energy for another show. However, her Grandma Abbie hadn't seen her latest show, and for her, Judith would do one last performance in the Big Easy, repeating the Dick and Condi skits. Abbie would like that a lot. Like most people, she'd disliked Dick from the moment she'd first heard of him, but she'd been very proud of Condoleezza Rice, a southern black woman, the first National Security Advisor to the President. However, when Condi joined the neocons advocating for the Iraq War, and the lies she told in the lead up to the war eventually came out, Abbie became tremendously disappointed. Joseph and Judith would dedicate this last show to her grandma but they wouldn't tell her what the show would be about. The old lady would get a big kick out of it.

Chapter 29

Lucy, Bill, Emily and Mark made good time in the Swift boat; it wasn't named that for nothing. It took less than a week to get to New Orleans. They passed one other Swift boat covered with "W" stickers, and when that captain saw their Kerry stickers, he gave the middle finger salute to Mark. Mark gestured back with an "up yours" gesture. Then the captain on the "W" Swift boat turned around, pulled his pants down and mooned Mark.

Mark shook his head and said, "Well, it's better than being shot at."

Bill laughed. "Yeah, you're right. We should just have wars fought by cursing and doing rude body language. No weapons allowed and a river between the two groups, so there's no physical contact."

The older man replied, "There'd be a few hotheads who'd jump in and try to drown the other guys."

"Okay. Well, let's have hot molten lava between the two groups."

"Cool. So we'll have all the wars fought in Hawaii, and after everyone verbally and visually abuses one another, they go off to separate islands with their families and have vacations paid for by their respective governments. Then they all go home and live out the rest of their lives. Would be a lot cheaper, and everyone goes home happy."

"Yeah, Hawaii is a lot better than Iraq. Why didn't you run for president, Mark?"

"I was too busy being crazy and drunk. I didn't have a wife like Laura to help me. Hadn't met Emily until after I sobered up. If Dubya had served in Vietnam he probably would have gone completely over the edge. Or would have gotten killed and then who knows who we would have had for president. Maybe someone even worse. Men can go to war and not learn a damn thing."

Mark jerked the controls suddenly and the boat shuddered left.

"Whoa, calm down, Captain. We still need this boat."

A few hours later they'd docked at a marina not too far from the city. Neither Bill nor Lucy had been to New Orleans, and when Mark and Emily realized that, they insisted on stopping to show the "Big Easy" to the young couple. "It's still not like it was before Katrina, but some of the real 'Naw Leens' has returned. You'll eat the best food and listen to the best music you'll ever hear." And that's what they did the next day, starting with strong coffee and sweet pastries at Café du Monde and ending with the blues at Tipitanas.

Lucy had only a sip of Bill's Hurricane, but the blues really affected her. She'd never heard music like that. Emotional music that entered her body as no hymn ever had. She watched Bill nodding his head, tapping his feet, almost dancing at the table. He appeared completely at home with the blues. Lucy felt that if she kept listening to this music, she might become a completely different person. Her eyes swept the crowd and she wondered if there were any Christians, much less Born Again Christians, there. It seemed doubtful. She felt a bit sick. She really wanted to get back on the river and get to the Gulf. She needed to complete her journey. She waited until the band took a break and whispered to Emily who spoke to Mark. Emily and Bill were both a bit intoxicated and would have liked to stay, but Mark, drinking O'Douls, agreed with Lucy and suggested they leave. There would be time for more blues after they finished the mission. Emily and Bill reluctantly rose from their seats and danced their way to the door as the singer started in on *Proud Mary*.

Mark and Bill slept on the boat while Emily and Lucy stayed at a nearby motel that night. Setting out the next day, Emily noticed a flyer for a show at a nearby comedy club. The comic was an Iraq War vet. Meeting up with Bill and Mark, Emily mentioned it. They could motor down to the Gulf, which was only about a hundred miles from New Orleans, and catch the show later that evening. Bill and Mark looked at each other skeptically. There wasn't much funny about the Iraq War. Not enough time had passed. It was still going on, Bill reminded her. But once Emily set her mind on doing something, she wouldn't let it go. She couldn't have lived in harmony with Mark all these years if she hadn't been determined. "How about *Catch 22*? *Hogan's Heroes*? Or *Mash*? Or *Good Morning, Vietnam*? I heard that the Iraqis have some kind of comedy show on TV that makes fun of the war. If they can do it, I don't see why one of our veterans can't do standup comedy. The war's over for that soldier. There'll be a lot of humor come out of this war. Here and in Iraq."

Emily, a retired teacher, had a master's degree in English, and when she wasn't tutoring kids or soothing her husband, she was reading. She had a huge private library in her home, as well as an extensive film collection.

Mark looked at Bill, who shrugged and said, "Why not?" Mark turned to Emily, "Okay. Tell you what, if we catch a big fish today, then we'll go with you tonight. The least we can do is heckle the fool."

"Yeah, he's probably Air Force or Marines," replied Bill.

* * *

George, who didn't know what to do after his failure to change his speech, decided to go fishing. His own pond hadn't recovered from the drought and he was just wondering where else he might go when he got a call from his buddy, Trent, who had rebuilt his home near the Mississippi River, after it was destroyed by Katrina. Trent had just purchased a new cruiser and was going to try it out the next day on the Mississippi. George had no obligations, so he made arrangements to meet up.

Trent's cruiser sported comfortable seats and a cooler full of cold (non-alcoholic) drinks. He had some good ideas about where to find bass, George's favorite fish. Accompanied by two Secret Service men, the former president and his friend settled back in the boat. They had cell phones and emergency radios and could call in a helicopter if there were any problems, but George wanted to go low key. He didn't want to frighten away the fish.

George was happy to turn the decision about where to fish over to the other man. He was sick of being the decider. He regretted using that phrase in public and wished for the thousandth time that he was more eloquent. But mostly he just wished he could follow through on his plan, which he considered as Trent chatted with the agents. George knew this would be the last major decision of his life, and his change of heart could turn not only *his* life around, but the lives of countless others. Maybe he'd even affect more people as a former president than he'd affected during his time at the White House. Even more than Jimmy Carter.

Later, as he watched his fishing line move in the choppy water, George thought about other presidents and their legacies. He really admired Abraham Lincoln. Honest Abe, he thought to himself and then muttered, "Damn," as he realized another thing he'd have to come clean about: the chain of events that got him the presidency in 2000. He knew he never should have been president. For much of his life he'd really only aspired to being the baseball commissioner, and he knew now that he would have been a happier man if he'd just stayed with the business of baseball. He would have had a lot more time for fishing and wouldn't be worrying about his legacy for the remainder of his life.

The cruiser's seats had safety belt harnesses but George had forgotten to buckle up. So when his line suddenly snagged, George, hanging on to the fishing rod, was hauled overboard.

It all happened within a few seconds. One of the Secret Service agents lunged but just missed the ex-president — although the agent probably would have been dragged into the river if he'd grabbed the other man. Whatever had hooked onto George's line was very, very strong and moving away fast from the boat towards the Gulf. The agent yelled into his radio, "SOS! Tumbler is overboard! We need rescue helicopters and boats right away."

George wasn't wearing his life jacket either, but even if he had been, whatever had the line was a real decider. So far he was mostly staying on the surface, thrashing about, but it wouldn't be long before he plunged downwards or out into the Gulf. Of course, he could have let go of the line, but in the frenzy of the moment, he didn't think to do that. In fact, holding on seemed like the only action that might save him. And so George was about to meet his death in the deep dark waters of the Mississippi...when suddenly, out of nowhere, there appeared a Swift boat.

Mark had seen the man fly out of the cruiser. He turned his boat to intersect the trajectory of the person and they were able to get close enough for Bill to slash the fishing line without running him over in the water. This all happened just before George lost his strength and would have gone under for the last time. Then Mark did his trick with the life preserver and the frightened man caught it. Bill and Emily hauled him out of the water. George collapsed on the deck of the Swift boat and then vomited water along with his breakfast. "Aw, shit. He barfed on my boat," Mark said and then muttered to himself, "Throw him back overboard."

Lucy wiped the vomit away from the man's face, and she and Bill turned him on his side so he wouldn't aspirate. He was breathing, so mouth-to-mouth resuscitation wouldn't be necessary, but both were prepared to give it, if they had to.

Bill was the first to recognize the near-drowned man. "It's Bush. It's President Bush," he cried. Even though he couldn't stand the man, it was an entirely different matter to meet a president out of the blue, especially after saving his life.

"What the...." Mark looked at the man's face. "You're right. It's him."

"And here comes the cavalry," Emily said, gesturing to the expensive cruiser pulling up next to them. She aligned the Swift boat with the cruiser and two Secret Service men jumped on board. They ran to George, pushing Lucy and Bill aside.

"It's okay. He's breathing. His heart is beating," said Lucy.

"Yeah, I'm okay," George said weakly. He appeared to be in shock. The agents instructed the others to stay back and then one agent worked on the near-drowned man and the other spoke into his cell phone. In mere minutes a helicopter thumped overhead, making waves. A cable was lowered and the Secret Service agents put George on a backboard and he was soon ascending up in the air. One agent accompanied the former president, climbing a rope ladder into the copter, and the other one stayed behind to interview the rescuers. They were obviously good Samaritans. He got their names and phone numbers and the name of the hotel where they planned to stay that night, as he thought the president would want to thank them personally. When it was finally all straightened out, the Secret Service agent returned to Trent's cruiser and roared off back to New Orleans.

Mark, Bill, Lucy and Emily observed one another with stunned looks. Then Mark started laughing. "We did it. We caught the biggest fish ever! Damn that we didn't do this five years ago right before the 2004 election. A Kerry Swift boat saving Dubya's ass. Okay, Emily, you win. We'll go to your funny vet show tonight."

As they traveled on to the Gulf, George was checked out at the hospital and found to be completely healthy. The ER doc prescribed some antibiotics and George showered to rid himself of the river stench. Laura arrived and he told her, "I'm never going on any boats ever again. Damn, I almost died. I don't want to die yet. I'm not ready to die." He started sobbing. His wife put her arm around him and George cried on her shoulder. Finally he stopped sobbing. "First things first. I need to thank those people who saved me. The Secret Service says it was a Swift boat, with Kerry stickers all over it." George chuckled.

While George was recovering, Mark made good time down to the Gulf. He guided his boat into the ocean and a short distance out, clear of the shipping lanes, he cut the engine and they rocked in the water. Lucy gazed at the ocean, which she'd never seen before. Then she leaned over the rail and threw up.

"Jesus, Lucy! Well, at least you didn't throw up on my boat, like damn Dubya did," Mark exclaimed as Bill and Emily went to Lucy's aid. What should have been a mystical experience after such a long and unusual journey was marred by the frailty of the human body. Mark turned on the engine and took the boat back to the river where the water was calmer. Lucy had nothing else to throw up and she felt better quickly. Kind of a letdown to the trip, although as she looked at her companions and thought about them saving the president earlier that day, she realized that was a pretty good end to her journey. She smiled at Bill, who was really the end of her long strange trip, and of course, the beginning of the next one. After she recovered from the boat ride, she'd talk with him about asking Mark to marry them, if Swift boat captains qualified.

Hours later Lucy felt well enough to eat. She'd talked on the phone with Maria and Charlie, who were actually in New Orleans. Winona had been a little too quiet. They agreed to meet at the comedy club that evening after dinner.

A Secret Service agent had called Bill and Mark at the hotel and they told him where they'd be dining, a quiet restaurant a few blocks away from the French Quarter. There were only a few other patrons there that evening, elderly couples who looked like mid-western tourists. Soon after Lucy, Bill, Emily and Mark sat down in a semi-private room off the main dining area, two limousines pulled up to the restaurant and the occupants were ushered in. Two agents entered the dining room first and visually checked out the occupants. None of them appeared to be threatening and, chattering away, the elderly diners didn't even seem to notice the scrutiny. One agent stayed in the room near the doorway and the other returned to escort in the former president.

Bill and Mark, who recognized the agent, rolled their eyes. "Here we go," Mark said to the others. "I refuse to stand up. He's not the king and I can't stand the man, even if I did save his life."

President Bush entered the room and walked straight to where his four saviors sat. He was casually dressed and had on a Texas Rangers baseball cap. The elderly patrons at the other tables didn't give any sign that they even recognized him. Perhaps they were Canadians.

The Secret Service agent hung back from the room where the foursome sat and George approached the table alone. He said to the group, "Excuse me, folks, but I'm here to thank you. Thank you for saving my life earlier today on the river."

There was silence as the four looked at the famous man. He had taken off his cap and was nervously licking his upper lip. His eyes shifted from person to person. Bill and Mark regarded George with long-standing revulsion for all the terrible things he'd done while in office. Especially for war veterans, starting an unnecessary war was the ultimate evil. It was okay for them to have saved his life earlier that day — it would have been equally evil to let him drown — but they didn't really want to invite him to sit down or even talk with him. Bill and Mark awkwardly allowed their gazes to drop to their plates. Emily pursed her lips. Like many other partners of war veterans, supporting Mark with all his Vietnam War problems, she'd also suffered.

Lucy finally spoke. "Would you like to sit down, sir? We can make a place at the table for you."

Mark and Bill looked irritated. George didn't move. It took a few moments but Emily smiled at Lucy and then at George. The two women moved over and made a space at the table for the former president. One of the Secret Service agents hurried over and pulled up a chair for George and he sat down. "I know you probably aren't my supporters. Uh, they told me you were on a Swift boat plastered with Kerry stickers."

Silence.

"If you'd known it was me, you probably wouldn't have saved me, right?" He nervously chuckled.

More silence.

"Well, I appreciate it very much. Is there anything I can do besides thanking you?"

Mark and Bill had their arms folded across their chests. They really didn't want George to be sitting at their table.

"Well, thank you anyway." George pushed back his chair and began to stand up.

"No wait, sir," Lucy said. Her whole life had been rushing

towards her as she sat there looking at the former president. If she still believed in the Rapture, she would have thought it was about to happen right then and there. "There is something you can do, sir. You can share a meal and then tonight you can accompany us to a comedy show."

Emily got the idea right away and smiled. It took a minute but then Mark uncrossed his arms and Bill lost the frown on his face.

George relaxed and sat back down. "Thank you. I would like that very much. Is it okay if I invite my wife and daughters? I'd like them to meet you all too. They're very grateful for you saving my life."

Emily responded. "Yes, that would be great. We'd like to meet them as well."

The conversation continued, but awkwardly. How could it not be uncomfortable for this group? Bill didn't say much but he listened intently to Mark and George, who were close in age. They were talking about fishing, perhaps the only mutually agreeable topic they could have discussed. And when things faltered, Emily spoke up. She was a very good conversationalist and she was determined not to have this end in anger. Lucy was filled with the spirit of the Lord. She just couldn't think of it in any other way. The Rapture was taking place but it was occurring here on earth amid the conversation at the table and what was going to happen tonight. She gave a silent prayer of gratitude.

* * *

So that's how Lucy, George and Judith all ended up in the same room that night at the Angels Comedy Club. Judith was on stage with Joseph and Ben and her grandmother sat at a table near the stage. Lucy, Bill, Mark and Emily came in with George, his family and two Secret Service agents. Other agents were stationed outside. Their group sat towards the back in an area with low lighting. George was wearing a baseball cap, Texas Rangers T-shirt and blue jeans, blending into the crowd. Laura and their daughters had also dressed casually. They came in right before the lights went down and only a few people recognized the former president and his family.

The spotlight shone on Judith. Joseph introduced her as Blue, the home plate umpire, for those who didn't know the nickname.

"Hi, ya'll. How many veterans we got out there tonight? Just clap or say something so I know." About half the audience made sounds, including Mark, Bill, one of the Secret Service agents, and George. "Okay, about half of you know what it's like to be in the military. How many of you were under fire at some point, in the military? I know you could have been under fire here in America, too. But I want to know if anyone else here could have ended up like me from a war? Just go ahead and raise your hands. My brother will count you. I think you probably guessed, but I can't see. I'm blind. No amazing grace for me. Thanks to that damn IED in Iraq. Thanks to that damn Bush who sent me over there."

George felt uneasy. He didn't raise his hand. Mark and Bill did.

"I count twelve, Judith."

"Thank you, Ben. Now I know a little about who you are. And I've told you a bit about myself. But this isn't a therapy session. This is comedy. So I need to get you to laugh, right? Anybody feel like laughing tonight?"

A few people snickered. No one at George's table was laughing. George wanted to leave. He remembered the White House correspondents dinner in 2006 when Colbert and Helen Thomas had skewered him in their video about Iraq. Boiling with rage, he'd had to sit there, hoping the C-Span camera wasn't on his face. That was one of his worst memories of the presidency, especially after having so much fun earlier that evening in the skit he'd done with his look-alike, Steve Bridges.

George looked at the people who'd saved him that day. They weren't laughing either. Maybe they did respect him. Or perhaps they were regretting inviting him to the comedy club. Laura put her hand on George's arm and his daughters whispered about leaving. George shook his head. Someone would recognize him if he left now. And he wanted to hear this obviously wounded veteran speak. George sipped his water.

"Yeah, when I was in my twenties I thought I was going to be an actress or a singer. But then 9/11 happened and I wanted to help my country. So I joined the Army. They sent me to Iraq, eventually. Three tours. And I made it home alive, but I left a lot of my pieces back there."

Judith, who was sitting in an armchair, wore her prosthetic limbs underneath long sleeves and pants tonight. "Joseph, can you get some help from someone from the audience?"

Joseph looked around and said, "You, sir, sitting there with the red beard. Could you come up here and help Judith?" An overweight middle-aged man with a thick red beard and a Saints T-shirt came up to the stage. Judith did her thing with him, shaking parts of her body, and pretty soon the fake limbs were spread over the stage.

The red bearded man apologized.

"Don't worry, you weren't the cause of this. I just wish that Bush was here to apologize. I went to Crawford to do my show, but he didn't show up. It's true, I volunteered to fight for the US and was unfortunate enough to lose my limbs and my sight. I guess it could have happened in a car accident. But it happened in service for my country. That goddamned war was wrong and I want an apology from the man who made the mistake of sending me to war. It would be easier to get through the rest of my life if he'd tell me to my face that he's sorry." Judith paused. "But he ain't here. And you all ARE here, which I appreciate. I'll tell you all some jokes now, but first I need some water. Joseph, can you help me out?"

Joseph retrieved one of the plastic bottles he'd earlier placed at the back of the stage and helped her sip through a straw. The audience watched her drink, a simple act for which, like so many others, she'd need assistance the rest of her life. Perhaps it was that simple act that prompted George to speak.

"I AM here. And I AM listening. And I am sorry." George spoke loudly as he rose from his table and walked towards the stage. He'd taken his cap off, and as he walked into the light, everyone recognized him. There was an audible gasp and whispers of "That's President Bush!"

Judith, Joseph and Ben froze. Laura and her daughters remembered what George had told them and realized this was the moment of truth, and they felt proud to be there supporting him. Abbie, sitting in the front row, was the only person in the room who wasn't surprised. She nodded. It was exactly right that he was here tonight. Her prayers and voodoo had worked.

George got down on his knees in front of Judith. He wanted to touch her but didn't know if that would be appropriate. "I do appreciate your service and your sacrifice. I would wash your feet if, if…."

Judith turned to Joseph. "Is it really him?"

"Yes, it is me. I am who I am," he said in that very familiar voice. "I'm not a Bush impostor. Laura, Jenna, and Barbara, could you stand up, please?" The spotlight turned to their table and the three of them stood and bowed slightly.

"Looks like his family, Judith," said Ben.

"He's right, Judith," said Joseph.

"That's them and that's him, honey," said her grandmother, who stamped her cane on the floor for emphasis.

"I wish I could see you," Judith said.

Silence.

"I wish you could too, ma'am."

More silence.

"Judith, I have some things to say to you, but they are also for all our fellow Americans. Do you mind if I speak to everyone in this room?" He knew someone in the club would have a video cell phone and that his words and image would be on the local news that night and everywhere tomorrow. It didn't matter that it was a Friday night. This would be the lead story for weeks, if not years.

"My fellow Americans," George began in a trembling voice. "This is hard for me to admit. But I was wrong. I was wrong about the weapons of mass destruction. I was wrong about an imminent threat of Iraq towards America. And I was wrong about the connection between Saddam and Osama. Iraq had nothing to do with that terrible day on September 11 2001. Absolutely nothing. So why did we do it? Why did I send our country to war?"

He paused. There was complete silence in the room.

"We wanted Iraq. Saddam was a terrible tyrant. I'd been determined to get him ever since he tried to kill my daddy." He stopped. "And, Lord help me, we did want the oil, absolutely essential to America. And we did expect most Iraqis to welcome us. And finally, God told me to go to war, which would eventually lead to Jesus' return to Jerusalem. Then we'd have heaven on earth, as well as democracy in the Middle East. I really believed this. And you have to believe me." Sweat poured down his face.

"I still believe we can have heaven on earth. God is still talking to me. But God has come to me in other ways over the last six months, and I've realized how wrong I was when I was the president. I'll tell you more about this in the days and weeks to come. But tonight I'm going to apologize for starting the war and I'm going to apologize to Judith. I am the real cause of her injuries."

George bowed down with his forehead on the wooden floor of the stage.

"He's got his head on the floor, Judith, in front of you," Joseph whispered.

The audience was shocked. No one had ever seen a president bow down. He looked like a Muslim or a Hindu or a Buddhist.

Remaining on his knees, George picked up his head and clenched his hands in the prayer position. "I have sinned against you, Judith, and I am asking your forgiveness. You and others have paid the price for my arrogance. And I am sincerely sorry."

Judith and most of the other people there could not have imagined this in their wildest dreams. "Are you sure you're George W Bush?"

Laura came up on stage and approached Judith. "Yes, Judith, it's him, and I'm his wife, Laura."

"I think they are who they say they are," Ben said. The Secret Service agents had moved towards the stage. "And there's Secret Service here, too."

Lucy, Bill, Mark and Emily watched the scene unfold in astonishment. They and everyone else in the audience knew they were witnessing the beginning of one of the greatest stories of the century. Something as momentous as Martin Luther King's *I Have a Dream* speech or the tearing down of the Berlin Wall. George's public apology in the Angels Comedy Club was the beginning of a story that would change history. In addition to a couple of amateurs with cell phones, there was a newly hired CNN reporter there that night recording the story. She'd been planning a story on Judith, and now she was getting the scoop of her life.

Everyone was looking at the former president, still kneeling in front of Judith.

Finally Judith spoke: "Sir, you have really done it this time."

George cringed.

"You've upstaged me."

Everyone burst out laughing.

When the laughter died down, Judith continued. "It's okay. I heard that you wanted to be a comedian. Might be a good way to get your new message across. People like laughter in between their tears. You and I have a lot of talking to do. And you've gotta a lot of talking and listening to do with others like me. But right now, we have a show to do, to get these people to laugh. So, for starters, that's what I want from you."

Judith began singing, paraphrasing an old Bee Gees song, *I Started a Joke*, substituting the word "*joke*" with the word "*war*."

Judith nodded and Joseph handed George a mike. George couldn't believe he'd have to sing in public. Judith encouraged him, saying, "Just sing like you do in church." She sang the line again.

A few moments passed and then George said, "I'll do it for you, Blue."

He choaked out the first line but then got stronger and kept singing. By the time they finished, he and everyone in the room was crying.

This duet would be replayed millions of times on YouTube and iPhone; pundits and historians would later agree that besides Obama's election, this was a major tipping point for change. Change away from American fascism. Change away from ignorance about the Iraq War. Change towards truth and reconciliation. Who would have thought that a mediocre Bee Gees song sung by the right people with a slight change in lyrics could tip the balance towards world peace?

That night, live at the Angels Comedy Club, everyone's eyes were on the stage, save for Lucy's. She looked at several tables that had been vacant before and first saw Maria and Charlie. They blew kisses to one another. The other tables she saw were now occupied by some new people, strangely dressed. There was a man who looked like Beethoven, another man who was Beethoven, a woman with books (a librarian perhaps), and a beautiful older woman whose chair looked like tree branches. And at another table, Machiavelli, Jesus, a Burning Bush, and Mother Nature sat, surrounded by huge sunflowers. In between stood Pat Tillman and some other terribly wounded soldiers and civilians, though they seemed not to be suffering. All watched with pride and amusement.

One young African American soldier smiled at his beloved family on the stage making history. Abbie felt his presence. She turned around and saw her grandson, alive again. She started to rise but Marty shook his head, blew her a kiss with his fingers and gestured for her to watch the stage. He was the past. There in front of them, on stage, was the future.

An arc of light flowed between the ghost soldier and the other spirits and Abbie, Lucy and the people on the stage. No one else saw this arc of light besides Lucy and Abbie, but most of the people felt the force as shivers in their backs and heads and as pricks of tears in their eyes. This experience couldn't be conveyed on TV, but the CNN reporter would later try her damnedest to explain it.

This event wouldn't be misrepresented. It was going down in history exactly as it had happened. And the former president would repeat his words for the remainder of his days.

The people who were there that night would talk for the rest of their lives about this experience with awe and wonder. Even those who weren't religious admitted that they felt the power of what others would call the Lord or Kwan Yin or Mohammed or La Virgin or Yahweh or the Great Spirit. If it could have been put into words, this presence might have said, "I am who I am. It is what it is."

At some point, Judith began to sing another song. The former president walked to his table where now sat a woman who looked like his sister, Dorothy. As he approached and the woman smiled at him, he saw that it was Robin, as she would have looked in her sixties if she hadn't died as a child. She was wearing a dress with a print of bluebonnets and her face glowed to see her famous brother, who sat down next to her in stunned awe. Robin tipped her head to the stage towards Judith, and holding hands with George joined the others in singing along:

> *Amazing grace*
> *how sweet the sound,*
> *that saved a wretch like me.*
> *I once was lost,*
> *but now I'm found*
> *was blind,*
> *but now can see.*

Acknowledgements

I want to thank the following family, friends, and writers who gave me helpful feedback and encouragement during the writing of this novel: Anya Achtenberg, Maya Elrick, Aeriel Emig, Barbara Fraser, Dana and Gary Goetz, Andy Hiett, Joanne Keane, Chris Kotur, Peter Kurland, Janet Page, André Pronovost, Julie Riechert, Joan Schweighardt, Dean Seibert, Dora Wang and others who remain anonymous.

My father is no longer living, however I think of him every day and my family will see his influence in *A Journey, a Reckoning and a Miracle*.

The earliest and most enthusiastic readers were my mother and my husband, who both first believed in the story itself and in my ability to write it. My agent, Joan Schweighardt, gave me invaluable help and her energy carried the manuscript forward to O-books. I thank John Hunt, publisher of O-books, for giving me the opportunity to get my ideas out to the world. And for everyone else at O-books, including Trevor Greenfield, Stuart Davies and Carolyn Burdett, I appreciate all your good work.

And I thank my sons, Alex and Tom, ages ten and twelve, for giving me time to write. They asked me if I was going to be famous, and I replied, "I don't know, boys. It will be up to the readers." As my sons and others of their generation will be dealing with the consequences of the past eight years for the rest of their lives, may Goddess help them all.

Namaste.

Author

Kathryn J. Fraser lives in New Mexico with her husband and two sons. She was raised in the Presbyterian Church but after a long search joined the Unitarian Universalist Church in 1994.

A *cum laude* graduate of Dartmouth College and graduate AOA with honors from Dartmouth Medical School, she is currently on the faculty of the University of New Mexico School of Medicine as an Associate Professor of Psychiatry. For the past seven years she has been the medical director of the Continuing Care Clinic where she does patient care, administration and teaching. During this time she has often been on the list of Best Doctors of America.

President Bush's 2004 re-election inspired her to write this book, which is her first novel.

BOOKS

O is a symbol of the world, of oneness and unity. In different cultures it also means the "eye," symbolizing knowledge and insight. We aim to publish books that are accessible, constructive and that challenge accepted opinion, both that of academia and the "moral majority."

Our books are available in all good English language bookstores worldwide. If you don't see the book on the shelves ask the bookstore to order it for you, quoting the ISBN number and title. Alternatively you can order online (all major online retail sites carry our titles) or contact the distributor in the relevant country, listed on the copyright page.

See our website **www.o-books.net** for a full list of over 500 titles, growing by 100 a year.

And tune in to myspiritradio.com for our book review radio show, hosted by June-Elleni Laine, where you can listen to the authors discussing their books.

MySpiritRadio